PLAINS of PROMISE

Alexis Wright is a member of the Waanyi people from the highlands of the southern Gulf of Carpentaria. She has worked extensively in Aboriginal agencies across four states and territories as a professional manager, educator, researcher and writer.

Her involvement in many Aboriginal organisations and campaigns has included work on land use agreements, publications, fundraising, land rights, and native campaigns for her traditional homelands. She continues to work in these areas.

Alexis Wright's other books in Australia are *Grog War*, which documents the achievements of the Waramungu people in their campaign to restrict alcohol in Tennant Creek, and *Take Power*, an anthology of essays and stories celebrating twenty years of land rights in Central Australia. Her short stories and essays have been published in anthologies in Australia and overseas. In France, she has published *Croire en L'Incroyable* and *Le Pacte de Serpent*, and her novel *Plains of Promise* was translated and published under the title *Les Plaines de l'espair*.

Her latest novel is *Carpentaria*. Alexis Wright works and writes in Melbourne and is undertaking studies in Aboriginal Storytelling for a Doctorate of Philosophy.

Also by Alexis Wright

Grog War
Croire en L'Incroyable (Believing the Unbelievable)
Le Pacte de Serpent (The Serpent's Covenant)
Take Power (editor)
Carpentaria

PLAINS of PROMISE

ALEXIS WRIGHT

University of Queensland Press

First published 1997 by University of Queensland Press
Box 42, St Lucia, Queensland 4067 Australia
Reprinted 1998, 2002, 2006

Typeset by University of Queensland Press
Printed in Australia by McPherson's Printing Group

Distributed in the USA and Canada by
International Specialized Book Services, Inc.,
5804 N.E. Hassalo Street, Portland, Oregon 97213-3640

This project has been assisted by
the Commonwealth Government through
the Australia Council, its arts funding
and advisory body

Cataloguing in Publication Data
National Library of Australia

Wright, Alexis, 1950–   .
  Plains of Promise.

  I. Title. (Series: UQP black Australian writers).

A823.3

ISBN 0 7022 2917 2

For my family

Contents

PART I
The Timekeeper's Shadow

1

The biggest tree on St Dominic's Mission for Aborigines grew next to the girls' dormitory. It was the only tree that had survived from the twenty-one seeds contained in a seed pod brought by the first missionary on the long and arduous trek to the claypans expanding across the northern Gulf country. The pod was a parting gift from his niece; it served a useful purpose on the journey as a rattling prod to strike a stubborn mule on the rump in the heat of the day, or to slap monotonously across the hand at night by the campfire, whenever the boredom or loneliness became unbearable. It was also a useful game to guess how many seeds were in the pod and keep a record, without resorting to opening it. Abstinence in praise of the Lord, until the time of celebration was right — when the destination for the work of God was reached.

So God's celebratory poinciana tree came into being, surviving the claypans, the droughts and the Wets to grow large and graceful in the presence of three generations of black girls laughing in their innocence as if nothing mattered at all. Its roots clung tighter to the earth when the girls cried out for their mothers or wept into its branches when they were lonely or hurt, enduring the frustration and cruelty of their times. The tree grew in spite of all this. Healthy and unexploited, unaffected when illness fell on all sides, witnessing the frequent occurrence of premature deaths, none of which affected the growth of God's tree.

Now a black crow sat in its branches, its beady eyes on the wait. Yes, someone else was going to die here. The branches swayed and creaked at night under the Milky Way, while all night long crickets screamed and frogs croaked back. Scarlet petals loosened their hold to fall on the carpet they were forming on the dirt below.

The crow would still be there in the morning. Several weeks the bird stayed. People looked the other way as they passed by. Everyone knew the crow was still there. It would stay until someone died. The precaution was always taken of looking the other way rather than taking the risk of checking if the crow was there. Unwanted bird. But no one was game enough to chase it away. The Aboriginal inmates thought the tree should not have been allowed to grow there on their ancestral country. It was wrong. Their spiritual ancestors grew more and more disturbed by the thirsty, greedy foreign tree intruding into the bowels of their world. The uprising fluid carried away precious nutrients; in the middle of the night they woke up gasping for air, thought they were dying, raced up through the trunk into the limbs and branches, through the tiny veins of the minute leaves and into the flowers themselves. There, they invited Cousin Crow to sit along the branches and draw the cards of death.

Every year when the flowers came the crow came too. Throughout the night the black shadow flew around the community to search for food. The girls in the dormitory prayed long and hard for salvation and tried to ignore the crow like everyone else — except the missionaries, who refused to be spooked by the Devil's work. The girls lay there at night on the brink of two beliefs, one offering the wicked eternal salvation, the other no more than the chance to be saved after the price of death was paid.

"Someone awake?" The girls' whispering starts.

"Watch that window now." Silence. "Over there."

They watched throughout the night until exhaustion finally took over, the whites of some two dozen pairs of eyes moving from side to side, from window to open window, on guard.

The corrugated iron windows, held out with long sticks, always stayed open before the Wet. If they were closed the heat of the humid tropical night would make it pitch-black and airless, impossible to sleep with them closed. Impossible to sleep anyway with that crow outside. But sleep they must to face each day of missionary zeal. But the door was left closed at nights in case snakes came inside.

"Someone awake?"

"Watch out it don't creep up on you."

"Might creep up on you and get you."

"Choose now. Which girl going to die here tonight?"

Singsong: "Which giiiirrrl going to die heeere? Might be you."

"Might be going to choose YOOOOUUUUU."

"Stop it. Stop it." Younger girls start crying.

"Well, stay awake then."

"Yep, you lot. Don't just leave it to some of us here to look after you."

It was already hot by seven in the morning and everyone was up and about. Errol Jipp, the missionary in charge of St Dominic's, with full powers for the protection of its eight hundred or so Aboriginal inmates under state laws, stood caught in the light of the sun streaming through the girls' dormitory window. He stood directly in front of Ivy "Koopundi" Andrews, aged about seven. She had just acquired the name Andrews. Andrews, Dominic, Patrick, Chapel, Mission — all good Christian surnames given by the missionaries for civilised living. "Koopundi" and the like would be endured with slight tolerance as long as they did not expect to use such names when they left to live in the civilised world, whenever they acquired the necessary skills.

"Your mother died this morning, Ivy," Jipp announced,

looking around the dormitory. "We are all very sorry." He used his high-pitched, sermonizing voice, staring down at the bowed head with its brown curls and sun-bleached ends.

Ivy did not move but gave a sidelong glance to see if the other girls were looking. She saw they were pretending not to notice. Her glance shot across to the open window. The bird could not be seen. "It's probably gone now," she told herself. She thought of her mother — that was about all she had done since being put into the dormitory a few days earlier. How her mother screamed, and she herself had felt abandoned, alone for the first time in her life. She could hear her mother crying, following and being dragged away, still crying. She did not know what had happened to her but she had not come back again to the fence that barricaded the dormitory after she was dragged away.

"Ah well, dear, we will give her a proper service in the chapel later on today." As Jipp spoke he formed the funeral arrangements in his mind. Things needed to be planned down to the last detail: that was his habit, his way of doing things. It will be necessary to find someone to dig the hole. Could he count on one of the men to bring over a plywood coffin, if there was one already made up, or should he get someone to knock one up quickly? No good keeping bodies around too long in this heat. Another thing, these people were far too superstitious. They might all try to take off in the middle of the night, as they did last time. Better secure the gates and make sure the children are locked in tonight. But maybe not. Old Ben, who died recently, was an important man. Law man, they called him. (Heaven forbid! These people never learn.) But the woman was not from around here. A loner. A real hopeless loser.

"When you hear the bell ring after class, come over to the mission house, child. Mrs Jipp will take you to the chapel." Best to make the day as normal as possible, Jipp thought as he gave the child a slight pat on the shoulder then turned and walked out. Ivy stood where she was, proud of the fact that Jipp had been so kind to her, hoping the other girls had noticed. She watched the middle-aged white man, the father figure, shaking out his handkerchief to wipe his hand, walking away into the distance.

"He's kind, that Mr Jipp," she said. Life isn't too bad here, she thought to herself, while the other girls said nothing but moved away from their eavesdropping positions to finish their chores quickly then race out of the door and down the road over the tracks fat Jipp had made to tell their families what had happened.

Everyone was talking about the crazy woman from another country that had killed herself during the night. The movers and shakers of the mission had a lot to say about her.

"If you knew so much, what was her name then?" No one knew for sure. No one would have minded if she had settled down at St Dominic's, even though she did not belong here — so long as she went about her business and didn't interfere with others. What could be the harm in that? Nothing.

But someone said she had "that look" in her eye. "Down at the store that day, remember? When you went down there for bread on ration day. You said you saw it. You told me that. Told all of us. Don't muck around looking like you know nothing now. You told us yourself — that one not right."

Another sister adds to the story: "Crazy. Crazy. Crazy one."

"Then you threw your hands up in the air. Then when we asked, you said, look for yourself."

"Well, I say, anyway she looked alright. Nothing wrong. But then I must have made a mistake. Seein' she goes and kills herself."

Another voice: "Just like that. You must have known that was goin' to happen. If you could see something wrong with her. You should have done something to stop it. Poor woman might still be with us now. Instead of waitin' to die. Waitin' for spirits to come and get her. You should have made someone stay with her at nights when she was by herself. And that poor little girl. She didn't even have that little girl for company any more. No good that. Woman being alone at night. She had nobody. Nobody at all. And you women didn't even lift a finger to help her. Poor little thing left up there now. No mummy or daddy for that one any more. All because of jealous women."

"Look, man. Don't you go around saying anything. Husband or no husband. Mind your lip, what I say."

"Yep, I know poor little thing alright. Kids here say she not too upset when Jipp told her this morning. 'Nother thing. You think I can be goin' around looking after every Tom, Dick or Harry here? How'm I to know she wants to set about killin' herself like that? How'd I know anyone want to do that to themselves? I only *thought* she was like that. Yep, crazy that's what. Lot of people around here like that. Can you blame anyone, hey? I'm askin' you that. Well, don't go around with your big tongue hanging out blaming me. I'm crazy myself — got kids of mine there too in the dormitory. That don't make me happy either. But what can I do? What can anyone do to stop old Jipp and his mob. They run everything here. They in charge. Not me, that's for sure. Do that make me go around wantin' to kill myself or telling other people to kill themselves too? Hey? So shut up your big mouth then. You got too much to say about things you know nothing about."

At that moment Old Donny St Dominic walked into the main camp where the argument was boiling hot about the death of the dead woman. A lot more people were drawn to the action by mid-morning. The main camp was where some of the most influential families lived. The families who truly belonged to this particular piece of country, the traditional elders where the real law of the mission was preserved in strength, in spite of white domination and attempts to destroy it, or to understand what really happens under their white missionary eyes.

The argument progressed into a lot of wrongs, which for some time had been left unsaid, floating around the place. There were facts to be aired, mostly to do with the inmates' attitudes towards each other. Somehow or other it all became interlinked with the woman's death.

Old Donny St Dominic, about the oldest surviving inmate of those last "wild ones" rounded up and herded like a pack of dingoes into the holding pen, now long pacified, sat unnoticed because of the developing commotion and looked on without speaking.

"You all know nothing!" one old *waragu* or madwoman yells in excitement, racing about excitedly and trying to hit people with her long hunting stick. She laughs hysterically at the top of her voice over the mass argument.

People weave and duck and dogs bark but the debate goes on.

"You the one now who sees things that not even there. Since when you cared about anything around here anyway? No wonder that woman gone now. Praise the good Jesus for taking her, what I say."

"Praise nothing. You churchpeople think nothing. Woman goes and kills herself and no-good Jesus got nothing to do with it. Bloody crawl up fat Jipp's bum — lot of good it will do you."

"Youse know nothing!" the old madwoman yells solidly into faces, and is told by at least a dozen people to well and truly shut up.

"At least we went to see her and talk to her — tried to settle her down."

"Sure you did. What did you tell her? 'God is going to look after you', did you? God's people take her child away and leave her there crying out like an animal for days afterwards. Only us here had to listen to her all day and half the night. Did whiteman's God hear that?"

"God heard. He heard her. And *you* can't say nothing. I see you down there after Jipp's God when it suits you."

At that moment Old Donny lifts his ancient frame clad in mission rags onto the tip of his walking stick that one of his nephews recently made to support his bulk. Slowly he draws himself into the centre of his balance, then moves one stiff leg after another into the centre of trouble. People watch him approach and stop saying whatever they were saying or about to say about the matter. Silence has fallen all around by the time he reaches the shade of the surrounding young mango trees.

"A woman killed herself here last night," he says quietly, then pauses for a few moments. "Down near Old Maudie's — under the mango tree there."

He stands leaning on his stick and waits before proceeding any further. "Maudie told me early this morning … said she been crying again for the child. The one Ivy … put in the dormitory with the others. Last night … she come and took Maudie's lighting kerosene … went and set herself alight."

Someone at that moment put a stool behind the old man and sat him down on it. No one up to this moment had known how the woman had achieved her aim of killing herself. That question had become enmeshed and lost in other issues — the reasons why and who was to take a share of the blame. The method was simply a secondary matter until Old Donny mentioned it: now everyone was dumbfounded, realising how bad the woman must have felt to go and douse herself with Maudie's kerosene then set herself alight.

The old man looked down and waited, thinking someone might want to say something. But the people gathered there either looked at him or down at the ground where the bull ants marched on regardless in their processions from one nest to another and said nothing.

"I went back with Jipp to see Maudie this morning. She's

pretty upset, you know. You women here, better look after that old woman."

Maudie was old alright; she looked as old as the land itself. The kids thought she was an evil spirit and would only go near her place to taunt her when their parents weren't around to rowse them. She lived alone, away from the main compound in an old corrugated iron hut and gum tree bower shelter, built by her last husband years ago before he died of smallpox along with several dozen others who fell at that time. Old Maudie never really recovered from his death and preferred to stay in the place alone, too old, or too previously loved and contented to want to share the rest of her life with another man.

The woman who had killed herself had chosen to move into the small abandoned shed beside Maudie's a week after she arrived at the Mission. She was not eligible for a mission hut — corrugated iron, one-room huts that looked like slight enlargements of outdoor dunnies. They were lined up in rows, with a single tap at the end of every second row. One tap for every two hundred people. They housed what mission authorities referred to as "nuclear families". That is, husband and wife with children, no matter how many. If the children had been forcibly removed to the segregated dormitories the couples made room for grandparents, or other extra relatives these people insisted should live with them.

At first Ivy's mother had been placed in the compound of large corrugated iron sheds which housed several families tightly packed together, as well as women alone, with or without children. This was where Ivy had been taken from her. The child was termed a "half-caste" by the mission bosses and therefore could not be left with the others. Their reasoning: "It would be a bad influence on these children. We should be able to save them from their kind. If we succeed we will be able to place them in the outside world to make something of themselves. And they will of course then choose to marry white. Thank goodness. For their children will be whiter and more redeemable in the likeness of God the Father Almighty."

But Ivy was all the woman had left. The child she gave birth to when she was little more than a child herself. The child of a child and the man who said he loved her during the long, hot nights on the sheep station where she had grown up. She had not seen the likes of a mission before. That was a place where bad Aborigines were sent — as she was frequently warned by the station owners who separated her from her family, to be an older playmate-cum-general help for their own children. So she was always careful she made sure to be good. Even to the man who seduced her by night she was good. She believed in love and he loved her just like her bosses did. With kindness.

At the end of the shearing season she was left to give birth alone, as despised as any other "general gin" who disgraced herself by confusing lust for kindness and kindness for love.

Years later, when the child Ivy was half-grown, the woman had to be got rid of. In the eyes of her bosses she was not a bad cook for the shearers. "Now she's had enough practice … since the time we had to put her out of the house to have her bastard child with her own kind." But the woman was often abusive to everyone. It was said that none of her own people wanted anything to do with her. She was too different, having grown up away from the native compound in the whitefellas' household. And having slept with white men … "That makes black women like that really uppity," they said.

"Now she wants to take her kid with her all the time. Even out in the shearers' camp. Won't leave her even with her own family — after all, she is one of them, isn't she? And the men don't like her either. You know what she went and did? She went and chucked hot fat over one of the fellas when he was just trying to be nice to that child. Caused a right old emergency." A shrug of the shoulders.

"Yes, might have been the father of the child ... who knows. Anyway, she's got to go — this sort of thing only gives the others bad habits ... if you don't deal with it properly."

A magistrate handled the assault matter and handed the finalisation of the woman's affairs over to the Regional Protector of Aborigines, and she was promptly removed. Under ample protection mother and child were delivered into their new world — an Aboriginal world, a world similar to that occupied by thousands of Aboriginal people at the time. In this case, the destination was St Dominic's Mission in the far North.

When Ivy was taken away, her mother had nothing left. The bad Aborigine became morose. A lost number amongst the lost and condemned, "bad" by the outside world's standards for Blacks. Sentenced to rot for the rest of her days. Even her child taken from her so that the badness of black skin wouldn't rub off.

Her heart stopped dead when they spoke to her just before taking the child, after they had shown her a spot to camp in the squalid stench of the communal shed. It was described as being "for the good of the child." Perhaps they were right — but how could she let Ivy go? She felt her whole body had gone numb. Vanished was any sense of the arrogance of the old days now for Number 976-805 on the state's tally books. Her arms and legs felt as though they had been strapped down with weights.

"No, don't," was all she could think of to say, but the words never passed her lips. Over and over after they left, she thought if only she had said the words out loud, if she had only tried harder, then maybe they would not have taken Ivy away. She had screamed and run after them and tried to drag Ivy away until she was overcome and locked up for a day in the black hole, a place for troublesome blacks. Her release came with a warning of no further interference.

"It is best for you not to be a nuisance. People like you

don't make the laws." She was told that next time she would spend a long time inside the lock-up if she still wanted to cause trouble. "And then we will be forced to have you removed to another reserve especially for the likes of people like you. Remember that."

Alone she saw the blackness of the night and the men who came, small and faceless creatures. They slid down the ropes from the stormy skies, lowering their dirty wet bodies until they reached the ground outside the hut while she slept. There in silence they went after her, pulling at her skin, trying to rip her apart. Taunting her as she tried to escape, to get out of the door of the hut. All the while pulling and jabbing her skin wherever they could with their sharp nails. Satisfied with their "bad woman's weakened state" they returned to the skies, beckoning her to come with them. Again and again they came back through the nights to enjoy another attack. Again and again they made her theirs nightly. But her final nightmare was to come.

Alone she can see the black bird fly in the night. See it hover, flap its wings faster to stay in one spot, swoop almost to touch the ground, then shoot up again to its hovering position. The process is repeated several times while the woman slinks into the darkness of the tree shadows. Frightened, on guard, she watches. Now the black bird has time for torment. It attacks in the darkness in the perfect moment — the moment of loss. Its attack is unrelenting. Face, back of head, shielding arms — the pecking persists as she crawls on her stomach into the shack which offers entrapment but no escape.

Hearing the screams, Old Maudie grabs her stick and hits the ground, over and over to frighten what she thinks must be a snake, while she finds her way through the darkness. She hears the flapping of the bird's wings and waves her stick frantically this way and that, striking air, twigs, branches, but the bird escapes. The frightened old woman finds only the terrified, incoherent victim bleeding and shaking, huddled on the ground.

Maudie told Jipp and Old Donny the woman knew she was being punished and would die soon. If anyone could believe Maudie. She knew a lot of stories like that. She said she told the woman not to go on like that, she was young, she should be thinking of finding a husband for herself and having more children. Only old people like Maudie herself thought about dying. But the woman kept saying: "I sick ... I sick ... sick." That's all she could say. She thought someone wanted her dead. She was a bad woman. Bad mother. Might be someone from her own country wanted her dead and came here secretly in the night to do bad business on her.

That's why Maudie said she did it. Poured the kerosene over herself before anyone could stop her. Before the clouds broke she threw herself in the fire. All the screaming when it finally came, and, by the time Old Maudie could get to the human fireball, it was over. Maudie said she tried to limp over to the mission house to get help for the woman, with only her lamp to see by in the moonless night. Then the rain came. But no one would answer the door there. Seems that as usual, whiteman's law did not want to know what happens in the middle of the night. Such are the spirits that haunt the night in Aboriginal places.

"Maudie came and got me to go with her in the night then ... nobody else to do it," Donny said, picking up the story. "Old Maudie and me sat all night long with her ... all night ... you savvy ... in the rain. But it did no good ..."

He looked up and waited for the silence to be broken. But all eyes looked at his and said nothing. Then he said: "That's all." Meaning end of story. The people left and went home.

Ivy ran to the mission house when the bell rang. Excited by the attention. And sure she would be told of a terrible mistake. It wasn't her mother dead after all. It was someone else. She was even sure her mother would be there to tell her they were going to leave this place for ever and go back home.

Jipp's wife, Beverly, sat in the shade of her front garden amongst the prettiness of the hard-won purples and pinks of petunias and button dahlias. An oasis inside a white picket fence that separated her from the bulldust outside. This was their eighteenth year at St Dominic's and it was home, even though she wished long and often they could get away for an extended holiday. But she could not conceive of their ever leaving the place. What would the people do if they left? These were their people: to serve God by saving these black souls from themselves, from paganism, was the highest calling for men like Errol. "Yes, of course such souls can be saved," she heard herself saying, as she often did to her churchwomen's meetings down South, on the rare occasions when they were down that way.

Proof was there already. One only had to look at the full congregation on Sunday and the devout faces of the little children. Strict rules set the guiding principles for these people to live by. Once you established that then you had no trouble at all. She recalled trying to explain life here to the churchwomen's meetings. It was breathtaking — how those women imagined life up here, Beverly thought. She smiled at the thought of how they followed Errol around, astounded by his stories of pacifying the natives, the troublemakers. Hanging onto his every word. "Are they really as black as you see them in books!" — and to her, in mock admiration: "How do you manage, dear, with only black people for company? It must be so hard on you up there, so far away."

And so it was. So it was. But to work and live in the grace of God is not meant to be easy. In time, just rewards will come to those who manage. It was worth the effort. Praise be to God Almighty for those who see His guiding light.

God's light sometimes becomes dimmed, however, Beverly Jipp thought as she watched in pity the child approaching under the stormy afternoon sky. The Devil's work still persisted here even after so much diligence on poor Errol's part. Still, the dead woman had been new to St Dominic's. That was the trouble. If only they could refuse to take in the strays the authorities kept wanting to send here. If only they could concentrate simply on the ones they already had, then their efforts might bear the proper fruits.

"Here child, eat this mango" — she hands the fruit to Ivy, who looks around in vain for her mother; but she is happy for the treat. Beverly is certain the gates of salvation will not open for the woman, but perhaps their prayers will be answered, and He will give absolution to the poor thing. She hands Ivy a white cotton dress to wear. It was a favourite of her own daughter, now grown up. Dot, now living down South, surely would not mind giving the poor child her old dress.

Ivy is forced to drop her sack dress in front of the white woman in broad daylight for anyone to see, and struggle with the white dress. She doesn't want to dirty it, although it will be impossible to keep it clean in the living conditions she is fast becoming used to.

"There! You look lovely," Beverly announces, scarcely believing her eyes, as she looks at the brown curly-haired child with her large, strange-looking brown-green eyes. "Yes," she thinks. "Quite beautiful."

"Put this around your neck and wear it all the time, child." The bead necklace is a gift which Errol would disapprove of. "Don't spoil the children, Bev, they are our only chance" — she can hear the familiar words of disapproval. The necklace is now in place over the white dress. Ivy, looking like God's own angel, dressed more for a party than a funeral, is ready to bid her mother a last farewell. There is no sign of her mother at the mission house: is it true, then, that she has died?

*   *   *

The electrical storm, typical of the tropics this time of year, suddenly broke, lashing out with all its violence at the lowering of the coffin into the freshly-dug hole. Ivy stood with the Jipps, next to the elders, who were secretly partaking in their own rituals but looking as though they were converts to Christendom. The others who came to save the face of the so-called community spirit on apocryphal occasions such as this were a few of the church-going groupers who hedged their bets both ways.

Ivy could not move her eyes from the wooden box, knowing now that her mother was inside it. The rain poured down on the box and Ivy could see the hole it was making — and soon she could see her mother's face smiling at her, a careful, peaceful smile that made her cry for the first time that day. At this moment lightning forked across the sky, and thunder shook the ground beneath their feet. Nearby a prickly bush was struck, so the funeral rites were hastily brought to an end by Jipp, with the coffin left to lie in the deep hole fast filling with water. After the storm ended some black souls would be sent around later on to shovel in the claggy clay.

Ivy was led away, back to the "redemption" dormitory, shamed that the sodden white dress now revealed every inch of her body, feeling the dirtiness of her brownness beside the middle-aged cleanliness of the white missionaries; feeling, above all, her loneliness.

2

Up North the clouds of night split fast at dawn. A dark-red dawn that crawls with increasing brightness over fresh green growth breaking through the burnt stubble roots of a claypan fire. A claypan covered in cobweb mist. And here they come. Through the track that splits the stubble, a track packed down hard from travelling feet. The so-called mindless ones walk on. They walk on the cutting edge between reality and beyond, placing new footprints in the thin layer of moist earth. They come separately, about five or six old ones, taking their routine walk.

No one cuts the white matted hair on head or face. Their long limbs of dry, sagging black skin are covered with dust. They are naked. Their chewing tobacco in its moist little lump behind the left ear or rolling in mouths with clicking tongues. Except for Old Eddie, who pushes bicycle handlebars attached to a pole fixed on tricycle wheels, they walk unaided. Their faces are mapped by the deep gorges of great wisdom and knowledge of their traditional homelands. Their eyes stare downward into an earth eagerly expecting their return.

They have nothing to say to one another about their institutionalised life. The old ones gave up talking about it long ago; they move in silence along the track. Others stare after them as they go past. What are they doing, wandering around with their dogs? No one goes to get them. The old ones themselves wonder, when they reach their destination.

They sit separately, and sniff the freshness of cut grass. They are prepared to wait. After all, everyone waits for something to happen sometime, sooner or later, don't they?

Errol Jipp sweats as he pushes the rotary mower up and down, up and down, concentrating his gaze on the spinning blades as the grass flies in a buzz of emerald jewels. He is sick and tired of telling them. He's determined to stop himself glancing up to the open ground around the corrugated iron shed that serves as the ration outlet. He is angry they are sitting there in the dirt in the heat. They always do it. Sit there in the sun for nothing.

He continues to mow Beverly's lawn. Faster and faster — nothing will stop him. Red-faced with exhaustion, he tries not to notice the old men. But he does. Errol Jipp's God keeps willing him to help the old ones. He knows selfishness is a sin; he feels obligated to tell them to go home. He knows Beverly is watching him through the white latticework of the upstairs veranda of their house and she is on the side of God. But he won't go yet. He is sick of telling them. Let them sit there. Angrily he stays on his side of the dust bowl and mows on. They sit silently, separately, until midday. Then they get up and walk back again over the scorched dusty track. Empty-handed. Independence intact. Another successful protest against whiteman's time.

Every Saturday morning the ration store is closed for the weekend. Errol Jipp mows Beverly's lawn because he must. Beverly is his wife and he ought to try to keep her happy. If mowing a lawn makes her happy, it is the very least he can do. Errol Jipp is a man for the main chance.

"Ivy! Ivy! She sits on his big leg so lively!"

"So lively … that's Ivy! Ivy!" The Chapel girls hiss.

Grace and Joan Chapel are beautiful, tall and slender, and their dark skin shines as though it has an all-over regular wax and polish. They are sophisticated, they read the *Women's Weekly* and they shave their legs like film stars.

Their legs are perfect and beautiful. Ivy Koopundi is fanatical in her desire to be like them and imagines there are similarities to herself whenever she chances a glance as they sit and gossip with the other girls in the dormitory.

She knows they don't like her, didn't like her to look at them and would slap her face if they caught her. Grace and Joan even act like film stars. Like those in movies about the killer women tribes in the Amazon jungle. No one dares offend them.

"My legs are a bit like theirs ... I think they are, anyway," Ivy mused as she looked at her scarred and scaly knees. She makes the comparison from her memory of those slender legs sprawled across the dormitory bunks. If Thelma Dogsface hadn't pushed her over again, she believes the scales on her own legs, infected and red, might have healed up by now. Unlike the Chapel girls, Ivy's own skin is too light in colour to shine, though she believes it does shine a bit.

Ivy thinks she may even be as tall as Joan Chapel; if she remembers to stretch herself out in bed every night, she believes she will grow taller. The other girls don't talk to Ivy. She used to try to copy their hairstyles, but her hair did not stay where she tried to style it. It was too thick and frizzy.

After the death of Ivy's mother there were more suicides. The Chapel girls' mother was the first. A lively woman with a strong will, you would have thought her well able to cope with life's difficulties without much introspection. She set fire to herself. It was inexplicable. Old Maudie thought about the men who came with rope ladders from the sky, those who had attacked Ivy's mother. But she kept her thoughts to herself.

The third death occurred a month later. A woman, a mother. Similar circumstances. This time the husband, a morose man who frequently beat his wife, was suspected by the Mission. But the man's family said different. A large family, capable of regional warfare if need be, people said. Old Donny agreed. "There is another way," he said. After that, when yet more suicides occurred as a sure, free way of leaving St Dominic's without permission, each time Old Donny stopped the troubles which flared up with the promise of "another way".

The suicides always by burning did not always bring instant death. These victims suffered horrendous burns, long and agonising pain while death crawled its way though to them. This was the legacy of Ivy's mother. Her only legacy.

Since the death of the Chapel girls' mother, no one in the dormitory spoke to Ivy except to taunt her and blame her whenever someone took their own life. The old people on the Mission watched these events; they said nothing openly about them. The kids called Ivy "the crow's Timekeeper". In fact they believed she had replaced the crow. Ivy felt the eyes watching her wherever she went. — whether she was walking down an isolated bush path, in church or at the store, the eyes never left her.

She even saw eyes watching her in her dreams. When a death occurred an uneasiness began mounting up inside her. She learnt very quickly not to call out in the night whenever she woke up in terror. Two pairs of eyes, one glaring directly in front of her, the other close behind her head. She saw evil in those eyes. When she opened her own eyes they were still there in the dark. All she could do was to stay awake and watch them hover around her in silence. Hours later, exhausted, she could not prevent her own eyes from being pierced by those spirit eyes. She fell asleep. At other times her resolve to stay awake worked but did not prevent her from screaming out. She screamed in agony as the pain swirled around and around inside her head, until the eyes left her alone again.

The other girls were not prepared to put up with Ivy becoming a major intrusion into a decent night's sleep. They talked about the "Timekeeper" constantly and attacked her whenever their tempers flared up. Ivy was often left semi-conscious after these attacks. A rib. A bone. A finger. Broken to mend by itself. No one bothered, not even the missionaries, to acquaint themselves with the child's injuries. Who really cared?

Here was a child with a sly look, the missionaries said. Who only looked at you obliquely. A promiscuous look, they said. *That look.* — "You know it when you see it." Said with confident ease. Such was the ethnographical data on Aboriginal people collected by white missionaries at the time. Not a likely recruit for Christendom, they decided, with the devil just lurking around the corner. "She has the Devil in her, that's for sure." Ivy cultivated a look on her face as if she was about to cry. She wanted people to feel sorry for her.

Whenever the mission staff spoke to her she would form tears in her eyes, even if all they said was "Clean the blackboard, Ivy!" Exposed from the cover of isolation she cried. It was as though people were noticing the ugliest thing on earth for the first time. If she was asked to answer a question she would look down to the ground and say nothing, and let her tears swell. She enjoyed the damp coolness sliding down her cheek. At the same time she knew the swelling tears made her eyes look beautiful. It was the look of the film stars she admired so much. She held the look before allowing the largest tears to fall. "It must be said," the missionaries declared, "this is a bad apple."

One time she was consigned to polishing the brass and silver in the mission church and overheard talk about herself, just after she had been told to stop being lazy and to put some muscle into the polishing. "It's what you expect from inbreeding," one voice said. Ivy felt the voice cut like a knife inside her stomach; she felt sick.

"Inbreeding produces the worst from both sides of the fence," someone else remarked.

"Mark my words. They're all the same, these half-castes. They are the ones that cause trouble. Can't help themselves. And the gins!"

"Take pride in nothing. Look at the way they treat their kids. Dirty. Disgraceful. Call themselves mothers! Isn't it obvious their race is sick and dying out? Just as well we're trying to do something for the littlies." Three opinionated men in the tub of the church, cleansing the sins of the world.

Ivy tried to rub harder with the polish rag but her arm barely moved. The chapel keepers went up and bowed to the altar, ignoring the child as they bristled past in their long black smocks.

Only then did she realise she should have said something. But what? That they were wrong about her. She wasn't like the rest of them? Yet somehow she did not feel they were wrong. How could they be? Anyway, it was too late now.

She planned to show them they were wrong. She stayed for hours longer than she needed to, until it was almost dark. Polishing and repolishing brass candlesticks, silver plates, vases, chalices. Even the statues, until the shadows sent her running. Brasso and Silvo spilt and left behind on the floorboards. Words firmly imprinted on her mind.

Down by the river Ivy watched the old ones walk past, never noticing she was there. In the middle of the day the crows soared high in the sky on pockets of hot air. Occasionally their calls broke the calm. She stood on the long dry sandbank in the branch of a channel country river running for the first time that year.

"Ivy … Ivy … You lively, Ivy?" The girls on the bank were laughing themselves silly. "You going to tell us, or what?" They looked hard at her, trying to act serious, and shrieked more lewd remarks at her. They turned their backs and wiggled their bottoms at her. Getting no response, they pretended to ignore her as if what they wanted to know was of no great consequence anyhow. Earlier, the Chapel girls, assisted by others, had dragged Ivy out to the sandbank and left her standing there. She looked really stupid, they thought.

The girls danced the hula. Round and round the broad perimeter of their highly stacked fire they moved after each other. Pointing the long sticks towards Ivy then back into the flames and running away from the heat. They went on laughing so hard they ended up falling onto the sand. Ivy wished it would swallow them. Picking themselves up, they spun around and around, specks of sand flying, reflecting like gold glitter. The party continued with joined hands and ran in a wiggling snake line around the edge of their fire. They loved the excitement of fire and the ideas learnt from the missionaries of faraway savages who burnt their victims.

"You move an inch. Just an inch! We gonna drown you."

"Or burn you too."

"Or both."

Laughing still, they finally disappeared into the bush and hid to watch what Ivy would do. In the shade they ate their tin can full of the baby fish they had swooped out of the shallow water and quickly cooked in the coals. Leisurely picking at the tiny bones while they watched Ivy vomiting and the vomit sinking into the dry sand. Ivy thought if she stayed there long enough they would go away and leave her alone. She listened to the storm miles away upriver and saw the heavy clouds rolling closer above the trees. She knew the river would flood. Fear was mounting as she saw in her mind the growing wall of water that would come rushing down the river and wash her away. But she did not move even a toe, otherwise it would burn in the hot sand. The sun caught the back of her neck and her skin felt as if it would fry. The girls' interest eventually died down to a pale smoke. That was when they snuck off through the under-growth. She hated them all. And she knew it was all because of what she did with Jipp.

Jipp used to appear in the middle of the night with a torch

to check the girls' dormitory, to make sure they were all asleep on their bare wooden bunks. He would walk down the centre and shine the light over the beds on either side. Sometimes he paused to look at the way one of his girls slept. Some nights he might do the rounds much later. At night he walked like a cat: a fat man who clomped around during the day, the lord of this little claypan kingdom was soft-pawed during the night. He knew every sighing floor-board to avoid for creaks and groans. In the sleepless nights, wet with sweat, he did not really need the torch, except to flick it on momentarily beside Ivy. He had grown fond of the child since her mother's death.

Beverly was constantly going on about wanting to take the child into their home. It had been a stupid gesture to give the child their own daughter's dress to wear to her mother's funeral, thought Jipp. Errol Jipp missed his own children and their nearness. Nothing felt close to him any more. He missed the energy and the fullness of life when they were small. Now it was only Beverly and himself in the big mission house. Silence, an undeclared agreement that there was nothing left to say to each other. She droned incessantly about time — how long things took, how time passed …

He had chipped her off about the dress. She always needed to go past the mark. She lacked the discipline of faith. And now she wanted Ivy in the house. "In God's name, they're not here for that," he warned her. Couldn't she figure these things out for herself? He told her she should examine her role in the Mission. He made some rough mental calculations on how long it would take to leave her figuring these things out for herself, before she came to him and asked his help. A muddling head he thought, driven by too many selfish emotions.

He knew Beverly had thought at first it was the death of Ivy's mother that was bothering him. He had to admit he was a little disturbed about the suicide. If he had his choice, he would have enacted God's law to the letter. He should simply have buried the woman without any service and made sure her grave was unmarked. She did not deserve any better. "The most valuable thing any person can have is the life God has given them," he told his wife.

Nevertheless, he was worried about the number of suicides. All he could hope was that these deaths did not create a problem with the mission administration down South. "Then, heaven help us, it will get into the newspapers," he told his staff. Adding under his breath, "and every southern bleeding heart will be up here breathing down our necks." Almost immediately he recognised and disliked his own fallibility in falling into the rough talk of a northern outpost.

He was rather pleased that he had managed to convince the doctor six hundred kilometres away to issue death certificates specifying natural causes. "What's the use of draining the taxpayers' coffers and sending the bodies off for autopsies?" Jipp asked on the radio. Jipp imagined the signature still wet, just signed on the death notice. "Over and out."

The doctor then complained in anecdotal terms about the ethics of the situation.

"They are always dying from something or other so what's the point in getting carried away with it? Over!" Jipp snapped, his voice sounding tinny over the crackling wire.

"But what if ..." the doctor responded, only to be interrupted mid-sentence.

"By the time you could organise to get the body off to the hospital, who would take it there? We'd be up and down with bodies like a bloody yoyo. We wouldn't make it in the heat. Two days drive ... Take it up with the authorities if you like. Over an out." Jipp was not prepared to be given the run-around by a small-town general practitioner.

The death certificate arrived in the next mail. "Death by accidental spillage of kerosene," Jipp mused. Perhaps that was all it was, accidental: he visualised a woman somehow spilling kerosene over herself then accidentally forgetting about it even though it smelled a mile downwind. Then, preparing her fire for the evening meal with sticks and car tyres, she set off a bonfire. It was possible, he thought.

But Errol Jipp's chief worry was his wife. She constantly introduced Ivy into her routine round of enquiries. Casually, but enough to make her point. Some general inquiry about time would include some comment about the child. "Will you see her before you come back? Will you be back by ten?" "Make sure she's alright." Later on, when he tried to figure out what had happened, he was unable to decide if his wife had the original fascination or vice versa — or whether they were both fixated at the same time.

Given half a chance, she would have the girl in the house with them. But that wouldn't do. He must remain firm. There could be no way he would allow that to happen. This was not his task to make pets out of these people and set back decades of mission work. His task was clear. To make Christians, and Beverly's duty was to fit into his work according to the Protection Act, and above all according to God.

Not only did Errol Jipp miss his own children, he missed a wife who shared his bed. Beverly slept in her daughter's lime-coloured room on a permanent basis. It began when she used to sleep there occasionally after Dot left for the South. Beverly wanted her daughter back with a force so desperate, she felt her own life had gone away the day Dot left. Asleep in her daughter's bed, curled up, she tried to remember the smell of her little girl years ago as a small child. She would lie with the sheet up to her chin and sniff the pillow, hopeful of a trace still buried there. But only the scent of specially shipped-up detergent with the freshness of bottled pine forests lingered there.

Beverly did not believe that she had intended to check on him. One night in the humid stillness before the Big Wet, when no one could sleep properly, she'd get up and go back to their room, only to find it empty. The house was empty except for herself; suddenly it felt cold. She had never forgotten this. Sometime — hours later, it seemed, he came back. She had simply asked him where he'd been, what had happened, because sometimes things did happen up here, in the night. Someone might get sick and you had to go and see what you could do. But she'd heard no knocking on the door.

"Go back to your bed. This is none of your business. Don't ask," was his response. Beverly felt as though she'd been spoken to by a policeman on duty at the scene of an accident — just a nosey bystander getting in the way. Now considered a person too ignorant to be of any use.

"I think we should talk," she said, not ready to be dismissed so easily.

"You have made me taste the filth. Get out of my sight," he hissed at her. She backed out of the room, as a sinner would struck down by words of the righteous.

Her cheeks burned by knowing her life, their life would never be the same again by forcing him to confront his guilt. In the same instant realising that her sin was even greater by having forced a man of God to break his vows to the Church. She had only herself to blame for the life they had lead ever since the difficult birth of their son. The son who had grown and gone away carrying their burden of silence with him. Yet even now she followed her familiar habit of never speaking about what was wrong in their life. How wrong now to have always assumed that they had both agreed on the changed order, or that it would be enough. The contentment of shared beliefs and Christian aspirations now soiled. She felt dirty but slept with it as her punishment.

Now the home took on a new meaning for Beverly. The house had to be clean. Errol was something filthy; she found it difficult to be near a man who always smelled of the Mission. She visualised herself packing, going to her daughter's place, but she knew she could never do it. She stayed. Always it was necessary to be on the alert. She knew the carelessness of men. Sometimes, for example, he might use her own towel, hung on her own rack in the bathroom, leaving his odour behind. But her compulsion to cleanliness kept her busy. Dust was always a hazard, however. It got everywhere in the evening and early morning when the wind blew up. And in spring. Dust storms preceded the electrical ones, as well as the rain in the Wet. There was always dusting for her Aboriginal woman helper to do. Dust caused an allergy that afflicted Beverly and most of the Aboriginal population of St Dominic's. She appreciated the "poor thing" sympathy her condition gave her within the community. Where the extent of her suffering scored higher when it was often compared with other asthmatics.

Running out of disinfectant was a constant problem for Beverly. The dormitories were a big hassle, the children always coming down with some nasty little germ or other. Some too nasty to mention in civilised company. It was a constant effort to keep the germs down, she wrote to her women friends who sent ladies' magazines that ended up in the girls' dormitory. There was not much you could do when the children would return from their parents' filthy camps and bring all the germs back again. Beverly reminded Errol constantly of their need to be vigilant, to take extra precautions. To keep themselves at a sensible distance, and not stay around the camps too long. Yet sometimes he did not even bother to wash his hands before lunch, after handling a dozen or so dirty babies.

Ivy was Errol Jipp's first little girl. He needed, above all else, to be discreet. "Idle tongues wag," was the recurring message learnt from past encounters with Aboriginal women he had put the hard word on. He received this message without words from some members of the community's Church Council. When the men started behaving in an over-familiar manner towards him, it was a warning sign that things had got out of hand. He always disliked any infringement of his absolute, all-encompassing authority over the Mission, but he was unable to put a quick end to the men's insolence.

He had previously spent years discussing this matter with God. He told himself (and God) that his situation was different, the use of black flesh a necessity. God knew he would never reduce himself to their level. As for the tribal elders — "Humour the poor simple-minded devils," he thought to himself. He pocketed jibes insinuating he was related like a son or nephew to the old men. "One big happy family," he kidded with a serious expression. Several visions rampaged through his mind of ways to force them back in their place in the appropriate time. By God, he'd make them feel the hurt even if it took transportation to the island penal colony for lepers and unmanageable blacks a thousand miles away. It would take only the stroke of a pen — "for their only good".

Authority mattered to Errol Jipp above all else. He had allowed a small amount of power-sharing by giving a limited number of the Aboriginal elders a place on the small Church Council of Elders he established to encourage cooperation. After all, he had a large population to deal with. His choice of the old fellas he put in charge included those he could manipulate. Those who dreamt and lusted over young women becoming their wives and indeed expected it. Individually, they had often confided to him about the girls they wanted. Their cooperation was on the basis of what favours he gave them. They knew he had the sole power to arrange marriages. So occasionally he would allow one of them to take a younger wife if he thought their argument sufficiently convincing. It caused considerable jealousy — and the desired cooperation.

Jipp chose Ivy because she had no family. She lay awake each night waiting for the torch to come and prayed to God the beam would pass over her bed. Sometimes he took her inside the church. He knew the place like a blind bat in its nest and would lead her through the pitch darkness of the closed building, up the aisle, past the altar, and down the steps into the vestry. These times Ivy felt more terrified than when he took her out of the dormitory.

His hands, fat and rough, never seemed to stop shaking as they moved over her and inside her after he managed to get her into the vestry and drag the sack dress over her head. She was sick, knowing her sin in God's place. Ashamed if her body responded but unable to move away beneath a weight that forced the air from her body. Desperate enough to keep living, she struggled to gasp enough air. But her worthlessness she swallowed to the pit of her stomach. She knew the sight of her nakedness sprawled out indecently in God's place would never be forgiven. Meanwhile, he would, by God, push the evil out of the "she-devil" who was possessing him.

Other times were better when he led her to the banana plantation. It was not just a place to grow bananas. It was a cemetery as well. Whenever someone was buried, a young banana plant was planted at the head of the grave. "Where there is death, there will always be life," Jipp would proclaim to his grieving flock. And in his diary he wrote: "The fruit is visual evidence that there will always be life everlasting in the whiteman's faith." A practical point to show the virtues of acquiring Christian faith: that here at St Dominic's, all could feel secure in the knowledge that no one would die of hunger.

But no one would eat the harvest when it came. (Except for the kids in the dormitories, who had no choice of refusing what was served up to them.) The bananas recalled those who were no more; buried and mangled up in the roots of the plantation. When eaten the fruit caused a head-to-toe rash that spread throughout the dormitories. Parents were outraged. Mothers came to yell and scream abuse outside the mission house.

Bananas by the truckload rotted and stank. A fence ran around the plantation and the huge plants drooped from lack of care and watering. The place lay abandoned and overgrown. A thick maze for snakes had been created. In the Aboriginal community it became known as "Jipp's Paradise". Everyone had a good old belly laugh. At the same time they were disgusted whenever the flashlight was seen wobbling around there during the night, accompanied by the rustling of dead leaves.

Now, standing on the sandbank, Ivy thought about what happened in the vestry and in the banana plantation, where, at least, the light of the stars and the moon gave her some comfort. She recalled how the remains of a banana bush rubbed coarsely against her back as Jipp pushed her up and down, her feet unable to touch the ground in his tight grasp. She was swallowed in his fat. A personal expression of his power over the Mission. Yes, it was better there than in the church.

The other girls were still taunting her. "Look out for the quicksand. Plenty of it around here!" Ivy did not know whether to believe them or not.

"You don't know 'bout quicksand. You come from rubbish country. You mother was a myall," they sang.

"This spot. That spot over there —" skinny arms pointing in all directions.

"Anywhere! 'Cause of all the sand round here."

Ivy did not know if they were joking about the quicksand just to make her stay where she was. She realised they couldn't care less if she died here in the sun. They could be saying the truth; no one would even know if she fell into quicksand. She would just disappear and people would think she just ran away, that some spirit got her, like her mother and the others. She thought she would just as soon disappear too, but she did not like the vision of herself drowning, her body trapped in quicksand anywhere between where she stood and the swirl of swelling waters to the bank.

"Don't think we don't know what's goin' on!" yelled Joan Chapel as the girls, sick of hanging around, prepared to leave.

"We's know what youse up too, no-shame slut-face!" Grace Chapel bellowed and laughed.

"Sneakin' off in the night with your man, old fat Jipp!" Hoots of laughter.

"We's can see for ourselves — But youse goin' to tell us what's goin' on anyhow. You hear that?"

Slipping and climbing through the damp buffalo grass, they left to go back to the Mission.

Ivy looked at the iridescent blue, green and red of dragonflies. Their awkward descent to the water's edge. Fast zooming lift-offs. Over and over. Hover, descend again. She did not yet feel hungry enough to test whether the quicksand existed or not. She thought of her mother, whose face she could only vaguely remember these days.

"They can hate me much as they like," she mumbled as she threw clumps of wet sand at the dragonflies. Soon she had a small pile of the shiny wings lying beside her. Those that tried to hobble away were squashed between her fingers and flicked back with the dead.

When she heard the grass rustle on the bank where the girls had been, she quickly covered the bounty with sand. The first time it was only Barney, trying to round up his pig Bertha. Although Barney was in his thirties by the time people stopped worrying about him growing, he had only grown to some 120 centimetres, and he was nearly as wide. In his usual high-pitched quick burst of words, he called out asking if anyone had seen Bertha though he was only speaking to one person. Ivy just looked the other way and did not answer. For a while he kept walking along the bank yelling at her. Smiling to herself she felt his desperation but continued to ignore him. Finally he gave up and went away.

By late afternoon the shadows of the ghost gums had edged their way over the waters. At the other end of the sandbank the crows had fed and grumbled amongst themselves in tune with distant thunder, sent the brolgas hoo-hawing away, then flown off in the nearby bush. The bare back of a black man flashed past some undergrowth on the bank: Ivy realised she had been watched and stayed where she was. With the storm edging closer, what light remained over the shaded river was suddenly overtaken by darkness. The thunder chased the headwaters into a wall of flood waters which gathered up speed, mud, dead branches, trees and dead animals as it moved swiftly down the river. In the light of the lightning forking across the sky above her head, Ivy saw the waters gathering strength from the flow of the passing debris. Now she felt too frightened to stay where she was and started to move off the sandbank to the side of the river closest to the bank. As she tried to manoeuvre the rising waters she felt the moving sand cause her feet to sink up past her ankles. Petrified she stood still. Echoes of the idle kids' talk bounced around in her head, at the same time she told herself she was doing the right thing.

The Devil was standing dead still there itself, thought Maudie who tried to rescue the child. The old woman unable to fathom why she would not move had to wade in to the swirling waters to get her. Grumbling to herself she had to ply the incoherent Ivy from the water. Then with her heart pounding from the little strength she could muster, she dragged the child to safety. Ivy was now screaming like a wild animal, almost making the old woman lose her balance and nearly drowning them both.

After that day Ivy never tried to be like the other girls in the dormitory again.

3

St Dominic's was now renowned as a place of evil.
From this place suicides spread throughout the Aboriginal world. The black bird lived in the poinciana tree.
Some years it seemed as if the bird would never leave the
Mission. In the 1950s St Dominic's became the place people
most feared being sent to. A place of death. A devil's place.
The elders kept the lid on their suspicions. They knew it
was some dangerous business associated with the death of
Ivy's mother.

Real grounds for fear existed. Who could initiate the
proper procedures to investigate the matter these days?
Several generations had slipped by since anyone had to do
this kind of thing. "Everyone lives mission life now," people
at St Dominic's said, in two minds about what to do. "Are
we really different people now or not?" That was the challenge. Had there been too much interference with the old
ways? But something had to be done. For a long while,
everyone had watched out for the power of Jesus Christ to
come and deal with this matter of evil. Nothing had happened. They got sick and tired of watching the Migaloo law
man, Jipp. He was useless. Wasted whatever he had in a
banana plantation.

The investigation for the truth would involve a number
of discreet visits to the dead woman's country. Secrecy was
essential. Someone inconspicuous enough must slip
through the net of the *Aborigines Protection Act (1911)*. These

included laws preventing Aborigines to travel around with-out a permit, or to move off a mission without a permit. Everyone knew Errol Jipp, as the local Protector of Aborigines, with authority to govern movement and all matters of life and death as he saw fit, was not going to be involved in "un-Christian" activity. But given the frequency of deaths the matter could not be ignored. Given the fact that the original source of evil — so everyone was convinced — stemmed from Ivy Koopundi's mother, people were prepared to reinstate their tribal governing laws over Christian institutional life to do something about it by themselves. It was a matter of survival.

The mission Whites, too, were suspicious of so many unusual deaths. Special prayer evenings were arranged twice a week in the middle of the community dwellings. Attendance ratings were poor. The missionaries felt the Devil had indeed come to live amongst their flock, in spite of the dedication of their work as God's servants to make St Dominic's the heartland of "God's paradise on earth". Church services became a more serious matter. A tally was taken before the service could begin to make sure everyone attended. If anyone was missing, everyone had to wait, sweating it out in their misplaced, European-style church, until those missing persons were fetched. Before too long anyone was quick to dob in anyone else. "Arthur waddim-name. Waddimname Johnson not here. Someone better go for him, or for her." No problem. "He's down by Well no. 7, your Reverendness. Youse find him easy there."

Everyone attended to hear the word of God spoken through the Reverend Errol Jipp. He told everyone straight out. "God is not pleased," he proclaimed in a loud, stern voice. "You. You. You and you" — indiscriminately pointing out people, inciting suspicion. He could not stay still, mov-ing about the pulpit with awkward sharp hopping move-ments, like a child at hopscotch. "You have all turned our paradise into a vile and evil place." He paused for a few seconds. "Let no man, woman or child, say I did not warn you against your evil ways. The Devil now lives at St Dominic's Mission. Here he reaps the reward of your wickedness. Will you join me to stamp out the Devil? Together we can do it! Are you with me on the road to paradise?" he belted out, clapping his hands.

"We are," came the reply.

He repeated the question over and over, the clapping growing louder as the congregation's enthusiasm grew to fever pitch.

"To live with Jesus?" — *Yes!*

"With all the Saints?" — *Yes!*

On and on he preached.

"Stamp out the Devil!" he finally roared again and again, pounding the flat of his hand hard on the pulpit. "Yes! We will do it!" He stared slowly around his flock, searching for signs in their evading eyes, thinking how sometime he was going to have to explain all the deaths to the authorities. "And by God's grace and mercy you are going to help me." Then he ordered all women with children three years and under to sleep in a separate compound he had fenced off, in order to keep the babies away from the Devil.

Church services became a daily event. The strain was obvious on the faces of people too afraid to discuss what they were thinking even with family.

The tally-keeper swore when bush names were accidentally given at the door instead of what was termed their proper names. "What's that? Look, it's not Poodnuti. Podnooti. Podnuckle. Or whatever you say it is." Absenteeism was punishable with twenty-four hours in the lock-up — a small room, 180 by 300 centimetres, with one small window up near the ceiling. An essential facility provided without compassion in mind. More than one inmate meant overcrowding. Still, there was always room for one more to complete the punishment list for the day. The door slammed shut on space and light. "Clean up your own mess when you leave!" Providing toilet facilities for a gaol was not part of the whiteman's burden in *protecting* its black population.

To exorcise evil was the battle to be won against all odds by Errol Jipp. He knew he was a good soldier, with twenty-odd years work behind him to prove it. He and Beverly listened to the screams penetrating the night air from the gaol. The frightened. The orchestrated arguments between families. Back and forth, well into the night. These days it was early to bed, early to rise for Jipp. He was ready for his daily onslaught of exorcism regardless of how little sleep he got.

Daily crowding in the small gaol resulted in an outbreak of dysentery which brought down the whole community. The Whites got it too. Babies died. Old people died. Yet the daily routine continued with the gastric-stricken, diarrhoea-driven, all attending church. The reverend was overcome with exultation. This was the first time in all those years he had it all in his grip. But everything changed the day he failed to turn up for service. Errol Jipp was unable to move from his sick bed for several days. The campaign finally slipped when the elders jacked up and stood in front of the church waving spears and nulla nullas, which they would have used if anyone had stepped within firing range. The Christian God was truly gracious in mysterious ways. Errol Jipp stayed in bed and another campaign began.

In secret, the elders arranged the surveillance. But a loose tongue ensured the secret was shared throughout the whole community. Whenever they spoke about Ivy it was in a hushed tone, even though everyone knew that everyone else was doing the same thing. In fact, everyone kept an eye on Ivy and knew exactly what she was doing at any given time. No one spoke publicly about it, and no one would admit to knowing anything sinister about her, but there was an unwritten dossier building up. Yet no one was any closer to establishing what it was about her that might be the root of the evil.

Maudie knew who was chosen to be the Traveller. But Maudie was not an important law business woman. She knew everything, even though she never left her own place to do any of the talking or gossiping. It seemed that no one visited her place either. Yet she knew who would be the Traveller even before it was decided. And she was able to anticipate the day he would leave and the day he would return.

The reason why Maudie never made law status was because of her preferred affiliation with her own country, not this country to which she had been brought as a child, this topsy-turvy world where, to establish harmony everyone had adopted local kinship status. But Maudie was always very staunch about where her true loyalties and obligations lay. Her seniority demanded respect, but she did not belong to the executive law council, which was a well kept secret from mission authorities. However, she still managed to give advice on important matters through various channels for people to consider. People believed that even though she lived in exile, she had never left her own country in her mind.

The Traveller left for the first time about five years after Ivy Koopundi's mother died. He went to the woman's country. His mission would have begun sooner but arrangements took a long time. The trip became more imminent with the increase of similar deaths, the last being a young woman of fourteen, with her newborn baby by her side. She had grown delirious when the missionary demanded she name the father. The perspiration ran from her hot body while she whispered that the spirit that looked like grey smoke was in the room, drawing the life from her and her baby. The next morning both the girl and baby were gone. The hut smelt as though it had burnt down. It was hours later before anyone could go inside because of the heat radiating from the destroyed bodies.

The main obstruction to the commencement of the investigation was the need for elders to mediate the perpetual disputes between local estates and family groups; not their traditional boundaries this time, but the complex nature of how to translate these time immemorial boundaries into the confines of their present circumstances. The mission authorites had no idea of this — since they did not speak the local language nor had any desire to learn it.

Family groups had been broken into husband-and-wife living quarters prescribed under European names, not by the preferred local estate groups. This meant that a redistribution of boundaries had to be decided before other matters could be dealt with. Nevertheless, the elders regarded their deliberations as a highly intellectual way of maintaining integrity over their lives, regardless of the white man enforcing his way of doing things. And this is how the Council of Elders saw it.

One or two others formed a "de facto" relationship with the white god. For example, Pugnose and Norman were both determined to give it all away.

"Bugger blackpella business, I say," Old Man Pugnose would assert stubbornly, sitting around with his greasy, dust-stained Akubra, brim now too big for his bony face; a faded memory of stockman days. It was his standard response when anyone tried to talk him out of Christianity. "All you mob want to do … is argue all the time. Me, I'm sick of it. Whitepella way good enough for me. Give me no trouble that one." At that he would wipe one of his bony arms across the front of his teeth, then shake the saliva off into the dirt to end the matter.

Norman Church was the same. He did whatever Pugnose decided to do. But Norman was prone to violence when anyone disagreed with him. So everyone let the two old fellas do what they liked for a few years. The only one who tried to reason with Norman was his wife, Gladys — even though she was a good churchwoman herself. "Well! He's only a man, you know, no prime minister so and so, not a god you know, and all that," she used to say. Still she wasn't prepared to let people pick on her man, and would brush them off like flies trying to settle on her face.

Her status throughout this period was not the best, even though she privately agreed that Norman had no business in God's business. Still, she considered her present predicament only a temporary set back.

Norman was particularly diligent in ensuring his clanspeople attended the daily services Jipp imposed. He made a point of being one of the last to enter the church, standing outside ensuring his family group were all accounted for. Once he frogmarched his own wife to the lock-up when she couldn't be bothered getting out of bed. She could have died of shame.

Gladys resolved the land space problem through the church council, of which she was an irregular but preferable member to her husband in the mind of Jipp. She settled the finer details with the senior women involved. When Norman found out she'd been plotting with Jipp he almost killed her, even though he favoured the movement of married children back near their parents, where their behaviour and grandchildren could be watched more closely. Days later, when Norman came down with the sickness, Gladys took her revenge and kicked him out in a public display of self-righteousness. What was the use of a husband who could beat her up but no longer perform as a man? She challenged anyone to fight her over the matter. No one did.

Norman limped over to Pugnose's place where he found his friend as sick as he was, flat on his back on his blanket with his four old dogs curled up beside him. They looked at each other as old fellas do when they realise they are no longer young. Living there together, it was they who planned the revolt against the Church which finally ended Jipp's "exorcism". As a peace offering from the Council, it was Pugnose's son Elliot who was chosen to travel the songlines to the dangerous country. Ivy's mother's country. He was to find out the reason for the big mob of sorry business affecting them all.

Everyone agreed Elliot was a good choice. In his early thirties, he was shaping up as a true Midinji law man. He would most likely have been the obvious choice even if no favour was owed to Pugnose. Elliot slipped away one night unnoticed by anyone except Maudie, who heard the steps softly crushing fresh leaves against dead pass by her place. She knew the investigation had begun.

Elliot journeyed discreetly, singing the songs taught by his father and uncle-fathers, each step through the song-map unlocking the land. Several weeks of travelling passed. Tiredness set in but still he threw himself forward into the night in front of him.

Sometimes his movements were as graceful as his totem, the brolga. A flock of brolga were now up ahead, quivering in a lake mirage across the plains, wavering in an eerie dance routine, there to greet him. He kept his promise to his father and ate only the food he saw the brolga eat on his journey. This meant he must stay close to the river, following the birds as they crisscrossed the Channel Country plains. Further into the landscape of brown-red earth they twisted, settling at last on a large lake where millions of birds had gathered to rear their young.

Elliot knew he had reached the home of a great spirit — the Serpent, the greatest ancestral creator being; he should remain on guard, for anything could happen in this greatest of places. He now felt unsure, not knowing for certain whether he had approached the place in the proper way. He recalled his journey. Watched himself crossing the land. How he had sung to the spirits he saw through the songs as he journeyed through the forever wavering landscape. He saw his footprints left upon the cracked, sun-baked clay. He had seen no other person in his journey there. He could go no further into the land of Ivy Koopundi's mother's people. This was the instructed destination: the song-map must end here. He could only go further if he was given permission by the traditional elders in this place.

The sun had disappeared twice and Elliot had walked twice around the edge of the lake, the second time in his own footprints. He walked inwards on the large expanse of the dry clay until his feet sank in sticky mud and eventually reached the water's edge. There he sat in the water amongst the floating black swans, pelicans, ibis and wild ducks. Then he returned into the bush to make his fire and camp for the night.

They came in the stillness of the night. It was the crows that sent up the first noisy alarm. A million squawking birds followed, creating a racket of such intensity it pierced the senses. At first Elliot thought it was just some dingoes he had seen in a small pack earlier in the day, robbing eggs from unguarded nests. He had watched them run off with the rounded eggs, unbroken, in their mouths. But now a roaring body created by thousands upon thousands of winged creatures lifting off in unison hid the light of the moon. Elliot imagined it was the Great Spirit troubled into action; he felt a cool change of the quick wind in the air touch his skin in the darkness and thought he was being struck down on the Serpent's path of destruction.

When the light of the moon reappeared it was the Chinaman he saw first. The old man stared back from under the heavy load he carried across his shoulders. He moved closer and threw the bundle down next to the red coals of the dying fire. Without saying anything, he started to untie the twine around the bundle slowly and unrolled his swag. It contained a blackened billy, rust-spotted pannikins, sweet biscuits, tea, sugar, spoons, and other bits and pieces. Waving his torch around he found enough wood to re-light the fire, then walked off to fetch water.

Elliot watched the torchlight gradually disappear and turned to see three ochre-faced women standing behind him. His look of fright set the women laughing. They explained they had just come back from a ceremony. They had seen his campfire earlier and had come to join him. They had a sugarbag full of dead goannas which they dumped on the fire; they were cooked by the time the old Chinaman returned. One of the old women, May Sugar, was the Chinaman's wife.

"You look like you long way from home!" the old man, who told Elliot his name was Pilot Ah King, ventured at last while preparing his tea.

Elliot told him where he had come from. The rest of the evening was spent in yarning and soon the old man and the three women fell asleep, exhausted from their travelling.

The next night, after he had helped to hunt and gather food supplies for further travelling, Elliot spoke of the reason for his trip. He needed to know what he should do now. The old sisters frowned and looked at each other with worried faces. "Better you stay away. Not go further," they told him. "Worry country way down that way." They pointed towards the South and solemnly turned their heads from side to side. This told him it was Sickness country.

Elliot called the women "granny". He listened to them and was patient. He could go no further, he finally must return. Then he asked them if they knew the woman in question, Ivy's mother, the reason for his journey. They said they did: she was a bad woman who got taken away. They also knew she was finished. But they knew nothing of any tricky business. As they spoke Elliot was aware of Pilot's face tensing up, his hands tightening into hard little fists, his right eye twitching. The women, seeing the old man like this, nudged each other and stopped talking. Finally, when

Pilot calmed himself, he confirmed there was a lot of sickness.

"Maybe the woman was sick before she left," the women said. They talked of seeing a few people still left alive in the sickness country. "Some here. Some there" — they drew maps on the ground to show Elliot. They knew there was big trouble in the ancestral world. "The spirits bring the sickness," they said. Each of the old grannies described the people dying, showing Elliot the sickness. "Here … here … here." Touching hand, foot, leg, arm, toes or fingers. "Here … this one … this one here …"

"Then finish up." Pilot looked put out by this sort of talk so he turned his back, tapped his pipe on a flat stone and concentrated on cleaning it. Elliot read the worried faces of the old women and watched Pilot finish cleaning his pipe.

"You don't want to believe liars. Too many around here," Pilot warned. And, when Elliot insisted it was his job to find out as much as he could, he said: "You people all believe too many stories …" The continuous tapping of his pipe with one shaky hand onto the other went on until it ended up breaking. "Now look at it! You bloody women … don't know why a man bothers to be burdened by you at all."

The women laughed. May Sugar rumbled through her bag and from among her squabbling kittens produced another pipe and threw it across the fire to land on his lap.

Content with the new pipe full of tobacco and lit, Pilot muttered: "They talk like this all the time … can't get them to shut up about someone getting something done to them … No one allowed simply to get sick."

"My people have to find out … It's not just the woman from old grannies' country here … Maybe someone is doing all this … We heard you mob down here think we are rubbish people … We don't keep the law properly, you say," Elliot challenged the women. He ignored Pilot, who was pretending he had no further part in the discussion.

The women looked at each other with heads bent, shamed that the accusation was true. There was competition about purity of culture and they saw themselves as the leaders in this respect.

"We don't know you people."

"We only heard someone say that."

"We don't know about any business goin' on."

"Maybe you can find out then ... Tell them we sick and tired of it ... We got business ourselves," Elliot continued, his tone indicating a revenge payment. He felt sick in the stomach for having to talk like this to the old women. He grabbed the billy and topped up the pannikins.

"We got business too," he felt compelled to go on, but in a gentler tone. He could only relate what the elders had chosen to tell him. He wondered if they were able to do anything about their trouble: it seemed the Great Spirit of this place was already angry with everyone, including this mob. He started to worry about making threats to these people, who might be more powerful than their appearances indicated. He wondered whether he would get home safely.

"We keep the law ... we always keep the law ... we do things different now ... that's all," he told the silent women. He wasn't sure how much he should tell them. Or if he should be talking to them at all. He remembered being told to go no further. Only to talk to the people of the dead woman's country. He suspected the old grannies knew more than they were willing or able to tell him. Perhaps they were messengers ... or even elders of their people. He did not feel easy about staying around much longer waiting for anyone else to turn up. Elliot reasoned he was doing his job the best way he could. He felt satisfied that he had been able to fulfil his mission so quickly. It might have taken as long as a year. He was pleased that he was not the one sent to avenge the deaths, although he thought he could have killed one of them if he had to. Momentarily, he pondered which one he would have chosen. Probably he would have got Pilot first.

Pilot, sensing the old women's uneasiness towards someone they knew was making a law inquiry, told them they had to be going right now. He turned to Elliot. "We can find out what you need to know for your people ... but I got to be very careful," he said, his voice growing so quiet it was barely audible. Then, as they moved off with their things he whispered: "Old grannies will let you know next time, young fella."

"The girl Ivy. She belongs to this country. We got to know what to do about her," Elliot said. He agreed to return in a year's time.

The four of them left in the night. Shortly afterwards, from the direction they had gone, Elliot heard what sounded like moaning; then the group of crows he had seen near his camp when he first arrived flew up, squeaking in delight, circled the moonlit lake, and headed South.

4

"Ivy! Look at me when I tell you something." The woman had come up to the dormitory to take the girl to Old Maudie. It was an emergency.

Ivy did not respond. She stayed sitting on a branch of the poinciana tree with her back to the woman, legs spread wide, feet dangling in mid-air. Why should she turn around to look at the old cow?

"You want to listen to me, girl … you show respect, hear me?" The large, irritable woman in her floral dress was determined to assert authority. It would be good to give the girl a flogging here and now, she thought. But no one was allowed to flog their kids any more. The missionaries did it instead. With a leather strap. Teaching and punishment in all manner of guises were their domain. "Get going! You little —" She bit her tongue.

Ivy did not move.

The woman felt like knocking the girl off the tree and giving her a kick, hard enough to send her flying into the dirt. Face first. That would teach her to go opening her legs.

Everyone knew what was going on between this girl and the Reverend Jipp. What sort of hussy she was turning out to be. And everyone blamed her for the affair. Ivy's intimate relationship with the one who ruled the life of the community caused a lot of unrest among the people. What potential did she have to influence matters, they wondered.

The woman hit out, but stopped in time to soften the

blow. Ivy was hardly shaken from the impact. She spun around and faced the woman with a contorted face. Her eyes were filled with bitterness.

The woman was taken aback. "Evil!" she gasped. Not many people got to see Ivy close up. The woman stepped back, realising that she had probably made trouble for herself and her family with Jipp. She said softly: "Old Aunty wants to see you."

"Who?" Ivy snapped back, as if she had no idea who the woman was talking about.

"Maudie! That's who … Aunty Maudie. She's very sick. She asking for you." God only knows why, the woman wanted to add, but bit her tongue again. "You better go fast now."

Ivy made no effort to move. She did not like Old Maudie much. That she was dying was of no consequence to her. She had been dying for ages. Each time she was sick everyone went into a big spasm. Always wanting to make a big thing of it. Who was Maudie anyway? It had happened before — each time Maudie thought she was dying she would call out in a quivering voice: "Someone get Ivy for me." Ivy thought Maudie just lived so that people could go on thinking she was dying. She was sick of all the fuss about her. All the dormitory kids would be marched off to church to say prayers for her. Everyone said Maudie was a saint. That she would be the first black person to go through the pearly gates to God's paradise. And those who believed in the Reverend Jipp's God knew that Maudie would have the ear of God after that. Not Jipp. Not anyone else. They would pray to Maudie and she would receive their prayers and tell God what they wanted. She would be deliverance. She would be hope. Because she would remember all the things they did for her when she was dying. No one had said any prayers for her mother, Ivy thought. Her mother might have been a saint, too. She just wished Maudie would lie down and die, get it over and done with.

Delaying tactics could only go on so long, however. Finally Ivy started to get up, scowling as she did so. The woman grabbed her arm and led her forcibly off down towards the village. Ivy walked barefoot with exaggerated casualness. She shook her arm free and averted her eyes from anyone they met on their way.

On their way to the old woman's place, Ivy remembered that Maudie had helped her occasionally. That time when she was caught on the sandbank it was Maudie who saved her. After that the old woman had even taken her fishing sometimes, before her knees packed up. But ever since everyone started talking about her affair with Jipp Maudie had avoided her. She was just like everyone else. "Thinks I ask for Jipp slobbering all over me," Ivy thought bitterly. Knowing what they all thought of her, she felt ashamed.

On the other hand, Ivy didn't really mind that Old Maudie kept away from her. "Never really liked the old black crow with the moley face anyway," she told herself. It was a proper shame job to be seen walking around with the old woman. She always made herself conspicuous, calling out to people on their way through the village. It didn't matter if there was nobody in sight. And always, someone would come out to see what Old Maudie wanted. Then the curious eyes would look Ivy up and down. Just keeping the mental picture up to date.

But Ivy also recalled times when she'd been so lonely that she had gone down to Maudie's. There was nowhere else she could go. If Maudie saw her coming she would sneak off through the saltbushes, spinifex and trees at the back of her place to hide. She shuffled so slowly that Ivy sometimes caught her in the act.

She'd seek Maudie out after the times when she got into trouble in the classroom, too. Ivy was never able to read like the others. Her best efforts consisted of stumbling over the words and muttering. The teacher would stand in front of her desk, her ruler slapping Ivy's arm and the desk top in turn. Arm. Desk. Arm. Desk. While the rest of the class just laughed. Ivy learned to cower into the deteriorating depths of herself from which she would never again surface. She just kept on making the same mistakes. And when it was her turn to answer a question, even though she knew the answer she stammered and became incomprehensible.

"Who is the Saviour of the world?"

Ivy knew the answer but was afraid of using the incorrect name. Was it God? Christ? Jesus? Was she supposed to say Jesus Christ? In panic the words went jumbling through her mind. Better to say nothing.

"Everyone —" bang on Ivy's arm "— tell this stupid girl — who is the Saviour of the world?"

The whole class sang out loud and true: "Jesus, Miss!" Repeating the answer over and over. Until Ivy would never forget it.

After such incidents Maudie's place was the best cure, even if Ivy never got to see the old woman. She could still sit under the tree where her mother had died and wonder about her. She found it difficult to remember now what her mother had looked like. Yet at other times, when she wasn't even trying, her mother's face would suddenly appear in her mind. Ivy knew that Maudie never went far. She hid behind a small rise covered with bush. Under the thin branches and foliage she sat in speckled shade with her billy of lukewarm tea. From there she had a good view of her place; she could see if Ivy was snopping around her things.

Sometimes, when Ivy went to Maudie's place, her thoughts passed over her mother's funeral. Being scared of the nearness of the thunder. Being cold from the rain falling on her while her mother was buried. "Was it like being a film star or something?" she would ask, tilting her head up to the sky. "Didn't you realise you would kill yourself with the fire?" The sky remained unchanged. "Well! Why didn't you take me as well?" She made a pointed stick and started to dig a hole for herself under that tree. In time the hole was big enough for her to sit inside it, a cool place to escape the heat. She used to lie in it speaking to the sky. After she left she would look back and see Old Maudie limping over to inspect the hole. With a scowl on her old moley face she would kick back as much of the dirt as she could. Then Maudie would flinch suddenly, and Ivy knew that old pussy eyes had seen her mother smiling up from the hole.

Today, after they finally got to Maudie's hut, Ivy sat on the upturned kerosene tin beside the iron-frame bed, feeling hot and uncomfortable. This death scene had been acted out so many times already; why did she have to be called in for some sort of kinky supporting role? Whenever she looked up towards the door those stern-faced women, the Christian stalwarts sitting around just outside spat icy glances at her. She didn't dare move, not even to scratch an ant bite on her foot.

Early that morning Old Maudie had known this was the day she would fail the final challenge. This time death would stay with her until the life was suffocated from her body. She did not feel so very different from those other times over the past few months when she thought her day had come. Somehow she had dodged the odds — until now. It was the Lord Jesus who saved her, the Christian women rejoiced. To be agreeable, Maudie conceded that Jesus might have helped. But now she was prepared to go. She was old enough.

"Tell Ivy to come," she managed to say in a weak voice. She slid weightlessly back and forth into unconsciousness. She could not stop the grey shadow wafting about the room, coming to take her away. When it descended she could not breathe. When it lifted she felt weaker. It was uncanny how the others remained unaffected. There was no air, yet they breathed easily.

Ivy felt exposed to the eyes outside. She thought the women were using her as an excuse so that they did not come too close to death themselves. She did not want to play her role in this event. She did not want to see anyone die. She twisted the wool fringe on the thin grey blanket bearing the government stamp that lay beneath the dying woman. Each member of the community was issued with one blanket a year. She remembered the assembly at Christmas time, when Old Maudie had walked up to collect hers from Jipp, standing beside the huge pile of folded blankets and ticking off each name in turn until the last one was gone. After that everyone waited for the Queen's Christmas message on the wireless set up outside. The other children giggled at the sound of the English voice, hiding their faces into their arms folded around their knees, but Ivy liked the different voice, even though she did not understand what was being said.

She did not look at the old face so close to her own, breathing in short, shallow gasps. She watched a honey-eater among the blossoms of the mango tree outside the window behind the clock at 4 o'clock. Inside the room flies were buzzing.

Ivy had not meant to slap Maudie's face: she only wanted to brush the fly away. Maudie's eyelids shot wide open, revealing brown-blue milky eyeballs surrounded by scarred tissue, the legacy of trachoma. The old woman's left arm came sharply across her body — in her hand the red-and-white spotted handkerchief that Ivy had given her one Christmas. Ivy's offending hand was captured; she stared at the contrast between the old, leathery skin against her own young arm covered with fine hair. She wanted to withdraw her arm. She wanted to run away. She could feel the urgency of Maudie's grasp, as if she was trying to steal her strength to boost her own exhaustion. *Why doesn't she just die,* Ivy thought.

"You, girl! You forgive Old Maudie, eh?" Maudie's eyes, all but blind, were directed straight into Ivy's face.

The women at the doorway almost blocked the last of the daylight filtering into the room. Their praying died away as they watched and listened.

Ivy could not understand why she should be asked for forgiveness by Maudie. She could only think that Old Maudie knew her thoughts as she had sat there all afternoon. Wishing the old woman was dead. Ivy looked at her, shamefaced, and tears swelled in her eyes.

"Old Maudie goin' soon now. Never meanin' you harm, girl." The old woman's sudden burst of energy deserted her and she fell back flat on the bed. Her breathing was short, panicky. "Your mother wanted to go," she muttered.

Ivy glanced at her with new interest, pulling her arm free and taking the scarf.

"I go in peace, please, my girl?"

The honeyeater had returned: suddenly it flew through the open window. Frightened, it flew back and forth, beating itself against the tin walls of the shack. The women at the doorway were stunned by this magic. Ivy just sat there watching the bird while the women's fat lips hissed orders to get it out of the place.

Instead, Ivy suddenly grabbed the old woman on the bed, stared into her eyes and shook her violently. She was not even aware of the bird pecking at them both as it swooped frantically about the room. The sun had almost disappeared from the western sky.

"Tell me about my mother," she cried — but Old Maudie's eyes were closing. "Tell me!" she screamed, beginning to shake her again — but this time the witnesses at the doorway dragged her away with slaps and punches. "You are evil!" they yelled. Ivy was pushed against one wall. Cups, tins, plates crashed down. Flour spilled over the floor. The bird, wings beating frantically, escaped in the midst of all this. Ivy was dragged outside by her hair and sent flying face first into the dirt. A big, heavy-set woman plucked her up again for further treatment.

"Playing your evil tricks on Old Maudie!"

"What did Maudie say to you?" — the question was put to Ivy over and over again.

Then the women, almost hysterical by now, began to accuse her of other things …

"You come here from your Sickness country. Spreadin' it all over this place here."

For the first time Ivy heard what the adults believed about her.

"Sick people there dying all the time. People with no hands. No toes. No fingers. You hear that, you disease carrier!"

"What you know? What you spreadin', hey?"

Ivy cannot believe this is happening. She has never heard this kind of talk about anyone. She does not remember ever hearing anything about her country. Dazed and shocked, she tries to put the puzzle of her life together. She cannot believe she is thought of as the embodiment of evil. Why should they think this? She has no power.

She began to feel faint. Surely it was a bad dream. She remembered comparing herself with the Chapel girls … wasn't she nearly the same as them? Then she thought of Jipp and felt ugly, exposed.

The women gradually stopped screaming and sanity returned. They went inside the hut again. Everyone had missed the exact moment when Maudie died.

"Poor thing. Poor old thing." The crying grew louder and Ivy felt sadness too. Sadness for Maudie, sadness for herself. She stumbled back inside the hut, through the thicket of weeping women and yanked the handkerchief off the bed, then walked out again. Swishing it briskly from side to side, she walked back in the dark to the girls' dormitory.

Elliot the Traveller, returned from his journey, watched her pass by in the dark.

"Your day will come, missy," he thought.

5

"Lift her out of the valley of darkness! But? Will she be accountable? Being accountable is profitable. Is it about money? Earning one's own living? No! Isn't there more to life? Nothing to do with money. Nobody should even think that. But I ask you … Can you lift her out of the valley of darkness? Will she then see the goodness … There … There! In God's grace. He who has given us His all … Given so much for us all. So we can live … All can live? Yes? She will be a Goddess there." They speak so many words. Their work is slow and laborious. Self-doubts frothing like polluted water trapped in a crevice or ebb with nowhere to go. The watertight Christian orthodoxy unable to suppress the multitude of disappointments that rages like a pack of wounded animals all through the night. And they ask questions for nobody to answer.

In her dream Ivy watches her body slip uncontrollably through the narrow darkness of a deep channel. It burrows deeper into the bowels of the earth. She asks herself if she is dying. She asks if she is already dead — if so, the occasion of her death passed without her realising it. She remembers the entrance to the channel. It was in the tree stump on the other side of the river, all that was left of a giant eucalyptus struck by the lightning of the Great Spirit. It had fallen into decay after death, one stick, one branch after another, termite-hollowed wood falling free with each rain. An ancestral entrance through the dark hole left there. — Or perhaps, if you looked at it another way, it was the white-man's traditional culture that put an end to it. *Hack, hack, hack!* Cut it down for the good of an unholy progress.

Ivy had seen a brown snake disappear down the hole once. On the day of Old Maudie's funeral, lined up there with the rest of the kids to form a guard of honour. For Maudie. All God's good black Christians and everyone else there thought a guard of honour was a lovely thing to provide for a saint who had died. Everyone saw the snake crawling towards the church. Trying not to get too excited, tapping each other on the shoulder to look at it, putting the fear of God into themselves when it flared up, mouth gaping wide open before it slid away.

The snipping scissors sound very loud in the quiet of the afternoon. It seems as though the cutting will go on for ever … Ivy's head, her lips are numb. Hold still in case of a slip! She hears the dull metal ends snapping and the crackling of the cut hair as it leaves her head and falls to the ground. "Nits and lice!" That is why her head is being shaved — so she has been told. But she knows the real reason. It is a punishment. She is not the only one to have her head shaved. All those girls who sneaked out at night and got caught have had their heads shaved too. Fuck them all! It's a good job they are forced to wear an old sugarbag dress to make them look uglier still. And they have to sweep the streets with everyone watching them. It is too light a pun-ishment for them, Ivy thinks. That pretty-face Dolly Dean even asked if she could wear a scarf over her head after it happened to her. She must really think herself!

When Ivy dreams she sees Old Maudie standing there and she is wearing the spotted handkerchief around her head, just like Mrs Jipp's "Old Mammy" teapot. Ivy wonders how the dead woman got the scarf back. She knows one of the girls in the dormitory stole it. In Ivy's dream, Maudie carefully unties the scarf and when she pulls it off she is bald too. How did that happen? Some loose bits of hair the colour and texture of chicken wire are still sticking to the scarf. Without hair she looks even uglier, but she is smiling at Ivy. Those loose girls never smile when they sweep the streets.

No boys ever wanted them girls any more. The boys just laughed and goaded each other about what a good time they'd had. Plenty others, they told each other. Always plenty other girls wanting someone to teach them a good time. Willing to sneak around in the dark looking for it. But no way would any of them boys want one of those baldy ones again. Used. Sugarbag sacks, they said. Old fellas could have them.

If only Ivy could find that spotted handkerchief she could cover her head. Let them laugh. They don't do it to your face. Not game. But she can hear them whispering about her. They always make sure of that. She tried not to notice the stones cheeky boys threw behind her back. She would just walk on through the village as fast as she could, with her head bent. Everything was just a dream. She was herself, Grace and Joan Chapel all rolled into one and everything was normal.

Ivy refused to acknowledge the spirit of Maudie walking beside her, keeping up, walking faster than any old person she had ever seen. Maudie, waving to everyone and not even noticing they never saw her, even shaking off the scarf, showing off. Her old bald head waves elegantly from side to side as if she had hair that flowed down to her waist.

Ivy goes to the mission house every day now to clean up for Beverly Jipp. She don't want no nits in her house. She says that to all of her "help". *He* don't want no nits around him either. Maybe some time ago his wife found a louse on him. Had Beverly quietly watched the louse crawl across his forehead while he spoke briefly yet glowingly of the normality of the platonic intimacies between them? Had it fallen into her breakfast cereal? Beverly Jipp would have had a surprised look on her pallid face.

Not knowing where the louse came from she still couldn't put two and two together. No wonder everyone had something to laugh about. Something like one little louse should have been enough sign for anyone else, but it was lost on Beverly Jipp, who only searched for the more insipid realities of life.

"You got to give it to old Jipp" — the men and women down in the village spoke about him often when they needed a distraction from their own concerns.

"Nah! Not possible, init."

"He's not much of a converter of black people for Church business. But talk about pricky-tricky when it comes to sinning himself and keeping his own property safe!"

"I'm waiting for the day she going to flog him."

"Maybe she still doesn't know. Poor thing."

"Nah! White women must be different. Mustn't be interested."

"Or something."

"Nah! He shouldn't go to so much trouble covering his tracks. Or trying to. Not for that sulky thing walkin' around with her head hanging down around the dirt. Up herself. Hasn't got the decency to acknowledge anyone. Don't think anyone would be wantin' to take that one on."

Ivy's thoughts had wandered back to the village, where she could vividly see the dozens of noisy tongues, slapping lips, making it hard to pick out one voice from the others gossiping behind her back. She sipped the cup of tea she had made for herself and Mrs Jipp. They sat at the kitchen table facing each other. Beverly Jipp never knew what to say during the tea breaks these days. It had become the least pleasant time of the day for her. One way of breaking the silence, if she could get Ivy to talk, was to say a prayer together. She thought sadly of how things used to be, when she sat down to enjoy her cup of tea and a biscuit or slice of cake with one or other of her previous helpers, chosen by herself — women who liked to talk about what was happening around the place. Women needed other women, no matter who they were.

Jipp was always glad when some domestic upheaval generally forced an early retirement of gas-bagging women from his house.

"That child of yours needs a firmer hand, wouldn't you agree, Freddy? Something must be happening at home lately. Everything going well?"

Setting the clock. Baking the cake. On average, he made a point of having a change of face around the house about every few months.

The trouble with Ivy, Beverly thought, was that she was too young for the job. What was she now — fourteen or fifteen? She would gladly have taken the girl into their family when she was a small child, after her mother killed herself in such a tragic way. At the time she used to think of nothing else except having Ivy in the house with her. She had felt such emptiness without her own children around her. First they had gone off to boarding school in the South, then they had left for good. She had thought that taking Ivy in at that time was a possibility and frequently imagined what it would be like. She recognised there would be some problems, but nothing she and Errol could not overcome. For instance, she imagined taking Ivy with them on holidays. The child was not very dark and could probably pass for white on certain occasions. (Better to save others from feeling ill at ease and embarrassed.) She had been such a slim, pretty little thing with her green eyes. She could easily have been taken for a Greek or Lebanese child, or an Islander.

But Errol had vetoed the idea. Had stared at her as though she'd gone mad when she broached the subject. There was no way he was going to let her turn their house, their very lives turned upside down by bringing "that child" into their home, he snapped. "Heaven knows where she came from. We don't even know who her father was. Judging by the mother it wouldn't be difficult to guess his type. Worst of both kinds, white and black. You know what you get when people interbreed up here. Haven't you ever taken any notice of those sort of women? What decent white man would go with one of them, eh?"

She knew now that he'd been right, of course, although at the time she did not want to think so. And look at the girl, now, already a young woman, sitting with her shaved head bent, a scowl always on her face. So painfully shy. Beverly could only think the reason Errol had chosen Ivy to help in the house now was to ensure she did not break the "them and us" line. She'd always tried not to, but sometimes it had proved difficult. She couldn't help becoming involved in the lives of her chosen help. She often felt guilt-ridden about what the women might glean from her over a cup of tea, then cart back to their own people as gossip. She would never knowingly betray Errol and the sacredness of their life together.

"Would you like a scarf to wear, Ivy?" Beverly asked suddenly. She had wanted to demonstrate some sympathy for the girl's shaven head. Poor thing!

Ivy nodded and Beverly went off to fetch the scarf. Ivy hoped that whatever she was given was not going to be hideous, causing her to feel even more shame. She would have to wear it. Ivy had no idea whether old woman Jipp knew about what went on between her husband and her. Maybe she did, and would punish her sooner or later. — White women are different, Ivy thought. They don't say nothing. Always polite. She could see for herself that Jipp and his wife did not sleep together. — That's the way white people are, she reasoned. Mrs Jipp did not look happy. Her mouth turned down and there was a permanent frown across her forehead. Ivy interpreted these features as the result of their separate bedrooms. She couldn't blame the woman, though. It was a better arrangement than having his stale, stinking breath all over you. She could smell him all over the house as she cleaned, especially in his bedroom. A woman like Mrs Jipp would be very particular about anything that interfered with her personal space, where she slept, dressed and ate. Ivy had seen how Mrs Jipp was able to force herself to cope occasionally with black babies — snotty noses, shitty bums — handed to her by laughing mothers who mistakenly believed she loved their children. She guessed this woman would recoil from the unpleasantness of her middle-aged husband, yet be incapable of coping with the worse unpleasantness of expressing her distaste. (White women don't say nothing.) She was incapable of keeping Jipp at home, Ivy thought scornfully.

Beverly was glad of the chance to do something to make up a little for what had happened to Ivy. Shaving the girls' heads in punishment was a barbaric practice. At the same time she was repulsed by the loose morals of the girl breaking out of the dormitory like bitches on heat. When the punishments first started she had felt sick in the stomach, while Errol had gone on and on about what he had to do to curb the temptations of young girls who behaved like camp dogs.

The tasteful mauve scarf with tiny white dots was okay, Ivy thought. Not too flash. (Though sometimes she had a vision of herself in bright colours like those billowing garments on clothes-lines in the village.) But the scarf was better than the drab colours Mrs Jipp usually wore. She took it without offering any further acknowledgment. It was, she thought, a small enough reward for doing this woman's dirty work. Her with the biggest mongrel dog she don't even know how to keep home … sniffing all around the place at night.

Ivy looked around the kitchen. She knew that in her whole life she would never have a house like this. So clean. With special cups to serve tea to guests. She would simply go on living the way the rest of the community lived. A prize in the garden of Eden! The prize of the Kingdom of Heaven! Was this it? The paradise they preached about on Sundays. They said that St Dominic's was paradise? Just who was Jesus, the statue? She recalled the way the old women talked about Him ...

"Je — sus! He born place belong far, far away. Overseas mob!"

"He gone now ... back to His father's mob along Heaven."

"Causin' them other mob killed him right off."

"Gone now! Gone and no wonder why, hey?"

"Hallelujah! Hallelujah! Hallelujah!"

"You got to really-eyes He died for you."

"What for? When He did that? I never hear 'bout that."

"It was before the Queen — you know that one Queen Elizabeth ... long time before that ... I don't know, I lost track. Anyway, long time ago."

That was the way they talked, the sort of things they said. Ivy compared the silence and neatness of Mrs Jipp's house to the laughter that went on in the women's camp out in the open, under the stars. A corrugated iron windbreak around several rusty beds piled high with tattered old government blankets. No scorpions or snakes wandered around there. The ground got properly slapped around at night. On cold nights the women's dogs slept alongside them on top of the beds, while spinifex skeletons rolled by below. Ivy heard their voices again —

"That lay-preacher, waddimnane — Jimbo Lainie. Gordon's son. He knows all 'bout Jesus."

"His name *De*-lain-y. Calls himself Delainy now. Don't you really-eyes — not Lainy, Delainy."

The women all cracked their sides laughing at their jokes. Really-eyes Delainy, he was the one all right. He made everyone think about a thing or two at the end of the day, when the women sat around talking about anything and nothing. You could put two and two together after listening to him. He told them God made heaven and earth and all the people. He made the trees and animals. God was really someone. He was even from the Dreamtime, if you thought about it. It was the biggest story. But white people needed to say God looked like them, to make them feel better than anyone else. So they made up their own story. Talk about thinking themselves! Really-eyes Delainy knew God was all the same one as Rainbow Serpent. All the jolly same. — "You better believe it, you women," he said.

Remembering the old women's talk, Ivy could hardly stop a smile crossing her face. She knew the Jipp woman would not be interested in what the locals thought about her wonderful religion.

The women's camp talked endlessly about Delainy. They often scoffed at him when they saw him sniffing around their camp at night. "What for? Nothin' round here except dried-up old grannies." Though there might be one or two amongst them who could still show him a thing or two — and they chuckled so hard at the thought that they ended up coughing and barking from their chest infections. If they kept up talking about him this way they'd probably all be dead by morning, they said.

Maybe Delainy was aware of all the talk about him. He was slippery, like the snake-oil salesman who came round with goanna ligament in his pockets. He would rub the oil into the women's sore knees and backs while they sat winking at one another. "Flashed-up dingo legs," the old women called Delainy. "Really thinks himself, talkin' all that church stuff." And why did he prowl around at night, they wondered.

The women couldn't stand the sight of Ivy's shaven head. They told her straight it served her right. She was glad to just dump their daily bag of food which the dormitory girls prepared for them. She was annoyed she had to take it down to them; the old hags could just have easily come up to the kitchen to get it for themselves. When they discovered their tealeaf was missing from the bag they began to wheedle her.

"Good daughter, good girl, go back quickly. Get the tealeaf for your old grannies here."

Good girl? Sure. But Ivy wasn't going to be bothered doing a second trip. Delainy the lay preacher was back again in the camp, standing in the smoky haze of several damp little fires. "Never mind. Never you mind now, old ladies," he said. "I will get your tealeaf." And when Ivy left he came with her.

"Do you understand why you are being punished, girl?" he asked as she walked uncomfortably beside him, wishing he'd go away. Early morning was the time when people were outside preparing something to eat, kids playing all over the place. The time of least concealment, when everyone noticed other people's business. She made no answer — she knew he would give her the answer himself.

"There are those on this earth whose wickedness is ingrained," he said. "They can't help themselves. You agree?" Delainy always sought agreement with his statements, pausing just long enough to strike the right chord in the listener's mind before moving on to another of his simplistic viewpoints. His voice had a convincing edge to it. Ivy was almost persuaded into believing whatever he said. Such people, he told her, sinned whenever they got the chance. He knew their kind because he'd been there once himself with girls like her, but luckily he had seen the light in time, praise be to God. She was one of those kind, he went on: he'd seen it in her face the first time he'd laid eyes on her. He didn't know if her present punishment was sufficient — it was obvious sin still burnt there in her eyes.

The lay preacher became more agitated as they walked on, grasping his hands behind his back to stop the involuntary flexing of his fingers. Ivy walked on swiftly, increasing her pace until they were both almost running through the village. Delainy gasped out the urgent need to speak to Jipp about her behaviour, to see what more could be done about her. Finally he rushed ahead of her to fetch the tealeaf for the old women.

After that encounter, Ivy felt that perhaps she did need to discuss her situation. This morning, sitting in the kitchen of the mission house, she was still aware of that need. But Mrs Jipp was the last person she could ever confide in, she thought as she sat in silence at the red laminex table. The ordeal of morning tea was making her feel sick. She longed for the break to end, if she had to sit there any longer she thought she would faint.

6

The elders' investigation heated up again after a string of deaths, two women and one man. It seemed an incredible story of love and jealousy. The two widows had set up separate camps in order to have a relationship with the same man. Some said it was the man who did all the enticing, to get the women to leave the widows' camp and then strangle them dead like that Jack the Ripper bloke everyone had heard about. The one who was still footloose, even after thousands of bullymen the world over had failed to find him. Some believed if anyone was on the run what better place to hide oneself than St Dominic's and prey on the widows' camp. A place freer of police keeping a eye on the law if there ever was. And Jipp was no artisan of policing.

It began when a man, a silhouette in the night, hung off some distance from the women's camp. The two he lured away had simply jumped up and gone off with him. At first the old women suspected someone like Delainy, Elliot or even some of the old fellas, still sowing wild oats. "Ah! She'll come back when she learns," they had scoffed when the first woman went off. Then another silhouette appeared for his rendezvous with the second woman. They had all assumed the two silhouettes were two different men, but after the deaths they told each other they should have realised it was unlikely two men would be loitering around their camp on some pretext of finding wives for themselves. But at the time they thought good fortune had finally struck where it ought to. Then goings-on had refuelled their opinions of men in general and added to their collective thoughts about men's disagreeable nature.

The old women rolled over in their beds to peep out when the first woman and later the second each returned alone, before dawn. "You won't get yourself a husband that way," they had goaded in the morning. Each of the two refused to name names. As the days passed, simple teasing turned into hostility, and the two women packed their belongings in a huff and walked off, shamefaced, to make separated, isolated camps elsewhere.

A charred corpse was all they found when someone went looking for the first of the two women. Jipp called it another suicide, cursing the shade of Ivy Koopundi's mother loudly enough to be heard throughout the village. A week later the other woman died in the same way. Fear entered the widows' camp: the women whispered to themselves at night and jumped up screaming at the slightest sound in the surrounding bush.

Jipp came to the camp to interrogate them, with Delainy close at his heels, hanging on every word. After Jipp heard their story, he kicked out at the cooking pots in the fireplace and at someone's dog for good measure before he grew calm enough to speak. He told them he was astonished they had not worked out what was happening for themselves. Delainy nodded solemnly. Then Jipp told them that he and Delainy would be patrolling around the camp every night from now on.

"If any of you want husbands," he said, "I will find one for you. Just ask me. I make the decisions here about marriages. See what happens when you go sneaking around behind my back in the middle of the night, leaving me to fix up the mess!"

"These women are sex-starved. Hungry all the time," Delainy told Jipp in a jeering tone.

"Don't talk like that," Jipp snapped back, wiping beads of sweat off his forehead.

"It's true. Tell him the way you talk to me." Delainy persisted, and whispered in Jipp's ear his long-held suspicion that this camp was full of black witches.

"Rubbish!" Jipp hissed; but he stored the notion in his mind all the same.

The truth was that in his night-wanderings, Delainy had a string of women who used him for sex for the hell of it. Afterwards they would swap stories, and now, when he came to the camp trying to hide behind Jipp, they leered at him with their hungry eyes.

The women just wished the intruders would go away. But it wasn't to be. The interrogations and lectures went on for days. Neither Jipp nor Delainy were able to decide why the two women had died. The widows' camp became the nerve centre for the two men to try to work out what was wrong with the womenfolk. It got to the stage where a list of potential husbands was discussed by the two men without any input from the women themselves. Eventually it all became too much for them, and one by one the women got up and walked away, while Delainy yelled in vain for them to come back.

Three weeks after the first woman had died, a married man with children and a good, decent wife who did everything for him, a man who was leading light for the Church, a man with a navy suit, hanged himself from the rafters in a foul-smelling toilet. Suddenly this dead man became the suspected murderer. His wife kicked off her new widowhood by publicly bewailing the shame of a husband who was a double adulterer. She blamed the Church, saying it was evil and made men act like animals, hanging around in the bush to sniff out women when a decent wife was sitting at home with his babies. There was murmuring amongst the converted about withdrawing from the Church. Both

Jipp and Delainy were mortified; the dead man was buried without fuss. The community was ordered to stop talking about the whole affair. It was to be forgotten. But the clandestine work of the forbidden Law Council of the elders continued. And now Elliot the Traveller embarked on his second journey.

It was a dangerous time to travel alone over the land: it was waking-up season. Elliot's journey back through the Channel Country and along his Dreaming line, intermeshing between snake-rivers to the Great Lake was carried out in the Dry. It was at this time that whatever powerful essences lay submerged all around rose from the earth. You needed to take extra precautions to remain safe. He was careful to eat sparingly from a limited amount of available food, so that he would not create any noticeable odours which the spirits would notice. Suspicious of every movement around him, even a leaf fluttering in the breeze, he starved himself to avoid the risk. The pathway he followed was dimly visible in his mind as a narrow, hazy tunnel. Should he penetrate its walls, even though soundless to his ear, this would create disturbance amid the serene surroundings and awaken the restful state of the spiritual environment and bring forth its malignant powers.

The most perilous time of all came early in the evening, when the dying sun beamed its last light onto the sandhills and over the dead grassland. This was the time you needed to take cover, when the last screeches of the black cockatoos with their red tails died away and the land was quiet. It was best to sit it out for the night. Beyond his camp, Elliot watched the bush pigeons fossicking amongst dry twigs in the red, glowing grasses. Although he lay with some sense of security beneath a gidgee tree, his father's totem, he was brooding about how he could get rid of the pigeons. No point in being cautious on the one hand then gamble in your camp at night.

Over the passing of many nights he repeatedly whispered to the pigeons, urging them to take flight and seek the safety of cover. Sometimes the birds took a moment and made head-wobbling movements as if they took notice of his words and actions, but they did not fly off. Mainly they ignored him. At first he tended to dismiss their lack of intuition, but as days of travel grew into weeks and he sat swathed in his sweat under a tree where the breeze did not penetrate, he heard the echoes of the great spirits thundering in the distant hills and started to have second thoughts about the nature of birds. He changed his attitude towards their presence. He felt he was right to do so, for he was trained in religious knowledge of the land by the thoughts of the elders, through a straight line of law since time began and the land and everything in it had been created. It was his duty to do his utmost to maintain harmony in the world that owned him.

As each day passed on his long journey he began to lose sight of the reality of St Dominic's and his own place in the Mission. He tried in vain to recall people's faces, the inside of his father's dwelling … try as he might he could not do it. It was like lifting his weight in lead. He had become obsessed by the pigeons. Before dusk each day he tried every evasive angle he had been taught — movements which were now an instinctive part of his nature — to try to rid himself of the birds. He had always been able to outsmart anyone: at St Dominic's people knew this side of Elliot's nature well. Some bore scars as reminders of times they had tried to call his bluff.

Try as he might, he could not escape the pigeons. He never saw them during daylight. It was only at dusk, when he made his camp, that they appeared. Sometimes he hid from them in low bushes. At other times he buried himself in the deep sand of a dry river bed, hiding there for hours until it was dark. He arose from his makeshift grave only to find the pigeons looking at him from a short distance away.

By now, the birds were cooing and scratching the dirt right next to the place where he slept. They would be gone in the morning, but Elliot never saw them leave.

Then night is broken into stages in the Hot. Early on the ground retains the stored energy of the sun and radiates uncomfortable heat — it is impossible to lie on this hot ground and sleep. Hours later, it cools: the dry, brittle earth sighs and expands in vast yawns. This is the signal for creatures and men, big red stony devils, to lie stretched out asleep on their sleeping mother. It is the time of the creaks and moans of the great spirits awakening. Rocks, trees, hills and rivers — all are awake at this time. Released from their sedated daytime state, the spirits of the land travel from place to place. The air, the sky is alive with the ancestral spirits of the land. As Elliot endured another night of restless sleep, he knew it was best to sing their songs and urge them towards good feelings.

No one was able to look after the land any more, not all of the time, the way they used to in the olden days. Life was so different now that the white man had taken the lot. It was like a war, an undeclared war. A war with no name. And the Aboriginal man was put into their prison camps, like prisoners in the two world wars. But nobody called it a war: it was simply the situation, that's all. Protection. Assimilation … different words that amounted to annihilation. The white man wanted to pay alright for taking the lot. But they didn't want to pay for the blackman's culture, the way he thinks. Nor for the blackman's language dying away because it was no longer tied to his traditional country … now prosperous cattle station or mining project. The white people wanted everyone to become white, to think white. Skin and all. And they were willing to say they will pay out something for that, even though they believed what happened was not worth much. They could not actually see the value for their money — not like buying grain or livestock.

Yet no one could change the law — so Elliot muttered to

himself as he crossed the whiteman's roads or stepped across tyre marks made by vehicles that had been bogged at river crossings. In spite of the foreign burrs and stinging nettles along the river banks — nothing foreign could change the essence of the land. No white man had that power.

Elliot visualised the hands of white people writhing with some kind of illogical intent to misuse and swallow up what was not on a map imprinted in the ancestry of their blood. Hands that hung limp when the land dried up. That buried dead children, set tables with no food to eat. Hands that tried to fight the fires that destroyed the crops and livestock they valued so much. The essence of their souls. He saw the same hands gesturing with self-centred righteousness, a backhand flick to explain hard times, without thought of the true explanations for disaster from the land itself. Good season, bad season! Their palms opened to beg for more government money to keep their stranger life afloat. Kill off whatever got in the way of it. Put it down to bad luck when things were bad. Put it down to good luck when things went right. A simplistic way of ignoring their own ignorance. Sit in one spot and eat it all away. A laconic race living on its wit's end in order to voice its demands and ordered others to fall into line.

The night might have been enjoyed once. He thought of the days when the spirits and the black people would have spoken to each other. But the blackman's enforced absence from his traditional land had inspired fear of it. They had to alter old, ongoing relationship with the spirits that had created man and once connected him to the earth.

As the weeks passed, Elliot the Traveller became convinced he would not live to be an old man. Cattle lay dead beside the mud-cracked waterholes of the dry riverbeds. Kangaroos and wallabies lay nearby. He had been sent at the wrong time. The restless spirits exchanged thunderous blows of anger, tying earth and sky into knots. *Wrong! Wrong! Wrong!* They raced up and down the sky in the pitch-black night. Giant arms struck out with a fearful force, felling giant ghost gums which nearly killed him as they crashed to the ground.

Why had the elders sent him in the first place? Yes, he was convinced they had hatched a plan to get rid of him. *"You won't get me,"* he repeated to himself a thousand times a day. He was no longer distracted by their attempts to cloud his thinking — for it must have been they who had taken away his memory of St Dominic's. Why did they want him dead? For the first time he imagined he saw deception in his own father's face. *This is a lot of trouble you have gone to,* he screamed. *Why? Why here and not there?* If the elders did have some sinister plan for him, Jipp the self-appointed augur would not have been any the wiser. Elliot traced and retraced every detail of his life for clues.

Perhaps it was his tendency towards violence. Surely not, when even the most demure of young women with babies in their tummies stomped through the village yelling at their husbands after they had quarrelled with them — "You wait! I'll be coming for you with a big knife! As soon as I get some money I am going to buy a knife for you." While the husband, looking like a piece of well-kneaded dough, trotted along after her at a safe distance. Then she yelled again: "to rip your guts out!" And you could believe it would happen. And alongside, her two-year-old, shaping up his little fists, kicked each leg back towards his father to demonstrate he was on his mother's side and he meant business, too.

No, it was not his violence. His magic then? Almost everyone in the community was wary of his knowledge of magic. When he was younger he would run and complete a somersault in mid-air, land on his feet and do it again up and down the road between the village and Mission. He made tobacco tins glow in the dark. Children begged him to show them. Watching, their mothers' eyes nearly popped out of their heads and they chased their kids away with sticks. He balanced stones on the tops of sticks and made them twirl around. The old men found interesting stones to challenge him. He beat them each time. He could sketch faces to the exact likeness, and left the portraits blowing around in the wind. That nearly frightened people half to death. Their fear was a source of amusement to him. They believed he was trying to steal their souls to serve himself. That he might be in secret collusion with the spirit world.

Elliot believed he could count on one hand the number of occasions when he had infringed the law during his thirty years of life. Trivial matters. Nothing to deserve this punishment. So what could it be? Perhaps some great danger threatened his people and his own life was considered inconsequential, a trivial matter in the greater scheme of things. Did the community fear of more suicides override one sacrifice? Had they agreed that he should provide that sacrifice? Who could know the true malevolence of Ivy Koopundi — or the combined force of her people, the guardians of the majestic spiritual being? Could their power, in some explicable way, stretch out to kill anyone, anywhere? Were they able to make those deaths appear as suicides? What pitiful chance did he have of confronting this power?

So, Elliot told himself, he was soon to become the sacrificial lamb for Ivy Koopundi. Why had not somebody simply murdered her in the middle of some moonless night? It would have been easy enough. He should have thought of it himself. He had no difficulty in recalling the way her sly face watched him everywhere he went. Jumping in front of him from right to left, left to right, the whole day, trying to send him crazy. Why had he not recognised the same sly look on the faces of Pilot and May Sugar and those other two old grannies? It was all as plain as day to him now.

Yes, it was her. He had been careful that she, above all,

should have no knowledge of his travelling — yet there she stood in the dark shadows the morning he left. Further back, he recalled the day Old Maudie died, and the side-long glance she had thrown him on her way through the village, a glance that chilled the base of his neck. She was a different kind. Not happy like his own people, who could joke about life, no matter what. They might be treated like dogs, but they could laugh just the same. They came from the spirits, and to the spirits they would return. That was the law. Always look above. Ivy played another role, and laughing at life was not part of it.

So be it. If this journey led to death then he must allow it to happen. But the pigeons ... were they a warning to him, a contradiction of prediction?

Travelling over a sacred Dreaming line, over the ranges sleeping on the surface of the land, Elliot caught the first glimpse of the Great Lake some hundred kilometres away. Each day the lake shimmered and grew larger in his sight until he reached its edge. There he walked on top of the white clay, cracked into slits that penetrated deep into the earth. The illusion of water kept its distance as he walked further into the basin.

Dead pelicans were dotted here and there on top of the clay. Kilometres towards the water's centre, the numbers of dead birds increased, until he was stepping over piles of stinking, fly-blown bodies. White feathers flurried around in the choking, foul-smelling hot air: it was almost impossible to see through them in the steamy heat. Elliot strained his eyes to see through the contrasting whiteness of feathers and clay. It was difficult to focus, to keep control over his balance. His throat was burnt and swollen from days of a dryness so great he could no longer prevent the hot air entering his parted lips. He was trapped by the enticing cool waters of the mirage, controlled by two competing needs: to rid himself of the stench and return to shore, or quench his thirst in the water that lay ahead. This, his greater need, dragged him forward. He realised his death was close when he came upon the mountain of dead pelicans stacked one on top of the other in the centre of the lake, the last waterhole — a pool of drying mud. Thousands of gaping mouths flung open in a final bid to find water before they perished.

Escape was impossible. Locked in a prison of his own delirium, he fell to one side of the stacked corpses. Like the birds, he had been deceived by the mirage. Seeing the immensity of this false expanse of water, they had imagined there was plenty of time to diverge on their long migratory flight and take some of the life-sustaining water. Mothers, too concerned for their chicks, misjudging the land. As Elliot slipped into unconsciousness, he had a mental vision of the flocks of pelicans flying on towards St Dominic's ... they had missed these dead on the long voyage North?

Everyone at St Dominic's knew of the pelican's flight. Each year they ran outside to wait and watch as the sounds of wings drumming against the wind grew louder. Until the birds were finally above them. Oh! if you could reach up and touch the white-feathered bellies above your head. Oh! if you could fly away. The ﾑousands of droning wings in close formation were like a cloud made up of white lines. It could take half a day for the flight to pass over the Mission. If they came at night, everyone stayed up and sang for their journey, to take their spirits across the sea and come back again. As a boy, Elliot wished he could fly with them. All together the boys would flap their outstretched arms and run, hoping for magic to let them fly with the birds. Nothing came of it but the clouds of dust they made. Near death, he smiled faintly at the memory.

The deep rumbling sound began softly then grew louder. Elliot woke suddenly as rain pelted against his body. Revived, he jumped up in fright. Another thunder clap shook the night. In a flash of lightning he saw the water shine, ebbing against his outstretched legs. Water splashed, swirled, sloshed, increasing all the time, while he ran and ran, stumbling over the damp bodies of dead birds, guided by flashes of lightning, until at last he hurled himself amidst the saltbushes growing high on dry land.

7

The land had turned into a brilliant carpet in bright shades of green moments after the rain finally stopped. As far as the eye could see, soft spikes of grass fluttered in waves. The dead clumps of old grass, charred black from bushfires months ago and smelling of moist charcoal, lay flattened beneath the abundance of new growth. The land rejoiced. The words of the world whistled by in an endless murmur of repeating rhythms. A mother's songs of quietness after the time of giving birth.

The new grass soon stretched upwards in the humidity, then the long flapping strands spun together to form a cocoon in the cool of the evening. The ribbon-like threads flickered ceaselessly over its hidden treasure, filtering air to keep the temperature cool inside. Elliot was entombed in a web of grass.

Throughout the day, flies fretted in vain for access, while trails of ants arrived and departed, their swarms too insignificant to carry Elliot away to the plains, where insects crawled on top of each other, endlessly craving space. Grey moths swam around in the jerky air currents until they had exhausted themselves enough to fall flat into their destiny.

At night the dead returned, marching over the flat land. This time they feigned their identity as mosquitoes, unrecognisable in their sameness as the stars in the sky. Their living relatives were safe from the retaliations of this battle, where lost spirits fought each other individually. The arms

and hands of fathers, mothers, brothers and sisters pro-
tected their own: Elliot, a messenger of his people's spirits.

Dying leaves blew in silent showers of pink, olive and
dappled grey and formed another layer above the grass —
leaves from last season, now diseased and distorted, thrown
down from an ancient riverside eucalyptus fed by cool
underground streams. They lay there until the winds blew
up over the plains at reckless and rocketing speeds, whirling
them away.

Slowly, painfully, Elliot awoke. His tomb a sanctuary of
dead clanspeople who left as soon as they felt the renewal
of life in the heat he began to generate. They were no
longer necessary; relieved of the urgency of family obliga-
tion, they could return to fighting one another. For Elliot,
reclaiming his body was a gamble. A toss that won over fear.
He feared the jostling of disguised spirits so close beyond
his clansmen's shield, eagerly awaiting one false move to
drag him off to a destiny of their own making.

Elliot gambled and won. He had won over the domi-
nance of St Dominic's and its ability to reshape mind. He
could now rejoin the deeper world of his birthright. A
fantastic world which only allowed occasional glimpses of
the ordinary to slip in and out from recent memory. Experiences not really worth remembering. He was in a place so
far away he often had difficulty in acknowledging the reality
of his physical being. It took time to regain consciousness,
to make any realistic connection.

The eyeless cavities of pelican skulls penetrated far inside
his mind. For some inexplicable reason they had somehow
moved inside his tomb. Their beaks pecked at his skin as if
they were feasting. He could not understand these surreal
happenings. Images appeared to him, on their faces the
expressions of any angry audience made to endure a dismal
show: they faded away without applause. Elliot knew the old
folk had tricky ways. They were clever ones. Like his father.
One day Elliot would be feeling almost himself again, the

next he was gone beyond the realm of a normal human being. He saw his father's face, shaded by an old, dusty Akubra hat. The face was blank, the eyes staring down as if into the depths of an empty well.

He had lain in his grassy tomb for an unknown period. A few hours? Many days? He thought it must have been considerable because of the red, blistering welts all over his body, caused by the shifting grasses which had covered him. It was the itchiness that finally led to his recovery from this clash with death. Eventually, he could no longer lie there, inert, in the cool, dark stillness; he tore the woven casket apart.

For a long time, his eyes blinded by the sudden light, he was unable to see properly. Meanwhile, he became aware of the smell of smoke rapidly increasing. And now he vaguely glimpsed tantalising movements as the smoke swirled its dance of suffocation. At the same time, he thought he could hear the sound of singing … but perhaps it was part of his dreams. At last he was able to see that the smoke came from grassfires raging across the plains. He looked ahead. A dust storm. Red dust and smoke combined, and the sound of grass crackling under fire. He would have to run for it. Towards the storm.

The distance was greater than he had anticipated. Too weak to walk, he limped and crawled away from the burning grass — yet he did not seem to draw any closer to the dust storm.

About fifty young dogs, bald with mange, pricked up their ears when they saw him coming and ran towards him eagerly, as if he was the one who fed them bones from a loaded sugarbag hanging over the shoulder on a bent back. But Elliot brought them nothing, their wasted saliva poured onto the ground and they quickly turned into snarling wild creatures, ears drawn back, cringing along to form a tight circle around him. They looked pitiful. Pissing on the ground, their horrible sounds, unlike the ordinary dogs on

St Dominic's, were so loud he could not hear the singing he had awoken to. Singing he had first thought could only have been part of his dreams. Elliot heard the flick from fingers somewhere a long way off and the dogs sat down and whined.

At that moment he saw a vision through the smoky haze. He had stumbled into the midst of a dancing ground where several hundred people, their bodies painted white, were dancing. It was the force of their stamping feet breaking up the ground and sending the red dust flying in the air that caused the storm. There were dozens of dancing, chanting groups in close proximity. Each one sang independently, not in unison with other groups, so that the sound was continuous.

The ground boomed with the stamping feet. The fresh green grass was squashed and flattened. Gravel loosened, ground by feet into dust which rose and whirled away on the wind. Smoke billowed from hundreds of fires continually heaped with dead branches: these had been previously prepared for the occasion, to disguise the identities of the white-painted performers from the spirits they had aroused.

Black and white pelican feathers, downy balls from ducks and swans jumped up and down with the movement of the dance: the feathers were attached to the dancers' limbs with twine. White cockatoo feathers floated effortlessly to and fro amidst the dust and smoke, swaying upon the dancers' heads.

Elliot knew he had no alternative but to limp through the dancers to keep out of the way. He did not allow himself to feel afraid of the grey-white faces whose expressions signalled "we notice you" then reverted to expressionless masks. He was not sure whether the dancers believed he was a spirit or a stranger — perhaps both. The singing proceeded in languages he did not know. He was surrounded by faces without expression or identity. Spirit and

man. Man and Spirit. All the same. Except for him. Yet he
was past the sense of personal danger. Why had those dogs
been allowed to act so freely, he wondered. Surely any
malevolent spirit could easily latch onto the back of one of
the dogs, burrow like a tick beneath its hair, then lie there
until the dog returned to its owner. As if there wasn't
enough trouble around.

Trying to grip onto the truth of his journey, Elliot knew
that up to this point all he had done was to become
increasingly anxious over all the untoward events that had
marked his progress. He believed these were deviations
designed to lead him away from his purpose. Even though
it seemed his life had been threatened at every turn, somehow something had succeeded in keeping him alive. He did
not understand any of the unusual events that had happened so far, and wondered what further danger he would
meet in the country of Ivy Koopundi's family.

He looked back over the plains and saw the cloud that
rolled off into the horizon. He listened to the language of
beating hands, hands against thighs, the sounds that were
calling the birds to come home. Hands telling the story of
birds and their successful journeys beyond this country and
back again. Letting them know that their waterless home
was once again a swampy inland sea.

As far as the eye could see the water had resurfaced and
covered the grassy landscape. It had poured over the smoking cinders of the burn-off in an inland tidal wave, steam
rising from the open mouth. Elliot caked the wet clay over
his body to disguise himself and to ease the rash caused by
the grass spears. Eventually, as the sun crept down over the
western skyline, leaving only the last light, he heard a
booming noise that gradually increased in strength until it
drowned out all other sounds.

The dogs had soon deserted Elliot and disappeared
under some trees; now they grew agitated, joining hundreds of other clanspeople's dogs in uncontrolled yelping

which grew wilder and louder until it took over the ceremony. Everyone stopped to look towards the horizon. The last low light of the sun gave the inland lake a shimmering effect with rippling specks of gold. The painted faces focused on the yelping dogs, which continued their noise oblivious of the abuse that was flung at them.

Gradually the wailing of the dogs was overpowered by that other sound as a black shadow formed across the sky, blotting out the moon and stars and finally crashing onto the water, sending spray over the people squatting close to the ground. Dogs raced for cover. Birds by the million had returned. The lake was reclaimed. The ceremony completed. People gathered on the shores to continue singing, more quietly now, and to wash themselves, laughing away their earlier concern that the birds might never return.

"You there! Come over here — come on, over here!" a voice yelled in the darkness.

Startled, Elliot swung round to find a group of dogs staring at him. And there in the distance, standing on a small sand bank, was the old woman called May Sugar, the moonlight highlighting the floral dress she wore. Slowly he walked up to her.

"You come back, what for?" she called down to him.

She gave him a hug when he reached her, then started to introduce him in a loud voice filled with irony, in her own language, to people neither he nor she could see. She jabbered on about relationships she invented to suit herself. She shouted over the heads of some of her own close relatives she knew were nearby, becoming more excited if she spotted those worthy of her comments. Then, after this had gone on for a while, she guided Elliot away to her husband's camp. Pilot, the old Chinaman. They walked on a narrow track made by animals through the grass countless ages ago, turning away from the lake.

Still she carried on an endless chatter, mostly to the pack

of dogs that followed them. Then she began to speak to the groves of native pines ahead. She told them how beautiful they looked, what good family she felt them to be, and how she was bringing this stranger towards them. She told them she knew nothing of him, what sort of a person he was. As they crossed a sandy rise Elliot saw that scores of people had made their camps here; numerous fires shone in the darkness like distant stars. Through this maze, lit by moonlight through the pines, May Sugar navigated the map of clan maps etched in her mind since childhood. Finally, in the midst of the encampment, they reached a fire that roared like a homing beacon beneath a huge pine with drooping branches. There sat the Chinaman, old Pilot, smoking his tobacco pipe, surrounded by more dogs.

He greeted Elliot with a smile. "Back again, young fella, hey?" He looked around, as if he half-expected someone else.

"I'm here alone," Elliot confirmed, sitting near the fire. The air had cooled since sundown.

Pilot muttered something, seemingly not wholly convinced.

Irritably, May Sugar told her husband to smarten up and stop worrying about this and that. She said she was sick and tired of people who had a big problem all the time. At this Pilot got up in a huff to rearrange the camp. Several times he insisted that his wife and Elliot should move from where they sat. Slowly he took the top blanket from a neatly stacked pile. Dust and dog hair flew everywhere as he shook each one in turn before placing it next to the fire for his dogs to sleep on. The next step was to carry out some fixed plan in his head of where each dog should sleep. He started with the most favoured and went on to the least liked of his numerous dogs. Errant members of the tribe were kicked in the ribs for not lying down when ordered, or for settling down on the wrong blanket.

Elliot, while he did not take much notice of the old man's

housekeeping, tried to stop the dogs milling around by prodding them with a stick. Suddenly he realised these were the very same dogs that had surrounded him earlier in the day, as he approached the bird ceremony. He counted almost fifty dogs, each one lying flat on one side.

"That's a lot of dogs you've got there, old man," he remarked, wondering why anyone could possibly want so many. At St Dominic's dog numbers were limited to two per family. A law enforced years ago by the missionaries. Puppies were handed in to be drowned — a task allotted to the boys' dormitory. There was community agreement; it was one law that suited everybody.

The camp was filled with Pilot's unhealthy, disease-ridden creatures. It was a repulsive sight. As Elliot watched Pilot fussing over them like children, he wished he had a dose of strychnine to put in the cooking pot. Looking at these hairless creatures with their pink, pig-like skin brought back boyhood memories. The nights when the boys slunk out to round up and stone such "pink panthers" out of the village and down to the Mission. A secret job the older boys allotted to the younger ones who had to prove themselves. He and his mates would creep around rounding up a dozen or so without waking up a soul. They started with the only two dogs his father owned. Quietly they lured them out of the village with a bag of meat they had saved up for days beforehand, laughing at the smell of it under their blankets in the dormitory. Watching Jipp waving his torch about at night, not knowing what the smell was and leaving quickly. Now they trailed the bag across the ground and stoned the dogs up to the mission compound, until eventually they grew tired of the fun. It was Elliot who came up with the brilliant idea of locking the dogs in the big freezer. They then slunk back to the dormitory, jubilant, to fall asleep. They paid a good price for their fun — Jipp made sure of that when he discovered the bodies next day. He took charge of their punishment himself, inadvertently saving Elliot from being half-killed by his father. Jipp wanted to teach the men how to deal firmly with boys. The public demonstration of his innocuous flogging with a leather strap was a remarkable occasion.

"A lot of dogs?" Pilot said, breaking into Elliot's reminiscences. "You bet, boy. Good dogs too. Kill anything. Cats, dingoes, rabbits, goanna ... plenty of snake. That's why."

"You old fellas! What about hygiene?"

"What's that, son? What you call it?" May Sugar asked.

"Hygiene is for white people, old woman," Pilot told her. "They build big houses for themselves. Don't let no dirt or dirty people like you or me inside. That's hygiene."

"That old man making fun of me?" May Sugar asked Elliot, who smiled and shook his head.

"Never mind him," Pilot said. "He wouldn't know about white people. Ask me. I've seen plenty sick white people. Cattle station mob. Town mob. Believe me, everything makes them sick. Always bellyaching, moaning and groaning about something or other. You can get too much dirt or too little. It's worrying about having no dirt makes you sick good and proper."

May Sugar looked at Pilot as though it wasn't worth arguing with him. It meant more to him than it did to her to have the last say. She started tapping the sugar bag by her side until the contents began to stir. Then she started to sing a song about four little kittens that lost their mother, reached into the bag and plucked four tabby kittens out of it. She placed them gently on the ground to wander around crying for food. The dogs took no notice, just went on sleeping as the kittens climbed over them. May Sugar asked Elliot whether he would like to take one home, but he declined even though she told him any one of the cats would be a good snake-killer. (It occurred to him a cat might keep the pigeons from haunting him on his return journey, though.)

After this Elliot began to tell the old couple the story of

his journeying. They listened until well past midnight without interrupting the flow of Elliot's thoughts. Occasionally, whenever a dog stirred in its sleep, they would give each other a private glance. As Elliot spoke the moon made its silent journey across the sky until it disappeared from sight.

Pilot announced he was tired and wanted to sleep. He looked at Elliot. "You are not safe here, either," he told him.

Elliot nodded. "You are probably right."

"People are already talking about it," Pilot whispered.

"What? About my coming here?"

Pilot shrugged. "More than that. About that other business, though only a few of them know about it. A good thing, if you ask me. They are saying you might be evil, like a devil, the way you appeared in a puff of smoke, standing straight up there in the middle of their ceremony."

Elliot shook his head.

"Well, it looked like magic," Pilot went on. "I can't work out how you did it. You just came out of the ground and walked off."

"But I've just told you how it all happened."

"They said they would rest on it tonight. Think about you. See how they feel tomorrow. After all, the birds did return. That's the most important thing on everyone's mind at the moment."

Pilot then suggested that they should both stop talking, so that Elliot would hear for himself what others were saying about him in the camps round about. After a minute Elliot said all he could hear were the distant squabbles of married couples and dog fights. Nearby, a jealous argument was rising to a high pitch. Elliot found it impossible to hear anything except shrill complaint about a worthless penis and a husband who could not father children in his own family.

But Pilot said he heard plenty — and when May Sugar refused to back him up, saying she heard nothing, he told her she should clean out her ears. He asked Elliot whether he heard the men talking. Elliot lied; he said he might have but he didn't understand the language here. In fact, he did not understand much traditional language at all. The missionaries forbade parents to teach their children their own languages. Instead, they were taught English.

"What did you hear them discussing, then?" he asked Pilot.

"I shouldn't say. You know I can't talk about those things."

"Were they saying something about me and the dust storm and the fire?"

Pilot nodded. "Could have been. And something about seeing a group of pigeons around here for days on end, until some kids went and killed them."

"Anything else?"

"No. Just talk. Just words. Go in one ear and out the other." But after a pause Pilot told Elliot he had better leave soon. "Get a bit of rest then go quietly before it gets light."

Elliot looked at him with a question in his glance.

"You want to die? You like a cat with seven lives?"

"So — what about the girl? What about Ivy Koopundi?"

Pilot said the elders had demanded he should bring the girl to her own country. Elliot decided not to say anything about the trouble and the deaths she had brought to his people, or how difficult it would be to steal Jipp's little girlfriend.

"It won't be easy, but I'll do it. It will take some time, you know." Elliot was determined to make that point clear. As he spoke, May Sugar grunted in her sleep. Shouldn't he be talking to someone else here, he asked himself, not some crazy old Chinaman.

"No," Pilot said, as if he knew Elliot's thought.

Elliot repeated the word, "No", and he felt as though that one syllable bundled his mind through a sieve. All that had passed through it before he lay on the ground like grains of sand. A neat, precise pile now regrouped after

rejecting the elements that did not belong to it. This gave
him a sense of contentment. Of finalisation. He knew he
had fulfilled the requirements of his journey. He had the
answer to take back. He had no power to question the law,
either here or in his own country. Nor did he want it. He
was now delivered safely. He had been heard, even if it was
through a mad old man who was not Aboriginal, alongside
his sleeping wife, who was.

"Do what you like," Pilot said; his tone indicated he was
no longer interested in the conversation. He struggled to
get to his feet, then went off into the bush to relieve himself
of the quantities of tea he had drunk all day. When he
returned he stood looking at the bundles of sleeping dogs.
"See that one there, the spotted one?" he asked. "That's
the greediest dog I ever seen. Never chews on anything. Just
rushes in, bowls the others out of the way and gobbles up
everything in sight. One time though he got real sick. If
he'd died I would've said 'serves you right'!"

Elliot yawned. He was falling asleep, but he felt a shiver
pass through his body as Pilot passed by him to stoke up the
fire.

"No place here for dogs like that." Suddenly Pilot picked
out the largest piece of burning wood from the fire and
hurled it past Elliot's left ear towards the sleeping pack.
Elliot rose to his feet while the startled dogs jumped up,
yelping. Then, with a strong smell of singed hair wafting
through the camp, they flopped down to sleep again as if
nothing had happened.

"May Sugar got one old man to fix up that sick dog," Pilot
said. "He knew what he was doing. Blackfella! He must have
shown us two or four billies of muck he took from that dog.
Like magic. Left no trace at all. — Wouldn't chance him
doing that to me, mind you. May Sugar used to go to him,
but I'd never let no witch doctor do those sorts of things to
me."

Elliot listened to old Pilot talking as he shuffled around

in his baggy clothes, scratching himself non-stop, keeping them both awake. And a little later, when Elliot had finally started to fall into a deep sleep, Pilot began to talk about Ivy Koopundi again.

"That girl. She was related to that old man, you know."

Elliot listened, startled out of his sleep as Pilot went on talking. "He's properly dead now. No one around could fix *him* up so that was it. I tell you, there was no one like him. He could fix up anybody just like he did for that dog there I told you about. You'd think if he was so smart he could have fixed himself up. But he couldn't. He got some sickness was too deadly even for him. In the end he just wanted to lie down and die." He shook his head. "Best not to think about those sorts of things."

"How come you telling me, then?"

"Well, maybe that girl, his relative, can help this mob here. Maybe that's why they want her back. They still got that sickness. After he died, more followed. Couldn't help themselves. Like they wanted to die. Some don't even wait to get sick, they find some other way to kill themselves to get someone else to do it for them."

"People die, you know," Elliot said, not giving anything away even though he was listening intently to what Pilot said about those who killed themselves.

"Those people get someone else to kill them tricky way. Tricking someone to kill you — that's something queer. So they don't even know they gone and did it. Then sometimes these people get so sorry for what they done, they do it to themselves as well. I'm telling you. I don't want to get involved with these things."

"You're the one that started talking, not me," Elliot responded.

"Well, I got to make you understand. Bring that girl back. She related to that old man, like I said. She got no business being in your country, even though it can't be helped what happened. You people responsible for returning her here."

"I don't know what I can say to convince anyone back there," Elliot told him, hoping for more clues.

"You tell them about my dog. That's what you got to tell them. They'll understand. If she don't come back it will get worse for this mob here, and for your mob as well. Just wait a little while — you'll see the evil spirits turn up at first light. You'll see that low fog crawling like a snake across the ground, sneaking around until it finds someone to take away. Someone not on the lookout. We all watch to see who those spirits will get hold of."

"No one wants to know stories like that," Elliot said, thinking somebody must be responsible for the deaths back at St Dominic's. All fingers pointed at Ivy Koopundi and her dead mother who had come from this country.

"Say what you like, I don't care. I don't sleep in the night — I'll be alright. Do what you like. They want you to bring her back." Pilot lay down on his blankets, having spoken his final words on the matter.

Elliot thought that this trip had been more than enough for him. Scary wasn't the word for it. One thing was for sure: no matter what decision was taken about Ivy Koppundi back home, he wasn't going to be the one to bring her back. He lay on a bed of needle spikes under the native pine. With eyes closed he followed the sound of May Sugar's movements as she stirred, but he did not speak to her. He thought about the difficulties and dangers he had encountered on this journey, which he had made not just once, but twice. Sooner or later his absence from the Mission would be picked up by the authorities. He had no idea what the consequences would be. Most likely a transfer to a state-controlled reserve on one of the islands. That was the usual treatment for absconders.

If he got back safely, all he had to offer was a story about a dog that ate too much. His father would really go for that! And a lot of dancing around with pretty feathers. Having been sent on the highest authority for his own people, only an old Chinaman was deputed to give him orders, as though he was not fit to talk to. He thought about Ivy Koopundi. He could see where her aloofness came from. Too good for other blackfellas! Just like the rest of this mob here. Everything pure here. Ceremony every year. These people believe they are all responsible for the strongest law. All law. Although, he thought, they never had to fight to keep it ...

The only sound Elliot heard when he awoke from his latest dream was Old Pilot's snoring. There was no chance of more sleep. Elliot thought briefly about serving a death notice on the old couple to catch them out for their lack of vigilance. For Pilot was right about the fog. Slowly it crept across the still water which he could see quite clearly from the faint light of the low moon lighting the surface of the lake.

The dogs stirred in their sleep as though they could sense the movement of the fog. Awake, they sniffed around the camp for scraps overlooked the night before, then moved off into the darkness. The fog arrived in the camp: its smoky film covered the two old bodies, burying them from sight. Elliot wished there were others present, a concerned crowd, to witness this, to watch the tailend of the fog disappearing with the spirits of the two old people into the mulga and dogwood forests on the southern horizon. A double suicide? He had seen a number of falling stars during the night. The next, he decided would be the signal for him to leave.

Suddenly two stars fell side by side across the sky with incredible speed and collided. The impact created a tail of burning debris that almost died before hitting the land far off across the other side of the lake. Elliot decided to go now, before first light, which couldn't be far away. He could see the embers of a hundred campfires all around him. He waited for the last dogs to return from their earlier disturbance and settle down again for their last sleep of the night.

After the fog dissipated a strong westerly wind blew. A monotonous song heard only in the dreams of the sleeping, through an orchestra of spiky leaves of desert trees and the plains of flapping grass. Movement on soft sand did not disturb this song before dawn as Elliot stole away. The spotted dog, its neck neatly broken, fell back into the sleeping pack. Elliot walked off, his back facing where he knew he would never return.

8

After two days Elliot was still walking along the eastern shoreline of the flooding lake without any hope of turning west towards his northern homeland. The waters lipped the red sandy mud, decoding the froth to reveal the dead bodies of insects and leaves.

His footprints joined those of the birds and dingoes that used the water's edge. On the third day he decided it would be pointless to continue in an easterly direction. The widespread flooding of the flat Channel Country could take weeks, months to dry out sufficiently to allow a northerly passage. The sheets of moving waters robbed the ground of negotiation. There was more possibility of movement towards the south-east: he decided all he could do was to head in that direction. It was like being pulled by an encircling hand closing the gap until there was nowhere else to go. He was aware of the lay of the landscape but not fully orientated with its dense saltbush and mallee plains. But he realised he was now not far from where he had originally set out towards the lake.

Each day the flood had claimed more dry land, though there was no further sign of rain. The bush pigeons had joined him again. "So you are not dead after all," he greeted them. Within a day there was a whole flock of them. He now walked with pigeons. They talked: *"A-kook! A-kook!"* from morning to night until he was maddened by their sounds. Far from their northern breeding grounds, desperate pairs of these birds worked on their private courtship, crushed beside each other up and down the shoreline. Eggs without nests appeared all over the ground. Some more resourceful birds managed to lay their eggs in a pile of haphazard twigs quickly put together. All the eggs in this insane hatchery served no purpose other than to be rolled along in the advancing line of water, which snatched them away with other debris. The eggs rolled forward until they shattered against each other and the yellow yolks and half-formed bodies of baby birds became mixed in the swell of froth.

Elliot ate some of the eggs, swallowing them shell and all in order to survive. He carried scores of others in a basket he made from bark, twigs and grass. After fourteen days the chicks hatched. He fed what he could of the season's young, discarding the dead while cursing the distraught adult pigeons who watched him. Three weeks later, just four fledglings, all the season's crop, took flight and joined in the dismal dispersion of the flock.

At dusk a chilly wind blew. The land rapidly grew cold. Downwind the strong smell of nannygoat flowers and dry dust spilled across the open plains. The nearest house of a group blended together in the distance with the saltbush and mallee flats now came closer in view. A rusted barbed wire fence laced into an overgrown dust-dry oleander hedge rattled helplessly in this neglected man-made landscape. These were the signs of spring at Tabletop Downs station, nestled amid the runaway clumps of nannygoat plants loaded with their four-petalled pink or white flowers.

That first house was clearly visible a kilometre away, but when Elliot reached it the high hedge blocked his view. In the last light of evening a charred skeleton tree, once a giant cedar, stood behind the dark mass of the hedge. In days past, the perfume of the flowering cedar would have spread over the entire house. There was life perched on the branches of the dead tree: a family of crows, silenced by the sound of the strong wind that blew, the telegraph wire, and the arrival of a stranger whom they had been watching from a long way off.

The uneasy rhythms of the wind parted the oleander thicket to reveal a well-used entrance secured by a weathered gate. Elliot unchained the gate and walked across the front yard, over the dogs that slept across the front of the house steps. He started to walk up the veranda with its flaking blue paint. The house was not as large as it had appeared in the distance. Above him on the veranda a pair of smart red lips caught his eye: in the early darkness they seemed to float down deep inside him. For the first time in his life, Elliot felt bound to something external from his own body.

"Better watch your step there," the girl warned with her blood-red lips. Elliot stared, willing her to keep on talking. "Next time sing out at the gate. Otherwise they'll bite you."

But the dogs hadn't moved. The girl turned and went back into the house. Elliot stood at the door and waited.

"In here! Come in here. And close the door, will ya?" she yelled from somewhere in the back of the house.

He found himself in a stuffy kitchen, filled with smoke from a slow-burning combustion stove. It tried to escape through every opening, even the cracks and empty nail holes in the tin walls. It poured up the walls to the corrugated iron of the ceilingless roof. At the kitchen table the teary-eyed family sitting through the ordeal started to introduce themselves.

"I told you to clean it out first," Mum Ruby Kennedy hollered. At the same time she pointed to an empty chair where Elliot might sit, while she went on glaring at her daughter Gloria, sulking by the stove, her red lips pouting. A cup of tea was poured and handed to him.

"She don't know how, Mum," Colleen, the older sister, snapped as she tried to hush her baby's screaming by wiping its face with a damp cloth. "Lighting the stove isn't her speciality. She don't know how you got to stand there and do it properly. Too busy runnin' off to look at herself in the mirror."

"Jesus, look who's talkin'!" Gloria snapped back trying to poke around in the stove to stop the smoke. "Too busy on her back with legs open, mother of five at nineteen, to light a stove herself."

Babies and small children were all crying from the trapped smoke burning their eyes. Colleen, struggling to manage her brood, had to yell to be heard. "Mum, you better tell her to shut up — Shut your ugly face up, I'm warnin' you!" she threatened her sister. The expression on her face might have been that of a mass murderer.

Mum Ruby yelled for everyone to get out of her way. She rose up with one thick arm pushed aside the slightly built Gloria, then set to work with a long stick and poked the ash through the grate. The ash-box was swiftly pulled out and she marched across to the kitchen door and threw its contents down the back steps. Finally she restarted the fire. "And leave that door open until the smoke goes," she ordered everyone.

Gloria checked with eyes and hands that her tight yellow floral dress had no soot marks, and that her stocking seams still ran straight up the back of each leg. She curled her lips over her lipstick, clicked her fingers in self-appreciation, then moved awkwardly on her high heels through the narrow space around the kitchen table, sat down and helped herself to some stew. She interrupted her eating to take another plateful served by Ruby and passed it on to Elliot with a wink. Colleen glared at her sister's brazen behaviour.

The arrival of Bob Kennedy and his son-in-law Big Blue Murphy Junior was announced by the thud of saddles and swags on the front veranda. They had been away for several days on the mid-year roundup of Tabletop Downs cattle. The two men came into the kitchen and a couple of children were nudged out of their chairs so that they could sit down. Both began to eat in earnest, breaking silence only to grunt responses to wifely questions about their trip. Several minutes passed before Big Blue looked up and noticed both Elliot's presence and the way Gloria looked. Mum introduced Elliot and Blue nodded at him, emitting another grunt. It was Gloria who interested Blue. His glance travelled from Gloria to Colleen, his wife, then back to Gloria again.

"What you doin'?" he snapped at the younger sister.

Gloria continued eating, her face tightening. "Nothin'!" she snapped.

"What's that you got on?" Blue circled the air with his empty fork.

"Jesus. Ain't you never seen lipstick?" Gloria glanced daggers at Colleen, sighing loudly with disgusted resignation.

Now Bob Kennedy looked up and he too stared at Gloria. Suddenly he reached over the table, loaded fork in hand, to grab at her perfectly curled hair with one huge hand. "You know what you look like?" he demanded of his daughter. "A slut, that's what. Just like your cousins slutting outside the pub in town. Get yourself cleaned up." He let her go and continued to eat his stew.

Gloria remained seated, an expression of determination on her face.

"Make yourself decent. Go on," Blue ordered through a mouthful of stew.

Slowly, cracks appeared in the mask of determination. Then Gloria began to cry.

"Oh, shit! Listen to her," Colleen said. She got up from the table and started clearing, banging plates and pots together.

Blue looked at Colleen in disgust, telling her to go and clean up the kids. "How come you let them get around smelling of piss and shit all the time?" he asked.

Mum Kennedy told them all to shut up. She struck the wooden table with the lid of the stew pot, then clanged it back again. The piercing din was enough to make Bob Kennedy stop eating. Now there was complete silence in the kitchen except for Gloria's hurt, soft crying. "Gloria's goin' out. That's why she's dressed up. With Kevin Shunassy. He comes up here on holidays to visit his uncle. A Catholic boy." Ruby stared straight at Blue as she said this. He was the only non-Catholic amongst them. And she had her suspicions about his moral standards when it came to her youngest daughter. She was letting him know that if she caught them together his life wouldn't be worth living.

Bob Kennedy gave his wife a questioning look.

"You know Kevin — that white kid that comes up from the city every year? Used to hang around with our Gloria when they were kids — until Old Mum Boss Lady thought they were getting too big, and told you not to send Gloria up there any more."

"Ah, ah." Bob's frayed nerves were subdued by his wife's soft speech following her clang of cast iron against cast iron to demand his attention.

"Well then, what's she doin' goin' out with the likes of them for now?" Blue growled.

"Might be she likes white fellas," Colleen snapped at her husband. She too had her suspicions about him.

"He's a nice boy," Mum Ruby went. "He came down here to ask me if it was alright. And I said — you go right ahead, son. So if I say it's alright, then it is. No business of yours, Blue. If you want something to do, chop some wood. Might save this one old woman from havin' to do it herself. Anyhow, you got your own family to look after. You look after your kids and I'll look after mine."

"I don't know about this. You should have asked me first. You know what sort of trouble this could lead to," Bob said.

"That's right. What you want to go out with a white boy for, Gloria?" Blue persisted.

"He asked her and it's okay. They're a good family." Ruby went on justifying her position.

"What's it to you who she goes with, Blue? She's goin' to start sometime and it's got nothing to do with you," Colleen cut in.

Blue glared at his wife with a look of disgust.

"Well! And fuck you, anyway," Colleen snarled.

"Where he takin' you to?" Bob asked his daughter.

Before she could reply, Ruby told him to a barn dance at Planet Downs, the next-door station, which had races on that day. Bob then told Gloria to get home early and go and clean herself up so that she didn't look like she been crying. "Fix your hair up, love," he added, in token apology for having messed it up.

"She's only fifteen. She don't know how to look after herself." Blue tried to put in a final word before Ruby took over the reign of her kitchen again.

She ignored him. "Well! And here's Elliot. He showed up just a minute or so before you two got back."

"Bob Kennedy. My son-in-law, Big Blue Murphy Junior." Bob offered to shake hands across the table.

Elliot sensed an authority in these people which demanded from him a form of politeness he usually reserved for the missionaries. He wondered what it was that caused him to react in this way. Perhaps because he was a guest in their home. He had never seen dark people in a house as substantial as this one before. He also thought his reaction might stem from the way they had spoken to each other moments before, as though he wasn't there. And it might be the effect of their daughter Gloria, her presence, her style, her red lips, had on him as well. He felt he needed her. Wanted her for his own.

"What you here for, Elliot — work?" Blue asked. "Not much of that here. Not with the flooding all around."

Elliot agreed that he was after work and told them he had

got caught up in the floods trying to get back up North, back to the Mission.

"Could see you're not from these parts," Bob said. He offered Elliot some work as an offsider, odd jobs and fencing, for a few weeks.

"You can always tell the desert rats, and you're not one for sure," Ruby told Elliot. "Your skin different for a start. It's on account of the heat's different here. They say the dust protects the skin, makes it browner. Not as black as up North. It's the sun coming off the ocean — well, that's what they say." She laughed.

"That's not true, Mum," Blue said. He himself was red-haired and freckled. He looked across at Elliot with a comic expression.

"Well, anyway, Mum, it doesn't matter — you shouldn't talk like that in front of Elliot," Colleen said, taking sides with her husband even though she still resented his attention to her younger sister.

Elliot said he didn't mind. He told them his people were able to pick the difference too, and told them that a lot of people from different tribes were sent to the Mission. They could even pick the different look of people from neighbouring tribes, from the size of their heads, their hair texture, their overall build. With the smaller-built people, people believed they had got that way because they never had enough food: over the years they had become small-boned so they wouldn't need to eat so much.

"You don't say!" exclaimed Ruby, pleased she wasn't the only one with the ability to make such comparisons. She said she knew every family from these parts. Especially all the mixed-blood ones. "Take the Murphys," she said, pointing to Blue. "They're all freckly-faced with ginger hair. Or the Morgans — they got a mad look in their eyes …"

"And what about the Moons, your own mob?" Blue asked her.

"You always picking around like a dog with a bare bone, looking for a row!" Colleen hissed at him.

"Why don't you mind your own business?" he retorted. "Like the state your kids are in, for instance."

Everyone looked at the kids, playing happily in one corner of the room.

"Sores!" Blue exclaimed. "They've got bloody things all over them again. If you had any sort of brain in your head, you'd know how to keep them clean."

Angrily Colleen got up and fetched some warm water, a roll of cotton wool and a bottle of purple iodine. "You're all the same, you Moodys. Want to argue all the time. Your dad. Uncle. Molly May. You want to have a good listen to yourself. Old Grandfather George even picked an argument with a dead horse once …" She rambled on with her expansive knowledge of her husband's family, which she would throw forth whenever the occasion suited her.

The pitiful screaming of the children stifled any further adult talk as Colleen roughly cleaned the open sores with damp cotton wool. The bowl of soapy water soon became discoloured by dirt, dry blood and scabs. Iodine was roughly dabbed onto struggling limbs. A sharp smack or two sent up more wails as each child was told to pull itself together and get off to bed — or else they'd get a good hiding. After the treatment was over the adults left the table, stunned into silence by the din and Colleen's horse-handling manner. Ruby was deep in thought about how much the children resembled her son-in-law's family — there was, she thought, a lot of truth in what her daughter had to say about them.

"We'd better call it a night," Bob finally said.

Elliot was told to camp on the veranda when he was ready. Blue mumbled on about how he could tell a mad Moon anywhere, at the same time making sure he was out of Mum Ruby's hearing. He added that no one was going to tell him anything about his own family. Mum Ruby, meanwhile, was busy washing up at the sink. In a low hiss Colleen told Blue to keep his trap shut. "Look, we all know about Mum's father."

But Blue told Elliot about Mad Morgan Moon just the same. "Old and mad. Even when he was young that's what they called him — Mad Morgan Moon. Of course, she claims to be a Jackson, not a Moon. Well, when I was a kid, all the old people used to say old man Jackson was killed by Mad Morgan himself — they'd even seen him leaving the scene of the crime. Walkin' down the footpath with the bloody axe right through the main street. Some nearly died of a heart attack when they saw him coming — they were relieved, I tell you, when they passed him by. When he reached the Town Hall the local constable stopped him and asked what he was doin' with that axe. And he replied, he was just goin' to clean it. The blood still dripping off it onto the newly laid cement outside the Town Hall. Beats me why they never locked him up. — All this was a long time before Mum Ruby was born."

There was a golden orange moon. Leaves whispered and the chill air smelled of the perfume she wore. It had dominated Mum Ruby's kitchen when the grey smoke died away. Lovers whispered close by. The boat-shaped leaves of the oleander rustled, the only sound in the quiet early hours of the morning. Gloria crossed the veranda in her bare feet. The moon was reflected in the patent leather of her high-heeled shoes which she carried in either hand, swinging them as she walked.

Under his blanket Elliot had lain awake listening for her return. Several times during the night he almost felt her slip in beside him. An owl flew down from the skeleton tree and hooted on the veranda, walking up and down the dry, splintery boards. Back and forth. Back and forth. Looking for something. Insects? Insects revealed on the pale wood lit by the moon. Shiny stink beetles everywhere. When the owl flew away its wings flapped with a sound like whips cracking, growing fainter until it was overcome by the even louder sound of silence.

Ruby's voice bounced from wall to wall, gathering force as they carried from the kitchen to the front veranda in the crisp air of early morning. Her voice, part of her whole being, belonged to this house. Her words, in fact, left the house via the front door with even greater strength than when they were first spoken. Other voices, familiar but hard to recognise because, in contrast to Ruby's, they were so faint, could also be heard. Elliot sensed a certain familiarity with the speakers, and as he lay there he wondered whether it was time to investigate or whether he should flee this place. His bed was slowly being abandoned by two stray cats and their kittens. The rest of his night-time companions, six or more dogs rolled in tight balls with tail-covered faces, he saw for the first time, still asleep in various locations across the veranda.

"Sorry we couldn't come though" — Ruby's voice boomed out as though she was talking to a deaf person. "But you're lucky you got back at all with all that flooding way up North." Ruby always regarded anywhere outside the boundary of Tabletop Downs station, a forty kilometre radius in either direction, as "way up North" or "way down South", "way out West in the desert" and so on.

Other voices were heard, but Elliot could not decipher what was said.

"You say what? *What?*" Ruby shouted louder yet — in fact, it was she who was half-deaf. "What type of person would want to do that?"

Walking up the hallway in search of breakfast, Elliot noticed Gloria in bed through an open door, sleeping soundly.

"Here's Elliot! Came here right out of nowhere," Ruby shouted as soon as she caught sight of him. "Come and get some breakfast, son. She indicated the two visitors who had turned up that morning. "Old May and Pilot here were just sayin' how some madman went and killed off their best workin' dog. Makes you wonder what sort of people there are around these days. Never used to be like that."

Ruby failed to notice the old couple and Elliot exchange looks of recognition, though they made no attempt to acknowledge each other. She went on to boast how her place would be safe from a madman or even a Kadaicha man, *her* dogs would see that. Though of course they didn't believe in Kadaicha men and all that kind of stuff any more. The past was buried with her grandparents, and a good job too. They needed to learn from the white folk if their children were ever going to amount to anything, she said. "We always have good dogs," she went on. "Trained by Mr Kennedy himself. Gordon is our best dog, though just by a margin to Red Dog. Yes, Gordon is the crazy one. Always after bird feathers. Kills chooks given half the chance. Chases ducks. One time we saw him chase emus until they got knocked up, and when they fell over he dragged them back home one after the other. Then he went out again and collected a dozen or more emu eggs and brought them back too. Didn't break one. Then he even plucked them emus. The backyard was covered in feathers. If I'd known better I'd have used them for stuffing but I didn't have any cushion material."

While Ruby spoke Pilot's mouth started to twitch, then his right eye. Finally he broke out into a loud chuckle. "God, how you know which dog's which, Ruby? You got that many dogs out there, lyin' around doin' nothing all day."

"Jesus, the cheek of who's talkin'! We got no more dogs out there than you got in that old cart of yours. When you goin' to get a new one anyway? That one's fallin' apart. One day it will break down proper and you an' May will get stranded God knows where and Mr Kennedy will have to go out and find you."

Their old weatherboard wagon stood under a tree a little way beyond the front yard. One one side a weather-faded picture of the Arnott's biscuit parrot could still be made out, with the cracker in the claw peeled away. Inside the cart was stuffy, stinking of old dogs and puppies packed on top of each other, and below them lay the couple's old rags and treasured belongings.

"You didn't see that blackfella wandering around outside last night, then?" Pilot asked Ruby, slowly sipping his tea and not looking anyone in the eye. Matching Ruby lie for lie. "He was all over the place, by all accounts. And so quiet, like an owl walking around. The dogs wouldn't get a chance to wake up. Only one kind of blackfella does that, you know. No smell, either. That's the other thing they said. He just walked right through them dogs everywhere he went. Looking for something. He musta come here too — he would've looked at you, Ruby, sleeping on your bed in the dark. So quiet you never heard him there." He waited for Ruby to react.

"You cut that out, old man," May Sugar interrupted him. She turned to Ruby. "You heard any more about your sister's girlie?" she asked her.

The interruption took Ruby by surprise and she forgot to answer Pilot back. She had just begun to enjoy herself, too — May Sugar had a knack of making people feel depressed. "No, nothing since the death," she muttered, beginning to clear the kitchen table.

There was silence for several moments.

"You know, that girl should go back to her own country now," May went on. Meanwhile, Pilot and Elliot pretended not to feel hostility towards each other over the incident of the dead dog in the Chinaman's camp.

"Well, there's nothing I can do about it," Ruby said. "She's up on that Mission now. If her mother had been more sensible none of this would have happened."

"There must be something that could be done," May said.

"I'd write a letter if I thought it would be any use. It's probably all for her own good now, being at the Mission. Considering the mother." Ruby wanted to finalise the matter.

"She was your sister." Bob Kennedy had heard part of the conversation from his bedroom and now entered to join everyone else in the kitchen. He greeted the old couple, saying that he hadn't seen them for months and would be glad to have them back at their old jobs around the station. He was pleased to see Elliot already up. Sometimes he made the mistake of hiring desert strays blown in by the dust who turned out to be real bums.

"Half-sister," Ruby corrected him. "She was a Moon. Morgan Moon's child he had with Mum. Before she remarried that other bastard and had the rest of us."

"That don't make much difference around here. None of us fully related to our brothers and sisters if you ask me," Bob replied.

"Well, no one's askin', are they? Sister, half-sister, one selfish bitch she was. She never worried about family. You could see it was only a matter of time before she ended up in trouble the way she did."

"Well, May's right. That little kid should be back here."

"And who's goin' to look after her? Who's to say she's not just like her mother? I'm not havin' some sort of nut-case on my hands. It's a bloody stupid idea. No, I've got enough to worry about right now. I'm buggered up enough already." Ruby made an attempt to laugh it off.

"Well then. Must get a move on. You ready, Elliot? We'll leave Mum here to sort out her family problems with Old May and Pilot. — You come up to the big house later, Pilot. Lots of couch to dig up, and the Missus up there says she wants only you to do it. Roots and all this time." Bob

Kennedy gulped down one last cup of tea and then he and Elliot left the house.

Elliot felt an excitement running loose inside him. The truths. The discoveries. The novelty of a different way of life. The unravelling of the mystery. The convenient concealment of identities. So this was Ivy Koopundi's family! And she was crazy, after all. Which explained why she felt no shame in being fat Jipp's woman. Mum Ruby was right, there was no point in writing a letter. Not to the likes of old Jipp. Elliot could imagine Jipp's eyes narrowing as he read such a letter, then screwing it up and aiming it for the bin by the door. If he missed he'd wait for someone to walk in, then ask them to pick it up for him. Left alone he'd try again, repeating the process until he succeeded.

Nor to Ivy, for that matter. Imagine the trouble Ruby would have with Ivy to look after. Sly thing creeping around her kitchen. No, she was better off thinking the way she did. She could see trouble coming, that was for sure. Elliot thought maybe she had a nose for it.

Elliot began to give serious consideration to how long he wanted to stay here. Even whether he might make the journey back again after all. He had to think about Gloria. In future, Gloria would be the motive for staying here, or going and returning. Idly he wondered how Ivy Koopundi would look with red lips. In his new frame of mind the world was filled with wonders.

At the big house, which was surrounded by lush greenery, Elliot caught sight of Gloria's fancy man, still a boy really, with nothing to do. The future king of a cattle station, its land extending in every direction as far as the eye could see. A boy-man sitting beneath a shady lime tree, reading a book to pass the time.

Overseer: the best in the business — that was Bob Kennedy's title. That's what the Boss said when he and Bob were in the company of others. Now Bob introduced Elliot to the Boss.

"A full blood," the Boss remarked. "Not many full bloods working here at the moment, hey Bob?"

Bob agreed, his gaze wandering to the boy under the lime tree.

"What, maybe four or five half-castes," the Boss went on. "Maybe a quarter-caste. What about that boy who chases up the strays as though he's flying over them rocky hills south of the property ... Billy, that's it. He's quarter-caste, isn't he?"

"Right," Bob agreed indifferently, still with his eyes on the boy who sat there reading.

Later that day, the dying bull lay on the ground, blood running from the bullet hole in its forehead. Its only sin that it had been the nearest beast in the rifle's sight. Its blood was the deep red of Gloria's lips as it poured over the ground towards Elliot's bare feet. In the butchering blood poured over his toes and swam between his fingers as he completed the job, while his mind swam in *her* redness sweeping across his face, over his body, drenching his clothes.

Later still he emerged from the brown water of the dam with yellow water dripping from his curly black hair. His skin cleansed through his clothes as it had been before he met her. All evening low clouds raced across the sky before a storm broke over the flat darkened land. A torrent of rain lashed the ground, throwing up splinters of red. In the distance the Arnott's parrots were on the move again. An owl came and walked quietly between blue and red sleeping dogs. And Elliot knew Gloria was gone.

9

The morning Elliot returned to St Dominic's was another of those hot days at the end of the Wet of '58. The dust flew in a blanket that laced across the horizon: the storm had started at dawn, leaving the day dark and sepia-coloured, and the residents were slightly confused about what time it was.

It was late December, and the dormitory girls sweetly sang the Christmas carols for the God-Jesus, who they believed would be born there that night. Their voices ran ahead with the dust like the cries of disoriented seagulls. Song filled the village as the little procession moved slowly through the dust storm over no-man's land, the open flat between the Mission's white area and dormitories and the village of the black inmates. Beverly Jipp carried the infant Jesus, a black baby presently being cared for in the quarantine area, away from its mother. Even though it was day the moon stood above and in its heavenly window sat a picture of the Virgin Mother holding her baby Jesus.

At the end of this day Elliot found his sister-mother, Dorrie, wailing death. The whole village listened to her — she had interrupted the Christmas carols and sent the choir home with a string of abuse. She still sat there as she had since morning, in the midst of ten or more dying fowls. She held the last of the dying, a bird with wet spiky feathers, close against her breast. When the procession reached her camp,

Dorrie had just discovered her hens and the rooster bat-tling for breath, thrashing around on their backs, feathers puffed, beaks agape for water. Nothing could save them. The dormitory girls, still singing, came to a standstill while they stared at the old woman's disorganised camp. Neither they nor Beverly did anything to help her.

Earlier, someone had spoken to Dorrie of a strange flock of seagulls seen before first light. Birds that shone like torches. The apparition was thought to be that of the dead spirits of birds lost before the storm. She would never have seen them herself — she could hardly see more than a few metres away. Apparently the seagulls had just kept hovering above the village, and as they swirled about, their white bodies caught the reflected light of the moon. A strange sight, and it was a mystery that all those fowls died so suddenly afterwards, even though they were old and de-crepit.

Dorrie's fowls were the survivors from her poaching expeditions years ago, when she was more up to such activity in the middle of the night. She was always allowed to keep what she had taken even when she was caught in the act. Nobody cared to subject themselves to the spiteful wrath and spitfire words she'd unleash on whoever she caught sneaking around "her" things.

Earlier, Elliot had found his own father sick. Another crook stomach, old Pugnose said; he believed the pain would be gone in the morning. He always said that, even though it always seemed to be there. But he refused to admit was the usual state of his health these days. A regular pain from too much chewing tobacco and other unhealthy delights. He took it for granted it was old age, even though both he and Elliot knew it was first caused from a bad batch of tobacco his son had given him.

This was a day when everyone had something wrong — either illness or misfortune with belongings, like Old Dor-rie and her dead fowls. This would be no ordinary Christ-

mas — even though an ordinary Christmas was little cele-
brated here. Everyone spoke amongst themselves of griev-
ances that came at this time with the dust, while overtly they
revered the ritual for the churchgoers amongst themselves
and the white mission folk.

This was the morning when the village's only rooster,
now departed, did not crow its blood-curdling greeting to
the morning. Instead, everyone found their own entry into
the day. Old Dorrie, sulking, saw Elliot but paid no attention to his return, as others had done. Now she sat with that
last dying fowl, a pannikin of cold black tea in one shaking
hand. Her body, shaking involuntarily, gave the impression
that the damp fowl was still alive. Elliot sat with her and
when she finally accepted the fact that the last bird was
dead, she broke her silence by asking him, in a voice
reminiscent of a cackling hen, whether he had seen her son
Matthew anywhere. This was in fact a son long dead. She
told him she had another son, Jimbo Delainy, and asked
him to go and find him.

Elliot agreed and walked away. Eventually Dorrie recovered from the worst day of her life, but in later years she
would always recall that she had not really cared about
Elliot's return, even though he had been away for eighteen
months or more.

There was a reason for this. Old Dorrie was someone who
listened to the messages blown by the morning and night
winds. Amongst the hundreds of voices and languages
passing by it was difficult to find the message meant for you
alone. But she had the ability. Today the voices had grown
wilder, louder and angrier with the intensity of the wind
and heat. Dorrie could also hear and pick out familiar
voices of deceased relatives whom she had never even met
when they were alive. These spirits could be relied upon to
impart important information. Dorrie's skills were such
that their messages were as clear to her as anything she had
learnt in childhood from her parents and never sub-

sequently forgotten. She did not pay any attention to other voices that only wanted to complain or make empty threats. Even when they made dangerous threats she could not do anything to help the people towards whom harm was intended. Wise women like Dorrie knew how to protect themselves. The secrets they heard were treated in the highest confidence by those who upheld the law: only in those circles could the information be acted upon in the proper way. It would be very dangerous for any ordinary person to approach people such as Dorrie and ask for information about what she had heard — or even about what they might think they had heard themselves.

It was known that Elliot's information would need time for very careful consideration before any action could be taken. Those like Dorrie who listened for the spiritual messages and others who were expert in interpretation would all have to be consulted. This would involve listening to the re-enactment of those messages in song many times before any final consensus could be reached.

So this was why Dorrie did not care about Elliot's return. The fact that he had been sent away as the messenger was of little consequence to her. She had already heard the answers given as a result of his journeying. Still, he was obliged to give her his account of what had happened and what was said to him. — "So, they want the girl returned to her own country," he had told her, finalising a brief account of his journey.

Now Elliot returned from his search for Jimbo Delainy, who did not want to see his mother because he was about to take part in the Christmas service. He said his mother could come to it if she wanted to.

"Funny thing you never seen Matthew," Dorrie told Elliot. She thought for a while. "It's funny how them girls wouldn't stop singing this morning, don't you think? You would've thought they'd stop, but they didn't … You sure you saw Jimbo? Jimbo Delainy? And you sure you never seen

Matthew?" Dorrie's questions were asked in tones that signified "I don't believe you" as she finally put the last dead and smelly fowl to rest.

"Where would I have seen Matthew, Aunty? But maybe I did and I've forgotten about it. But I just seen Jimbo alright. He is a lay preacher, so he should be up at the church. It's their big Christmas celebration, after all."

"You know, those girls just kept on singing. You'd have thought they would have stopped and helped an old woman, wouldn't you?" Dorrie carefully avoided any further talk of her sons. She had had a long day. She had a lot to think about, and she wanted to sleep. She had little joy out of asking Elliot the key questions in response to his story. And she had had a lot of trouble hearing and remembering the sequence of the events foretold through the spirits today because of the powerful tricks that had caused interference. Her age and susceptibility to the elements of wind, heat and dust made it easier for the tricksters. So had today's misfortune and the distraction of her grief. What would be made of the information gathered on this day of important ritual for the white man? — That in itself was another interference at this time of year; a time when hot winds blew across the claypans, and important and practical information must be obtained.

The gathering of the magic people such as Old Dorrie began a few days later; their deliberations would continue for several weeks. They searched for the meaning of those voices from the winds — a meandering riddle of jumbled phrases and words. There was no use in trying to rush the process: this was important information for the future of the land and its people. All the magic people seemed to have physical disabilities. Dorrie herself suffered from the shaking disease, yet it did not stop her efforts to analyse the messages she had heard. She met each day with the likes of Old Eddie Mosquito, dependent on his wheel contraption to get around and Noah Two-By-Two, who had been blinded as a boy from a missionary's cane. There were always one or two others who claimed powers of interpretation, or else faked such ability. Some, who were thought to be suffering delusions, could not be excluded from the group simply on this basis. Yet it was risky: the confidential nature of the discussions might well be breached by such people. However, if this did happen, the others felt their power would be insufficient to convey a correct interpretation to outsiders. Dorrie's son Jimbo Delainy shared this gift of being able to listen to the winds, but he was not included in the circle since he had turned towards the mission God. As for the general community, most viewed the circle of magic people with scepticism, yet at the same time held a guarded respect for it.

Gabriel and Mervin, the left-handed twins, were included in the circle. They presented identical accounts of low smoke coming from a southerly direction. They said it reminded them of the morning glory cloud — like a fire, destroying whatever it touched. This interpretation of a foreign voice heard in the wind could not be ignored by the others, especially Dorrie, who had heard Elliot's account of the low-lying fog from Ivy Koopundi's people. She herself had a similar interpretation, and when she had reached her conclusion her body had turned strangely cold; the numbness she felt momentarily stopped the shaking she had suffered for thirty-five years. Likewise, Two-By-Two and Old Eddie Mosquito eventually agreed with her interpretation, although at first their thoughts were centred around clear visions of long stretches of river banks flanked by dying river gums. They recounted their joint vision of bare branches arching to the skies as though beckoning for rain.

While these matters were being reconciled, Elliot found new and lasting joy in being back home. He had avoided detection by the missionaries and melted back into family routines, doubling his load of tasks on occasion to recompense those who had covered for him in his long absences. And now he had something much better to concentrate his thoughts. He had been reunited with Gloria Kennedy, who had actually arrived at St Dominic's weeks ahead of Elliot.

Running away with her white lover had seemed the right thing to do for a bored young black woman from the cattle station. To begin with even the white boy imagined that with true love he could conquer the world and the odds against them. However, their romantic quest could only be condemned through the racist viewpoint of the conquistadors. The boy, Kevin, represented every white person's hero in the country towns: a beef baron's son, a member of the bloodlines of the pastoral industry. Gloria's style, her very existence, were completely out of place. And soon she was abandoned, driven to win fickle hearts in dark corners at the side of the pub. Soon she was begging the local nuns to show mercy and send her home. They, in turn, contacted the Protector of Aborigines — the local police.

The police sergeant in a small country town presents a powerful presence in his uniform: a big man not open to persuasion. His understanding of the law is by the letter. He understands the harshness of the townspeople, arising from a community dependent on limited industry — cattle, in this case, being the name of the game. An industry run under difficult circumstances. Each year of a decade of drought strengthens that harshness, which flows through to everyday life.

"He did the most practical thing under the circumstance": that was the general consensus uttered through pencil-thin lips after the event. Keep the town clean. That was the sergeant's job. He already had a number of Gloria's kind destined for the northerly road, a consignment of "mixed bloods" who needed to be put into care for their own good. It simply made life a lot easier to include a girl who was already seen to be making her own way in life. There was no question of sending her back South.

"Too bad, girl," he told her. "Ya shoulda known better to know ya shoulda kept ya nose clean and outta town."

Mrs Police Wife's social committee, over rose-flowered teacups, had even stronger unofficial laws for women of "other backgrounds" than those legally enforced upon them. It was clear to them that Gloria needed to be taught a hard lesson to know her place.

"Everyone was watching her."

"Out in the open!"

"Without even a shred of decency."

"Hasn't she already caused more than enough damage to a fine son of one of our most important families, that keeps this town going?"

The white womenfolk were seriously offended by any blatant attack on their territory — attacks that seemed on the increase.

"The cheek of these black girls flaunting their tarted-up looks to *our* kind!"

Gloria was like a nasty, dark picture of a baddie in a storybook. Or a walking badge that warned about ugly pollution hitting your town. A sight that affronted the decency and status of all white women. Small towns. Churchgoers. Caucasians. Apartheid.

At St Dominic's Gloria was very relieved to see Elliot again. She was attracted to his maturity, his good looks, his capability. She had been shaken by the force with which her destiny was taken out of her hands. It was not so much the white boy with his fatal weakness for conformity. An attribute quite foreign to herself. She had soon forgotten Kevin. She believed she was made of stronger stuff, well able to take care of herself. And she was convinced that her current misfortune was only short-term. If Elliot had been able to leave the Mission, then so would she — somehow, they would have found love and happiness and all the rest of it together. In the meantime, being at St Dominic's with Elliot would suffice.

Elliot's passion for Gloria was all-consuming. "See this thing straight," his father warned him. "Jipp will find out." But Elliot was not interested in secret, infrequent meetings with Gloria arranged through the Chapel girls. "You're a fool," Pugnose said. "There are spies everywhere here." But Elliot's pride in his love affair would not allow him to away in the bushes at night for a quick screw. "I am a man, not a boy," he told his father. And Pugnose agreed it was time his son had a wife.

Gloria was beautiful, and it was predestined which company she would keep at St Dominic's. "You should look after your cousin Ivy," Elliot tried to persuade her. Instead, she made friends with the Chapel girls, not with her mousy cousin. Elliot was correct in his opinion that Gloria could be easily led astray and he wasn't sure he would be able to tolerate that. "I will kill any man who comes near you," he told her, and she smiled.

Elliot was aware that all the young women and even the older, married ones were eager to be led astray by him. And he continued to fall in with their wishes behind Gloria's back, using his good looks, his physical attractiveness and his intellect to seduce whoever took his short-lived fancy. When he boasted of his conquests Gloria smiled as if it meant nothing to her. She was a match to his own fickle nature: he did not know whether she would destroy him before he destroyed her … but he thought it would be a long time before that time came.

"Let's be perfectly clear about this. No one makes any decision about marriage before I have been spoken to first." Errol Jipp made this prouncement when Dorrie came to him to talk about her dead sister's son, having agreed to do so at Pugnose's request.

"Elliot would be very good to his wife," she told Jipp in a conciliatory tone.

"I have already agreed to a request for that new girl, Gloria, because it was made in the proper way," Jipp responded. He was not going to agree to this request from Pugnose's family. He'd had enough demands from them over the years. — "Jimbo Delainy, your own son, came here first and spoke to me himself. It was the right thing to do, under the circumstances …" Jipp broke off, letting it be understood that he knew everything that happened on the Mission, even at night.

Fallen leaves were everywhere, rustling noisily as they flew past. Some came through the open door of the building, rolling across the floor and tap-dancing against the walls.

"Well, I don't know what to think. Elliot's really got his heart set on that girl, Mr Jipp Boss." Dorrie, head bent, eyeballed the floorboards.

"The decision is made. I can't help it if Elliot chooses to do things his own way. He should have come here first. Jimbo Delainy is as good a man as you'll find anywhere. He'll be a good influence on a girl like Gloria." Jipp spoke quickly to match the new idea formulating in his mind. He needed to carry out the decision he had just made as soon as possible: after lunch he would get it over and done with. "Send Elliot up here to see me after the lunchtime bell," he told Dorrie. "I'll see what can be done."

Old Dorrie was worried. She wanted to reassure herself that she had done what was expected of her. Off alone amongst the grey saltbush that grew everywhere on the flat plains, she listened for endorsement from the whistling wind. Her quirky shakes disturbed the clustering waves of small blue butterflies that hovered over the sticky stems of saltbush.

Jipp's intervention in the matter of Elliot's marriage was a fact of life. Ideally, it was what the elders themselves would have wanted, given their way with Elliot. For, having overcome the obstacles placed by the spirits during his journeys in alliance with unknown forces there, Elliot had become a big-head. Dorrie knew that he did not even trust his own father, that he had no fear about what Pugnose might do to him — or any of the other old fellas, come to that.

For some time she walked around seemingly without aim. Her hobbily leg soon caused an ebb and flow of pain to radiate down her left side in time with the dance of the blue butterflies, which were accumulating in increasing numbers drawn as if to magnets, to ride on the invisible waves.

She was not sure whether chance brought about her meeting with Elliot out there or not. She had no memory of making any arrangements with him. He seemed to appear out of nowhere: suddenly he was standing in front of her.

Elliot watched the words come through the gap in her gums between the few brown stunted spikes that stood like lonely soldiers guarding the wisdom of age. "You'll be getting married today," Dorrie told him.

He looked at her in stoic silence.

"This is a special day. Don't you forget that. It is time for you to be true to your mother, my dead sister. Hear me?"

"Who says I'm getting married?"

"You go and sort that out with Mr Jipp."

"Well! Who am I supposed to be marrying, then?"

"That's for him to tell you."

"No. You tell me, Aunty. You know, don't you?"

"We agreed. It's better you have a wife than go chasing after sluts. We all know what you been doin'. Sneakin' around in the middle of the night. There are eyes everywhere here. You should have watched out, been more careful."

"You all want to mind your own business. I done enough here. Gone off looking for nothing. Two times, all for nothing. I am a man. I can do what I like."

"Say what you like. You do what I say."

"What agreement did you make? You shouldn't do that without letting me know. Do you think you own me?" Elliot's temper was beginning to seethe.

"You have no mother then, is that what you are telling me? Of course you have a mother. If you have no mother, where do you live? Not here — is that what you are telling me? You have no mother and you do not live with your mother? I speak as your mother and you do what I say."

"Are you threatening me, Aunty?"

"Do what I say. That's all."

Dorrie's squinting eyes shifted from Elliot's hardened face to a slight movement on the ground close by. In an instant she moved as if she belonged to the wind. Body bent forward, she reached out with one arm and grabbed the piece of earth that had moved. A slender, translucent snake about a metre in length revealed itself from under a shallow layer of dirt. Into the sack she carried it went, to join the others she had captured, all tangled in a tight knot.

The capture of this snake released a chain reaction in the surrounding earth: dozens of the hidden creatures simultaneously surfaced in fright. In their efforts to escape they attacked each other, becoming entangled in a wild frenzy that grew even wilder as other snakes were attracted to the scene. Dorrie had never seen this happen before. She had never felt as frightened as she did at this moment. She trembled even more uncontrollably as she moved closer to Elliot, while the knotted, writhing serpentine ball grew ever larger beside them. Elliot felt his own heart beat harder as he tried to drag Dorrie away. It was like moving a stone. Her bare feet had become firmly planted in the ground and the strength that held her there penetrated her whole body. Shaking as she was, she could not be moved. It seemed as though hours passed before the mass of snakes stopped growing, and then Dorrie calmly rolled the lot into her sack.

"The Chinaman will be here tonight for them," she said, grinning. And she told Elliot it was the same one he had seen in the dead woman's country. "He comes here about this time every year — I always have a bag of snakes for him." She told him she had left it a bit late this year, but she had been so busy with her meetings, and not up to walking around too much. He used to take them up to the coast, she said, where his own people came fishing and hunting dugong, and made their own medicines or magic.

After the amazing event that had just occurred, and Dorrie's account of her longstanding knowledge of Pilot the Chinaman, to Elliot the news of his marriage seemed almost mellowed. If there was to be a marriage, he would comply. It would not change a great deal in his life. It could have advantages even. It was not unusual for marriage to be enforced by the Mission. By Jipp. To most people it meant nothing. It was just for show, a formality behind which you went on living. Maybe you got to like it later on. Maybe not. Life went on just the same. Men did what they wanted, and so did women. Elliot knew that Old Dorrie's mob had something up their sleeves which he would find out about sooner or later. Meanwhile, he would go along with what she wanted. It wasn't too big an imposition after all.

He walked off with the speed and lightness of one who had received good news. Dorrie eventually got her crippled body back to her camp about an hour before midnight, then crawled under her blanket. The plan was almost completed. The marriage would serve its purpose and provide the key to the future. The track whence evil came would be closed. People would know there was still honour and strength in the Council of Elders. There would be widespread respect for their strategy. Not even a powerful white man such as Jipp could prevent Old Dorrie's powerful magic. The marriage was right and could not be prevented, and would proclaim the power of magic. She fell into exhausted sleep.

Elliot reported to Jipp's office as requested and waited. He sat down inside, then leant on a veranda post outside. Hours went by, when evening came he was ready to give up and go home when Jipp finally appeared, and told Elliot to come inside. He opened his files, pulled out a couple, then sat down at his desk. The sweat of the day poured from his forehead; droplets fell onto the open pages of the flimsy buff-coloured files. He began to fill in a form which he took out of a drawer. When he had completed putting in dates and cross-referencing details from the files, he turned the form towards Elliot and told him to sign it.

Elliot signed his name carefully but did not read the document — he was not asked to do this, and Jipp quickly took it back. Together they went down to the girls' dormitory and collected Ivy Andrews. Back in Jipp's office, Elliot watched as Ivy signed the form. She did not look at either of the two men. Elliot continued to conceal his anger while Jipp read the script for the marriage ceremony, making them repeat the necessary words to complete the formality.

In Jipp's most pious voice Elliot and Ivy were pronounced man and wife. Jipp gave them words of encouragement, worn-out, often repeated sentiments. They were a family now and must live by the standards encouraged by the Mission and the word of God. He spoke of marriage as sacrosanct and warned Elliot to live by the example set by his father, who had turned to God and godly ways. Turning to Ivy, Jipp told her that God had helped him to choose a good husband for her. The past was now the past. She was a married woman now and should live by the will of God. Then he filed the completed form under "M" for Marriage in the filing cabinet. *Slam*: the heavy drawer returned to its closed and locked position. Jangling a loaded keyring, Jipp walked out of the door. The newlyweds followed him outside. Jipp shone his torch up the road as an indication that they should go now, signalling farewell. Once they were out of sight he turned the torch towards the mission house and went home.

10

The wind suddenly disappeared in the last light of nightfall. The contrasting quietness brought to the newly wedded couple a more intense realisation of the gravity of their incongruous marriage. Ivy: legally bound to follow this man across the darkened claypan division which would close the door for her between white and black. Elliot: contemplating future life with the "booby prize" when he had surely earned the right to choose from the top shelf.

Ivy heard words of accusation sent through the mimicry of night birds. Small children's voices that spoke of bad deaths ... of babies without heartbeats inside dead women with white eyes. They whispered of ways to inflict the pain of birth and mimicked the screams of women in labour. Rambled on about ugly souls looking around the saltbush for their little human bodies. Squealed and sniggered about slothful pregnant sluts ... Ivy followed as close as she could to Elliot, whose determined footsteps seemed to signify that he would not welcome her beside him. She felt squeamish and needed to vomit.

After walking a while through a narrow path flanked by darkened scrub they stopped. Here Elliot pushed Ivy into a clearing he knew well, behind some prickly pear bushes. Moonlight gave diluted dimensions to the surroundings. The Christian marriage was consummated on the ground in silence — save for the mimic sounds that only Ivy could hear. Hours went by, it seemed, with no reference to love or affection from either the man or the woman. The only words Elliot spoke were violent threats to induce encouragement whenever he moved his teeth from biting into the closed, bloody lips or swollen nipples of his pregnant wife.

Many others used this track, driven by emotions that swayed between love, lust and violence. Although Elliot made no attempt to conceal himself, he covered Ivy's face with his arm so that she would not see those who came by. Ivy heard her heartbeat pulsate louder; she was afraid of not being able to breathe, of vomiting, of shame. The other couples who passed by Elliot's patch giggled softly and joked about Elliot fairly motoring for it this time.

Deeper into the night the quietness quickly changed to a howling wind. Its velocity sent rapid squalls in all directions. The mimicry grew louder, as if an amplifier was being used to get the messages heard over the howls of the wind.

Ivy was taken home to share the dirt floor partly covered with putrid blankets in the semi-partitioned corrugated iron humpy where Pugnose lived with his dogs. The daytime temperature of over 40 degrees Celsius managed to survive inside this aged construction for most of the night. The loose tin roof and walls flapped and banged in the wind like a wild drummer until the rain heralded another summer storm.

In the early hours of the morning, after the storm had subsided, the dogs left the shelter first. Shortly afterwards the old man, his swollen joints creaking, slowly moved outside to squint at another brand-new day. Inside the windbreak, a semicircle of sheet iron of various shapes and sizes, he set about his usual tasks of making fire and brewing tea to soothe the pain in his head. After a while, with the tea running through his veins, Pugnose felt civil enough to call out Elliot. "Son, come out here!" he called.

When he did not receive an instant response he grabbed whatever was nearest at hand and threw it at the humpy.

The din started the dogs howling. "What's that smell you got with you there inside?" he yelled out in anger. Pugnose's short fuse was a renowned trait of his personality. Usually he lost his temper as a result of some wild stretch of his imagination ... a thief was trying to rob him ... some woman was trying to trick him into marriage ... jealous men were lying in wait for him. He provided plenty of incidents as fuel for the community to gossip about.

By the time Elliot woke up and made sense of the noise outside, Pugnose had interrupted the sleep of most people in the vicinity. Everyone got up, and people came outside their camps to sit around in the darker shadows and find out what was happening. Some of Pugnose's relatives, having recognised his voice, wandered across to his place for a closer look at what would occur between father and son.

"What's that inside there?"

"A wife. Organised by your churchman, Jipp. That's what." Elliot had finally come outside to face his father.

"You get her out of here. That's not a wife. I got no time for the smelly harlots you like around here. Told you before about that."

Elliot grunted something like "Fuck off". Angrily he threw a few pieces of firewood towards the neighbouring huts and loudly issued the instruction to "Fuck off, and fuckin' mind your own business!" The drained look on his face and the hard set of his eyes spoke more vividly of ill intent than any words ever could. Unwillingly the neighbours went away. Conjugal arrangements were no joke. No matter what any of them thought about Ivy, no one would want to cross Elliot's harsh and unforgiving nature. His sharpness of temper never faded into insignificance once the moment was past. He did not forget, once offended. It was impossible to make a reconciliation with such a man.

Pugnose had not noticed the outside world looking into his home. He went on mumbling — "She stinks. You can't smell or something? You must be able to … can smell her from here!"

Dorrie, awakened like everyone else, had continued to sit around after Elliot sent the others away. "You'll get used to it so stop your useless whingeing, like an old mongrel dog," she told Pugnose.

Elliot, boiling up the billy, remained silent. Meanwhile, Pugnose kept hopping past the entrance to the humpy and taking a shifty look inside. Elliot had switched off. He took no notice of his father's complaints of never being consulted about what was to happen in his own home. He drank a mugful of boiling tea straight down and left for work before the seven o'clock bell tolled for the men to parade outside Jipp's house.

"Even my dogs have gone off now," Pugnose moaned to Dorrie. He shouted after Elliot as he walked away down the road — "She can't sleep inside and that's it! I'll go and talk to Mr Jipp!"

"Come out here, Ivy," Dorrie called. She hit Pugnose lightly on the knee with her stick as an instruction to sit down and be quiet. "Keep your tin lid on, you useless old fool. Someone who knows nothing and never did. Stop complaining about nothing. You can sleep outside."

Slowly Ivy came out and sat on an upturned tin with rusted labels. She looked younger than her fourteen years, and in the light of day her pregnancy was obvious. Both she and her father-in-law sat there with sly, downturned faces, trying to cope with this change that had come upon them. The smell of the invisible vapour that somehow emanated from Ivy grew so strong that Pugnose could no longer bear to stay there. Dorrie noticed that the smell diminished with his leaving, as if it had followed him away. She took note of these matters, to discuss them among her group later on.

"We can get rid of that one," she said, pointing her digging stick towards the girl's belly once the old man was beyond hearing distance.

"No, thanks," Ivy said.

"That one will have no place here. Your mother was not from here. That baby got no father here either. Better you let me help you before it's too late."

Ivy continued to refuse with "no's" and "no thank you's", not saying anything more. She trusted no one. She was bearing a Christian child. A child of the Church?

Old Dorrie warned her that Elliot would not accept this baby. "He will make it very hard for you. I know that boy," she warned.

Ivy believed that the missionaries, Mr Jipp in particular, would not allow any harm to come to her or the baby.

This was Boxing Day. It was breathlessly hot by ten in the morning, when the body of the Chinaman, Pilot Ah King, was found in the bridal suite, hanging by his broken neck from a low branch amongst the thorns of the prickly pear tree. His body was trapped in a snare of straggly under-growth and covered with flies. The badly lacerated body had to be roughly pulled out of the thorns and buried immediately, without formalities, before the blood drip-ping out of the torn body even had time to dry.

Errol Jipp did not attend the burial, nor did he even bother to report the death. There would be no official investigation by the Mission. Whatever the connection be-tween the Chinaman and someone at St Dominic's, it was now over and done with. No illegal non-Aboriginal person had ever been found on the Mission before, and Jipp bemoaned the fact that it had happened now.

He knew the root cause of this trouble. "Those cattle station people," he would say. For their part, the cattle station owners had no time for those mission people. Less than twenty years back, it was unusual to see Chinese in the area — perhaps a handful or less in the townships. Most would have "married" Aboriginal women, alliances con-doned by the owners of the surrounding cattle properties.

They provided the pastoralists with a stable workforce, after all. A good Chinese was not likely to go walkabout for weeks at a time at the drop of a hat. He would make sure his "wife" caused no trouble for the boss or the missus. The Chinese gardener could be depended upon to actually work the ground and make the green stuff grow, no matter how much loading, carting and plain old slog it took with bended back. The thin brown men knew how to make wells and dams and provide irrigation wherever they set down. This appealed to a pastoralist's longing for the green acres of the old country ... the subconscious minds of homesick souls could almost reach out and feel that luscious greenness in the hot dead of the night. The Chinese possessed the secret ingredient to mix continents to fool the eye of the so-called "tiller of the soil". The large numbers of children that came from these liaisons were considered good assets towards the future workforce in these isolated places. Tied to the cattle station owner, there would be nowhere else for them to go. They were a social minority which would be hard pushed to find acceptance elsewhere. And the illegal mixed-race marriages were kept secret by the property owners whenever a police patrol rode in to round up the "coloured" babies. The only future for the Aboriginal Chinese family was to stay where they were born and work and, if there was no trouble, where they would die in old age.

The history of these cattle stations was forged by Aboriginal men and women who lived in slavery, bound to the most uncivilised and cruellest people their world had ever known. Those enslaved were the Aborigines who had escaped the whiteman's bullet, his whip, his butchering and trophy collections — the sets of severed ears decorating the lounge-room wall. There was the Aboriginal girl, not killed with all the others, young enough to tame, brought back to the property to work.

"Strap her to a tree and leave here there until she's tame enough to start."

How long did it take? One month? Or two?

Nowadays, there were more Aboriginal people who could claim Chinese blood in the Gulf country than there were white. The Gulf was filled with Aboriginal Chinese families, a kaleidoscope of colours between black and brown.

When Jipp saw the dead Chinaman that morning, he was instantly repelled. He regarded the dead man as a feral alien who was outside his jurisdiction. An alien who had fornicated with the pure stock of his Aboriginal people.

"Get it down quickly then bury it somewhere," he ordered the work gang he had chosen from the assembly line that morning. It included Elliot. At first the men were inclined to treat the dead man with some gentleness, out of respect, but when Jipp saw they were getting nowhere he swore at them: "Rip it down and stop wasting time," he told them.

As soon as Jipp turned his back the men started to talk amongst themselves.

"Must have been murdered, I reckon," said Allie Green-frog, a young man who spoke through his nose and always wore green socks with Jipp's old shoes. He had been picked up by the police at Lost Lagoon some time back because he had no occupation. For his "care and benefit" he had been delivered to St Dominic's wearing a limegreen, skin-tight suit: this was how he acquired his name. He had not stopped talking since he arrived — some said he did not stop even in his sleep. Most people were alarmed by those who talked with loose lips in their sleep. It was common knowledge that conversations in the night between the unconscious mind and spirits wandering around looking for such a thing to happen could be extremely dangerous.

Allie, so far as anyone knew, had no authority to deliver communications to the dead — or to the living, for that matter. He had been told to stop talking in his sleep by Dorrie's group, who determined everyday law matters. He had tried to obey by sleeping very little, although sometimes, being so overtired, he simply could not stop himself falling asleep. Then, immersed in deep sleep, not able to be woken, his talking was incessant and his ideas so numerous that no one was able to recall very much of what he said. Sometimes Allie could be blamed for bad news of moderate significance. For instance, there were times when he would mention Christian names, which resulted in a person who happened to have that name suffering a headache or migraine or even influenza next day. Sometimes a person's bad mood or quick temper was said to be caused by the Greenfrog. Generally no one took much notice, though there were times when Allie became the subject of heated debate.

No one knew why he always wore green socks, which he obtained from the Mission with his charming chatter. They came in various hues of green. To some, it seemed a miracle for anyone to be able to persuade the Mission to undertake a personal favour. He was often seen darning his green socks — there were never any holes even in the oldest pair. People often looked out for them while they listened to him talking. Whenever anyone took up the subject of his socks — or Jipp's old shoes for that matter — Allie would change the subject in such a way that he easily gained the listener's interest in another topic. Perhaps no one really cared: shoes and socks were of no great concern to any Aboriginal person in the tropics.

The other four men engaged on dragging the Chinaman's body out of the bushes agreed that his death seemed like murder.

"Must have been a few fellas involved in it, I'd say," Allie remarked, keeping up the dialogue while they all sweated and strained over the task.

"It's taking all our strength to get him down, so I reckon

there's no way he could have hanged himself up there. Others were involved in this — that's what I think. He couldn't have got himself jammed up in this mess by himself."

Finally they broke the body loose of the prickly foliage and it lay on the ground, a multi-coloured signature to violence fully exposed in the sunlight. It was obvious to the men looking down at the face, arms and other exposed parts of the body that the old man had been beaten up in a relentless and vicious attack. Several open gashes had been caused by some sharp object much larger than prickly pear spikes. The black-and-blue bruises mingled with dirt told of a struggle which ended with the victim being dragged, maybe face down, to this spot.

"I know this fella!" Allie claimed. "This is the old Arnott's parrot man — you know, the old Chinaman who travelled around all over the place in that wagon of his with the biscuit label on the side. He traded things for snakes — goannas, too. Ah! You must know him. I saw him at Lost Lagoon. He's been around these parts forever, poor bugger."

Nobody there admitted ever seeing him at the Mission before and it may have been true, in spite of the fact that Pilot had visited St Dominic's many times in recent years. He came at night, never staying very late, and always saw Dorrie. She was not only one of his suppliers and a customer, but also his agent in these parts. It was a good arrangement for a small-time snake-oil salesman of the bush. Not a lot of money in it, but a viable way of life. At the end of the line Pilot sold the oil to a white bloke who visited Lost Lagoon two or three times a year to collect whatever snakes and goannas he could for a shilling or two each. These were then sent down south for the venom to be milked from the snakes for medical purposes. The goannas provided jars of medicinal oil and grease, extracted from the fat off their slain bodies. All that was left in the boilers at the end of a good boil-up.

Pilot had known a lot about medicines and plants. He came from a Chinese family with a long line of doctors. For generations his forebears passed on information, carried out medical research and cared for the sick. At a price. Money was necessary, of course, to obtain rare ingredients, update equipment. The family business was sponsored by royal dynasties in China for hundreds of years. Intricate operations were performed by the younger doctors in the family and cures found for many diseases pronounced "incurable" in the Western world.

The reasons why Pilot had left China, never to return, were complex. He was in his early thirties when he left, and considered one of the most brilliant doctors produced by the family. The Chinese revolution had its effect on the family's status in the medical profession. The family was forced to share their knowledge and wealth, and other compromises had to be made. Communism created yet another dynasty, breeding nepotism and dispensing favours in return for loyalty. Merit was never the single reason whereby a person's worth was judged. The family prospered as it had always done, simply by exercising compassion, always its guiding force. New conditions: the same sicknesses.

But all families suffer wear and tear. One or other of their members is a disappointment like a cold breeze on a sunny winter's day. Pilot went against the habit of thrift in a wealthy family and lost badly. He loved unwisely, committing adultery. He experimented where obedience was required — this was malpractice. The family reputation for medical excellence had little carrying ability for flaws, and there were known methods of elimination for an unsatisfactory member.

Pilot faced a hard decision. Voluntary exile was not the ideal alternative to death. It was a coward's choice, an acknowledgment of failure in a proud family which had produced generations of highly principled sons: this was its most prized inheritance.

So Pilot came to Australia. Almost at once, although he was in a foreign country with totally different flora and fauna, he was identifying the scientific properties of plants. In no time he was once more again able to produce medicines for most illnesses. He might have fitted into the white world of any Australian city but had no desire to do so. In the bush towns he often attended the sick, then moved on. He preferred to live in the bush with the Aboriginal people, whose culture of traditional ownership he had no difficulty in understanding. In their country he behaved always as a guest who has been showered with the very best hospitality. He was always eager to understand the local language, since it gave him access to the medicinal properties of plants. And he was able to gain information for the application of cures, and operations.

As the body lay in the sun it was soon covered with a thick sheet of black flies once again. A green frog crawled out of a pocket in the dead man's jacket, then crawled weakly away in the sun, through the broken pieces of prickly bush scattered over the ground.

Allie, surprised, was struck with a nervous twitch in his left eye. For once he had little to say as he and the others watched the frog's slow movement. It made its way into Allie's shadow and then tried to buy itself underneath the place where he sat. Nobody said anything, but they all wondered about the significance of the frog and the coincidence that it had favoured Allie. Could it have been attracted to his green clothes? Perhaps it thought he was another frog — or a green bush. Allie himself, though he was shaking, did not move and allowed the frog to burrow beneath him. Meanwhile, the buzzing of the flies increased in volume, and eventually the men got on with the job of carrying the body away to be buried.

*   *   *

Lay Preacher Delainy, dressed in a long, starched white gown, beads of sweat pouring from his forehead, was waiting in the cemetery at the head of a line of twelve vacant holes in the ground as the men arrived with the body. Jipp had relented after all and told Delainy to conduct a brief burial service. Most of the holes were filled with stagnant storm water. The driest hole was chosen by the workmen. There was no coffin. No blanket. Quickly they lowered the body into the hole, two of them standing inside it while the others manoueuvred from above. Intent on their efforts, they ignored Delainy's presence.

"I am the resurrection and the life, saith the Lord: he that believeth in me, though he were dead, yet shall he live: and whosoever belieth in me shall never die," Delainy chanted.

"Be fuckin' careful, I can't take all the weight. So fuckin' hold it!" Greenfrog shouted from below, inside the grave.

"I know that my Redeemer liveth. Praise the Lord," Delainy continued.

"Jesus Christ! Hold it, until I can bloody get a grip on him. Fuckin' hell! Hold on!" — the other man had dropped the body and pulled himself out of the hole. Greenfrog was trapped underneath in the mud, panicking for the others to get him out.

Through the cemetery, that held at least two hundred graves, old Dorrie came limping along crying loudly with all the spirits in that place. She was supported by Noah Two-By-Two, blind to the living world, who saw the spectacle of the spirits rising from their graves, moving towards the funeral humming the old song for the dead, levitating in the hot sky, going towards the unfilled grave and descending into it. Both the old people were accompanied by the twins Gabriel and Mervin, who were softly singing a mournful Christian hymn.

At the edge of the grave the four of them stood sobbing

quietly while Delainy concluded his service. He had known nothing of Pilot's life, nor did it occur to him that there would be any need to console any of the living.

The earth was piled high beside the grave, as the shovelling into the grave began, dozens of spirits ascended from the hole through the falling dirt, and without a sound carried out the soul of Pilot. Noah was that close, he felt the breeze from the upward spiralling of black spirits, some still in mission dress, some without clothes, some clothed in grass or paperbark. They moved that close to him that he stepped back to let them pass by. They smelt of those familiar yet strange aromas that come when you break leaves or the twigs of certain bushy plants. There was the smell of wetness, of the damp mud of the riverbank. The smell that comes when you are digging mussels from clay mud with your bare hands.

Noah leapt forward as the incandescent spirit of Pilot left the ground, his neck supported by a spirit's hands. Indeed his neck had been broken. His eyes were closed. Blind as he was, Noah had to shield his eyes from brightness of that ascending soul. Squinting to see with his hand over is brow, and although the words were barely audible, he heard Pilot speak: *"Draw no simple conclusion, my friend. All are implicated."*

At that moment, seeing Noah teetering on the edge of the grave, Elliot screamed to the others to pull him back before he ended up in the hole as well.

Shovelfuls of dirt fell onto the body until it was covered and earth filled up the sides of the hole. By this time the stillness of the day fell upon the cemetery and Noah's visions had disappeared. With the hard heat of the day gone by — it was now late afternoon — only the noise of a rake tidying up loose gravel in a slow, easy manner could be heard.

But Noah did see one more vision after this. A small group

of Chinese people wearing traditional clothes in warm, rich colours came walking towards the grave. They intoned a sad chant, a long chain of unchanging rhythmical passages. They were mostly old men and women with long grey hair, and with them was a handful of small children, one ringing a small bell while the others awkwardly carried baskets too big for them to handle properly. Noah growled to Dorrie and the twins to stay with him for a while. He watched as this strange group, with forlorn faces, inspected the grave. Some went into the grave and inspected the corpse; finding Pilot's soul already departed, the old men regarded Noah and his group with disgust. Then the women and children planted dozens of small red candles in the ground and lit them. Next they sprinkled the grave with flowers and blossoms which Noah had never seen before. They spoke briefly in their language, then walked away softly in their silken, embroidered slippers.

Noah felt great sympathy for Pilot's relatives who had come to take his soul home — but, because they had come from so far away, had arrived too late. He wondered whether Pilot would have waited for them if he had known they would come. Perhaps they would be able to catch up with him later on.

Then Noah told Dorrie and the twins what he had seen and what Pilot had told him: *"All were implicated."*

"Well," Dorrie said, "I knew something like this was going to happen."

"Why did you think that, Aunty?" Allie jumped in, wanting to find out everything.

Dorrie ignored him and pointed her finger at Elliot.

"Don't look at me. I had nothing to do with it," Elliot warned her.

"Aunty's right. You must listen to what she tells you," the twins said together. They often spoke identical words in the same instant. It was only natural, since they both shared the same thought. But when they were children they had become too frightened to do this, for everyone had believed that one of them was a devil spirit the other had allowed to exist. Often people would avoid them, sometimes running to get away from them. Only their mother, who was struck down with sickness as she gave birth, disbelieved the myths about twins — or at least her own, and even though she was abandoned by most of her family, she struggled on alone, in great pain, to bring them up. The missionaries, even though they still carried some of their own superstitious baggage about the Devil's hand at work in either the conception or birth of twins, supported her with words of praise and ridiculed the simple beliefs of her relatives and others. But they too left her alone to rear the children herself.

Both had survived and grown to manhood, in spite of the generally held belief about what would become of them. Most people predicted that the devil would lure the real child to run away and return to Tabletop Mountain, where their devil spirit ancestors resided. It was by sheer, simple accident the mother had conceived a devil spirit in the first place — it was generally understood that someone, perhaps the father, in a moment of great melancholy which caused a predisposition for the lighting of large fires, had thereby ushered a malign spirit into the community, where it disguised itself as a children's playmate, and then was unwittingly called by an unborn baby to become its identical self.

After the mother died, Dorrie's group had taken the grown-up twins into its care, because it seemed that their existence should no longer be ignored. There was some reason why they were a pair, but the original theory remained unproven and had by then been forgotten.

Elliot faced Old Dorrie and the twins. "What are you getting at?" he asked.

"You know, you bring that one now, right in the middle of things. That's dangerous," Dorrie told him.

"For Christ's sake. You really get to me. Wasn't it your idea in the first place? You set the whole thing up."

"We wanted to get her out of here — don't you understand?" Mervin blurted out impatiently.

"Old Pilot was set to take that woman Ivy last night. Take her back to her own people," Gabriel added in a flat voice.

"Well, you should have told me, shouldn't you? After all, it is my wife you're talking about," Elliot snapped.

"Your wife?" Delainy was curious.

"That Ivy thing. That's his wife," Dorrie told him. "Jipp married them. All legal and correct."

"When?"

"Yesterday, if it's any business of yours," Elliot said.

"Well, it's too late now. We missed out. You should have left her there," Noah said.

"Things will get worse unless somebody does something about this business," the twins remarked together.

"It's up to you now, son. You'll have to do something. I've tried. But she's too smart to trick." Dorrie spoke directly to Elliot.

Elliot told them that Ivy was up the duff with Jipp's kid. He blamed Dorrie and her mad friends for getting him into this situation. Said he wouldn't listen to a bunch of screwballs, and from now on what he did with the mess his life had become.

Delainy challenged Elliot for speaking to his mother as if she was nothing. Elliot responded by knocking Delainy to the ground with one sound punch under the chin. He told him he was just as crazy as his mother, the way he masqueraded as a Christian preacher made him the laughing stock of his people.

When Dorrie managed to insert herself between the two of them, Delainy not only told her to get out of the way, but to remember that he would be watching her in future. "Making sure no crimes like this are committed," he said. He would find out who were the criminals. "And when I find them I won't try to expel any devil, I'll make sure the police come to take them away to a proper court of law

where they will be tried, found guilty and justly punished."
Not even his mother would be spared, he warned; they lived
according to strong laws made by the Australian government.

"This is the Law, you fool," Noah told Delainy. "You are
looking at the true Law, your Government, right here. For
this land and our people there is only one Law and this is
it."

"Well, you figure it out, Preacher man. I'm going home,"
Elliot said. He gestured for his workmates to go with him.

"Nothing like family business, that's what I say," Allie
muttered.

"Yep! Well, if you are married, as you say you are, mind
you keep your vows," Delainy yelled after Elliot. "I know
your type. You mistreat your wife and I'll be on to you!"

Elliot made a backwards gesture with one upraised arm
and walked on.

The job of burying Pilot was finished by six o'clock in the
afternoon.

11

The sky was full of clouds: more and more clouds passed overhead until the sky grew thick with the build-up of unshed rain. Dull, shadowy days, quiet and heavy, sticky with humidity and heat. The nights were alive with electrifying storms that lit up the darkest crevices of every part of the land. The earth shook like a captured animal with each clap of thunder. Trembling dogs panted and whined all through the night. Nobody got any sleep. Squally winds bent tall trees back and forth until they snapped. No rain came out of any of this for St Dominic's, although in the late afternoons heavy rain storms could be seen a long way off in all directions. This is how it was each November. And in the middle of the night, on the twenty-fifth day of this month, Mary Koopundi was born.

The marriage of Elliot and Ivy was not one the Christian Church could point to with pride as one made in heaven. That would have been an extremely misleading notion. In the real world of St Dominic's, established for Christian usage, the very widest of interpretations would have been required to pluck any sense of goodness from the depths of mutual despair. Within this environment there were very few examples of ideal marriage. On the other hand, this particular marriage was not always the "hell on earth" of Christian metaphor. It was to prove a paradigm for their ultimate life experiences.

Ivy spent the last weeks of her pregnancy mostly alone,

sitting outside the humpy and using only enough of her low
reserve of energy to keep moving her heavy body into the
shade. From early morning she stayed on the east side; by
midday a little shade could be found at the back of the
humpy, and here she would lie down and sleep for a while.
Then she moved again to catch the shade on the west side.
But on the final days she scarcely moved from the dirt floor
just inside the door. Here she sat up wide awake all day and
for most of the night.

She spent a lot of time watching the large, fat babies of
clouds that passed overhead, darkening the day. They came
across the sky, building up their numbers until they were
jammed together, crawling on and on, unable to stop. At
night she listened to these babies scream with an anger that
grew deafening as they flung fiery rods back and forth
across the sky in utter fury. Occasionally these rods fell to
the ground with a force that made the earth on which she
lay rock and moan from within.

Life was frightening. Both Ivy and her unborn child cried
continually, with the depression of those who want to die
yet stay alive. Ivy had lost any physical power. She was the
victim of the small being that struggled and shoved its solid
little body against her ribcage, which had already been
pushed so far forward that she felt sure it must be broken.
Furiously the child beat its fists and kicked its legs towards
her heart and lungs. Ivy thought it was trying to kill her by
strangling itself inside her body. Her fright developed into
paranoia. Over and over she slapped her swollen stomach
to stop the baby's pummelling, only to hear the child cry
louder and fight even more desperately.

Eventually Ivy fell into a long sleep one night during a
storm, and did not wake until late afternoon the next day.
She was surprised the storm had stopped and amazed that
she had fallen asleep amidst its din. But now she felt at ease.
And she was aware of a strange silence. Something different
about herself. She seemed to have regained a sense of her

former self, a sense of normality before the baby. Before her marriage. Now the tortuous being within her had stopped moving. Nothing. Only silence. The seemingly endless storm within her body had passed. It was a wonderful revelation and she lapsed into more luxurious sleep.

Next day, when she still felt no pain, she assumed the baby had died, and was happy. That was the truth. Relieved that her life might be endured without the burden of a child. A monster that had grown inside her and caused internal damage. After all, she was only fourteen. She hoped that things would get better in the future. Surely it was only a matter of time before something would be arranged for her. Work had been organised for some of the other girls in the nearest township or as domestic help on cattle properties. The fact that she was married did not loom large in her mind. In fact she hardly considered herself a wife.

She had scarcely seen Elliot for the last few months. He had not touched her again after that first night of their marriage. At first he stayed at Pugnose's camp, but the bickering between father and son finally became too much. Now he came by infrequently and never stayed long, just sitting around for a while. Although Ivy was the cause of many of his arguments with the old man, he did not bother to take her to his new place.

Over time, old Pugnose became obsessed with his daughter-in-law. Alone in the camp day in, day out, she was all the company he had. She became a wonderful source of complaint about the many trivial concerns that occupied his mind: supposed thefts of food and other small dishonesties. He quizzed her continuously about these and often she lied for the sake of peace, or else tried to ignore him. Above all, Pugnose assumed the interests of the unborn baby and exerted a powerful authority over her in this respect. Every day he spewed forth a litany of complaints about her behaviour, although she seldom went anywhere and was solely occupied with the basic necessities of existence.

Pugnose would begin his complaints at sunrise, when he woke with the sun on his face from the makeshift camp he had made in the wrong spot outside the old humpy. He refused to make it easier for himself by shifting his blankets to a shadier spot. The inconvenience served his nature. Besides, he needed to wake up earlier because he had so much to say. He paused only to drink more tea. The main source of his complaint concerned the taboos that Ivy broke. Food she ate, for example, which he thought was not good for the baby.

For almost the full term of her pregnancy, Ivy had morning sickness. As soon as she awoke she would dash out of the humpy to vomit into the saltbush outside. Every time this happened, Pugnose would offer his thoughts about the causes of this, and how to cure it. He would ask her what it felt like to be vomiting the poisonous venom of the snake-witch, which he declared he had watched her eating. He would tell her she was killing the saltbush. He told her she came from a tribe of gluttonous people who cared nothing for family or the poor little babies they brought into this world. This was the reason her mother had been brought to St Dominic's, he said.

Then he would reach the main issue of his discontent at having Ivy as his daughter-in-law. "Another thing," he would say, and then begin his ravings on the subject of her adultery. He enforced the taboo of running water on her, saying he had caught sight of Ivy swimming with "a group of young, sex-starved sluts looking for a poke down in the river". He told her: "Pregnant women shouldn't go near running water. If you do this, something will happen to that baby. Or you. There's a bad fella living there disguised as a crocodile. He wants babies because he has no children. He will take you down to his underwater den. You'll be trapped there. His slave. He will rape you. If you go to the river, this is what will happen to you."

He went on to talk of other water spirits who stole the life and spirits of babies by ripping them from their mothers' bodies. He entered into considerable detail about their large, warty hands which could change into a scissor shape, sneak up and reach inside a woman to extract her baby without her even feeling it. "Terrible, poor things," he said. "But they got only themselves to blame." He said those women never made it back to camp — and serve them right. Some drowned. Others died on the spot with their insides hanging out or else crawled away leaving a trail of blood, to die in the nearest bush.

Then he would quiz her about her exact whereabouts throughout the previous day. Bubbles of saliva ran down the sides of his mouth as he fabricated accusations against her. Eventually he would tire himself out and drift into sleep. Other times he might go out, or his inquisition would be cut short by the intrusion of visitors.

Pugnose held most power over the issue of sex. Ivy could not handle any allegations about her involvement in any kind of sexual activity. In the beginning she would clumsily try to defend herself with complete denial, taking care to speak respectfully, for she had learned that she must show respect to the old man. Pugnose did not need much prompting to hit her across the head or on her back or legs with his walking stick. Even though she tried to stay out of reach, she often nursed an array of bruises that lasted for days.

There were times, when she first came to the humpy, when she tried to run away. Pugnose would limp around the village to tell Elliot what had happened and he would bring her back. Ivy had learned that no one would help her, not even the Jipps, who handed her back to Elliot when she looked to them for help. When she began screaming accusations at Jipp she was quickly silenced by the mind-numb-ing blow of Elliot's fist in her mouth. It took weeks for the swelling infection of her gums to heal without any medical help.

Beverly Jipp, shocked to the inner core of her being with what she heard and saw, walked back into the mission house and spent the duration of Ivy's pregnancy knitting and sewing everything needed for a baby's first year. All these things she put into cardboard boxes, then mail-ordered more wool and cotton and began all over again.

Those times when she ran away were the only times Elliot flogged her. He did this in full anger in front of the old man, using his bare hands while she doubled over to shield herself and her unborn child. When he finished, usually after intervention of neighbours who could not take the shouting and screaming any longer, he shoved her inside the dwelling and told her it would get worse every time she upset his father. Then, threatening to come back later to finish off the job, which he sometimes did, he would walk off. Inside the shelter, Ivy cringed in one corner, nursing her pain for several days. She came out briefly only in the dark night to feel her way to the communal latrine.

How should she respond to the ongoing allegations of sexual misbehaviour hurled at her by the old man? She said she was sorry. She even elaborated on the stories he made up. Did she do it? She said she did not remember — she thought she must have. She agreed to having had sexual encounters with all manner of men, and went along with any details Pugnose dreamed up. She submitted to his blows. She swallowed the medicines he concocted and other potions brought by Dorrie to dispel the evil from her body. These often increased the nausea that left her so weak and listless and caused more vomiting.

Ivy grew thinner while the baby within her grew larger and robbed her of health and energy. At night she lay watching while the old man stood above her without speaking, shaking his penis, exposed through one of the holes in his tattered trousers, until eventually a few drops of semen fell on her. Then he would limp and grope his way back outside.

Sometimes Elliot caught bits and pieces of the adulterous gossip spreading through the village about his wife. Fabrication that had become substituted for fact. Usually it was his lover Gloria who told him, whenever he showed indifference towards her. To her, indifference was the most intolerable offence perpetrated by men. On such occasions Elliot would go round to his father's camp. "So what's been happening around here lately, old man?" That was how he began the game of verifying Gloria's information.

"Nothing much," Pugnose would reply, then launch into trivial accounts of neighbours' noise, how one of his dogs had killed a snake, and how weak he was in the legs. He liked to think up what he would say to Elliot when next he saw him, to let him know how he was suffering, and how neglectful Elliot was in his duty towards his old father.

"What's *she* been up to, then?" Elliot would interrupt his father's self-indulgent conversation in mid-sentence.

"Nothing much," Pugnose would answer absent-mindedly.

"That's not what I've been hearing." Elliot's irritable gaze would settle on Ivy, clumsily going about her tasks, stoking the fire, cooking and pouring out tea for both men while avoiding their eyes. Then, as she was handing him a pannikin, he would pull her down by one ear. "So what are these stories going around about you, hey?" he demanded. When she stumbled and dropped whatever she was carrying he felt justified in starting his direct attack.

At the beginning she had half-heartedly defended herself, in the simple belief that this was supposed to be her husband: she had the strange notion that he was actually showing the strength of his feelings towards her. This man who, though she did not understand why, had married her. And he was good-looking and strong, after all: she was not entirely opposed to the idea of being his wife. Any other woman would have thought the same way.

So at first she had behaved in an upfront manner in a sly sort of way, even answering back Elliot's claims and making frivolous challenges concerning his own extended absences. Half-joking, half-crying, she made flimsy references to things she had learned about him. She did not say it was Pugnose who first told her about Gloria and many other women.

Elliot did not care whether she knew these things or not, but he made her pay dearly for the knowledge. He liked to twist things — the truth as well as physical things. He liked to twist Ivy's ear, sometimes both of them together. In this way he was able to force her to reveal that it was Pugnose who had given her the information. Then he descended on her with more abuse about her supposed infidelities. Finally, as she lay semi-conscious, he held a knife across her throat and told her the next time she lied about his father she would be dead meat. "That will go too," he added and ran both sides of the knife across her stomach.

Nowadays Ivy had learned to say nothing. She waited out the accusation and abuse and pitched her screams as loudly as she could, even before the pain inflicted by Elliot began. Over time, she had learned to manage the pain by dramatising her fear at the start. If she merely succumbed to the physical pain, she was unable to create attention. But if she could generate enough attention before she was attacked, she could force Elliot to stop.

Sometimes Pugnose intervened. "You stop it now!" he'd yell, hitting Elliot with his stick. "You nothing! You bring me shame. You're no son of mine! You can't even look after a wife. You too busy fuckin' anything like a dog to even understand about a wife." Then he would shout out for everyone to hear. "This is no son of mine! This is a mongrel! You hear that. So don't you people say this animal is related to me. You hear me?"

When Elliot stopped his abuse and walked out, Pugnose would run down the road as fast as his weak legs could manage, waving his arms and yelling after Elliot not to come near his place again.

At other times, enough onlookers would gather around so that one or two might risk telling Elliot that a man who beat his wife was complete and utter scum. A man called Lawrence, who lived close by, would always tell Elliot or any other man who beat his wife that they were the scum of the earth, if he was around when things were happening. But one day Lawrence overstepped the mark with Elliot. Elliot released his grip on Ivy, and flung her towards that crowd that had gathered, so that she almost landed in the camp-fire.

"Where's that motherfucker?" Elliot's eyes were protruding out of their sockets and a froth of saliva ran from his mouth.

"Here! Come and fight a real man!" Lawrence challenged him.

Elliot lunged at the crowd, scattering people in all directions until he connected with Lawrence, who stood there waiting for him. Though quite tall, Lawrence, a man in his thirties, was of slender build and no match for Elliot in a fit of rage. The struggle lasted ten minutes: dirt flew across the village as the two men moved through other camps, knocking down whatever lay in their path. It looked like a dust storm before the rain. Elliot was deaf to the shouting of the other man's family, who struggled vainly to pull him off Lawrence. Finally it dawned on him that Lawrence was dying of suffocation in the dust, with a broken neck.

After this time, Pugnose learned to protect Ivy from much of the violence Elliot was capable of inflicting. At least to make sure a son of his own blood did not commit murder again. The verdict of "accidental death" following this incident was helped by the fact that it had been Lawrence who incited Elliot to fight him, as many witnesses were able to testify. For a long time afterwards, as he slept at night, Pugnose saw the spirit of Lawrence sitting by his bed weeping for his family. The old man told Elliot to stay away and not come back until the baby was born. After that, he said he should take his devil woman and her baby right away. He was sick and tired of having to put up with all the excitement at his age and coping with the damage Elliot was causing.

"Then after you are all gone I hope to be left alone to die in peace," Pugnose concluded.

After that Elliot did stay away, but he paid out elsewhere. Unsuspecting people whose names had been used in the fabrications of sexual melodrama invented by Pugnose — and, in self-defence, by Ivy — became his targets. They were viciously beaten up, and the attacks were often repeated, until the victim became predisposed to some common illness, which caused them to die within a matter of weeks.

Dozens of complaints were made about Ivy and Elliot to Errol Jipp, particularly by the relatives of Elliot's deceased victims. Jipp maintained his silence, listening to story after story of how Ivy had promoted the fighting by her promiscuous behaviour, which caused a good man like Elliot to do these things. Finally he thanked them for coming, expressed his gratitude that people were letting him know what was going on, and promised to do something about it. In fact, he was undecided as to what he could possibly do. So long as neither Ivy nor Elliot caused any severe trouble for himself, he thought he would simply let the matter ride for the time being.

Jipp did go down to Pugnose's camp once, to see for himself what was happening there. He tried to talk to Ivy, but received no response. Her face remained blank. She looked straight through him. He gave up, realising he was talking to a brick wall. She had turned out like most of the young wives in the village, who he thought could have made something better of themselves. First he found them acting like sluts on heat. Then he arranged marriages for them with men from promising families. Jipp felt that he managed these people skilfully. But he was at a loss when it came to the lack of sense these young girls showed. He created the opportunity for them to make better lives for themselves and they simply failed him.

Seeing Ivy there, Jipp felt justified that he had forgotten to bring the neat piles of baby clothes that filled Beverly's sewing room. He told Ivy about Mrs Jipp's good hard work on her behalf. Then, as he was leaving he quipped: "We'll be better shipping them off to a hospital to give to real needy people who will appreciate them properly. Instead of giving them to people who can't be bothered to help themselves."

Ivy awoke from a deep sleep, startled by the realisation of what she believed was happening. "What if it is dead?" she said out loud. She thought it was morning. It took her a while to decide why the shadows were not where they should be. She struggled to lift herself to an upright position.

Pugnose was nowhere in sight. He had more or less abandoned her in the last few weeks, determined that he would not be present when the baby came. He felt he had no business being around during childbirth — and he was afraid of what would be born. He waited nervously over at Dorrie's place until it would all be over and someone could tell him about it.

"Go down there and have a look," he kept telling Dorrie, but the old woman went on with her own business. The more he harassed her, the more determined she was that she would suit herself when she went. She was fed up with the old man's nagging. She hadn't asked him to come to her place, and now he expected her to look after him all the time.

"Look here, you old fool," she told him, "babies get born

here all the time. Believe me, I will know when it comes. I know about these things. You got nothing to worry about."

She refused to discuss it with him any more. Her ears were ringing from the way he kept talking all the time.

Ivy could have shrieked for help. The baby did not stir when she tried to move it into action, pressing both hands on either side of her stomach. No movement. Harder pushing. No result. She had no idea what this meant. What happened to a dead baby inside its mother's stomach? She had never wanted a baby, though sometimes she thought it might be alright. At this point she started to panic.

What if she died with the decaying baby inside her? Would they say she was a murderer? She imagined throngs of hard, angry faces moving towards her, coming to get her. She felt the sticks they carried beating her to death. She must escape. Swallowing in huge gulps, she began to walk away, then ran as far as she could, struggling with the weight of the baby inside her belly. In fact she only made it across the floor of the hut, where she lay down exhausted, thinking she had completed a long journey.

The second journey was more difficult. She saw the mine shaft amongst the stony rubble. She had to cross the chasm of a sheer drop into a well of darkness. She must focus her thoughts on that far-off place she considered to be her real world. A world where she was alone and not pregnant. A place vaguely remembered from childhood, locked in the subconscious world of the distant past. Before she had been abandoned in a life that was not hers. Here she would find her former self and reach reality by thrashing about with her arms through the layers of cobwebs that formed screen after screen across the landscape. There at last she entered a room where curtains of Chantilly lace flowed in the light breeze coming through the open window. A woman was there, laughing with a child whose arms were covered with cobwebs. They laughed as if they would never stop. This was where she would get help if she shouted out for it.

She did not remember whether she shouted before the pain began or whether it came first. Then her screams flowed from the pain. Pain that sprang at her from deep inside her groin and raced down her thighs. She lay breathless while the pain subsided for a few moments, then lashed back at her, piercing the base of her back with tremendous force. Over and over the pain rushed upon her. She felt as though her body was being split in two with the baby being forced out of her body. Her legs shook involuntarily and went numb. She heard a baby cry loudly, then the sound gradually faded away. The room of happy laughter had disappeared.

When she woke she found it was dark and she was back inside the humpy. Alone.

Later Dorrie came. "Where's my baby?" Ivy managed to say when Dorrie asked her if she was feeling better now. The old woman held a cup of water to her lips and told her the baby was being cared for by Mr and Mrs Jipp, because it was very sick. Ivy felt so exhausted that she went back to sleep.

Next day she managed to get up and was able to eat a little, and take a few unsteady steps outside. Back in the humpy she drifted once again into a deep sleep. On the third day the milk filled her breasts. She felt she would burst from the liquid that could not escape fast enough through her nipples. The painful gorged milk glands forced her to react to the fact that she was a mother. That evening, alone, she managed to walk the distance to the mission house.

"Mrs Beverly," she called out.

Again she called, louder each time. She waited. Nobody came. "I want to see the baby, please!" she called again, scared that they might fetch Elliot.

Then she heard footsteps over the wooden veranda and Jipp came thumping down the stairs.

"Sorry, Ivy, but the baby is not here," Jipp told her the baby had been flown out with the flying doctor soon after it was born, because it was gravely ill. "When it is better it will come back from the hospital," he said. In the meantime, she should get better and not worry — the baby was being properly looked after. When Ivy asked if she had had a daughter, he answered, "Yes." Then he told her to go home.

Several months after her baby was born, Ivy had regained a little meat on her bones. She was fifteen now. Elliot had returned to reclaim married life. In the meantime, Gloria had given birth to Elliot's child. When she married Jimbo Delainy, following his request to Jipp, she was pregnant to Elliot again.

Both Jipp and Delainy knew what Gloria had been up to with Elliot, but they both felt that the marriage should go ahead. Delainy was no fool. He took marriage seriously and firmly believed he could turn Gloria into a good Christian wife. The first time she ran back to Elliot, Delainy came with an armed band of Aboriginal men who formed the unofficial police force of the Mission. He dragged Gloria home and tied her hands and feet with rope which he had earlier requested from Jipp for this purpose. Then he gagged her blaspheming mouth with a rag that smelled of rotting fish.

Over the following five days he chastised her with lectures on virtue, and with the rod before he left home for his day of Christian work. Gloria was left to contemplate a new beginning to permanent life at St Dominic's, sweating it out inside a hot room in the summer heat. On the fifth day Delainy ungagged his wife and left her with some food and water. A few days later he released the ropes. From then on, he kept a close rein on his wayward wife, making sure she was beside him all day long. At night, in order to get some sleep, he tied one end of a dog chain to the door post, and locked the other end around her ankle, leaving the key on a nail driven into a tree outside the hut. Even when Gloria was defecating Delainy would stand next to her, besotted by her every action. No sooner after her second child was born, she went on to have five more children who were all raised as Christians and well educated by the Mission.

Unfortunately, Ivy had grown to hate Elliot. She was not ready to resume marriage. Pugnose stayed away; he now lived permanently at Dorrie's place. Ivy cried a lot for the baby girl she had not even seen. Her baby never came back, although she repeatedly went to the Jipps' house asking for her. In the end, Jipp got tired of inventing stories about how it was getting better. All the time he was speaking to Ivy he could sense Beverly watching him through the veranda blinds. As he walked back upstairs he would hear her walk back to her own room, which she rarely left these days. When she did come out, she went about her business without acknowledging his existence.

Jipp went down to the couple's humpy. He did not speak to Ivy. He told Elliot that his wife was making a nuisance of herself about her child; it could not be brought back to St Dominic's because of its ill health.

"She is too young to look after it," he said. "You must understand that. We are doing what is best under the circumstances." He explained that the child's sickness was due to the fact that Ivy had left it unattended at birth. "It now needs expert care and attention. Make her understand, would you? There's a good chap." He told Elliot that if he couldn't make her see sense, he would have to consider placing them elsewhere. "I have already let a lot pass by in your case, haven't I?" he said, fixing Elliot with a meaningful gaze.

The next day Dorrie came by to borrow tealeaf. The humpy lay flattened. The whole dwelling, tealeaf included, lay scattered to the four winds. Amid the ruins she found them side by side. Both were unconscious. Congealed blood from wounds to Ivy's head encased her face. Blood still oozed from a stab wound to Elliot's chest.

Both left St Dominic's in an emergency evacuation by the Flying Doctor that same day. The plane flew across the landscape that Ivy had seen in her mind's eye from the window with the flowing curtains. Her home. They never lived as husband and wife again.

Many weeks later Elliot went home alone. He eventually married Joan Chapel, although he carried a lifelong passion for Gloria in his heart. Over the next thirty years he would father many children, but none with Joan.

In later years, after the missionaries left, Elliot and Joan became the leaders of their community. Many of Elliot's children would follow in his footsteps. Everyone believed they had inherited their father's strength and quality of leadership. Perhaps they had. However, they were influenced by the remarkable achievements of his two firstborn, the love children of Elliot and Gloria. These two received strict discipline throughout their childhood from their step-father, but benefitted from their mother's nurturing. They were Gloria's precious jewels, all she had left of her dream of freedom before she was forced to succumb to Delainy and conceived her other children by rape. In secret she taught Elliot's children the joy of love. She gave them the gift of hope.

PART II
Glimpses of Distant Hills

12

lowing crepe paper streamers oscillating in a kaleidoscope of vivid greens, yellows, pinks, reds and oranges,
literally flew out of the windows overlooking the rose
garden at Sycamore Heights.

Rows of large terracotta pots containing double red
flowering geraniums, signalling mid-afternoon September,
stood in perfect harmony with the billowing streamers. The
fast rhythmical beat of Eastern music on the record player
was being played full blast, filling the landscape of European sycamores and oaks surrounding the Sycamore
Heights Mental Health and Research Institution. The foun-
ders of St Dominic's Mission station a thousand miles to the
North were of the same religious order responsible for the
administration of Sycamore Heights.

On an improvised stage the assembled audience watched
the jelly-like movements of variously shaped white bellies
moving with tantalising speed. Some rippled folds of fat up
and down like rolling waves. Others were either sunk deep
in ribcages or disappeared within the pit of empty navels.
Belly-button eyes stared at the silent audience. This was the
first performance given by the nine patients — eight
females and one male — who were students of Madame
Sylvia Sadaan, a remarkable woman who had been a professional bellydancer over several decades.

Madame was in her mid-fifties, a handsome woman of
Arabic origins. "Much too much of the good life" were the

words she used to describe her body. But she knew how to make a fat body fabulous. All year round she covered herself with flowing gowns, caftans and ponchos in vivid patterns, like large pieces of brightly coloured material carelessly draped around her. She walked on tapering high heels. An eye-catching behind so broad its wobbling was mesmerising to anyone walking behind. She was perfectly aware of this as she passed along the narrow corridors of Sycamore Heights. Wobble, wobble, wobble, almost bumping into the walls each side. What male could resist the temptation? It would take a very dull man, Madame Sylvia thought, not to feel an irresistible temptation for her magnificently pursed lips, painted to perfection in crimson red. To watch her dance was a feast *par excellence*. The grace of a swan gliding over still waters. The speed of a jaguar in full pounce. A phenomenon. And always wobbling. If she had been the size of an elephant she would have caused earthquakes. As it was, maintenance men had to nail down the floorboards after each performance. She used to say she became carried away by the mesmerising calls of some mythical Eastern prince who joined her body as she danced, pounding her heart with his hands as he faced her. Whenever this happened she needed to be resuscitated quickly when the music stopped. A portable respirator accompanied her whenever she performed … or whenever she went to bed with a man who was game.

Medical fashions and fads, including bellydancing, were considered by the progressive board as a foremost form of treatment in modern psychotherapy, its introduction at Sycamore Heights formed part of the ongoing research work. The Chief Administrator was Mr Des Penguin, a small, plump, middle-aged man with thick black hair rapidly receding from his forehead. Sceptical to the core, he had been hard-pushed to give his endorsement to this performance, though he had known he would have to give in eventually, to keep pace with the more innovative board members, particularly his colleague Quill. But Penguin still lacked conviction about this unconventional concept, which replaced the recreational two-step and Pride of Erin on the lawns on Saturday afternoons. He didn't mind admitting he was something of a traditionalist; in years gone by, as a mere junior nurse, he prided himself on his ballroom dancing skills. And he felt he knew what treatment worked and what did not. He had been in this business for a long time. He distrusted the claptrap solutions of the academically trained professionals who sat on the board. What did they know of the mundane sphere of reality?

It had taken Des Penguin almost a decade to perfect the art of manipulating the other members of the board to his satisfaction. As administrator, he had attained a position of sufficient power to make it impossible for what he called "the enemy of God" to touch him. Now he had reached the summit, where he sat warmed in the light of God's countenance. His methods were often controversial and unorthodox — for example, he had found it easy enough to stack the annual general meetings. He would also persuade older members of the board to resign, after carefully recording their incompetency and absences from meetings. (He was adept at manipulating the agenda of meetings where he knew certain older members would not be present.) He would point out the older members' lack of contacts compared to younger members of the Church who were employed by large business firms. Sometimes he would present flow charts showing a decline in predicted growth for the institution, dredging up lost contracts for peg dolls or wooden carts produced by the inmates. To Penguin, all this was like playing kindergarten with a straight face. And whenever he had secured the resignation of one of these older members, he would triumphantly plant a kiss on the notice of retirement before the signature had time to dry.

Serious discussion had taken place with Madame Sadaan

at several meetings of the board concerning the design of the costumes for the inaugural performance of bellydancing. Madame's rough sketches of ample fleshy forms, scantily clad, were passed around the boardroom table, to be carefully viewed by censoring eyes.

"No, Madame, all the dancers must conform to standards of decency," the administrator told her. At the next meeting, Madame Sadaan presented a Barbie doll clad for bellydancing as a model. — "More modesty for both top and bottom, Madame," she was told. An instant refitting of the doll was carried out by Madame's dab hands, and it was passed around again. One or two members made further adjustments, pulling the panties up further (which only succeeded in revealing more bum). In the end, Madame offered more scraps of material and these were attached and readjusted with pins before the board reached a concensus. — "That's the ticket!" they agreed in the end.

"Oh yes, that's just fine! Over normal underwear, each dancer will wear a black bra and pants of plentiful proportions," Madame Sadaan said in a sarcastic voice.

For the performance, the dancers were also adorned with gold bangles and chains, and sported nylon scarves in colours that matched the streamers decorating the stage. Their faces were not beautiful, nor did they have flowing cascades of wavy hair as seen in Hollywood impressions of the belly dancers of a thousand and one Arabian Nights. Instead, white, middle-aged faces below beehive hairdos stared forward into outer space above the heads of the audience. Nine bodies shook, nine pairs of hips swayed, eighteen feet slid in perfect synchronisation, following Madame's choreography.

Not many Aboriginal patients came to Sycamore Heights. Ivy Andrews was an exception. She was an oddity. The decision to place her here had been made some twenty years earlier; her file began with an undated, handwritten order from the most senior elder of the Church. It consisted of two sentences concerning Ivy Andrews, a ward of the State. The first read: "Not to be returned to St Dominic's." The second: "To be constrained at Sycamore Heights until possible medical discharge." There was no information in the file about her admittance, no medical notes on her condition, no note of her age or anything about her background. The file did contain copies of requests made over the years for information that might have helped her case. Following the last request, a reply came from the Mission: the person concerned was not known there, and no records concerning her were held. Possibly this was due to a fire which had destroyed St Dominic's central office.

There was a file note of a telephone call to the State Administration of Aboriginal and Islander Affairs inquiring about the former Minister at St Dominic's. The reply received was that he was very old and long since retired. He refused to speak to anyone about his years at the Mission. His attitude resulted from a decision made by the State, backed up by his own church, to have him forcibly removed by the police, so that new policies might be put in place insisting on Aborigines managing their own affairs.

Ivy Andrews, prematurely aged, lived in the women's ward. Except for fears of some bogeyman, she was mostly contented enough, seemingly as oblivious to her surroundings as a fish on dry land. Des Penguin, as the longest serving staff member, had had the most opportunity to observe Ivy's progress (or lack of it). But Ivy was already at Sycamore Heights when he arrived. She did not speak much, except to answer "yes" or "no" to questions, or make simple requests. She stared through anyone who spoke to her.

Penguin told Madame Saddan about Ivy when he showed her around the women's ward to choose patients most likely to benefit from the bellydancing therapy. As he spoke, Ivy repeated each word in her mind. Prattle, prattle, prattle!

She also imitated the noise of their footfalls on the linoleum floor … *"Kerlip!"*

"She is so shy," Penguin told Madame. "For instance, the nursing staff have found her perishing for water in the night and whispering to her own shadow to get it for her. She cannot remember where the toilets are located — she is unable to retrace her steps from one end of the ward to the other without help. Yet she will ask for something — a cake or an orange, perhaps — which she has seen in the possession of another patient as long as a week ago — it can take her that long a time to pluck up the courage to do so. These are just examples of her behaviour."

Ivy smiled in her mind as Penguin spoke. No one knew that she was in the midst of a massive sulk which had lasted for each day of her more than twenty years at Sycamore Heights. Each morning she woke up unaware of how she had left the old familiar room she recalled with the curtains at the window. She did not understand why she could not return to the laughing woman with the child that she remembered. So she was in a permanent sulk, with her face always downcast and dour. Her everyday look of twenty years, which to the changing staff on the treadmill of the institution appeared "normal".

In a place like Sycamore Heights, Penguin told Madame, Ivy was the typical inmate trying to find a missing person: herself.

"I can understand that. She cannot know who she is inside a building with white walls, being organised by white people." Madame felt herself drawn into explaining Ivy's situation. "I understand alienation well," she added, as Penguin's rubbery lips moved in appreciation of her words.

Ivy's sense of herself was contained in far-off glimpses, like remembering distant hills seen once from the window of a car moving through the landscape. She saw a small child with her mother's arms around her. She could not make the bits in between fit with the face of the young woman she saw reflected in the window. She tried hard and often to bring back the lost memories, only to sense her mind revolving faster and faster into a black vortex, disappearing into nothing. There was nothing there to remember.

People were not particularly unkind to Ivy at Sycamore Heights. In the gardens, if the gates were open she would run back inside. Once or twice she was encouraged to walk towards the gates, but failed the test, so overcome by fear that the staff took her back to her room. Only Ivy knew of the hands waiting to drag her away. The open gates represented a bigger trap than the one she was in already.

"Ivy is our challenge," Penguin continued, as if he were explaining the difficulty of growing some exotic vegetable. "Very occasionally she has wandered away, even caught the bus to the city."

"Fancy."

"She would be found by the staff, or else brought back in the police car. The city is small enough to be familiar with its mental institutions. The managers of most city shops will do the civil-minded thing and call around to find whether someone is missing."

"Bad girl!" — Ivy would be lightly scolded when she left the police car that took her back. She'd toddle inside like a child with her dour face, carrying the small purchases she had made with the few dollars tucked into a knot in one corner of her handkerchief.

"Ivy is here permanently," Penguin said. "She has nowhere else to go."

In the beginning, all the right tests had been undertaken and appropriate treatment prescribed. Although Ivy never showed any improvement, the medical department did not give up; any doubts they may have had were put down to their inability to communicate properly with an Aborigine of tribal background. New tests were ordered, new treatment tried. Ivy did not like these strange men and women prodding and poking her, but she knew she was incapable of stopping them. If she struggled — as, for instance, when excessive voltage was used in treating her — she would be strapped down. She often cried, but the words "You're a good girl!" could pacify her, together with a few Minties to take to bed with her.

The physical examinations were another matter. Ivy felt constant shame and was unable to look any of the staff in the face for days afterwards. She lived in fear of her next visit to the examination room, and after it was over would sit trembling in her bed. At night she would sit alert, eyes wide open, staring into the darkness until she fell into a fitful sleep. Then the night staff slapped her until she woke up. "Stop your bloody screaming, you bitch!" The other patients, with terror in their eyes, would be sitting upright in their beds staring at the window, where a crow pecked the glass, trying to get inside.

When Ivy was young, when she first arrived at the institution and it was found she had given birth not long ago, there were constant examinations.

"How did this girl survive it? She should have died from loss of blood." The unsutured rips carried infection — a complete mess.

They tried to push her ribcage down, only to see it rise again. Her breasts were squeezed to see if any milk came from the nipples. She presented an interesting case. More tests were taken to discover any diseases she might have. Tissue was scraped from her uterus, swabs taken of internal fluids. Her pubic hair was shaved to give access to her genital area for a rough clean-up each day, until the doctors were satisfied that no infection survived. Ivy gulped down solid balls of air to block out the pain of the stinging disinfectant. Ivy was on show for the medical profession. The doctors re-examined each other's findings, perplexed by the fact that her stomach showed no stretch marks, and puzzled about what had happened to the child. Ivy herself could recollect nothing; she could not answer the simplest questions about her sexual experience, let alone childbirth.

Over the years routine examinations continued, conducted every three months. "Pants down, lie down," a voice of unrecognisable gender would order. "Feet together and drop your legs." A screen placed across her stomach prevented her from seeing what was happening. She was aware of her vagina being swabbed. Surgical lights beamed down on her; she kept her eyes closed. She twitched as ice-cold instruments entered her body, and again when their manipulator pinched her flesh. A strong hand held her down, increasing the abdominal pain. The masked face of the manipulator of this procedure remained a shadowy form. "Get dressed now. Into the wheelchair. Quickly!" Then she'd be wheeled back to her ward and receive a couple more Minties to add to the precious collection she kept in an old biscuit tin. In bed she curled her thin body into a foetal position to ease the pain. She swallowed the tablet that would make her sleep, and in the morning she woke with the nice feeling of the Minties still locked in her hand.

It was Ivy's case which finally gave Penguin his ultimate power. When he took over the administration he had initiated an inquiry into her treatment. Amazingly, that inquiry was able to establish wrongdoing and to dispose of the guilty party. The verdict was a botched abortion, without witnesses or evidence, followed by a cover-up completed by the former administration. The victim was, of course, unable to talk about her ordeal. A detailed confidential report gave the name of the suspect and options for appropriate courses of action to be taken. The author of the report remained unknown. A one-sheet summary was given to each member of the board at a special meeting, and collected again afterwards. All written evidence was then destroyed in one gulp of the shredding machine in Penguin's office.

In the shake-up that followed Penguin shuffled staff

around, retrenching some and transferring others to places as remote as St Dominic's. Members of staff completely lost track of each other. Industrial arbitration was a luxury for such employees not part of the fellowship of a religious institution. They were all missionaries with a shared belief that through their joint efforts they could save the world. They had no option but to do as they were told. The reorganisation of Sycamore Heights was completed within six months, and Penguin was able to assure the board that there would be no more trouble under his management.

It was Ivy, more than anything else, who made it possible for Sycamore Heights to become a showpiece. Penguin was the proud beneficiary of contributions made to the institution based on her case. Visitors came from near and far, praising the research, social consciousness, community integration and reconciliation achievements of Sycamore Heights. There were visits from politicians and state funders. And always the star patient was Ivy.

"And here is my little Ivy" — Penguin would have her brought in to meet important visitors and recite the well-worn story of the mystery surrounding Ivy's former life. Mysteries still to be resolved, he would add sadly. Then, as though turning the page to a better story, he would explain how progressive the institution was towards the study of Aboriginal mental health. "Take the case of Ivy," he would continue, telling his visitors about similar people he had encountered in the missions in Asia, the Pacific and Africa. Native people born with particular genetic material that set them apart — something that happened within every culture. He would pose the question: "Can these inherited genes be turned into traditional qualities?" He seldom received an answer: if he did, he would manage to incorporate it into his own theories. Then he would answer his own question: "Yes, I believe they can."

But Penguin was not prepared to explain an unnatural phenomenon he and other staff had observed over the years. A group of crows would appear at precisely the same time every year — the anniversary of Ivy's arrival at Sycamore Heights. They sat on a tree outside Ivy's ward and stayed there for weeks. At times staff had reported the crows pecking at the window beside her bed in the middle of the night. All this had become a legend, and each year there were whispers of deaths associated with the crows. Penguin always dismissed such whispers, convincing himself the staff used them as a ridiculous excuse to avoid night shift.

"I am simply a layman in these matters," Penguin would tell his visitors, "yet I have a feeling it is only a matter of time before Ivy comes out of her melancholy and will be able to tell us who she really is herself." At this point he would place a fatherly hand on Ivy's shoulder. "One day she will tell us why she is so sad."

For her part, Ivy enjoyed the moment when she was displayed before such visitors. The nice room filled with pleasant furnishings. The actual people were only a blur. She heard a jumble of words, drank her tea and fidgeted on her chair. Then her thoughts, irresistibly kleptomaniac, eventually led her to grab at whatever she could while Penguin apologised on her behalf. "Be a good girl, Ivy, and give back what is not yours." His kind, soothing words were a pre-taught trigger, enabling her to respond appropriately. Then, having thoroughly duped his audience, he would lead her outside, where an orderly was waiting.

Madame Sadaan was quick to understand Ivy's importance in the scheme of things. She observed Ivy watching the inaugural performance of the bellydancing, slumped in her chair, the usual dour expression on her face. The *challenge!* Ideas ran through Madame Sadaan's mind as she turned her observation to other members of the audience, anticipating which of them would become her first six students of dance. She had agreed to instruct six inmates for the pilot class. The remuneration offered was "magnifico" and she would become "world class" if the experiment proved sucessful.

Penguin was enthralled with the performance, and the inmates clapped even more enthusiastically than their minders. Next day, Madame's quota of students was delivered by men in white to Bellydancers Inc. Ivy and three other women slowly came into the large room and stood huddled together.

"What? Only four students?" Madame turned to the two men in white.

"Two of them bailed up." By this they meant that after being dragged from their wards, only four were in a fit state to be presented to someone outside the institution.

"In that case I will start now with these four and this is how the class must remain, with the same four pupils."

The two minders helped themselves to seats against the wall, but Madame swiftly asked them to leave the room, requesting that they remain outside the door in case she needed assistance. She beamed at her students. "But it should not be necessary."

During the weeks that followed, she built up a program of muscle toning in exercise routines that began quite gently. As the initial anxiety diffused itself in one pupil, she would wait until the others caught up before moving on to something more strenuous. She saw the four women for one and a half hours each weekday morning. In this time she would take the phone off the hook and lock the front door, hanging a sign that said *Do Not Disturb* on the knob. If one member of the group was sick and could not come, as happened when Ivy had influenza, Madame would go to the institution to spend the equivalent time with her, speaking of what the others had achived during the lesson. She likened them to the great bellydancers of the world, living their lives on the rim of a normal existence. She spoke of the great life the four would have when they left Sycamore

Heights and described the grand performances she had planned for them.

Eventually, she had her four stars in perfect physical fitness: they looked like top devotees of the aerobics scene. She taught them to massage each other with sandalwood oil, while they told each other how beautiful they were. "How beautiful," she would coo. "So beautiful," they would reply.

Then they would make a circle on a large piece of olive silk spread on the floor, join hands and talk. To begin with Madame had talked mostly to herself. She asked questions and if she received no response she would dream up a reply, slowly building up their confidence so that they would respond. Ivy was the slowest one to gain Madame's confidence. From complete refusal to respond she moved towards reluctance, then to doing what was basically necessary. By that stage the others were more than willing to move on, but Madame waited until Ivy was ready.

"You must all believe in me," she told her pupils as they sat on the silken floor. She would hum an Arab serenade while the others coaxed Ivy towards response. The room was dimly lit, curtains drawn, redolent of the shared odour of perfumed oil and perspiration. Madame related fantasies of famous bellydancers, saying these would be their stories if only they would reach up to capture them for themselves. Each step of the way, Madame Saddan, the skilled artisan, was able to retrieve beauty, no matter how deep it tried to bury itself. She was a woman possessed of such wilful eyes that she could surely have convinced a retreating worm to reveal itself, had she chosen to use her powers so uselessly. Within five months she had made impressive progress. Ivy managed to revive a relatively dependable short-term memory. It was, however, selective, and as she began to remember, she mostly kept her thoughts to herself, rarely letting others know about the concerns of her small world. It was only because she was able to recite word-perfect the stories of the dance and remember exercises in correct chronology, recalling her own place in the scheme of the happenings in the dance studio, that Madame realised the progress she had made.

"I knew it! I knew it!" And Madame flapped her arms in the air, excited as the Church would surely be to witness a miracle. "My little Ivy remembers all. Don't worry, dear. Do not tell me if you mustn't. There is much beauty in mystery, let me tell you. You are my beautiful blazing star."

She had conversations over the telephone to Penguin. "I have moved a monolith, inch by inch, with my bare hands," she declared.

"I shall be running some tests. Let us see the result of those," he told her in a choppy voice.

"I shall be eager to find out. Let me know the results quickly," Madame responded.

The usual psycho tests, involving cards of different shapes and colours, were carried out. All proved positive. It was true. Madame Sadaan had far exceeded all expectations. Ivy had been Penguin's own nomination from the "too hard basket" when the dance training began. He really had no choice, since he was financing the project from funds donated by the government for training Aboriginal people — not to mention some Aboriginal health funds as well.

And now Madame Sadaan announced to her students that they had met the challenge. She would go on to teach them the dance of the night. The dance of romance. The dance of love. Soon they would be cured for life, because they would be sharing her deepest secret.

"Off with those clothes!" she commanded, making the four women strip to their white bras and pants. "You are beautiful. Believe in your beauty," she ordered.

From a large wooden box she sorted through a heap of costumes and took out the garments they were to wear. The women dressed themselves precisely as they were told.

When they were ready, Madame revealed her own costume, removing her huge satin caftan with its pattern of red roses, then moved swiftly across the floor and turned on the music. "Now we dance. Dance for the love of ourselves," she repeated over and over, until her words took charge of every thought, muscle and molecule of earthly existence in that curtained room.

The four women followed her around and across the room. Together they were five floating spirits that swayed and wobbled as if they were once small hills that grew into mountains and became volcanoes on the verge of erupting. Each woman felt her body drip with perspiration which fell to the floor; its slippy film re-entering her body when it massaged the soles of her feet. Their pants were soaked with the hot flow of lava from subliminal sex.

Madame whirled past the light switch and turned the spotlight on high beam. The harsh illumination travelled deep into every open pore of skin, into their hair, into every cavity. It beamed through the transparent costumes to drag out and burn away every sense of inhibition and shame, the prison each of these women had created for herself. Madame Saddan had reclaimed from a world of inhibited humanity these four women. They could now rejoin a society where the walls were much more expansive than the inner walls of their safe cell which had previously held them prisoners to their own minds.

13

Within twelve months the pilot project collapsed like a punctured balloon. The doors of Bellydancing Inc. closed for good. The government funds that had initially poured in, initiated by politicians on the lookout for vote-winning photo opportunities, dried up. The rush to be involved with an astonishing "medical miracle" evaporated. The "wonder cure" slipped into oblivion after conservative forces finished kick-butting government departments concerning lack of probity in the advice they received. Likewise for Aboriginal communities dependent on government funding, the wait can be like standing on the edge of a precipice screaming "push me off!". Collapse of scheme. End of story.

Bureaucrats blamed each other with copious memoranda and counter-memoranda that flew between the ivory towers of the state's capital city. All blamed the administration of Sycamore Heights — churchy people were always good targets, particularly reformers. Information fell "off the back of a truck". The newspapers confirmed that the Missionary Order was under investigation by the police for bribery, distortion, corruption, mismanagement, and theft of public funds unaccounted for.

At some stage along the way, Madame Sadaan tossed her life into her carpetbag and disappeared. The note she left behind stated that she was fed up with lies about her stealing money, about how she conducted illicit sexual relationships and was no more than a common trollop, that she had defrauded the institution — when she did not recall receiving any payment for the work she had done. It also stated she was now permanently bedridden as a result of cruel slanders, and that her mind had been plagued by demonic words from the "dark side" ever since she commenced her relationship with Sycamore Heights, and that she could no longer think straight. Her life was now a major catastrophe. *Etcetera.* Her lawyer would be in touch soon, to negotiate a settlement for all the damages listed above.

The collapse of the four "stars" came within months. Gradually, each woman awoke from her bellydancing trance as a permanent trampled tragedy of her former self. All except Ivy. She was the last to lapse out of the dancing frenzy. It had, after all, been simply a live-for-dance experience, as one might imagine the life of a highly charged pop star addicted to drugs. Her withdrawal reached the stage where she had to be strapped to her bed. Penguin ordered this procedure to save everyone the embarrassment of encountering Ivy cavorting all over the establishment in a state of undress revealing her crater-shaped stomach. There had been complaints by visitors, patients and staff. Once she shook herself so violently as she lay on the bed that she broke the straps. The staff replaced them and made her lie on a flat board instead of the mattress. When she stopped shaking and lay babbling the bellydance music, the minders placed tape over her mouth. At last, having completely worn herself out, she fell into deep sleep. With the gag removed, she stayed asleep for four days.

"Can I eat now?" Ivy asked, looking the nurse straight in the eye and speaking in a coherent voice instead of the rhythmless babble they were used to.

The nurse, stunned and slightly frightened, looked over the straps in case by some extraordinary means Ivy might leap up at her. She then backed out of the small room where

Ivy was being kept. Moments later, the nurse, a doctor and Penguin were running through the corridors with the nurse breathlessly explaining that this one was not a zombie, like the others had become. When Ivy saw them burst into her room, she gave a thin smile and repeated her question, "Can I eat now?" They were amazed.

"Well, even if she's short of the full quid, at least we're one short of a full catastrophe," Penguin announced in a dull voice, summoning up whatever relief he could find in the circumstances. "Still, heads will roll," he sighed, looking at Ivy and tossing over in his mind what he would have to do to get her out of the way.

The subsequent inquiry into Sycamore Heights led to further embarrassment for governments and many politicians of the old guard. Information generated by Civil Liberties groups flowed wide and fast. For weeks press releases concerning the exclusivity of the religious order and its undue influence inside the government, clogged fax machines. Abuse of power backed by public funding was against common decency and created crimson-faced consternation. Many hoped they would not be publicly linked to past decisions. The revelations became a continuing obsession for newspaper readers, who followed more "dirty laundry" in weekly magazines. The great bellydancing fiasco initiated the finish of those powerful arms of exclusive religious sects (as well as others not so exclusive) which kept themselves financially afloat by imposing missionary zeal on voiceless minorities.

Ivy Koopundi never knew she had caused the toppling of mission control over so many Aboriginal lives. In future years, if the lives of Aboriginal women such as Ivy are unravelled, their names may be remembered like latter-day Joans of Arc or Florence Nightingales.

In an economy carriage on the Sunlander, Ivy held on to

the small cardboard tickets. One, pale pink, was for the Sunlander. The other, pale blue, was for the Inlander. That was what he'd said. Hadn't he? Ivy thought hard but couldn't remember which was which. After they'd found her a seat, the male nurse, wearing street clothes, placed her luggage in the compartment at the end of the carriage, then returned to check that she was alright. He went over the details: where to go for meals, and in particular the changeover of the trains in two days time. Ivy nodded her head, looking around anxiously. He kept patting her hand, telling her she would be "just fine". The waiting seemed endless. He wondered whether the administration was doing the right thing. No one really knew whether the latest policy of integration of patients back into the community would work. But Ivy had agreed that she wanted to go "home", and a thousand miles from Sycamore Heights was the closest to "home" anyone was prepared to arrange. Penguin, in charge of the arrangements, was confident that Ivy did not have any true idea of where "home" was.

The train was at least forty minutes late when the whistle finally blew. Ivy was beside herself with worry and held on tightly to the nurse's arm as he desperately tried to disentangle himself from her in order to leave the train.

"I don't want to go home," Ivy whispered then, looking around warily to see if anyone was watching her.

"Don't be silly, Ivy. We've been through all of this. You know what to do." He saw the conductor, a pot-bellied man in an olive-green uniform, walking towards him. "Conductor!" he called.

Unfortunately the conductor was deaf and kept yelling "What did you say, matey?" and looking hard at Ivy while the male nurse quickly explained her travel schedule and asked him to be kind enough to keep an eye on her. "It'll be okay, matey!" the conductor finally shouted. So without looking back the nurse left the train, which was now moving slowly down the platform. At the entrance to the compartment where Ivy sat, the conductor kept talking loudly to those who tried to squash past him in the narrow aisle. He stood with his rear end, smelling of train travel, almost brushing Ivy's face.

The last thing Ivy wanted was to create a scene, but she felt she had to leave the train immediately. She knew she must stay calm, otherwise she would begin to smell and then people would stare at her. Once the conductor walked on after clicking her ticket, she glanced around quickly to see if anyone was looking at her. The train had gathered speed and was moving at a faster pace. She stayed quiet and looked out of the window, catching a glimpse of the nurse weaving his way amongst the people walking away from the platform. She saw the cold grey backs of old city buildings and tri-coloured city pigeons — black, grey, white — strutting on sooty rooftops or flying away from windows of broken glass. The train sped past the industrial side of town, with huge, mysterious sheds. Vast petrol storage tanks with a large shell painted on the side threw long shadows across the track. The train twisted past suburban homes of flickering light. The day grew darker and gradually suburbia dropped away.

In the morning she woke to find the train heading past farms with dairy cows in green and yellow fields. More towns. More farms. Then plantations of pineapple ... banana ... sugarcane ... mangoes. Ivy watched it all, and that night she looked out at the blackness until she fell into fitful sleep.

She did not use the dining carriage, where people would have noticed her. Instead she bought sandwiches and cups of tea at stops along the way, making sure she was first back on the train in case something happened. She continually checked her Timex watch, a gift from some of the older staff members who were sad to see her go. Whenever the time was announced over the intercom on the train she made sure her watch tallied with it exactly. And again she checked the time on the platforms of the towns where she alighted, deciphering it through the high-pitched buzz of what might be important announcements for travellers. She thought that people who worked for the railways must learn to speak a special language — *huh, huh, ha* — the result of listening to too many trains. And in fact trains and railway employees were the only ones that understood each other.

Early in the morning of the third day's travelling, Ivy made the switch in trains, from Sunlander to Inlander, without the problems she had been dreading. The pot-bellied conductor had in fact recorded in neat printing in the log book precise details of the request the nurse had made at the beginning of the journey. So when the Sunlander reached its destination, he set out to find her. Ivy was at the platform snack bar, and when he did find her he had to spend some time convincing her that he was just trying to help her onto her new train.

"Keep an eye on her, mate! Just make sure she gets there alright," he told the conductor of the Inlander.

This was the country of Ivy's dreams. The train sped on, whistling past black men working on the track, past workers' camps and worn-out sidings. The land was flat and featureless except for the occasional tree-lined, dried-up river beds. Buffalo grass like pale yellow straw covered the grey gravel and clay. Here Ivy spotted families of emus running away on long, strong legs. The odd dingo half-hidden in the long grass winked at her as the train whistled past. Even flocks of grey brolgas, sometimes a hundred or more, flew alongside the train turning their red faces to look at Ivy, until, tiring of the sport, they turned to fly further northward.

"I've lived in this house nearly all my life," said the black lady of eighty-plus, who stood on the footpath beside Ivy in her stockinged feet. She was about four feet nothing, with long grey hair neatly combed into plaits wound around her head. She led the way into her house, then took out her false teeth and popped them into a glass of water beside the unused stove, which was covered with opened and unopened tins, mostly bearing labels such as Pal, Chum, Whiskas or Snappy Tom. The kitchen table and every other flat top, was loaded with plates, cups and more cans, vases of old plastic roses in fading colours of summer. Large bright plastic butterflies were attached to the pole in the centre of the room and hanging from a nail in the post was a current calendar with a picture of cows in green meadows. Above that hung an old picture of the Queen.

The old woman was wearing her best dress, of pale pink terylene with a pattern of little white dots. It hung loosely over her thin body, held in place with a narrow belt.

"My late husband, Bob, built this house. He was a good man, my poor old Bob, God bless his soul." She sighed, then started to fill the electric kettle at the sink, moving pots and pans and dirty crockery to get the spout of the tap into the top of the jug. She said she never worried about what the place looked like any more, not since Bob had passed away, and she asked Ivy to call her Bessie, because that was her name.

The house was made of reused corrugated iron with pop-out windows of the same material, each one held in place with a short stick which at night became a large bolt, threaded through a couple of rings. The front and back doors were also made of iron, nailed to timber frames that fitted fairly neatly into the door frames. Both doors were secured at night by a chain wound through a hole in the door and wall and locked with a padlock. The dirt floor where they stood comprised half the house area. The other part was raised slightly; dirt-filled kerosene tins were covered with lengths of timber of different sizes which left gaps in various places. The raised floor was semi-partitioned to form two unclosed bedrooms, and a piece of cotton material separated the remainder of the space. Bessy showed Ivy which of the bedrooms was hers; Bob's, still with his belongings scattered around it, remained as it had been on the day he died years ago.

"He always said to me before he died, my Bob, he said: 'Bessie, if anything happens to me don't stay here alone, will you?' That's what he'd say." And she sat down on a chair, first shoving a great fat black-and-white cat off it onto the floor.

At that moment the electric jug started to boil and Ivy turned it off. She moved around the kitchen, finding cups which she had first to scrub clean at the sink. Bessie pointed to an open box of teabags perched on a bench, then to the centre of the table, where Ivy saw a bowl of sugar with brown lumps in it and a tin of Sunshine milk.

"You know, Bob died about eighteen years ago. Funny thing, that. He was a churchman, so I don't know why he did it. He said, 'Bessie, I'm goin' for a walk' — and he never came back. He went as far as the second bridge crossing. People saw him there looking down at the flood water. Next minute he was gone. People talk all the time in this town. They say he took his own life. I don't know why. You'd think he would have said if he was unhappy. But he never talked much. It's a funny way to say goodbye to someone — 'I'm goin' for a walk.' So that's why I wanted you to come here and live with me, because Bob said it will be alright. That church down South was his religion too, you see." And this is how Bessie explained why Ivy was sent to live with her.

Before it got dark, Ivy read aloud Penguin's letter addressed to Bessie and her husband. Bessie was unable to read a thing — she could recognise labels on the foodstuffs she bought, and frequently ate her share from the same can of Whiskas or Pal she opened for the cat or the dog. It was a short letter, an official introduction to Ivy which offered Bessie appreciation for her Christian charity. Nothing more.

The old woman just said "Huh", swallowed her piping hot tea and went off to a ricketty wrought-iron bed under the mango trees in the backyard. The dog slept on the ground next to her and the cat beside her feet on the bed.

Pal was a fat, three-legged mongrel with a piebald brown-and-white coat. During the day he slept in muddy holes he dug under the fruit trees. He snarled at Ivy whenever she passed by, but did not move. He just hated the sight of her. So did the cat, which bolted outside if the old woman was not around.

"How did you sleep?" Bessie inquired the next morning as Ivy came down the one step into the kitchen.

"It was alright, I suppose," Ivy muttered. In fact she hadn't slept at all. Her head ached and she was in no mood for chitchat. She'd spent the night in total darkness. "One switch here, another over there," Bessie had told her the evening before, "You'll need to see up here in all this mess." But neither of the electric lights worked — they probably needed new bulbs. Ivy had groped around, feeling the walls to find Bob's bedroom.

All night long, whenever she was finally succumbing to sleep, she would feel a cold shiver run down her body as the branches of the cedar tree scraped over the roof. She was convinced that the old woman was up there, sweeping with a broom, and, when the overripe cedar berries rattled along the grooves of the iron roof, that she was throwing stones around. An owl, a permanent resident in the cedar, hooted most of the night just above her head … unless, again, it was the old woman. Ivy lay staring up at the ceiling; once she believed she caught the gleam of the bird's eye captured by the light of the moon, peering down at her through one of the nail holes in the roof. There were other sounds, like people crying, from somewhere up the road, but she could not pin down their precise direction.

"There's nothing wrong with that room, is there?" Bessie asked, obviously wanting reassurance. She made some effort to clear space on the crowded table as Ivy made tea and found some cornflakes.

"No, I don't think so," she lied. She knew the old woman was fully aware of what was wrong with the room. *Yes, she knows,* Ivy thought, *she only pretends to sleep outside because it's cooler.* She served the tea and breakfast cereal to the old woman — she knew she would not do it for herself. Ivy did not feel hungry; she sipped her tea beside the unused stove, sitting on an upturned kerosene tin with a small cushion on top. She felt ill in the stomach. The dead Bob was to blame for that.

Bob might be dead, but he was making a lot of fuss about it. He had appeared the previous night disguised as a little terrier sniffing around the room. Ivy lay perfectly still. She hardly breathed. She knew he was looking for the old woman, and hoped he wouldn't see her lying on his bed. It was unusually high, one of those old-fashioned steel-framed types you need a leg up to get onto, unless, like Ivy, you are tall.

"It's not me you're after. She's outside," Ivy tried to tell him, but the words did not come out because she was so frightened. Eventually she screamed out to the little dog: "She's outside!" She wondered if the old woman had heard her. The dog pattered out through the curtained wall and she waited in the darkness, repeatedly looking around the shadowy room. The only illumination came from small rays of moonlight through various cracks where the walls joined the roof. Finally, she could stand the darkness no longer and groped her way to the kitchen in the hope of finding some matches.

"I'll get some for tomorrow night," she promised herself when her effort of feeling around the table for the familiar Redhead box proved fruitless. The small dog followed her back to the bedroom and sat in one corner near the locked front door.

* * *

Occasionally it growled, as though there was a prowler outside. Ivy heard Bob's voice in her mind, the grizzly voice of an old man gibbering complaints about his wife …

"You poisonous bloody so-and-so. You poisoned me. I wasn't the first, nor the last …"

Ivy pretended to be asleep, curled up tightly, her legs tucked under her.

"Is she still breathing?" he asked then.

"Yes." Ivy ended up answering automatically, giving her presence away. She was terribly frightened.

"Good. I don't want her humbug." The dog lay down and went to sleep for a while. Ivy lay watching it. There was something not quite right about its hairy coat. It had old, grizzled grey patches in otherwise bald areas.

"What are you doing here?" The next question suggested he had only just realised someone else was present. Ivy didn't know whether he meant in the house or in Bob's bed. She didn't move. She fell into a moment of deep sleep, only to be awakened by the dog sniffing at her feet. But was it? She jumped to one corner of the bed and saw that the dog was still asleep in the far corner of the room. She drifted back to sleep. Suddenly she huddled in a corner of the bed again. This time she thought it had whispered in her ear …

"You'll be next, you know. Sick enough to die. Jump ship! Go on."

Ivy did not say anything to Bessie next morning. She felt the old woman could not be trusted. *She wants to know if I can see her guilt*, Ivy thought to herself. She decided she would prepare everything she ate herself, so that the old woman didn't bait her food with poison. But she had to stay here because she had nowhere else to go. She had begun to feel sick already, unable to eat. *Might be I'm poisoned already*. She almost spoke her thought aloud.

After breakfast Bessie left to go shopping in town, dragging an old pram along behind her. Ivy refused the offer to go with her. Why would she want to go into town and put up with people staring at her? The first thing she did after the old woman left was to visit the toilet right down the backyard. She felt she had to go, but when she got there she couldn't do anything because the man next door was watching her. A big bloke, must be twenty stone, just wearing navy shorts. He just stood there, looking over the fence and watched her as she went into the toilet.

Why is he staring at me? Ivy saw him through a nail hole, still peering at the toilet. After this experience she decided she would go down there only at night, never in broad daylight. Bessie's place was in fact quite isolated from any neighbour — there was no one around as far as the eye could see, but that did not deter Ivy from making her decision. She was convinced that man lived next door, in the grass. Having a shower in the bathroom was another daytime ordeal. Someone might peek in there as well. So she decided this, too, would take place under cover of night. And she would wash her clothes in there, instead of using the twin concrete tubs exposed to view outside. She got into the habit of hanging up her washed clothes at night and sneaking out of the house before daylight to bring them inside again.

Ivy took over the running of the old woman's house. As soon as Bessie left for town, to shop for whatever they needed, Ivy would clean up, sweeping the dirt floor and making everything tidy. Then she would cook a meal, usually a stew with cabbage or sausage or curry. She would leave it on the side of the warm stove, and each woman would eat separately whenever she was ready, adding rice and bread and margarine, so long as they had enough to pay for it after pension day.

Ivy could see that Bessie was pleased and enjoyed the aroma of food cooking in a warm kitchen. Nor did she ever complain about Ivy's strange smell. Yet without realising it, the smell triggered a long-ago memory. For no apparent reason, Bessie would often recall a visit to an inland lake she and Bob once made when they were young — "About fifteen or seventeen," she'd say. Every time she talked about it her age would differ. Sometimes she was twenty-two, sometimes thirty. The days of her youth were so long ago, she said.

"It was a beautiful lake in a flat country, with stubbly plants and small flowers. The lake was full of birds, ducks and waterfowl. It was the first time I ever saw a pelican." She never remembered where it was — it was like a dream now, she said. "And I never seen a pelican again," she added. She felt that something terrible had happened there, but she couldn't recall what it was. "Maybe Bob killed it," she said once, her voice trailing off. Ivy wasn't interested in her stories.

Every weekday Bessie went to town in her best dress, the pale pink one with the white spots, and wearing heavy stockings. It didn't matter whether the day was forty degrees plus or minus two. She went to town about ten and came back two hours later. First thing she plonked her old bones on a chair, had a bite to eat, took a shower, changed into an old work dress, washed her town clothes, and had a sleep for two hours, no matter what. She did not need to shop every day but she liked to see people, anyone — she would stop to talk and find out the latest news about various members of their families. After being given a cool drink she would be on her way to someone else's place for a cup of tea. She knew the town and the town knew her. She was an identity figure.

The backyard of Bessie's house was long and narrow, with the back half fenced off. The first part contained her vegetable garden and pot plants, which she religiously cultivated between six and seven each morning. This work was a celebration of new life. She moved her pot plants about with remarkable strength. One day they would be gathered beneath the cedar tree, then moved again to the mango trees around the back, or under the chinky apple or the citrus trees. Next they would appear around the other side of the house, under a jacaranda that never flowered. It was the only tree in the yard that Bob had planted.

There were no weeds in the yard. Part of Bessie's gardening time was spent gathering them — mostly bindi eyes, chickweed or dandelion, poking up through the rich river loam of the ancient river route where the house stood. The limp tangles of green were banished over the fence of the chook pen. Buffalo grass was removed as soon as it showed one blade. Bessie had a good eye for it, having originally dug the stuff out of the dry, packed earth to get it all out of her yard. She grew flowers as well as vegetables, and at the end of each plant's season she collected the seed heads, then started the growing process all over again. People would come to her place to take whatever she had to offer.

"Bessie!" they'd yell over the front gate. (No one came past the gate, held shut with Pal's dog chain.) Ivy watched them through a nail hole in the front wall of the house. Fat white women in floral tent-dresses, fat white men with Brylcreem'd receding hairlines, in off-white Bermuda shorts and pale-coloured shirts, with white kneesocks. "You got any of those cabbages left?" (Or lettuces, beans, parsley ...)

Bessie was pleased that people wanted what she grew. She always parted with the best and the last if it was there, and always grew more next time so that she would not disappoint anyone. At other times she would yell out to anyone walking past and give them all the eggs she had collected and left in an old tub outside the chook pen. She said that when Bob was alive, she used to throw hundreds of rotting eggs over the fence even though it encouraged snakes and crows. "Bob never liked giving anything away," she said. "He never liked strangers."

The back half of the yard contained a few old gum trees. This is where Bessie kept her goats. The herd fluctuated from between fifty and three times that number when a lot of kids were born. It took Ivy a few days to realise there were goats in the backyard, because Bessie let them loose at daybreak, after she had milked them. But these days she usually gave up the job long before they were all milked. She left the milk in a container at the back gate to be collected by a pig farmer, who paid for it. She told Ivy this had been Bob's job, and she was annoyed that he had died before first doing something about all the goats. Yet it was obvious she was fond of them simply because they reminded her of Bob. The goats would graze all day in the bush along the river, returning at dusk.

Before Ivy realised the different uses of the backyard she had begun her new schedule and gone down to the toilet in the concealment of night. Once she had bolted the door, she heard rustling noises and knocks on the tin wall. She was too afraid to light a match from the box she now carried with her at night. She imagined a madman was out there, waiting to get her. She felt sure Bessie had told everyone about her, and now they all knew she was living here.

Bessie had told Ivy stories about three or four solitary men who had set up semi-permanent camps on the river bank. She said the people up town reckoned they were mad and had often reported them to the police for wandering around the streets at night or else sitting around on the pavement in front of the nicely decorated shop windows. But Old Bessie knew different. "They alright folk," she told Ivy. "Prospectors. They go into hills to a secret opal mine." From time to time, one or other of these strange, unkempt men would call out to Bessie and hand over a sugarbag to her. Who knows what was inside those bags. Sometimes it was a bush turkey which the old woman would gut and pluck by herself. In return, she handed back the sugarbag filled with eggs, fruit and vegetables.

When Bessie went for walks in the bush on weekends she often visited these men and chatted to them over a cup of tea. She'd started talking about the men at the time of Ivy's arrival, because shortly beforehand she had discovered one had died in his sleep, leaving an undrunk cup of tea beside him. It seemed to Ivy that Bessie was more worried about the undrunk tea than the fact that the man had died. "Fancy," the old woman said, "he left his cup of tea behind, poor thing!"

Trapped in the toilet, assailed by strange noises, Ivy stayed there until finally Bessie rattled on the door, wanting to be let in. When she told the old woman about the noises, Bessie fetched a torch and a big stick. Ivy didn't know what was happening. All she heard was the noise of the stick thrashing the grass in the backyard and crashing against the toilet walls, until Bessie satisfied herself there was no snake there.

"Must have been the goats, that's all," she told Ivy. It was the first time Ivy had heard of the goats. By this time the creatures had become restless and broken out of their pen. Pleased to have the old lady in the yard at night, they were trampling around out of control.

"Git out of here! Nicodemus! Stop it, Elijah! Rebecca, Bathsheeba — stop pawing me!" Bessie had names for all of them. Coming out of the toilet at last, Ivy wrestled with the swarm of goats, shoving them away wherever her hands landed on their hairy bodies or hard-boned heads. Shielding the old woman, she got both of them out of the yard and into the house. Bessie, badly shaken, slept indoors that night. Neither woman spoke to each other for days afterwards, and it was a long time before Bessie felt relaxed enough to sleep outside again.

The little dog continued to visit Ivy's bedroom at night. Ivy was always too frightened to communicate with it, apart from telling it that it was Bessie it was looking for. Weakly she would point to the next room, for this was before Bessie began to sleep outside again. The dog would trot off and she saw it curl up at the feet of the frail old woman, who was fast asleep and snoring.

*   *   *

Life went on this way for several years, during which time each woman created a world full of suspicions against the other. Sometimes Bessie made veiled threats about getting rid of Ivy. She would accuse Ivy of trying to kill her by leaving things in the wrong place, where she might fall over them and have a serious accident which could affect her heart. Often Ivy was harangued about the goats. Bessie tried to get Ivy to milk the creatures, telling her that the milk money was needed to keep the place going. "You know I'm just an old woman. I can't do it all on my own," she complained. "I used to be alright by myself. Now the money just goes with all the things you want, running up more debt at the supermarket." She sighed then. "Bob always looked after the money side of things. We never wanted for anything."

She always managed to turn any topic of conversation back to Bob, until eventually Ivy felt she was in direct competition with the dead man so far as companionship and concern for Bessie's welfare were concerned. In the end, Ivy got up early each morning to help milk the goats. This joint effort slipped on Bessie's part until she only milked one or two of her favourites; then she would merely stand around, complaining about the nuisance Bob had been and making sure that Ivy got it right. Soon she tired of supervising and didn't come down at all, taking an extra hour's sleep before getting up to do her gardening. But Bessie made sure she collected the money left for the milk. Sometimes there would be less money than previously. It didn't occur to the old woman that the goats might have produced less milk — only that Ivy stole her money.

"I might be reporting you to the police when I go up town today," she would tell Ivy. She refused to discuss any of her accusations, and Ivy had become so used to the old woman's incoherent threats that she ignored them. "I know Constable Long. He always says 'Hello, Mum' every time he sees me. So don't think I won't!" Then off she'd go, trailing the pram behind her.

It was true that Ivy often stole from the old woman. The goat milk money she took she would add to her "rainy day" savings hidden in her room. She would help herself to fancy items like soap or talcum powder, stashed away in the old suitcases for some occasion that never came. Standing well back of the bedroom window, Ivy would watch her disappear up the road. Then it was action time. While Bessie was away she would carefully sift through the old woman's belongings yet again. Under the bed. Through the suitcases on top of the wardrobe, stuffed with old clothes and photograph albums. She searched the cupboards in the kitchen, reading the labels that had *POISON* on them. All bottles and packaging that looked suspicious got thrown in the bin — until Bessie started to check the rubbish bin every day to see what was being thrown away. What Ivy did not know about were the cardboard boxes filled to the brim with bottles, tins and packets of life-threatening poisons hidden in the roof. Each year when the storms came the boxes got wet and the cardboard disintegrated into pulp.

Ivy had lived in fear that she was somehow being poisoned ever since Bob, disguised as the small dog, had made his accusation against Bessie. As a result, the younger woman generated enough acid in her stomach to withstand the increasing dosages of poisonous substances she imagined Bessie was secretly adding to her food. Ivy's stomach upsets were usually nothing more than a feeling of nausea, but sometimes she had bouts of debilitating vomiting and diarrhoea. Every day she would examine her phlegm on a saucer for suspicious signs. Remembering from her years at Sycamore Heights how to self-monitor such symptoms as dizzy spells, double vision and systolic functions, she carried out self-examinations according to the annual calendar that arrived each year from the baker's shop.

As time passed, Ivy's skin grew paler, ending up looking

like the pale flesh of a lemon. Her uncut hair turned snow-white, and resembled the texture of a horse's mane. Except for a general lethargy that increased over the years she lived in Bessie's house, she was always able to perform her daily tasks. She would take her time and rest each afternoon.

Eventually, Bessie guessed that Ivy suspected her of trying to poison her food, but neither of them ever mentioned this obsession. Instead, Bessie began to tell Ivy stories of how Bob used to try to poison her. "But I was too smart," she gloated. She would smile while Ivy agonised whether to eat the stew or not, knowing what was running through the younger woman's mind: *Had there been time to do it while Ivy fetched another piece of wood for the stove?* It only took about thirty seconds to nip around the back door and take some wood from the neatly piled stack. Phlegmatically Bessie would calculate how long it would take Ivy to overcome her fear and eat. She knew poor Ivy must eventually lose out to her own command of tactics.

Talking about Bob once more, she said: "He was a good enough man, I reckon, but not too smart. I wouldn't let him in the kitchen in the end. I'd take his food outside to him. If he wanted anything he'd come to the door and ask for it. That's why I got the padlocks for the door. Whenever I went out I had to lock the doors — the old fool couldn't be trusted. Maybe it was him went around town poisoning people's dogs. The folk in town reckoned it was them prospectors. I can't remember now if it stopped when he died or not. Anyway, he was always talking about who he didn't like. This one. That one. It was probably their dogs that got poisoned."

Lately she had begun to talk about how Bob always threatened to blow the top off the town. "He went around the miners' camps at night, stealing explosives, then hid them somewhere. He'd say, 'Bessie, I've got a secret place. That's where I'll be if the police ever come lookin' for me.'

Oh yeah! You know, he had funny dreams, that man. 'Then I'll escape down the gullies and that's where I'll be if you ever want to find me.' " Bessie would make her voice growl whenever she related Bob's words.

"It must be acid," Ivy convinced herself. Then one day she found it. It was a late November night during the build-up to the Wet; she was washing her clothes and swearing to herself that Bessie seemed to go through a cake of soap a day. Her torch shone on the Sunlight packet and she read the label. This was it! The label listed several forms of acid. And she realised that there was always a taste of soap in her mouth. A taste she'd got used to over the years. Now she had discovered the reason. "The rotten old cow!" she said aloud. She went back into the house and woke Bessie up. The little dog who was Bob sat on the end of the bed and watched.

"You've been trying to murder me, you old fool!" she yelled into Bessie's face in the dark.

Bessie couldn't understand what was happening. "You're a madwoman, that's what you are," she told Ivy. She tried to remain calm, but realised she had probably always been scared of this strange woman, ever since she arrived all those years ago.

"And this is Bob! Here he is!" Ivy pointed to the dog with the old face at the end of the bed.

The old woman looked terrified. She couldn't see Bob. Ivy took hold of the neck of her nightdress and forced her down the bed to look at the dog. Unable to speak, Bessie just shook her head.

Ivy laughed wildly. She told Bessie that Bob had told her he'd been poisoned by his wife. "And now you're trying to do me in too. Go on, admit it!" she yelled, slapping the old woman over and over again on the face. Now Bessie began to scream out to Bob. The little dog ran out of the room and Pal, outside, reacting to the old woman's cries, began to bark and scratched at the tin wall, frantically racing round and round the house, trying to get inside.

In the midst of all the screaming, barking and scratching and the wild dust storm which was blowing up outside, Bessie escaped from Ivy's grip. Ivy, completely out of control, began to swing punches, screaming incomprehensible threats to kill the old woman. Bessie hid under her bed in the pitch darkness. Outside, thunder rumbled in the distance, but the lightning was still too far away to light up the room.

Cursing that there were no electric lights in working order, Ivy stumbled off to the kitchen to find the matches and light the carbine lamp. This was a light attached to the end of a pipe — the other end was welded to a large cylinder of carbine gas. "I'll get you in a minute! You wait! You murderer, I'll get you!" she screamed, laughing wildly over one shoulder towards the bedroom. She began to shake with rage, and kept colliding into the furniture and knocking things to the floor. On all fours she scavenged around the kitchen trying to find the matches and the disused lamp.

Bessie, meanwhile, struggled out from her hiding place and managed to prise the window stick out of its bolted position. With her remaining strength she shoved it towards the window, until it was wide enough for Pal to come in. The old dog forced his fat body out of the storm through the gap in one swift leap.

Three things happened in the next few moments. Lightning from the dry storm struck the roof. The pile of rotting boxes filled with congealed chemicals in various stages of frothy disintegration exploded on impact, igniting another box containing gelignite cylinders. The blast tore the house apart catching Pal in mid-air as he was about to attack Ivy. The white tip of his tail was all the police found the next day. The house burnt to the ground leaving no trace of the two women.

All emergency services were outside the old woman's place within minutes, such was the explosion it had shaken the whole town awake.

"Jesus Christ!" was all those looking on could say over and over as they stood back from the flames in the rain that had eventually come.

Beams of light cut back and forth over the scene as the emergency services searched for bodies they knew they would not find. Each searcher felt driven by the hope of a miracle. The town would not be the same without the old lady they all loved. She was a part of what made the town home for them all.

Afterwards, they all stood in defeated huddles cursing Bob. It was a good job and good riddance that he had committed suicide they all agreed. If he hadn't been found floating in the Two Mile, nobody would have bothered dredging to find him. Everyone in town had suspected he had stolen the explosives but the sergeant could never put the finger on him. But Old Bessie! They hated him more. When nobody could say anymore, they all went home, promising to help in the search the next day.

Later in the night when occasional torches were haphazardly shone over the back yard, only the yellow lights reflecting from the eyes of the frightened goats shone back. Ivy lay semi-conscious on the ground under the herd that had gathered around her.

The local police sergeant, his offsider and two or three volunteers turned up next day to search the place for whatever remains could be found. They found only blackened earth covered with bits and pieces of corrugated iron that creaked under the weight of searchers' boots. The scarred and blackened jacaranda was in full flower.

The goats came back at the end of the day, after everyone had left. The gate to their yard was shut, so they settled down outside for the night and went off again early next morning. They returned three or four days in a row, camp-

ing for the night then going off again. After that they would
come back every now and then, but since no one was there
they began to stay in the prickly bushes along the river bank,
on the other side of the river to town side, a few kilometres
away. The rubbish tip was close by, and after the rains
stopped a few months later, the goats would rummage
through the garbage bags in search of scraps of food.

The townspeople made several complaints about the
goats to the Town Council. In four years the goats increased
to a herd numbering some three hundred. It would have
been very unusual for the Council to take swift action
without due consideration of the factors involved. It entered into prolonged negotiations to have the goats moved
interstate for slaughter: with several rounds of re-tendering
completed, the contractor just happened to belong to the
most influential family in town.

Another significant consideration for the Council was the
continuous speculation about the Aboriginal population
that lived on the edge of town, and their illegal fossickings
at the tip. It was assumed this was how diseases were spread
around the town, and for a while it was thought a pretty
good solution to this problem to allow the goats free run
there. "Let it be," stamped the hammer of agreement at
bi-monthly meetings. But then there was a tuberculosis
scare. It was alleged the goats would spread the disease, and
that it would become rampant throughout the town. The
local doctor wrote an article in a medical journal. A petition
was got up.

At the same time, reports came in about a wild woman
who lived with the goats. She wore baggy clothes, obviously
taken from the tip. "I saw her wearing my old shirt," the
town butcher swore. Most of the town kids had caught sight
of her over the years, and she had become the target for
playing dares. The kids thought she was a ghost. "Long
white hair like a goat's, down to the ground" — "All bent

over, and she runs just like a goat." — "White skin, like she got no blood." Black or white, the kids all said the same.

Only the black parents believed what their kids said and told them to stay away from that place. Stories spread over card games and cups of tea. "She lives in an old refrigerator box — true as I'm sitting here," the storyteller would declare, retelling the yarn. One day some kids went too close to the box, and out shot a bony white arm. "Must be full of TB," everyone said. "And she tried to drag the kid inside her den — he got away in the nick of time."

Everyone in the Aboriginal camps agreed it was only a matter of time before a TB epidemic broke out. People would give themselves a look-over to see whether their dark skin was turning yellow, and look sneakily into other people's eyes for signs of yellowing there. Children were kept home from school, just in case. Everyone began blaming the Aboriginal community for spreading the disease. At last the Council was forced to take direct action as a result of the townspeople's petition and the doctor's medical article. The doctor, interrupting a Council meeting through an open window, threatened to demand a state of emergency in the town and get the army in to remove the goats. Next day the Council deployed every bulldozer in the vicinity into action, and marshalled every man holding a gun licence into the Town Hall for instructions and bullets.

At dawn, every Aboriginal camp on the edge of town was flattened. People scattered in every direction when the bulldozers came roaring in, almost on top of sleeping families. The noise was their only warning. The drivers made short work of all that those people had in life. The doctor and medical staff from the hospital were on standby to give injections after the police force rounded up everyone there, separating any who showed signs of illness. They would be sent to a remote quarantine island established by the State for Aborigines with diseases.

Now bullets sprayed the rubbish tip. Back in town, people heard the sound of bullets ricocheting over the dump for hours on end. They thought it would never stop. The goats had nowhere to go except towards the centre, to be shot dead on top of all the others. The fingers that fired the bullets were red-raw when the last goat, with her kid, fell on top of the pile of corpses. At this point the bulldozers came in again. The tip was ripped to pieces from edge to centre, with the gunmen still in position for any final strays.

In the last light of the day, amidst the roar of engines and choking dust, one gunman saw a movement amongst the tumbling piles of cardboard. He took aim, but just in time realised he was looking at a woman's face through the white, burr-tangled hair that surrounded it, so like a goat's. If his finger hadn't been so painful, "If I wasn't so bloody tired" as he said afterwards, he would have fired without pausing.

As it was — "There's a woman!" he yelled, trying to be heard above the roar of the bulldozers. He dropped his gun and raced between the nearest bulldozer and the woman, risking his life to drag her to safety.

Ivy was kept in an isolation room at the hospital for several days until tests confirmed that she did not have tuberculosis. She stayed in the hospital for several weeks, while the doctor tried to restore colour to her skin and bring her out of her state of shock. At the same time he tried to decide what was to become of her. When she finally recovered, the jacaranda was flowering once again in the ruins of Bessie's abandoned block.

PART III
Victory Lane

14

A whistling wind blew in from a sea choppy with winter storms. Its damp breath hurled itself down the city streets, through the concrete valley of multi-storied office blocks to cut into the chafed faces of clean city people in winter clothes.

The No. 27 tram was coming at last. A giant neon clock registered that it was already twenty-eight minutes late. *12.43 pm Thur 15 Aug*— lit in red. But the tram that lurched over the horizon, stopping at each of the intersection traffic lights along the way, kept pace with a former era. At last the carriage with its slatted windows and pictures of happy faces celebrating the Bicentenary painted on the side panel ground to a stop. The lunch-hour traffic was dense in mid-city. Black slush sprayed up from passing vehicles along the line of head-bent passengers. Mary waited anxiously near the end of the queue. The tram doors crashed open.

"Move down the back there! You blind or what? Other people are trying to get on, you know!" The tram conductor hollered over the heads of passengers in the chaos of getting on and off, mumbling in disgust about people who wouldn't budge from their safety grips. You couldn't blame them — it was a frightening experience, travelling on an overcrowded city tram as it jerked and swung around corners, the driver crunching his way through the traffic trying to make up the delay.

Most passengers just wanted to go a few blocks. By the

time Mary reached her destination she had almost the whole tram to herself, apart from an old derro hugging a bottle in a paper-bag beneath his grey overcoat, and a couple of trendy young lovers dressed in black.

She missed the Victory Lane stop in the heart of Apperson, an inner-city suburb that had as yet managed to escape the development profiteers. She left the tram at the next stop, walking quickly uphill past second-hand stores that gave way to more tacky shopfronts whose broken windows were sealed with boards or tin. "Victory Lane," the voice on the phone had told her that morning. "You can't miss it."

It was almost one forty-five by the time Mary reached the office of the Coalition of Aboriginal Governments. She should have taken a taxi, she thought.

Buddy Doolan sat the reception desk, busy on the phone. He looked at Mary and glanced at his watch. The wind slammed shut the door behind her. He waved one hand towards a chair and lit up another cigarette while saying "Yes", "No", "Probably" to the person doing most of the talking at the other end of the line.

After a few minutes Lesley, the secretary, returned from lunch. Buddy tapped his watch at the tall, willowy young woman with her dark skin and yellow dreadlocks. She rolled her large brown eyes. "What are you — the timekeeper?" she snapped. Dropping her bag behind the desk, she began to fuss around, separating her work from Buddy's scrawled notes. Mary was fascinated by the attractiveness of these two people. They seemed far more confident and assertive than she could ever be.

"You want a cup of coffee, Sis?" Lesley asked. She grabbed all the cups in sight, and motioned with curled lips for Mary to come with her behind the office. Mary followed the chink of jewellery adorning this vision of beauty, admiring the ancient Aboriginal rock art patterns on her blood-red dress, its full skirt held in with a black belt.

Now Mary heard the sounds of other voices in the front

office. The rest of the office staff had returned from lunch. Lesley poked her head around the door and simply said, "They're back early." The place was soon buzzing once more; coffee cups were handed round and telephone calls were answered as the staff yelled at one another, carrying Lesley along in a flow of office talk. Lesley came back to Mary and said: "Come on, Sis, your show is about to start."

Lesley led the way up the narrow stairs of the old building, her perfume wafting behind her. Mary was acutely aware of the sound her high-heeled shoes made on the bare wooden steps. Lesley, in rubber-soled red, black and yellow boots worn with matching leggings, moved in silence. Mary wished she'd worn something else; her little grey suit, a snatch at a sale at the most exclusive department store in the city, seemed too elegant.

"In here." Lesley left her at the door of the boardroom, and Mary walked in to be greeted by the interview panel of seven Aboriginal people.

Buddy Doolan, whom she had already encountered downstairs, spoke first. "I'm the Director of the Coalition. Take a seat. You are Mary Nelson, right? Well, this is our Operations Board: Johnno Scott, Mervin Lee, Dave Stingray, Steve Rivers, Mavis York, and Gillian — what name you go by now, Lilly or Cogan?"

"Cogan."

"Right." Buddy Doolan turned to Mary again. "By the way, please accept our apologies. We are not always this late. I have to be honest with you, Mary — you are the only applicant, so we are pretty keen to know a bit about you."

Mary told the board that she had worked for a high-tech computer company for twelve years, doing contract work. They set up programs and trained the staff of companies that purchased their computers. She'd joined the firm straight from high school after completing matriculation. She elaborated on the different types of computer programs she had established for various companies.

The members of the interview panel grew nervous, tapping the table with pens, the floor with their feet, drinking glasses of water, making notes on paper, twiddling their thumbs and staring at her straight suit. It was not going well. But Buddy Doolan noticed none of this: he had meantime dashed off a memo to Lesley, telling her to be more punctual.

"Well! That's fine. Very good," he told Mary. "But it's all a bit different to what we do here. Why do you think you can do this job?" Buddy slapped the papers in front of him in an impatient gesture.

Mary felt like slinking out of the door. She felt out of place. Who were these people? Just what did they want? She needed a moment to think.

"Take your time. We have time to listen," Mavis said firmly. She was the oldest person there. She wanted to give another woman a chance.

Mary went on to explain her newspaper research on Aboriginal issues. Most of the problems seemed to be about funding, with the Aboriginal people saying that the return of their land and self-determination presented the only solution. It seemed that the rest of the country was a long way off being reconciled to Aboriginal Land Rights and autonomy. She explained how her financial programming knowledge would be useful in analysing the economic and other needs of Aborigines to be self-governing. She had recently completed university studies, majoring in politics and anthropology, and she thought this should prove useful for them as well.

A couple of the men raised their eyebrows at the word "anthropology", and both asked the same question, whether Mary had been involved in Aboriginal organisations before. Mary hadn't. More eyebrow raising. Mavis fiddled with the long strand of beads around her neck. "Why should you want to work for us? Seems like you have a pretty good job uptown."

Mary told them that recently, following the death of her parents in a car accident, she had learned that she had been adopted. In their will they had asked forgiveness for not telling her. Her father was unknown. Her real mother was Aboriginal — but her birth certificate stated that her step-parents were her real parents. Somehow, all traces of her past had been removed. Mary told the board she wanted to be Aboriginal. She wanted to find out who she really was. For the first time she understood why she had felt different all her life. Perhaps her mother was alive ... She thought that working for an Aboriginal organisation seemed the best way to achieve her aims.

"Well, girl, it sounds as though your heart's in the right place," Johnno Scott remarked. "How much does that job of yours pay up there in the city?" When Mary told him, Buddy Doolan cut in to tell her she would be looking at about a third of the amount with them. "Still interested?" he asked her.

Mary said that would suit her, quickly carrying out dollar calculations in her head. Her step-parents' will included a house and other assets, as well as money in the bank for her as sole heir. Then she waited outside the room while the board came to its decision.

After a while Buddy Doolan came out and told her she had the job and could start on Monday. "I hope *you've* made the right decision!" he called after her as she left the building. She smiled all the way to the tram stop.

It seemed that the job and Buddy Doolan came together. Their affair started the same week. Was this the sexual harassment written about in intra-office bulletins under the heading "Equal Opportunities in the Workplace", which went out unread in the daily rubbish? It began with invitations to lunch and dinner. At first she said "no": she knew a try-on when she saw it. Nevertheless, she had never received such attention before. Men did not usually consider

her attractive enough to pursue. Certainly not good-looking men like Buddy Doolan. Mary was flattered. And she
didn't want to let her new colleagues down. She was aware
of the huge struggle just to keep the organisation afloat.

For Mary, it was "on the job" training from the first day,
learning to become Aboriginal as well as beginning a career
in Aboriginal politics. The team was made up of highly
motivated project workers consigned on request to regions
throughout the country to coordinate special political
tasks. There was no putting off anything until tomorrow.
Just long days and long nights, including lunches and
dinners. "Be prepared to work fourteen, sixteen hours a
day, not eight, just to make the mean yard," Buddy warned
her.

One night towards the end of that first week, Buddy, tall,
dark and handsome, decided to drive Mary home to her
small, embarrassingly upmarket flat, several suburbs away
on the better side of the city. They'd had dinner together
and it was nearly midnight.

"You know, Mary, I'm pretty wrecked. I'd better have a
few hours sleep at your place before I drive home. I need
to have my head together pretty early tomorrow morning,"
he told her.

What Mary didn't know was that he had been literally
thrown out of his own place by a long-suffering girlfriend,
after which he'd camped at the office in Victory Lane. Next
day he'd found his belongings dumped on the footpath in
front of the wrong premises. Across the duco of his red
Commodore parked by the kerbside a rusty pipe had
scratched the message: *Fuck off mongrel.* What you might call
a pretty final situation. But Mary was not yet jaundiced in
her view of Buddy Doolan. She thought a man who worked
so darned hard must be completely above board. He could
have her bed and she would sleep on the lounge. She was
so innocent. After some initial protest about not wanting
to inconvenience her, they slept together. His body was

warm, after all. And he was better in the bunk than anyone else she'd slept with. They'd all been one-night stands, in any case.

Not Buddy: he moved in almost immediately. It turned out that he had his belongings stashed in the boot of his car. He didn't even mind living on the flash side of town. But Mary, who was resourceful, found a cheaper place, a spacious flat above the Cauliflower Hairdressing Salon, in the trendy street around the corner from the office. She managed the move herself while Buddy was away at an important meeting.

"Those buggers up at Canberra can't get a thing right," he declared on his return. He meant the Aboriginal bureaucracy in the federal capital. "A bunch of fuckin' no-hopers without a brain between them." This was how he greeted her as he entered the new place for the first time, slamming down his overnight bag. Once he'd cooled down, he said it was all the same to him where they lived. Mary used a more reasonable approach to life in those days, always seeking the middle ground. She'd want to find out why people acted the way they did. So far as the "fuckin' no-hopers" were concerned, maybe Buddy had done something to upset them. She could see how bad-tempered he was.

"Perhaps there's a better way of dealing with them," she suggested.

"How would you fuckin' know anything" — that was how the arguments began. "Can't you see what's happening? We have wholesale suffering in every aspect of our people's lives. You can read about it if you haven't yet seen it for yourself. There are fundamental reasons for this. The record shows that government programs and control don't work. Yet these buggers in Canberra still want to work with our biggest enemies, the state governments, who go on squealing about their sovereignty over our lives. Chances are, we're on the way out. The old assimilation theory is still alive and kicking, and now it's even being peddled like hot cakes by our own mob!"

Mary found this difficult to understand and insisted on maintaining a mediatory role. After arguing the toss, with neither of them getting closer to any understanding, Buddy just threw his arms up in the air. This happened wherever they happened to be: at home, in the office, at a restaurant or the pub around the corner. He told Mary she was glued to her fixation about the perfect life, and screamed at her in exasperation.

Finally he'd relent. "Oh, give the world a break, Mary," he'd say, but all the same he'd sulk until she apologised.

At other times he would wake in the middle of the night, screaming. He told her this was when the devils came. What were they like, she asked. No different to the devils of the day, he answered. They all had to be fought. It was a fight all the way, a struggle to be Aboriginal. There were no free rides. Other times, he told her that evil spirits were everywhere, even in the cities. They knew how to manipulate your mind until the day you died. They knew all about modern-day matters and were able to use any disguise to carry out their evil work, as they had done all through the ages. Another of Buddy's theories was that in the early days, the black man had sung the Whites, to make them greedy and miserable in the blackman's land. But then he'd laugh, as if he only half-believed this. "It's a war of the mind, to tell the truth. The mind must be in harmony with the land. We do not need to have a society bent on ripping up the ground pouring whatever they find into sustaining an over-supply of humanity."

At this stage Mary was keen to abandon her former life completely. She believed implicitly in Aboriginality, where Buddy had doubts expressing what he knew in his heart. He failed his own conditioning. Mary became his doormat, which was unfortunate. Buddy made good use of her. She was always there in the wings, waiting for him to return from conferences, meetings, Parliament House, extended visits interstate or even overseas, social occasions, one-night flings, confrontations with dejected former lovers ... Being there was all-important to him. He had to carry on the fight and she was still learning the ropes. By now she had learned quite a lot about love and nature, but she didn't know how to fight back. "It's never on a plate, Mary," he repeatedly warned her, telling her not to expect anything of him.

By the time Mary's daughter, Jessie, was born, Mary was alone — except for two of Buddy's ex-girlfriends, who visited her at the maternity hospital, no doubt hoping to catch Buddy there. No such luck. One was like a crow, the other a lark. At Mary's bedside they bitched about Buddy. Then, noticing the baby, they twiddled its fingers and raved about the image of Buddy in its every feature. They left happy.

The birth had been a long and painful experience. An eighteen-hour labour. The father was notified, but did not come. Mary lay there trying to reconcile her mind to his non-appearance. The staff kept promising that he would come soon, for sure. The pains were excruciating. An electric storm, like an explosion above the city, caused a power cut in the hospital and Mary spent an eternity in complete darkness. A young Indian intern stayed with her the whole time, holding her hand. He looked like a black crow in the darkness. The baby stayed inactive and she was convinced it was dead. The intern told her she was doing fine. Using emergency power, they monitored the baby's heartbeat, but she was still not convinced.

"Take it out of me!" she screamed.

The intern damped her with a moist sponge — a gentle touch. Mary cursed them all. In the end he held one of her legs apart in the forceps delivery. He gave her the baby. She imagined she had fallen in love with him. Then he went away. The Sister cursed because there was blood spattered all over the floor. "This is not India," she complained as she bathed Mary with warm soapy water. "Your baby is just like its mother, dear," she went on. The intern would be reported for not doing his job. Still the father did not come.

During the last few weeks of her pregnancy Mary had stayed at home. No one from the office came to visit her. They were all so busy, as usual, and no one noticed the time passing quickly. It wasn't like that for Mary. Time dragged between morning and night each day, and still Buddy did not come to see her, as he'd promised to do before she took maternity leave. By this time he had not only left the flat above the hairdressing salon but several other shack-ups as well.

When it was time for Mary to leave hospital, Lesley arrived in her hot-pink, customised Falcon XB GS sedan with its twin exhausts to take Mary and Jessie home. Lesley often boasted about what this car meant to her. "It's man, woman, baby all rolled into one — and it's all mine," she says. And: "Get your fucking ride elsewhere," she'd tell the boys who wanted to use her in order to use the car. "This is a fucking woman's car and you need special privilege to soil up my upholstery."

Lesley apologised on Buddy's behalf. "He's sorry, truly Sis. He's been away for days, and as soon as he got back he had to catch a plane for the US. Don't hold it against him too much." And she warned Mary, as she often did, that he was just a man.

In the car the pale-pink upholstery of the back seat was laden with stuffed animals, flowers and baby clothes — all from Buddy, Lesley said. Glancing at the pile of tiny garments, Mary was reminded of the unused baby clothes, neatly folded in dozens of sealed boxes, which she had found in the ceiling of her adoptive parents' house.

Lesley declared she was thrilled to pieces to be able to drive "their" baby home in style. Jessie, she said, was the child of their vision. "You can just tell this is a very special child," she told Mary.

"How?" Mary asked, even though she thought this too. It seemed a strange child that seemed to stare all the time. But perhaps all babies did this. How would she know?

Lesley shrugged in reply and said she just was a special child. "Believe it," she told Mary. "You always ask too many questions."

"I just wondered what you see in her, that's all."

"It's not what I see. It's what I feel. I feel her power. She will be a powerful woman one day."

Back home, with the baby occupying most of her time, Mary was able to come to terms with being a mother. It was just her and the baby and she loved the fact that no one could intrude upon their cocoon. She burnt perfumed oils. Bergamot and cypress during the day. Geranium while they slept. She taped classical music for her contented child. Mozart's piano Concerto in D Flat, Weber and Rossini clarinet concertos. Beethoven's Violin Concerto in D Major. Tchaikovsky's Serenade for Strings. The beautiful voice of Teresa Berganza. The "Possessed" Belinski Quartet, because she and the baby were in total possession of each other. After a while the few visitors who came to see them stayed away. In their place, Mary encouraged butterflies, moths and other winged creatures to flutter around the bedroom where she and the baby slept under an enormous mosquito net.

She kept in contact with the office by phone — rather, they kept in contact with her, seeking her advice on any number of internal issues. The other senior staff were often away, and Buddy had embarked on a series of visits to other Indigenous nations to examine their systems of government.

Mary would set out reluctantly to do the shopping. Never an uneventful business. It was okay going out with the baby in the stroller, all rugged up. But she resented the admiration and touching of strangers. A stampede to touch the newborn. Mary hated it. Bad enough to engage in baby talk with total strangers. One old white woman even tried to take off with Jessie in the stroller, while Mary was busy checking the contents on a container of nappy softener in the super-market. Would it be better to keep on using Sunlight and Electric Soda? ... It took only a moment offguard. Then she was yelling and screaming abuse at the old woman when she caught up with her. Onlookers stared at Mary in disgust as she accused the old lady of having orang-outang hands. And once Mary cooled down (which wasn't until a few days later), she guessed the woman was just a poor old thing. But the incident upset the timeless, lullaby life she had created. It was like the intrusion of a mighty orchestra over the sweet-sounding timbre of a Mozart violin concerto.

The Aboriginal mob was no different. Those jealous former girlfriends of Buddy's sniffed back their jealousy. They were all bitchy — Buddy must have a predisposition for this type of female, Mary thought. Some pretended the baby didn't exist, holding their heads up so that they could ignore it and moving into top gear as they walked past in the street. It was a real ordeal going past the corner pub. The doors swung open to see her moving past, accompa-nied by whistles and abuse. Could Buddy really have so many relatives? Out they came announcing their skin clas-sification and relationship to Jessie. Pulling her out of the stroller and disappearing into the pub with her. Mary soon put a stop to that. She began to give sermons about grog, handing out pamphlets about Alcoholics Anonymous. "Keep your drunken fingers off this healthy child!" she had other drunk people saying. She raised a lot of consterna-tion. The fat publican waved the index finger of his right hand at her. It was missing the top joint. "What happened to the rest of it?" Mary called out. He yelled for her to fuck off. The rellies hobbled or swaggered back inside. "Don't want to cause no trouble," they muttered.

Pub talk about Mary was a bit extreme at this time.

Everyone decided she must have turned into some kind of evangelist, a weirdo type, a religious nut. It was hotly debated whether she believed alcoholism was contagious. She most certainly had a righteous streak about her. It all died down: in the end, Mary passed by the hotel untroubled, receiving only the occasional meek wave.

Her more favourable excursions with Jessie were to collect bottlebrush, wattle or eucalyptus foliage and blossoms from nearby parks, or from the front gardens of gentrified inner-city dwellings. Sometimes there were roses. She would create a natural bush setting inside her flat, starting from the back window. The winged creatures who came inside soon included honeyeaters, sparrow and pigeons, who all ate from her hand while Jessie looked on, wide-eyed and laughing.

When Buddy Doolan returned from his overseas trip months later, he caught up with news about Mary and his child from the pub. The office staff said "Bullshit!" when he told them the news about Mary becoming a religious fanatic.

"Get real!" Lesley told him. "Get your butt together and go and see for yourself. You still haven't seen Jessie yet, have you?" she spat. She decided she'd save it for another time, to tell him what she thought of black men who didn't support their children. *What a louse.*

Late one afternoon, Buddy appeared at the office with his father, Frank and his younger brother, Donny, both down for a visit. Buddy announced he was going over to Mary's. The grandfather needed to see the baby, he said.

Lesley knew they were all looking for a place to camp. "Too scared to go over by yourself?" she hissed in Buddy's ear.

"Fuckin' shut up, Lesley, and drive us over," he snapped, his eyes wild.

"What's wrong with your car?" she hissed back. She didn't want to be drawn into this.

He told her it was being used by someone else, out of commission, whatever. Lesley knew he'd planned this. He was like a snake charmer. Nothing was coincidental with him. Nothing happened on the spur of the moment. And what he decreed was always on the line. So they all went. The family, the team, together.

Mary let them in and greeted Buddy as though he'd just returned from a ten-minute outing. She went straight back to her comfy chair to continue feeding Jessie, while distant echoes of male voices chanting in French wafted through the room.

"That's nice," Lesley commented.

"Gregorian, French monks," Mary responded.

They all came close to look at Jessie sleeping at the nipple, but Mary waved them away to distant chairs. No one spoke. They were allowed to watch. Lesley pointed to the kitchen and Mary nodded for her to make tea. Buddy didn't know whether he liked or disliked what Mary had created in the flat. He wanted to take the child, since he had now worked out a way to be part of her life. But he knew he must wait. He would have to put off holding her until later. First, Mary must relent. Then Mary put Jessie into her own bed and allowed the men to look at the first grandchild for their family. When she saw the pride in their faces she felt satisfied and left them alone with the baby.

Lesley and Donny went out to fetch Turkish and Greek takeaways, and they all sat down to eat. Lesley wondered how long it would take for the showdown. She didn't want to stay here all night. She thought it wouldn't take this long if some mongrel did this to her.

The mood at dinner was somewhere between formal and casual. Buddy was an expert in handling situations and Mary always maintained her cool. Now Buddy began to talk about the acknowledged inherent sovereignty of the American Indians and what this meant in the USA. His father, a small, white-haired man, prematurely aged beyond his fifty-

something years, spoke of family matters and their disinte-
grating community. The lines on his face deepened as he
spoke of the illness and deaths of adults and children. It
was like hearing a documented report from the front line
of a country torn by war and famine. Then Jessie woke up
and Mary fetched her. Changed her. Fed her. Then popped
her into her father's lap.

Frank Doolan kept on talking. "That school is useless,
the children aren't being taught anything. I went there and
looked for myself. 'There's nothing there for those kids of
ours', I thought when I saw what they were doing. It's being
run by a couple of airheads sent up from the city. 'We are
trying to teach them respect for Aboriginal law,' they told
me in their high falutin' way of talking. 'We want them to
respect the environment.' — 'What are you?' I asked them
— bugger if I knew. And bugger if they knew how to teach
our kids to read and write, either."

Frank had been employed as one of the health workers,
but lack of funds now meant he had lost his job — "Well, a
paying job, that is. I'm still at work there," he said.

"He does it both ways, Sis," Donny explained to Mary.
"Dad is a traditional healer."

"We buried four children last week," Frank continued in
his bland voice. "Died of poisoning themselves. A whole
group of kids playing with aviation fuel. They broke into
the warehouse during the night. The rest of them are still
fighting for their lives. Can you imagine that? I found them
myself. Terrible! None of them could move. They just lay
there, eyes rolled into the back of their heads. The Flying
Doctor came up in the middle of the night and took them
all away. We had to light the drums with fires so he could
see where to land. You could hear people crying all night.
A week later he brought the dead boys back — I knew they
were dead when he took them. He shouldn't have done
that. But you reckon anyone listens to us? Families are still

fighting and putting blame on each other. Luckily we Doolans aren't involved … this time."

Frank stopped talking to think for a while. Then — "Give me my grandchild," he told Buddy, who handed over the child he'd been cradling. Frank began to sing a traditional song in his language as he looked down at Jessie and she stared up at him. When he had finished he looked at Buddy, glanced quickly at Mary and said, "Um!" Then he closed his eyes and went on singing for a long time. Donny went to sleep on the floor rug just listening to his father's voice. Lesley waved goodbye and left quietly. Mary tidied up and made more tea. Buddy helped her. Finally, Mary placed a pillow and a spare doona beside Frank, placed a rug over Donny and gave Buddy another rug and a pillow. Then she took Jessie, who had gone back to sleep, off to bed with her. Thinking how easy it had all been, she quickly drifted into sleep snuggled beside her child.

Frank dreamed he was travelling inside a spinifex fire, being carried along with it. As it travels forward his line of vision is just above the height of the spinifex plain: he is able to see the flame engulf the vegetation that lies ahead. Farther ahead still, he sees the fire raging on all sides of his community. Then he awakes in his own house, screaming as he swirls about in the flames engulfing all the dwellings with fiery arms while people sleep inside. He sees his own house explode and is part of the flames that have grabbed his home, where his family are sleeping. He is screaming for them to wake up. To get out. But no matter how hard he screams, his voice is unheard …

He was still screaming "Get out! Save yourselves!" when Buddy woke up. Somehow he remembered where the light switch was and jumped up to turn it on. In the sudden flood of light the three men dossed down in the kitchen saw a crow sitting on the table looking at them. It squawked twice, then flew out of the open back window into the night.

Frank was pretty shaken by his dream and the crow. He'd

never known a crow come inside someone's place like that. Buddy made tea. Donny tried to stay awake but eventually went back to sleep on the floor. The other two men stayed awake, sitting at the table and talking for the rest of the night. Buddy talked about changing the world. Frank talked about death and powerlessness.

In the morning Mary came into the kitchen to find Buddy cooking breakfast for everyone. He told her about the black bird in the night.

"Oh! That's just Norman. I found him in the park one day. Some kids had stoned him and broken a wing. He's recovered now."

"A crow!" Buddy was surprised that anyone would want to make a pet out of that black bird.

"He comes and goes. I don't like crows either, but Norman's different." Mary opened the kitchen window; outside, several gulls, pigeons and sparrows perched on the electricity line. None of them answered her calls. They saw the men who had invaded the kitchen.

"Where did you say your people are from?" Frank asked Mary casually. For the first time she noticed that he spoke in a strange way, moving only his lower lip. Mary knew she had never told him anything about her tribal people — how could she, when she did not know herself? She explained why she did not know. Frank was anxious that she should find out. He believed Mary was Buddy's permanent woman — Buddy had only given his father a sanitised version of his private life.

"How come you haven't helped her to find out about her family?" Frank asked Buddy now. He felt annoyed that his son was such a know-all but ignorant about important matters of life and death. "With all your contacts you should have been able to do something."

Buddy interpreted this attack as an implication he should be back home, helping his own people. He guessed this was the whole point of his father's rare visit to the city. Soon it would be out in the open — he estimated it would take half an hour for Frank to get going, quickly followed by excuses to catch an earlier train back home.

"I will help Mary to try to find something out when she returns to work next week," Buddy said, sipping tea and eating toast.

Mary was surprised when she heard this, she hadn't thought of returning to work so soon.

"Make sure you do," Frank told his son. "You have responsibility for a family now. Me and your late Mum were married thirty-five years, almost to the day. We were always satisfied to stay in one place with our family. Not go traipsing around. You got to be with your family when you got young 'uns, you know. It's no good bringing up children in the city. You should be thinking about coming home soon, Buddy, and bringing Mary and the bubba with you." He turned to Mary. "You'd love it up there," he told her. Then, swivelling back to Buddy — "Listen! You find out today where your little baby's people are from. You're supposed to be the smart one in the family. And let me know straight away. You hear what I'm saying, son? Straight away. Today, if possible. Where is my grandchild, anyway?"

Mary glared at Buddy, wondering what nightmare she had walked into. What had happened to her life? She went to check on Jessie and decided to stay in the bedroom to calm down. Work! Moving! A bossy old man she didn't even know, who had no connection with her so far as she was concerned, just coming in and taking over. She realised by now that Buddy had used her for his own convenience. Yet even after the way he'd treated her, she just let him walk in and take over.

Buddy came into the bedroom. His face was set hard. He and Frank had had the argument about why he should or should not go back to his community. Mary had heard them shouting. "I'm sorry about all of this, Mary," Buddy told her.

He picked up Jessie and cuddled her while Mary folded clean nappies ready to use.

"We'll be leaving soon. Dad needs to catch an earlier train. We need you to come back to work, Mary. You can bring Jessie. — Yes, Jessie, you can come and sit on Dad's lap all day," he told the baby.

Oh sure, Mary thought. She faced Buddy. "Why does he want to know where I come from? Aren't I good enough to be the mother of his grandchild or something?" This seemed the easiest thing to pick on at that moment.

"It's nothing like that. But it's important to him — Jessie is his first grandchild. It's natural he should make a fuss over her." Buddy decided not to tell Mary how suspicious the old man was. Nor that he had already organised a check on Mary when the organisation initially employed her. He had some details of her background, but would tell her all in good time, on a need-to-know basis. That was always his policy, formulated from often bitter experience.

That night Buddy returned to Mary's place alone. He brought presents, food, details of a project the organisation wanted her to start working on, and his belongings waited in the car outside. Before long he convinced Mary of the need for a reconciliation between them. Firstly, there was the baby to consider. He was the father, and Frank was right about family responsibility. He and Mary needed to work together. Regardless of all else, they were a team. They shared the same vision. In the past these factors had worked in their favour. Yes, it was time to start family life.

Mary agreed to a trial period, knowing in her heart it would not last. She went back to work, taking Jessie with her. Her team began to work on organising regional conferences for Aboriginal communities on methods of negotiating land settlements as well as self-government agreements based on practices used by Indigenous groups in other countries. This, of course, was based on Buddy's overseas research. Other teams, meanwhile, were working on lobbying the federal and state governments, industry and other groups such as the Trades Unions.

While Buddy was at the flat even the birds prospered. He took over most of the domestic arrangements, which included changing the water bowls each day and buying birdseed. He liked being there, and was annoyed whenever he had to travel. He began to spend more time at home with the baby than he needed to. The flat became his alternative office, as well as the coffee shop nearby. His colleagues were agitated by his sudden lack of drive.

Then, a few months later, on one of Buddy's stay-at-home days, Mary came home from an up-country day trip to find the flat empty. He'd have taken Jessie down to the coffee shop, she thought. Several hours later she started to phone around. — "Seen Buddy?" — "Nope" — "Not since yesterday" — "Don't worry, you know him, probably talking to someone." The problem was that Mary did know him. And she did not trust him. Lesley came over. She did not trust him either, but she didn't say that. She had even checked out all Buddy's old flames by phone before she knocked on Mary's door. Contacting the police brought no news. They sat and waited, Mary jumping up at every sound outside. It was Jessie and what might have happened to her that filled her mind. She was distraught.

At a quarter to midnight the phone rang. — "Sorry," Buddy said from a distant payphone. Frank had called to say Donny had been in a car accident. Badly hurt. Car had gone up in flames and the others with him were dead. Donny was still unconscious. Bad burns to most of his body. "I'll bring Jessie back in a few days," he said. The Aunties were looking after her. — "Yes, she'll be alright. This was her family. No, don't come up. There's nothing you can do. Too many people here already. Okay? — See you, then."

A few days later one of the Aunties, a stoic-looking woman in her late fifties wearing a purple suit and looking like she'd be a hard one to win over, brought Jessie back. Yet, Auntie was a nervous woman, obviously glad to end her responsibility by handing over the child. It was clear she had rehearsed what she would say. She told Mary that Donny would pull through but needed a lot of care. His recovery would take a long time. Buddy had decided to stay for a while to help out. — No, she said in reply to Mary's question, Buddy had given her no message, just told her where to bring the baby. "But Frank said I was to tell you something," she went on. "He said you must take the baby back to her country. Why? I don't know. I didn't ask him, dear."

Auntie went back the same day, saying she didn't like the city. Better to be out of it than in.

At times Mary thought of going up to see Buddy, but thought she would probably just make a fool of herself if she did. Obviously he wasn't serious about their relationship, otherwise he would have contacted her. She wrote a couple of letters but received no answer. She wrote others, but did not send them. After some months had passed it was plain to everyone that Buddy had no intention of returning to the city.

Johnno Scott and a couple of the other directors of the Coalition of Aboriginal Governments went up to ask Buddy to come back. Johnno offered to take Mary, but she declined. She was tied up with the regional conferences just about to take place. Johnno felt sorry for her and thought she deserved better. It was too bad the way Buddy always screwed things up with women.

"He's not coming back for a while," Johnno reported when he returned. "Reckons he has to look after Donny. The family's in bad shape, pretty shaken up by what happened. Donny looks pretty bad an' all. Buddy's looking after the whole lot of them, including old Frank. He has plans for the community. I reckon he'll move it ahead. He's

already negotiating for direct funding for most services —
he's told the government they're not accepting anything
less. Made all kinds of threats about international exposure.
Strikes me he's organising a self-government movement on
the spot," Johnno grinned. "He's even found something to
negotiate. Mining. He won't agree to cooperate with the
government until it's ready to negotiate on an equal basis,
government to government. We have to support him from
here ... can you get together a national meeting within two
weeks?" He gave Mary a rather shamefaced smile. "Sorry I
couldn't bring better news for you."

15

An entry in Buddy's old desk diary read: *Mary born St Dominic's*. Mary stared at the page. Other notes for that day filled the page in Buddy's hasty scrawl. Indiscriminate notes. Meeting times. People to call. All to do with the business of the organisation. No clue to show where he obtained the information about her.

"And he won't tell you," Lesley warned her when she shoved the diary on top of her computer keyboard. "You know what he's like."

Mary phoned Buddy. "What are you doing looking at my diary?" he asked. He sounded pretty casual, like she should have better things to do. She challenged him about keeping the information a secret from her — information she had been desperately trying to obtain. "Don't you understand? I've been trying to find out about myself for ages — with no result whatsoever."

"God!" Buddy sighed in disbelief. He knew there had been more talk about discovering her identity than action. "Go on, admit it. You were just hooked on the romance of it. You're not connected with reality."

Mary thundered on in defence of what she had tried to accomplish in her life, accusing him of trying to hijack and belittle her Aboriginality. "You are lower than a piece of dog shit!" she yelled. She could picture him — raising his bushy eyebrows, rolling another cigarette, waving someone out of the door with a sigh, as if to signify the heavy duties of life at the top. He should be willing to talk to her about this. She asked him to call her back if he was too busy to talk to her.

He had a moment, he told her, though the usual line-up was waiting to see him. "Look," he went on, "I don't even remember writing anything in the bloody diary, for Christ's sake. I was flat chat at the time."

Mary suggested someone who came into the office may have mentioned it. He couldn't remember. It was true he'd made inquiries about her — but, like herself, he'd come up with nothing. "It was routine," he said. He had to check on new staff. "What did you expect?" No, he could not tell her who he contacted. "It's a case of friends knowing friends," he told her vaguely. "Look, I gotta go. I can't keep these people here waiting. When I remember I'll be in touch."

Mary knew she had no hold over him. He would not contact her. He hadn't even asked about Jessie. His ego, his people and land came before anything, or anyone else. While they needed him, he needed nothing else.

It was late at night when the phone rang. Buddy. Said he was calling from somewhere in the city. He apologised for the earlier conversation. He told her he'd remembered it was some old drunk fella who told him where she was born. "Came in looking for a few dollars and saw you in the office. When I put him in a taxi he told me that he remembered your mother, and you were from St Dominic's. I wrote it down so I wouldn't forget the name of the place. That's all he said."

"That's bullshit and you know it!" Mary screamed into the phone. She was worn out. Jessie was feverish and they were both getting little sleep. She was on breaking point with the job, too. She urgently needed to finalise their relationship. He seemed to feel he could walk in or out as he pleased. It did not really matter to him. So long as he had somewhere to put his dick. Momentary love. Wherever, whoever, without ties. He said he would come over to her place tomorrow and they could talk when she had calmed down. She told him not to bother. He said he wanted to see the baby. No, she said, she couldn't handle it at the moment. Some other time. Then she hung up.

Later he rang back. She had calmed down enough to ask about Donny.

"Donny is in a wheelchair for life. What you get when you drink and drive, I guess. Killed the others. Off his face and bashed into the back of a road train for the hell of it. It's a pretty bad situation up here for the Doolans. That's why I'm staying. Apart from the fact that I have a responsibility to look after Donny. No other bastard wants to do it."

"What do you mean? What about the rest of your family?"

"They're mostly too old. The rest you wouldn't spit on." His voice was hard.

"So what are you down here for, then?"

"Just some business to attend to."

"What, now, in the middle of the night?"

"That's right."

Mary figured the "business" was another girl friend. The reason why he wasn't at her door. "So, who is she this time?"

"Aren't there other options?"

"Well — tell me, Buddy. Have you been involved with other women since going home?"

"Yes, one or two." He sounded bored with the conversation. Then he said she could go back home with him if she wanted, but warned her she wouldn't like it. That was why he hadn't asked her before.

"And be a doormat for you." She told him this was the truth. "The moment of truth, Buddy. Before I start to turn into a liar as well. Can you imagine trying to bring up Jessie around a man like you? To be a decent person? Someone has to teach our child the truth — and it won't be you."

He managed to get another word in. He knew Mary in full swing. "Just remember I am her father. Always remember that."

"What! You trying to threaten me?" Once again she hung up.

She arrived at work next day feeling bone-tired and a little disoriented from the incident with Buddy. Had she handled it properly? Could she have handled it better if she hadn't lost her temper? Would it have made any difference anyway? Commonsense prevailed with a big "No". But the other questions still nagged her.

Wrestling with her thoughts, she missed seeing the police cars double-parked near the office. As she walked in, she was confronted by about six policemen, some in uniform, others in plain clothes, in the reception area. A shouting match was taking place. As soon as Lesley saw Mary, with Jessie in tow, she just about hurled herself on top of them and pushed them through to the back kitchen.

"Quick, upstairs to your office," Lesley ordered. She sounded out of breath.

As they ran upstairs, Mary looked down and saw the rest of the staff yelling abuse at the cops. More people were coming in through the front door. Two older plainclothes detectives were making a futile effort to speak to the staff. Once inside Mary's office, Lesley locked the door behind her and grabbed a telephone directory. Her hands were trembling so much she could hardly turn the pages to find what she was looking for. "Bloody television. Channel 11. That's the best, isn't it? Fuck! You can't find a bloody thing when you want it." Lesley was panicking and getting nowhere.

Mary flicked her teledex and pointed to the number. Lesley started dialling.

"If you've seen Buddy, for God's sake tell them you haven't," she told Mary as she waited for the number to answer. "The police are raiding the headquarters of the Coalition of Aboriginal Governments!" she snapped into the telephone. "... You got it. Right! Get your people over here immediately. Send a helicopter. Hurry!"

Slam went the phone. She started dialling again. "Legal Service? Lesley here — you know, good. On the way — good. Ring the Race Relations, Civil Liberties, Social Justice mob, will you? Tell them to get over here." *Click.* "Fuck! they've cut the bloody phones off."

The locked door bulged with the weight bashing against it and flew open. Mary couldn't believe what was happening. It was like the final scene from Cop Shop, when the baddie is apprehended. About four policemen burst into the office.

"On the floor!" — "Face down!" — "Fast!"

Mary froze on the spot, while Jessie's cries were drowned out by the police thrashing and trashing through her office. Lesley fell to the floor at once. She saw Mary's purple shoes next to her face and pulled her ankle. "Get down, Mary, for Christ's sake. Get down."

Mary hit the floor with the help of a policeman's shove. She lay with her body shielding Jessie. She had no idea how long they stayed there. Jessie cried the whole time, while around them the building echoed with thumps, crashes, screams and the sounds of splintering furniture. Books and papers flew around, some landing on top of them.

Then they heard the helicopters buzzing overhead. Maybe they were trying to land in the park next to the high-rise flats. Television, the newspapers, the police — maybe all three? A few moments later she heard Aboriginal voices dominating the scene.

"Get up, Sis," they urged her.

Mary, Jessie and Lesley were helped up from the floor. Jessie was in the arms of big Jack Stuart, a Legal Service field officer. Then they were ushered downstairs. Aboriginal faces were everywhere. Aboriginal flags were displayed inside and outside the building. The main street was jammed with traffic and trams were piled up back to the city. There was an incessant hooting from bad-tempered commuters. And all the while the Aboriginal demonstrators raised their fists, chanted loudly and refused to budge. The police formed a line between the demonstrators and the immobile traffic. Newspaper reporters and photographers scurried through the increasing crowd of onlookers. Ambulances and fire engines wailed in the distance, negotiating hazardous paths to reach the scene. Mary could smell smoke — it was billowing high across the street, but she couldn't see where it was coming from. Helicopters from the TV channels hovered overhead. Another police helicopter was booming orders for the media to move away. They did not respond. The police helicopter began to airlift wounded policemen from the park.

"Well! Why not create something none of them will forget!" Johnno Scott boomed in his gravelly voice. He stood there, hands on hips, beaming. "Call the PM. Get him on the line."

One of the Legal Service people called Canberra. "They won't put him on," he told Johnno.

Johnno grabbed the mobile. "Listen, fool." He pointed the phone towards a commotion outside. After a few seconds he handed the mobile back to the Legal Service representative. "Now ask him again."

The representative waited for a response, then turned to Johnno. "Sim Shaugnessy. Senior Aide. Want to speak to him?"

Johnno took the phone. "Watch the news and get this straight. Get the State off our back. Get the police out of here. Or this will get worse. Got it?"

The firefighters had got through and began dousing major fires in abandoned buildings along Appleton's main street. By three in the afternoon, amid the damp, smouldering remains of the fires, the police made their exit. The Aboriginal demonstrators stayed on for several hours, and so did the media. The office staff tried to calm each other down. The Coalition partners had been assembling all day as the news of the raid travelled farther afield. They were meeting in another building, made available to them by the Trade Unions. They were convinced that the issue of State rights versus Aboriginal rights must be dealt with immediately following this new outbreak of harassment.

At the end of a long day, Johnno called Mary into his hastily restored office. He and other members of the organisation's core leadership sat on every available chair. Mary had never met these people, even though she had now been with the Coalition for some time. Some of them had caught planes from interstate and others were still arriving.

"Sorry about today, Mary. Not good for you and our little Jessie here," Johnno said, pointing to an occupied chair. Someone got up so that she could sit down. "You were both very brave and we are proud of you. We are determined to sort this out. We will be meeting with the PM next Monday. It will be a hard struggle, but I believe we got somewhere today. But what we are concerned about now is Buddy. The police will get around to questioning you. When they do, you must have Robbo present." Mary knew that Robbo was the lawyer who acted for the Coalition. "And, Mary, we have to ask you a big favour. You must tell them that you haven't heard anything from Buddy. Okay? It's very important."

"I'll do that if you want me to. But was all this because of him? What has he done?" She saw them all staring at her as she asked the question.

Johnno breathed deeply before he answered her. "Alright. The newspapers have described it as inner-city warfare involving several major gangs that rampaged throughout the city last night. A number of people were killed or injured. Didn't you hear my radio reports this morning?"

Mary shook her head. She had heard only Mozart that morning as she got up.

"And you see," Johnno went on, "there were Aboriginal gangs involved."

"Buddy is not involved in gangs," Mary protested.

Johnno breathed heavily again. This was going to take a while. Why couldn't women settle for what you chose to tell them? "No, he's not. But the police think he is. That's why they came here looking for him. Witnesses! But we want to eliminate any connection with what happened last night. We know about these gangs, but only from outside. Their allegiances shift as quickly as you pinpoint them. Black against White. Black against Black. Black using White to fight Black. White using Black to fight White. And so on. A lot of family quarrels are sorted out in gang warfare. I don't know if last night's events involved traditional payback or what. I don't want to know. None of our business. But whatever the situation, Buddy won't be around for a while. Whether the cops catch him or not. It's a loss to us and to this community. Too bad. That's the way it goes with people like us."

Mary was speechless. By now the other members of the leadership were moving outside to go elsewhere. Johnno always talked too much once he got going, always with an admixture of fiction among the facts. Now he picked up his bag of confidential papers, patted Mary on the shoulder, and left with the others. He looked back at Jessie ruefully. He'd promised Buddy he would look after Mary and the child.

As Johnno drove away, he thought about the days when he was young. A young black man who followed the same escape route as Buddy through deserted city buildings. He could still recall the exact route they took, and the smells of disuse, of damp, rotting timber. Tripping over a mess of decay … something to laugh about later when they were safe. Down to the underground system of sewerage pipes. Lighting a trail of minor fires for the secret organisation that looked after all the others … His thoughts jerked back to the present. Later on he would meet Buddy and talk about today's events, and how they should tackle the PM next week.

Mary took Jessie home. The birds did not come to her flat and she felt even more deserted. These days she was too busy to buy seed and put it out in the trays. The water dishes were empty. There were no more leisurely strolls to collect stolen flowers, blossom or berries for birds. Late that night she sat waiting for the arrival of Norman, the crow. Soft Hebrew melodies played in the background, sounding incredibly sad tonight. The big black bird had all but disappeared after the incident with Buddy's father. Sometimes he came, stayed a few days, then disappeared for weeks. Much later she was able to admit to herself that it was not the bird but the man she was waiting for. To hear the sound of the phone ringing.

About one in the morning Norman came through the kitchen window. The flapping of his strong wings startled Mary. He didn't go straight to the kitchen table, as he usually did. He flew through the flat and around her several times. She felt the strong air currents stirred by the frantic movement of his wings. "You are not a graceful bird, Norman," she told him. Unable to sleep, she fussed over the bird for several hours. She played one of her favourite CDs and talked to Norman, raving on about most aspects of her life, past, present and future. Finally she slept, hoping the bird would stay.

It did not leave until next morning. It watched from the kitchen sink as Mary stumbled around, half asleep, dead tired, mechanically doing what was necessary for Jessie, sitting her in the highchair for breakfast, making porridge and squeezing orange juice.

"Jesus, Jessie," she exclaimed, struggling to keep up with the child's demands and clear up the mess she made while she got herself organised at the same time. Another work day. And she felt as though she needed to sleep for a month.

She opened the flat door to leave, Jessie on one arm, baby bag loaded with nappies and food swung over her shoulder, together with a second bag filled with papers, purse and car keys. She was about to close the door behind her when she glimpsed through the stair rail faces that had shouted into her face yesterday. Plainclothes police, four of them waiting downstairs. She thought it amazing they did not look up and see her. She backed into the flat again and closed the door, then sat Jessie down next to the bags and waited. What to do? She was trembling. Her fingers shook as she tried to dial the office. No answer. Too early. Who else could she call? No one. It was her own fault. She'd made no life for herself outside the flat. Her relationship with Buddy had reinforced her solitary life.

Twenty minutes later there came a knock on the door. Mary had kept on dialling the office, but there was still no answer. Now the blood drained from her face. Should she open the door or pretend she was out? At that moment Jessie started crying, and Mary suddenly remembered she could call the Legal Services. She flicked the directory pages. *Calm down,* she kept telling herself. She heard voices on the other side of the door. "Open up!" *No way,* she thought. She'd rung the wrong number, so hung up. Then she got through, heard the right number ringing. *Thank goodness ...*

"Open the door!" This time she recognised Lesley's voice.

"Who's there?"

"It's alright. Just us mob. It's okay."

Abandoning the phone, Mary opened the door. Lesley and several other people crowded in.

"Right! Mary, you're leaving today. Johnno said to tell you to pack your clothes. You leave on the plane after lunch. Everyone here will pack up the flat. A removalist comes this afternoon to put everything in storage. In a few weeks it will all be sent on to you. Johnno wants you to know everything will be taken care of and you are not to worry. 'Trust me': that's what he said to tell you."

Mary gaped at her. "Shit! Fine! 'Trust me'! Just what I need. I don't know who to trust anymore. Lesley, I don't know if I want to leave. Not today. Not right now. Don't I have any choice in what I do anymore?" As she spoke her arms flapped like a crow's."

"Come on. Calm down. I'll make a cup of tea. Just sit down. Hold Jessie. That's right. — Everyone else, start in the bedroom. Pack all the clothes first, then the bed stuff." Lesley's hidden talent for household removals came to the fore, her supposed role as receptionist for the organisation fading fast. Mary wondered at her professionalism. She was completely in charge. *What was her real role?* Did she have one? She was always there to handle all the difficult situations, carrying out instructions to the letter, able to ignore any emotional upheaval caused to others in the process.

"Lesley, am I on the run now as well?" Mary asked finally, feeling completely defeated and exhausted. Jessie sprawled across her lap, asleep. She watched her life disappearing into cardboard boxes, with just a few treasures she insisted on taking with her piled up in a heap beside her. Framed photos of her adoptive parents, Jessie, Buddy and herself. Some books. CDs — classical. Not his taste. Some of Jessie's toys.

"Pack all these in one box for Mary to take on the plane. Not much time left, Mary. Anything else you want to take with you? Alright. — No, Mary, you are not on the run. It's just better, Johnno said, for you to be away from here for a time. You know what the cops are like." (But Mary probably didn't know much about the sleazy side of life, Lesley reflected.) "They'll be pestering you all the time if you stay here. They're already hanging around downstairs. Been here all night. Outside your door, trying to spook you. It's a wonder you never heard them …"

(Bird talk: it had taken the cops a while to figure out who

"Norman" was as they listened through the door to Mary raving on.)

"... No, I can't tell you where you're going. I don't know everything. We've got to get you to the airport first."

As Mary left she put a bowl of water and some pieces of bread on the kitchen windowsill before she closed the window. Farewell to Norman. Her only friend, her only family. She had good memories of being here; she had learned a lot about herself in this place. The organisation had helped her to do this. Perhaps it was best to stay with them. Not that it seemed as though she had any choice.

The plane flew over the city. From her seat Mary could see the red neon light of the Town Hall clock. *3.20pm Thur 17 Aug.* She looked at the airline ticket again. Her destination scarcely seemed to matter. She had never thought of moving away from the city. Everything she needed was there.

Life took a hectic turn for Mary. She was always on the move. She spent months in the West, moving from cities to isolated communities. Then North, from the islands to the desert, spending little time in each place before she was required to move on. It was more than a year before she established a home base for herself.

Her job, as Johnno explained often enough over the phone or in instructions sent by airbag, was to explain the policies of the organisation and demonstrate how these matched local knowledge and aspirations of autonomy. The national organisation, Johnno reiterated, would continue moving towards a direct and equal relationship with the federal government. She was to gauge what support was required and work out political strategies to move communities towards achieving their goals of self-government and autonomy.

Mary threw herself into this work with great enthusiasm. Eagerly she took on new tasks, holding the organisation in the highest regard. It was her life. She felt she owed the organisation the air she breathed. If she heard criticism of the membership, particularly of Johnno, she would spring to the defence. And there was criticism. Plenty of it.

"Keep that to yourself," Johnno might say, after giving her the lowdown on some place where she was to work. Or, "This is what you need to know ... we don't think anyone else needs to know," another executive member might tell her on the phone, late at night. Mary should have thought about what they were not prepared to tell her. But she did not have the confidence or experience to know when she should challenge them. Her knowledge was more academic, theirs grounded in the evolution of local folklore. A former local bogeyman, for example, would now be recognised by the organisation as a political deviant — "Uncle Tom" or "Coconut". Grades of Aboriginality replaced former acceptance procedures in contemporary Aboriginal organisations or political processes. Mary was a fast learner, but she was a long way from becoming a hardened political operator of the Aboriginal movement.

Nevertheless, it was obvious to Mary that she was a favoured staff member, trusted to the letter to carry out instructions. Many more experienced staff members did not rank so highly. Yet Mary believed that allegations of cronyism were unfounded. In fact, the leadership had long memories for unfavourable incidents, particularly anything involving betrayal of their management or policy.

She learned to be extremely careful to respect the fact that work and family were inextricably linked. People had relatives everywhere. She saw how debts were paid out on those who gossiped out of context. "Remember, information is a valuable weapon": this was another of Johnno's homilies. He had others. "Been in the eye of the cyclone lately? Don't wait around for the wind to blow you away." — "Words travel faster on Telstra where family relationships are concerned." This was his oblique way of speaking.

With no family of her own, Mary's life was as solitary as it had been in the city. For reasons unknown to her, the few Aboriginal men she met along the way were unprepared to form a relationship that would last longer than a one-night stand of passionless penetration. She talked about the dilemma of her sex life to Johnno one night over the phone, during a friendly chat, his only response was: "Buggered if I know, Mary. Older men might be worth a try." He suggested she needed a mob of family in order to keep a young fella in line. And babies created a bond, he said. He had eight himself— "not all by the same wife," he laughed. Yes, he could laugh now, but it wasn't funny at the time, he said. When Mary mentioned Buddy she got nowhere. Just the enigmatic response: "Well, my dear, he was the acid test." End of conversation.

Try as she might to fit into the organisation, she was still alone at the end of the day. She had no family strength to back her in the life she had chosen for herself. She perceived a denial by Aboriginal people wherever she worked to accept her Aboriginality. She believed that if her life was to change for the better, she must gain their full acceptance. And this, she was certain, depended on finding her mother so that she could claim family and land affiliations.

It was Johnno, the father image, who introduced Mary to Pastor Delainy. Johnno had flown North to attend a regional agreement conference. He was to speak to the delegates about how their region could be included in a comprehensive agreement. The State had a policy of blocking land claims and most forms of Aboriginal autonomy — an offshoot of old-fashioned notions of State rights and total sovereignty over all matters. The State sold land to any foreign investor rather than allow Aboriginal people any involvement over resource development on their own land. Because of the need to set precedents, national headquarters of the organisation considered this conference very important.

Over a cup of coffee Johnno was explaining to Delainy the need for shared sovereignty. "No one in the world these days can claim the right to full sovereignty over land, resources or people," he was saying when he caught sight of Mary, wearing a blue dress. — It was time to do something about her situation, Johnno thought as he called her over.

"Mary, come and meet Pastor Delainy," he said, indicating the frail, white-haired man sitting beside him.

Mary shook the other man's hand. "Glad you could come, Pastor."

"Most folks just call me Delainy. I'm not much of a preaching man any more. Retired from it." Delainy looked at Mary with interest.

"Mary is one of our best workers, Delainy. You can count on her for anything."

"Good to hear of young people working hard. None of mine turned out well. Pack of bastards the lot of them. — Sorry for swearing, dear. But it's true. Makes me sick every time I think of the lazy mongrels. If I was younger I'd flog 'em. Used to do that. I'd chase them around with a stock-whip twice every Sunday. Even after they were grown up. Doctors say I got to take it easy now. That's why I gave up the preaching. It made me too angry, trying to save the wicked." Delainy broke off to cough hard and long, a smoker's cough. Saliva trickled from one corner of his mouth. He looked hard at Mary through his one remaining eye. The other one was made of glass. "You from these parts?" he barked, wiping away the drool. In the process the yellow discharge from his nose was wiped across his face.

Mary looked at him. She was terribly disappointed. All the people of this region she'd met so far were mean and hard. The women were big and hard, spitting chips at each other all that morning. A fight down the back lane had been temporarily postponed when Johnno asked her to tell the participants that the meeting was about to continue. When she said "Excuse me ..." they glared at her, then dusted themselves off and returned to the conference room. Participation in the conference had been silent so far. The men stood around in their oily Akubras, bent fags dangling from their lips. Most of the women had the dangling fags as well, even at the conference table. Unlit. Just dangling there. Men and women alike showed fighting scars. An ear missing, perhaps. Glass eyes. Lopped fingers. One had a missing arm, amputated at the elbow.

"Delainy is from St Dominic's," Johnno said, feeling pleased with his revelation.

"I know," Mary responded in a flat tone. She'd had great expectations — that was why she'd worn her blue satin dress.

Johnno turned to Delainy. "Mary was born there. Then fostered out. She is looking for her mother."

Delainy took a good hard look at Mary with his good eye. She did not remind him of anyone he could think of, he told Johnno. He tried to carry out a mental calculation of her age and where that would place her in the history of births and deaths at the former mission. His calculations were not correct, because Mary looked younger than her age — and much younger than survivors of her age-group who had grown up under mission conditions.

Mary, looking at his lopsided mouth with its continuous drool, hoped to Jesus he wasn't her father. Or that any of the fighting-hungry women here was her mother.

Delainy had a reputation for recognising family members. He might meet someone for the first time, particularly a younger person, and he could tell them straight away which families they belonged to anywhere in the Gulf country. He loved doing this and would chuckle to himself for hours, recalling the occasions when he had inadvertently fouled up. Sometimes his recognition of family came as a shock. Skeletons might be successfully locked in the cupboard for decades — until Delainy put his foot in it. He had caused a number of brawls and had often been threatened. More than once someone had wanted to kill him. But he was an old man now, a respected elder. People shrugged and accepted him for what he was, being a Pastor and all. There weren't many of his generation around these days.

"Maybe you should stay and work here for a while," Delainy suggested to Johnno and Mary. He chose not to challenge Johnno's political assertions, but he was suspicious of him all the same. He'd heard things about the way his organisation did business. They were a bit too sharp, mixed up with city gangsters, he'd heard. Arson in the cities — he'd seen it on TV. The city Blacks didn't understand how things worked up North. They just came in, spouted a whole lot of nonsense, then went away again. Just like the government people or politicians who would swoop past in their flash cars. Promise this and that, then they'd be off once more. Delainy didn't believe in anything he heard from strangers, including harebrained theories of autonomy. Autonomy! Where did it get Aboriginal people anyhow? They were too busy fighting among themselves. It had only got worse since the missionaries left. He wished they would come back. They all needed the Church. Being clean for God. Learning how to get into God's paradise was more important than destroying each other with booze, he thought.

Delainy couldn't believe it when he heard himself inviting them to stay up North. And this woman in the blue dress … he'd get it in a while, he told himself. If it was true she had been in St Dominic's. A lot of babies were taken away directly after they were born. The Church kept all the records. She could have been anyone's, he thought, staring at Mary all through the meeting for the rest of the day. He even speculated that she might be his, though he wasn't aware of any strays he'd fathered. Well, he thought, if they turned out like her, it was proof it was better for them to be taken away. You could tell churchpeople. They had a clean look about them. A sheen that glowed. They cleaned them-

selves up inside and out. Not like that other pack of bastards, his own mob included. He went on surveying Mary,
his good eye almost closed in his wrinkled face.

Johnno jumped at the invitation to St Dominic's. He
would send Mary up. She had clearly made an impression
on the old man, and that was all he needed. They had to
break the intransigence of Church and State influence in
this region. It remained about the most isolated and neglected area of all, until now pretty hard to get a foot in.
The old Christian soldiers still guarded the gate. State
influences, little incentives offered here and there, ensured
the community opposed outsiders pushing for stronger
autonomy. And then the State used the communities in the
region as a lever to maintain power over resource development, continuing to oppose Land Rights and recognition
of Aboriginal sacred sites.

Johnno was quick to make a firm arrangement with
Delainy. "We'll be up again quick as a wink," he said,
shaking Delainy's bony hand in his own plump palm.

"Well, let's see how it goes for a while," Delainy replied,
beginning to wonder about the implications of his invitation.

Johnno knew it would take some convincing to get Mary
up here. She seemed uninterested and said she had to
consider Jessie's schooling, now she was almost four.

"But Mary, these people are Jessie's kin," Johnno insisted. "It will be good for both of you."

Mary just looked at him and walked away.

PART IV
Plains of Papery Grass

16

Any twisty road in the northern Gulf country will take you through kilometres of gravel winding through plains of papery grasses. It is said that there is nowhere to go except to farther flung, yet more unimpressive destinations. After a while the grass reaches out to snare you if you are not careful; it is better to keep on driving your old ute in case the old Aboriginal man who lives anywhere at all comes into the car to sit down beside you. He follows cars at night; you can see his yellow eyes looking at you. He might spring out from a clump of grass; he might be sitting in the middle of the road.

Sometimes, driving along these roads late at night, a ghost car will suddenly appear in the distance. Its headlights beam ahead of you across the claypans but it takes ages to pass by. At other times the lights just fade away. This is scary country at night: you must keep going just in case. Finally an old rust-bucket of a truck passes by, travelling slowly, like an animal on the lookout for its prey. Over the tray dozens of dead kangaroos, looking like a pile of dead grey wood, weigh the vehicle down. But then the eyes of the dead creatures catch the light and shine like distant stars, and you can see tails and legs hanging over the side, almost to the ground.

If you tell the locals what you have seen along the road, they look around as though there must be invisible people watching them. "What time was it?" they ask in slow voices.

"You say you seen it again?" It's like a recurrent tune, hearing them talk. Why should the time matter? It's really a matter of indifference. You can tell the same story to someone else, changing the time, and they'll still have the same response. They'll tell you about a couple of brothers in the bush that married into the local Aboriginal tribe. They existed like hillbillies, kids and all, living off kangaroo meat. Real wild people. One day the rest of the family was murdered while the brothers were away. Wholesale slaughter. The brothers came back, saw what had happened and went crazy. They've travelled the roads looking for revenge ever since. Never finding the time to empty the stinking 'roo carcases off their truck. It happened over fifty years ago.

"Well! Those two must be dead by now, by crikey," the locals remark in a dreamlike state.

"By Jove, that old truck was old even then, wasn't it? They must've died out there somewhere — yet by all accounts it ain't over for them yet."

The significance of such stories is that although many people try to avoid going to the Gulf, once they get there, there's no turning around. So you go on and on without reaching any particular destination yet unable to break the spell that binds people to stay there until they die.

Johnno Scott used to tell these sort of stories about the Gulf country. He'd come to believe in them. He'd tell them when he spoke of Mary and the many months it took to move her to St Dominic's.

"Why the hell won't you go?" Johnno would ask her impatiently in his weekly phone call. Mary unnerved him but he impressed himself for not losing his temper with her over the issue. It was worse when she stayed silent at the other end of the line. Moments would pass. He would imagine he'd lost the line. *Tap, tap, tap* with his finger on the mouthpiece. Nothing. He'd always end up asking if she was still there. She got him each time. *Bloody scary woman*, he thought, wondering why Buddy had got so hung up about her. He almost began to think of her as though she was a bogeywoman of the Gulf roads. Mary gave her usual practical reasons for not wanting the transfer to St Dominic's. Telling a few lies if necessary. The truth was, she felt uneasy about going there.

Sometimes Johnno went on about the lack of Land Rights in the Gulf. "You know, the poor buggers don't even have matchbox Land Rights. You know what I mean. Not even room to swing a cat. Not even room to bury themselves — the government even makes them pay for that. It's time to count the beans, Mary. It's time the beans paid dividends." This last remark Mary interpreted as a veiled threat concerning staff performance, as measured by Johnno.

"Don't you want to know your own people?" he'd ask her. She wished he'd stop the jargon and leave her alone. She never told him that the people she'd met at the conference had unnerved her. — "Can't you see they'll be happy to have you back?" Johnno persisted. Mary felt quite certain that would not be the case. The truth of the matter was that she felt superior to the yokels she had met there. Any feeling of empathy, which she normally had with people in their communities, was entirely lacking. — "You got to do this for Jessie": another of Johnno's tactics. Obviously those people were her relatives in some degree, but she felt a loathing for them. As an Aboriginal person she knew her feelings should be very different, and she thought of Buddy's total acceptance of his family. She knew about the importance of families and family connections. Yet she felt nothing where these people were concerned. She kept her feelings to herself. There was no one she could trust sufficiently to discuss the problems she was experiencing in identifying with her Aboriginality.

Finally, Johnno coopted Lesley to clinch the matter. He was determined to foster the prospect of pan-Aboriginality

in the Gulf. He was worried about the organisation as it
rumbled along under his leadership. Since Buddy's departure it had become an ever-weakening force. Places like St
Dominic's were being used by his opponents to undermine
his own leadership. It was a case of win — or face defeat.
Mary did not understand what was happening, but he knew
someone who did. Lesley, the good-time girl, an image of
black beauty combined with trendy efficiency, and a special
talent for carrying out particular jobs. Lesley had been away
for months overseas, and had only recently returned to the
office in Victory Lane.

"Mary knows her own mind," she warned Johnno. She
was pleased with his offer of travel and the chance to see
her old friend, but she knew Mary was no fool. "She'll smell
a rat as soon as I get there." She knew Mary's power of
analysing a situation.

"Just do your best," Johnno told her, his words cutting a
double edge.

Mary's present location was a provincial city on the eastern
seaboard where the rain drizzled more often than there
were clear days. She had become used to her life and felt
quite comfortable with the distance and isolation from the
power brokers of the Coalition's headquarters.

Now she was amazed when Lesley walked into her office.
She had just switched off the lights and was about to leave
the darkened building. She hadn't seen Lesley for years and
now she had suddenly materialised.

Lesley laughed. "Gotcha! Didn't expect a blast from the
past, did you, Mary?"

Mary smiled and gave her a big hug. "What are you doing
here? The latest I'd heard was that you were travelling
around overseas with some French or Polish bloke. Half
your luck."

"You can't always believe what you hear. He was Dutch,

and he ended up being a big pain in the butt. So — how've you been?"

"So-so. Can't complain. I run around a lot. I've a live-in woman who helps with Jessie. It's such a surprise to see you! You on a job, or just passing through?"

"Bit of both. I'm here for a few days." Lesley knew she wouldn't be able to fudge it for long.

"Johnno?"

"Johnno."

"Mmmm. Thought so." Mary lapsed into a sombre mood, and started to outline her case. "Why doesn't he listen? *One* — I'm a single mother. *Two* — I have a child nearing school age. I can't keep running about the country. *Three* — I have a responsibility to see that Jessie has somewhere to live, with the security of one place and one parent at least ..."

Lesley cut her off in mid-sentence. "Let's go out, Mary." *For God's sake,* she thought, *who wanted to know.* She knew Mary was all fired up to explode into the same old story that most of her black women friends told about their failed relationships with men.

Mary organised a baby-sitter over the phone. Lesley had borrowed a car. She drove past the docks, where container ships reflected the last glimmer of sunset in streams of slime over their rusted paintwork. She parked the car up a narrow alley behind dilapidated terrace houses with broken windows. Such a deserted location was definitely not Mary's style. Lesley said she needed a moment to see an old flame. "Haven't seen him for years," she told Mary. She gave three sharp beeps of the horn, and a moment later they both jumped at the sudden slap on the car bonnet.

"Boat people!" Lesley whispered to Mary as she wound down the window with a grin on her face.

A good-looking man was standing beside the car, at Lesley's side. Soon half of his long body was inside the window, wound around Lesley in a passionate embrace.

Mary, with pangs of longing for strong, long arms, thought he might be Vietnamese. "He doesn't speak any English," Lesley told her. Mary watched the man burrow his head into Lesley's neck while he reached one hand down the front of her dress.

"Wait for me. This won't take long," Lesley told Mary, interrupting the embrace and jerking away from her lover. The two of them extracted themselves from the car, rejoined outside, and departed through a maze of broken fences.

Mary waited a good half-hour, checking her watch constantly, flicking on the car's interior light. She sat in the dark listening to loose fence panels snapping in the wind. Down the alley, cats were fighting. Mary became worried — freaked out, in fact. "I'll tell her where to get off, bloody tart, as soon as she gets back," Mary growled to herself. Then she'd get Lesley to drive into the city and take a taxi home. Home to the sanity of her life and her child. (A sanity clouded now by the recurring vision of that wandering Vietnamese hand.) Insane Lesley! Insane organisation! They came into her life without notice, always finding ways to dominate her while she tried to maintain a separation from them. She knew the separation was necessary to stop her blood from racing wild, her mind from working overtime. To keep the devils away in the middle of the night. The dreams of being lost in the traffic, unable to get home … the homeward train whistling past at incredible speed, with faces of strangers staring out at her, leaving her stranded on an abandoned platform in an unknown city.

The squeal of tyres up the far end of the lane broke into her reverie. Headlights tore into her vision as the car roared towards her. It swayed sideways as it braked to prevent a head-on collision. A group of hooded youths jumped out. Mary realised they were armed with knives. They crouched forward as they ran, and began circling Lesley's white car. Mary felt the blood drain from her face as they forced open the door and dragged her outside. She was slammed face-down on the bonnet of Lesley's car. A hand held down her head. Fingers were jammed into her face. Her hands and legs were tied, she was blindfolded and gagged. Then she heard a man screaming. Lesley screaming. Then a sudden pain in her head. She realised she'd been hit, then the quiet resounded inside her skull. During lapses into semi-consciousness she was aware of shaky movements, of being inside a car travelling at high speed.

The car stopped. A hand ran lightly over her clothes, smoothed her cheek. A deep voice whispered in her ear: "I think we're home, Mary. Be a good girl, won't you? Don't call the police." The cords that bound her were undone and she was led to the door of her own house. "Very nice little girl in the photograph, just like her mumma. Jessie is a nice name, too." It seemed he was looking at her Medibank card. Was that a threat — might something happen to Jessie if she didn't keep quiet? "Goodnight, Mary. Maybe we'll keep in touch. No police, remember?" Then the car sped off while Mary, full of fear and hurt, let go of her feelings by kicking at the front door.

"I'm out, Johnno, I quit." Mary poured more of her hurt into the phone late that night, after she had calmed down enough, stopped shaking and gathered her wits sufficiently to tell someone what had happened. She still half-expected her door to crash open at any moment.

"Trust me, I'll fix it." Johnno's response was soothing. She would never have admitted she needed to hear him say that. He spoke slowly, effectively. "Take a break, leave town, have a holiday back here with Jessie, then go for a few months to St Dominic's. Get to know your own people. It will be safe up there."

This time they reached agreement. Mary figured she needed to regain strength in her life. How she used to be before the death of her adoptive parents. She had become both dependent upon and empowered by the organisation, but she had a greater sense of loneliness and being separate: she had lost the ability to trust either herself or others. She finally told Johnno that she did need to acknowledge her family. To connect the threads and overcome her intuitive fear of the unknown.

"Then leave if you want to," he said.

As before, she left in the morning, and the organisation cleaned up in her wake. Just as she was going out of the door the phone rang. Long distance.

An urgent voice: "Mary, are you alright?" It was Lesley.

"What about you?" Mary found herself almost speechless. Her earlier anger was gone, along with her rehearsed words of disapproval. She had feared for a friend perhaps murdered. She felt that she had reached a crisis point in her relationship with Lesley. No apparent harm had been done. Yet wounds of the heart take too long to heal.

"No worries!" Lesley said. "Sorry, Sis. I can't talk about it right now. One day when we catch up again … Best you leave town for a while, anyway. See you soon. Love." The phone clicked.

17

With the wind behind her, Jessie Doolan raced up the gravel road that wound its way through the lemon-coloured grasses. Long dead grass rustling its stems in the discordant winds of September. She was unbridled by reason. It could not be otherwise than to run with the wind, to belt up the road breathless, without care, the full sun shining straight into her face: as if to arrive half a minute later would be too late. The short burst of energy it took to reach her self-appointed destination, to run that far in the heat seemed entirely worthwhile.

Forty or so crows that usually frequented the neighbourhood were perched in the old rivergums next to the road. Now they had Jessie to contend with.

"Git! Go on" she yelled up to them. The trees looked downwards from the sun, and so did the crows parked well out of her reach. "Bloody crows!" Her nostrils burned from the running, forcing her to blow her nose hard and rub the runny discharge a few times over the back of her hand.

"*Auk! Auk!*" chorused the crows.

"You want to git it I'm tellin' you. Git. While you got a chance."

"*Auk! Auk!*"

"Christ, youse are dumb. Dumb crows," — muttering, while she wiped her hand over the back of her new red shorts.

"Yuk!"

"*Auk!*"

"Auuu — uk off. Go on!" she screamed over and over, but still no crow gave flight from the white branches high above.

She was left with no choice but to take drastic measures. She dropped to the ground on her spindly legs and began to scamper around on her haunches, a bit like a crow herself. Her hands slid around in the loose dirt to select the missiles — hot, dusty, red stones. The right ones. Those you can hold easily between a small finger and thumb. Good size shanghai stones.

Mary Doolan walked slowly in her thonged feet, some distance back. She watched her child's brightly coloured clothes shimmering through a heat mirage wafting up from the road. Thongs were not the most practical footwear; her feet ached. Another whirly spun thousands of seeds from the dry grasses into the air, gusting and swishing across her face. The harvest wind joined the mirage to create a further barrier against a clear view of the road. The child had disappeared altogether this time.

But the woman could hear the determined young voice cursing the crows, wafting up from the grasses. The maternal connection was intact over the space of a barren road between them. She stopped to survey the situation. Forced to squint, she peered ahead with the side of her hand across her forehead. She slapped dead several stray flies that hadn't moved fast enough. Hundreds were free-riding on her back. As she dusted them off, she watched the dying insects convulsing on the ground, their broken bodies spinning around. She walked on. In her mind she was deciding whether she should call out to the child. *Not yet — she knows how to look after herself. I can't be there all the time.*

The crows fussed and hopped, exchanging gossip on the branches of the narrow-leafed gums. They had lived in the area for several generations. A bit like the town where the woman and child had spent the night, with its staunch families who gave no leeway to outsiders.

"Auk! Auk! — look at her."

"What's she doing here?"

"What she here for?"

"How long are you staying ... dear?" The town's busybody had asked Mary, wondering whether the town was being overrun by more of them yella fellas from the city.

"*Auk! Auk!*"

Mary remembers someone telling her once that crows pair for life, and look after their young for a very long time. Children. Uncles and Aunts. Grandparents, great grandparents maybe. Cousins, brothers. No possibility of divorce. No losing your parents or someone you care about. A real traditional, tribal life. All sitting up high in the gum tree together. Resting in the heat of the day, talking about crow matters ...

"Yep! Not much happening under what they call a change of government around here."

"You can say that again. Wouldn't remember what their own political party stood for even if they fell over it. Nothing there for the family man. You can tell that simply by looking at the pickings around here. Don't need much of a brain to sort that out, hey?"

"Survey the rubbish bins. A sure test of rising interest rates, mortgage losers, marginal losses on the all ords, lopsided economies."

"*Auk! Auk!*"

"Well, that's right. Still, what can you do. Beggars can't be choosers, can they? With all them half-castes, radical types from the city walking around town here dressed up better than us. Half of 'em are living off our taxes."

"No wonder things are always getting worse."

Lost in a parody of narrow-minded country towns, Mary felt some empathy, if only momentarily, for the predicament of black crows. The parallels of discrimination. Same as Murries. No Land Rights. No Crow Rights. Stereotypes the same. Black is negative. Stands for *no*. Crows are negative. Even if they have a family life. Similar to an Aboriginal community, tribe, kin-group. But crows were blacker, and as far as Mary was concerned it didn't matter who discriminated against them. She had hated crows for longer than she could remember (Norman was the only exception). It didn't matter if Jessie learned to hate them too.

The child shoots up from the ground amidst the swarming flies disturbed for the first time in days. Crow girl visible again. Ready and taking aim. Left bony arm, reaching up in a straight line from her head. Other hand gripping the neatly cut fork of the shanghai. Left hand stretching back as far as it could pull the black rubber sling joining the patch that held the right-sized red stone. Perfect.

Jessie's eyes darkened into a squint, concentrating, selecting, focusing on the one crow at that moment making a sound. She waited. Still. Only the flies buzzed around her face, separating her human smell from the rest of the bush. She waited for the right moment. The bird stopped squawking and looked down at the small statue in red. "What? Me?" *Now. Pow*! Stone released. Missile firing upwards.

Crow girl yells. The crows scatter. Black magic wings flap wildly, swoop low above the child's head, beady eyes analysing the image in the collective memory. Black feathers attached and unattached polka-dot the sky and the road.

The shanghai that Mary had made for Jessie earlier that day from a branch of a young gum tree has worked.

Mary allows herself a smile.

The group of Murri kids approaching from the opposite direction stand some distance away and watch what's happening. They yell out to Jessie to stop as they ran up to her. The first to arrive, a couple of girls some years older than Jessie, shout: "What you think you're doing?" Jessie is frightened. The rest of the kids arrive and are closing in around her. Her instant fear is of being locked in and beaten. Reasoning with the enemy is beyond her. She looks around in vain for her mother. She says nothing but hears her small heart thumping loud. She wonders if these kids can hear it too and will start laughing at her cowardice.

"What did them crows do to you, hey?" The bigger kids demand, while the smaller ones deliver shoves.

Nothing. Only her eyes respond with the swell of tears that begin to leak down from the corners of her eyes. Jessie was embarrassed that she cried so easily. The tears end up as dirty droplets on the parched dirt.

"Hey, dummy? We's talkin' to youse." They shout over each other at her although they are standing only centimetres away.

Nothing. The group stare at the relatively clean-skinned Murri girl in her bright clothes. And compare them with their own from the bin at St Vinnies. They have identical hair styles, courtesy of the winds. Young faces grimy with dirt set in the tracks made by tears from days gone by.

Arms reaches out to give the dummy a few more shoves. "Lost your tongue? Come on. We's askin' you — why you shootin' at our crows? Come on. Don't belong to you. Miss High-and-Mighty. What you gotta say for yourself, then?"

As Mary draws closer she can see what is happening. She feels drained. The surge of panic rushes through her body and out of the pores in her armpits. She finds herself running with surprising fitness towards the commotion coming from the small bend in the road. She almost falls on top of the little group before the children notice her.

"What do you think you're doing!" she screams as she lunges in and grabs her child to her side. "You leave her alone. Go on. Pick on your own size if you want to have a fight." She speaks quickly, trying to regain her composure, still breathless from running.

Jessie's four years of life, all it had been, tumbled out of her now in loud wails of crying. Her mother bent down to hold her but was unable to stop what she knew took so long to let go. She, too, felt the urge to cry but held back the tears — *Think of why we are here. Think of what you have got to do. Don't cry. Not now. Not in front of these kids. Probably his relatives. Cruel little bastards.* Her mind raced on way past where she was now, to where she had been and where she wanted to go. Nothing better than self-reprimand. She was able to regain her composure.

"We sorry, lady," the eldest child told Mary in honesty, although the smaller ones stood back with broad, shameless smirks across their faces.

Glaring at their defiant faces Mary could almost see herself turning around to walk back. Right away. She hit out at herself — *God, it was a mistake. A bloody mistake that's costing a packet, to come to this place. Why did I think I could bring Jessie out here with this lot?*

"It's alright," she said firmly, fighting reason, as she wiped Jessie's face with a clean tissue. She looked at the group and said matter of factly, if coldly, "It's alright."

"We's not allowed to touch the crows," said one child of about Jessie's age. Others joined in. "We're not even supposed to look at them." — "That's why" — "They can be dangerous. But these ones are our friends."

Jessie started to recover. From the comfort of her mother she retorted: "But they frighten away the little birds and I'm not frightin' of crows. They aren't dangerous."

"You wanna bet?"

"What can they do?"

The children from the old Reserve looked at one another and straight at Mary. They are surprised she does not say something to stop her smart aleck daughter. She is as brown-skinned, as "coloured" as themselves. Dark but well-dressed in her flash floral sundress. She is carrying a large brown-and-gold vinyl carryall but wearing thongs.

Mary had decided to wear the cheap footwear picked up for a few dollars in town. It would save her good sandals from the gravel road and red dust. She didn't want to appear flash. And she knew what the road to the Aboriginal side of town was usually like. Murries could not afford to pay rates nor were they on town councils, so their roads were bypassed, even though the one or two main streets in town were resurfaced on a yearly basis. Same all across the country.

But these kids knew the difference. They were not easily fooled by appearances. The smooth evenness of Mary's skin said she was different — flash. Her haircut was definitely not how Auntie Josie would do it for the ones who thought themselves the "flash women" at home. Auntie did everyone's hair: men, women, kids; and charged everyone a dollar. She could dye women's hair, tint short ends gold — even if it all ended up looking dreadful on the oily-skinned girls with pimples, once their mousse-glued strands collected the dust around them. Not even those white people in town, with a proper hairdresser, had hair cut like Mary's. And there was Jessie with her long hair. Girls were not allowed to have long hair here.

The woman and child were Murries alright, but not from anywhere around this place.

"Crows can make people die," came the slow, guarded answer to Jessie's question.

Jessie smiled. Her eyes were red from crying. She took a good look around the empty trees, wishing there were more crows she could stone. No one could say anything to her now her mother was here.

The Reserve group stared back, wondering if the child had any ability to understand anything at all.

Mary released her hold of Jessie and asked the kids if they knew if Buddy Doolan was around.

"Yep. That's my uncle" — "And mine" — "Mine too" — "He's uncle of all of us. He's here. What you want him for?"

"You sure he's here — today?" Mary asked again.

"Sure. Just seen him a minute ago. He's down the Walducks."

And this was how Jessie received her first introduction to any of her father's relatives since she was a baby. Kids were usually pleased to be united with blood kin. Jessie despised her cousins for what they had managed to do to her. The power their bullying tactics and laughter had over her. She could not remember ever bullying another human being. She wouldn't know how to begin. Mary had told her to be kind to everyone.

She remembered long ago her mother saying, "Be kind to people, Jessie" when all around her were desert kids with snotty noses who looked like they never had a bath and had no intention of playing with her. Instead they called her names she couldn't understand. But Mary didn't have time to notice the other kids taunting her daughter. All she said was to play with them and not to humbug her while she was busy. Jessie thought it over again now. — *How could I have played with them. Played what? They didn't even speak English. Mummy didn't care. If she did she'd know I was frightened, but she only got angry with me all the time and told me not to make her shame.*

Jessie clung by her mother's side as they continued their way to the town's former Aboriginal reserve where her father now lived. Some of the cousins raced off ahead to spread the news. Others restrained themselves and stayed behind as escorts, out of politeness. A bit for Uncle Buddy's sake and a bit for the lady walking alone.

Mary wished she could have made the unspectacular visit she had been mentally planning for some time. In and out is all she wanted. Do her business and leave quickly. Now she felt the visit was going to turn into a nightmare. — *It's going to be another of those vulgar times whenever I have to see the man. Only this time with every one of his damn relatives milling around.* She was alarmed at her own inability to remain detached.

"Let go my hand, Jessie," she said quickly, her temper surfacing. She snatched her hand from the child's tight grasp. "It's too hot and you're big enough to walk by yourself."

"Fat bum bitch," hissed the child under her breath.

It was too late to turn around, too far back to town. Mary could just picture Jessie whingeing all the way back again. Did she had enough mental reserve to persevere with gentle encouragement? No.

The child let her hand drop awkwardly down by her side: it felt uncomfortable not having anything to hold onto. She tried another familiar tactic, taking hold of the back of Mary's dress in the hope of not being noticed. Mary persevered with this for a short while until she began to feel the typical dragging that signified Jessie's endless need to be propelled along. She gave her dress a sharp jerk and Jessie was left to fall back and walk alone, some distance behind the little entourage moving up the dusty road.

The vicinity of the old reserve became obvious to Mary as they passed broken-down car bodies strewn on either side of the road and left to rust. Some showed signs of temporary habitation: green garbo bags flagging in the wind had been used to provide privacy for the occupants from outside elements. Perhaps young lovers looking for time out from overcrowding, with twenty or more inside whatever housing existed on the reserve.

Corrugated iron pinned across other car bodies with thick gauge wire and held down by rocks helped to create the much needed shelter for "drunken people". Those who wanted a chance to see things differently but were not tolerated inside the biggest social experiment in the world. Beer bottles: broken, intact, splattered, all brands, lay everywhere amongst paper, cartons and assorted plastic containers. The socially engineered Aboriginal community — the result of decades of government interference.

As they passed through this wonderland of nonconformist reality, Jessie's heart raced at the discoveries unfolding one after another on this long walk her mother had told

her would be special. Fascinated with these special mysteries, she was overcome by the urge to explore the car bodies,
but not wanting to lag behind too far, she made the effort
to keep up with the others. She knew Mary didn't like to
backtrack looking for her all the time. "Keep up, child!"
she would yell when in a stern mood. When she said "child"
instead of "Jessie" she meant business. She would usually
wait for her to catch up no matter how far ahead she had
got. But you could count on Mary never to go back for
anyone, anything, including Jessie.

Instead of exploring, Jessie decided to make a collection
of the bits and pieces of smooth, rounded, glass of various
colours that lay everywhere, glistening with light caught
from the sun. Pieces of springs from clocks were collectable
as well as the systematic boards with colourful wires from
broken-down and ripped-apart transistors. Dead beetles
with shiny bodies and parrots' feathers were also picked up
to give to her special mother later on, all carefully placed in
the plastic bag that carried her shanghai and a few leftovers
from the snacks Mary had bought her before leaving town
on this special walk to see her dad. Yet even the excitement
of seeing this father she barely knew, her real father, could
barely be sustained over the heat and distance.

There was nothing to show they had arrived at their
destination. Just a high fence laced with barbed wire. Probably there was a sign years ago, when the place was run by
state authorities. Most likely it would have stated "Burkes-
ville Aboriginal Compound, by Authority of the State Department for the Care and Protection of Aborigines" —
something like that, Mary thought.

Now she waited for the dawdling Jessie to catch up while
she wondered why such a high fence had been left there.
It was obvious from the extensive rust patches that the fence
was originally a part of the protectionist era of a few decades
ago. Its purpose to keep Aboriginal people inside and white
people out. Both. One could never be too careful. The

voices of authority, for the sake of decency, for the good of the town, for the prevention of disease, would have been well pleased when the fence was brand-new. Such were the echos of the good old days — when you could do something about your Blacks being an eyesore around town.

Now the fence was left standing to keep white people, small-town yobbos, outside, particularly at night, when the young hoons like to imagine themselves gung ho as Ku Klux Klansmen, trying out things like throwing petrol bombs into the houses where children slept. Or firing an odd round or two of rifle shots for practice or the sport of it on their drunken way out, driving their revved-up Falcon utes, flashlights blinding, to go and shoot up the 'roos.

"Hurry up, Jessie!" Mary called, feeling the heat, wanting to be out of it, watching the child take her time, with her bag of excuses for not mixing in with the other kids. The bag she knew she would be lumbered with on the way home.

"Mummy! I found something for you," announced Jessie on arrival.

"Not now, Jessie. Come on. Show me later," was the impatient reply, cutting short Jessie's chance for a breather, as Mary started to move off again across the fence line. Into the home of ex-lover, ex-husband, ex-father of Jessie — dirty rotten cheating bastard, Buddy Doolan.

What a life, Mary thought. Chaos all around. The ramshackle ruins referred to as houses, assorted small tin humpies with broken glass windows. So this was the real Buddy. The true Aboriginal. Something he pushed into my face, night and day she thought. No one could beat Buddy, understand anything the way he could. He came from an Aboriginal reserve and only people like him who come from an Aboriginal reserve really knew what it was like. According to Buddy.

— God, I'm sick of people like that, she thought. *The bloody know-alls. No wonder we can't get it together and get*

anywhere when all we do is argue about how much more oppressed
we are than each other.

She smiled to herself at the cynicism of the whole thing.
It was rather amusing for a race of people to have stooped
so low on the oppressors' terms and money and to have
created their own secular power bases, cheap and nasty,
based on a competition about who was the most oppressed
and most severely dispossessed. Reduced to grovelling after
government like a bunch of beggars.

She speculated on where Buddy stood in the beggar
games these days now he was living in his home community
away from the city. Would he still be pushing the community line, living under a system of community control which
he had always espoused as the correct way of doing things?
Community — what a welfare term, she thought.

The children turned up a side road and continued on,
past the stares of onlookers and free-ranging chooks. Dogs
began to bark from every house or dwelling. People must
own several dogs each. Other dogs snarled as they lurked
inside dark holes under the floorboards of their owners'
houses. Others sprang out of their holes and started running and circling around: brown, black, white, all colours
and sizes, but invariably ugly, with sharp teeth. Mary
grabbed Jessie's hand and tugged her close, using her vinyl
bag as a shield, and together they frog-marched ahead. Now
she was thankful for their escort — the kids who knew how
to deal with the local pack.

"Gone, you dogs. Git outta 'ere!" they threatened in loud
voices.

"Gone! Where's a stick? Give me a stick, someone." A
huge bamboo stick was found and the dogs were sent
howling, cowering, tails between legs, back to their dingy
hideaways along with a flurry of stones and rocks.

Buddy Doolan had moved on several times that morning
doing his social rounds. He wasn't down at the Walducks'
camp on the bank high above the river bed, through the

cut in the back fence and along a zigzagging track that led away from the rest of the community. So they trooped through mazes of other narrow footpaths barely visible through the long buffalo grass, through camp after camp. Some had seen him, some had not.

Mary felt exhausted and annoyed. She could not believe this grand parade was necessary. At each place she and Jessie would be introduced, and Jessie would back off from over-zealous, stranger-relatives. This was just like Buddy, never to be where you expected to find him. Wasn't it always like that? Buddy never at home. Never where you needed him. Buddy so responsible — yet responsible for nothing.

One track eventually led to a grove of mangro trees in full blossom, their fragrance filling the surrounding hot air with its sweet pungency, while the tiny flower heads opened up to the buzz of working bees. This is where Buddy was finally found, along with some of his brothers, cousin-brothers and uncle-fathers, partaking in the serious business of the card game. What else would he be doing, Mary thought.

She could see his face as she approached. Expression serious. Brown hair, curly and longer than usual. Still the handsome one. Momentarily, she allowed sentiment to take over. The same way it had happened when she'd first met him years ago, when they started working together. Knocked overboard into the sticky, sordid mess which he, and only he, could control. Quickly she pulled herself together. — *Times have changed, lady.* Bringing up the guard in her imagination was a huge woman in steel armour who announced in a voice of thunder: *"What did the prick ever do for you expect fuck you and leave you holding the bundle?"* Mary responded likewise — *"I wouldn't even give him the opportunity. Bastard."*

When Buddy looked up at the approaching figures rustling through the grassy track the first thing he saw was Mary's icy stare looking directly through him. It sent a shiver up and down his bare back, finally settling to form a tight ball choking in his throat.

From thin blankets spread over the ground, the cross-legged brothers, cousin-brothers and assorted uncles looked up at that icy stare as it approached. They said nothing, realising it was the sort of look all Buddy's jilted women usually gave him. They knew it had nothing to do with them, and after a few uncomfortable moments they continued with their game. Best not to notice these things, although they all had identical thoughts about who this one was. Flash, too. But all eyes determinedly concentrated on the dealt cards in front of them.

"You took a chance coming here," said Buddy as he slowly rose to his feet. "Might have missed me altogether."

Mary waited moments before responding: "I knew you'd be here. You live here now, don't you?" Chisel cutting steel.

Buddy did not reply but remained standing in the exact spot where he had been sitting. Across from the sitting card players. Across from where Mary stood.

"Good to see you anyway, Mary," he said at last with some honesty.

Normally Mary would have shrugged her shoulders at a remark like that. Who cared what the "anyway" meant? "I brought Jessie to see you."

Buddy's eyes etched the question *why* into Mary's face, then turned to the small child trying not to be seen behind her mother's skirt. His own child. He had not even noticed her. She was very like the cousins gathered around, his nieces and nephews of about Jessie's age.

Jessie watched the strange man put on a worn checked shirt before moving around the card players. Meanwhile, an old black man with a wrinkled forehead was looking at her hard while rolling a cigarette. Slowly he finished the job and popped the cigarette into one yellow-stained corner of his red lips. He was trying to remember where he had seen the girl's face before ... seeing the brown water lapping the shores of his traditional country. Jessie's gaze was transfixed by the old man's as he struck his match without looking at his hands. The red flame shone above his nicotine-stained fingers while he lit the cigarette.

Buddy snatched up his daughter to hug her, calling her his little Sultana Princess, a nickname Mary hated which he had given her at birth. Jessie hung limply. She was not used to physical expressions of affection towards her except from her mother. She tried to see what the old man was doing and to hold her breath at the same time, so as not to smell the odour of sweat and alcohol that personified most of the men she knew. Certainly it was a trademark of the man now holding her.

"We found her, Uncle Buddy. Stonin' our crows she was," announced the cousins.

Those on the blankets raised their eyes to focus on the mother. Jessie stared at the old man, who had looked away and was now concentrating on his cards. A sudden change to his morning's winnings … now his hand held misfortune.

"Shouldn't do that, honey. Bring bad spirits," said Buddy lightly. Quickly he continued to introduce his daughter and Mary to his next-of-kin.

"Want to finish the game, Buddy?"

"Not now. I'll come back later. Better go up to Moodie's for now."

Mary allowed herself to follow him silently, to watch his tall, slim frame as he walked ahead of the others, Jessie high on his shoulders, to Moodie's, his Auntie's place. Jessie felt like flying. If only she could stand up she would use his shoulders as a launching pad and fly away to the moon! A special journey she had frequently undertaken in her mind. Mary saw the goats, dog-collared, eating the long grass at Moodie's place. They raised their heads to stare at her daughter. It sent shivers through her. Their eyes looked at her in funny ways is what Jessie always told her. Goats always did that to her.

Moodie was home, an older woman with greying hair surrounded by a lot of kids. There too was Molly — Buddy's new woman? Introduced simply as Molly. A young woman heavy with child. Mary thought she appeared disturbed by the intrusion of a part of Buddy's past. She stared at Mary and Jessie with an empty expression.

"How long will you be staying?" Buddy asked. It was probably what Molly wondered too.

"Not long," Mary replied, glancing at her watch, trying to make the appropriate gestures of formal distance between herself and Buddy, to maintain family stability for the other woman's sake.

They all sat down with cups of tea and Mary listened to idle chitchat and irate voices until Buddy announced his departure. No one inquired about her or Jessie so she offered nothing. Buddy said he had some work he'd promised to do with his brothers. He would be back in a while.

"You can stay here as long as you want," he announced at the door to everyone in the room. Full of the same old Buddy responsibility, covering years of separation as if nothing had happened in the meantime.

Mary just looked at him. Blood draining from her face. A feeling of dizziness passed through her body. Something that happened whenever she was taken by surprise. She still could not accept his casualness. *How can I respond to him and keep any dignity? How to say yes, thank you, I will, to the one person who might have wanted to know what had happened in my life?*

A passing vehicle going back to town presented the quickest opportunity to escape meaningless politeness with the relatives. Mary and Jessie had the night train to catch. They must both go. No chance of leaving the child with her father for a while. People like Jessie had to forfeit next-of-kin while passing through this world.

18

It had been a big mistake to think she could leave Jessie with her father. She thought of their train trip away before leaving for the Gulf. Buddy had pursued them to the train when they left, argued with her on the platform. The pregnant girl had nothing to do with him, he claimed. As if it mattered to her any more, Mary thought. There was almost a tug of war over Jessie as they boarded the train. Buddy's face was set in stone, his eyes staring hard at Mary as the train left the station.

Later on the DC9, with Jessie curled up asleep beside her, Mary looked down on green veins crisscrossing the brown plains. Land she felt she knew although she had never been there. After the plane touched down at the airstrip Mary made inquiries and was told that the "old fella", Delainy, was up at his house. Jessie was whingeing with the heat and had to be carried in one arm while Mary checked her neatly piled-up luggage. Mary felt the heat herself. Then the camp dogs started a fight and scattered the luggage. Finally someone with a truck took her up to Delainy's house. Mary sat up front. Jessie on her lap. Some other passengers from the plane sat in the back with the luggage and freight. They drove over corrugated streets with the dogs snapping at their wheels, past tired-looking houses and other makeshift dwellings. People were dropped off along the way, and finally Mary and Jessie were left outside a tropical house on stilts built in the 1970s, surrounded by pawpaws and banana trees. One stunted mango tree with a few wrinkling yellow leaves stood isolated in the middle of the front yard.

After the truck departed there was silence. The house was quiet. Mary found a tap at the bottom of the veranda steps and sprinkled some water over Jessie and herself. The light breeze on their wet skin gave new life.

"Anyone home?" Mary called out several times. There was no answer.

They went under the house to sit in the shade, and there Mary found Delainy asleep on a bed. She sat on a chair, deciding what she should do, while Jessie played in the dirt. It seemed pointless to wake the old man. Was she to sit out the three months? Or three days, until the next plane out?

Some time later the old man stirred on the bed. It wasn't his movements but his moaning that alerted Mary. She went over to him, expecting him to get up. But Delainy lay still. Only his eyes flickered. Mary stood there uncertainly, looking around, hoping someone would come. A moment later, she saw a young couple come out of a house across the street. They walked over to her.

"Victor's the name. This is my sister, Victoria. You know Dad?" He looked down at Delainy.

"Yes. I met him at a conference earlier this year. Is he alright?"

"Nope. He had a stroke on the plane, coming home from that conference. Can't move or talk. He should be in hospital, I suppose, but the family knew he'd rather be here, so we brought him home."

Mary looked down at Delainy. His eyes glared at her. She looked away. He scared her. She put an arm around Jessie and distanced herself from the bed. Victor propped his father up, putting pillows behind him. Victoria said she would get some food for him. Victor sat in an orange plastic chair beside the bed. Mary sat on another. She explained that she'd come here to set up an office for the Coalition, as agreed by her boss and Delainy. Victor was surprised, because he knew his father didn't agree with the politics of the organisation, with its pan-Aboriginal expectations of united action. His father had always been a regional man.

"You certain of this?" he asked Mary.

"Well, I wouldn't be here unless it had been arranged first. We don't just barge into a place. But if there's a misunderstanding, I'll leave as soon as I can." She felt uneasy, hanging around in the middle of nowhere with no place to stay. Would she and Jessie have to stay in Delainy's house? What should she do? She felt she could kill Johnno and all the rest of them. Or, perhaps she could last a few weeks somewhere without a job.

Victor shook his head. "No. You may as well hang around until we sort something out. Tomorrow I'll see what we can fix up. I'm on the Council, and as far as I'm concerned, it might be a good opportunity to have someone like you around. We need to be looking at all the options for more self-determination. I believe we should have more control, some autonomy over our lives."

Mary started to relax … so long as she avoided looking at Delainy. Victor noticed the way his father was looking at Mary. The old man grew more agitated when Victoria came back and tried to spoon-feed him the soup she had prepared. In the end she simply said "Bugger you, Dad," and ate the soup herself. Victor kept on talking about the state of the community and what they were trying to do to improve things. He spoke about the frustration they were expecting with one government department or another. Then other members of the family came over with their kids, and the brother and sister took Mary and Jessie to their new home.

It was an old fibro cottage raised on blocks, its wall ingrained with the red stain of mud from many seasons of tropical rains. The oleander shrubs around it and the house itself were covered in a fine layer of dust. On the small veranda they found every piece of their luggage neatly stacked, with Jessie's doll, teddy bear and bag of sticky lollies resting on the top.

Victor opened the front door and went inside, turning on all the fans inside the dusty house, which was full of storage boxes. When the overhead fans began to move spiders scattered from long strands of cobwebs.

"All this stuff must be yours," Victoria said. "It arrived here a little while ago."

"We didn't know whose it was," Victor went on. "One big removal truck fella brought it. We left it here to see who would turn up."

Mary opened one of the boxes and found some of her kitchen things. Jars of spices and herbs. "Yes, these are ours."

There was enough furniture in the house to make do. Mary started to clean the place up, and unpacked a few things, with Victor and Victoria helping her. Mary had brought food in big eskies and this was stacked in the fridge. By mid-afternoon tiredness set in and they all took a siesta. Brother and sister parked themselves on lounge chairs and Mary and Jessie lay down in the main bedroom. The fans droned overhead, a mechanical lullaby to turn on deep sleep. Mary woke with a start. She'd been dreaming about Delainy and his wild eyes. He had been desperately trying to give his family messages about her. He had too much to say, and only a few little slips of paper, no bigger than a matchbox, to write on. In his weakened state he had great difficulty writing. He became more and more agitated, not knowing how to put all he wanted to say into a few words. He was dying with the biro in his hand …

It was now late in the day. Victor and Victoria had gone home. Jessie was still asleep. Mary found an old hose in the front yard and began to spray off the dust from the house and the oleanders. Then she sprayed the dust to settle the ground. An old woman came across the road, first looking this way and that, taking extreme care that no one was about to run her down, even though there hadn't been a single vehicle for hours. She introduced herself as Kathie and followed Mary around the yard, watching the water connect with the dirt.

Presently the two women sat on the top step of the veranda and told each other their stories. Kathie told Mary she wouldn't know who her mother was. Lots of children had been taken away. Might be anyone would claim her if they got the chance. Lots of men and women were still waiting for their children to come home from a long time ago.

"Mind you, there are others who won't admit they had children taken from them. They too shamed to admit it. Keep blaming themselves and think others blame them too. Lot of people bury these things in the past. No one can keep records on other people around here." She tapped Mary on the knee. "But never mind, you are not alone, dear. Good many people came here after they had been taken from their families. I was taken from my parents on the cattle station where I was born. I think they brought all the children here. It wasn't always bad. Not always good, either. I want to go back home still. I have no idea what it would be like. I must have dreamed of that for over seventy years now. But I married a local man — a good man, but I could never give my children the law, the language of their mother's country. I saw them become alcoholics in this place. I had to watch when one son of mine was killed in a drunken brawl. I couldn't give them their past. They lived with the fear of the unknown. They have no future and I cry for them, because they cannot go back to their country."

Mary felt a lot of empathy with this wise old woman. She told her that she also lived in fear of the unknown. "When I try to reach out I never find myself in others."

"One day you will, dearie." The old woman looked up as a car screeched to a halt outside her place across the road. She said it was her youngest son. The last one left of four sons. "Looks like the canteen's closed. That crazy boy ran me over one time when he came home after the canteen closed. Blind drunk, didn't even see his old mother. I suppose I'm lucky to be alive. But each time I've asked the Lord, 'why not take me, not my boys?' ".

Jessie woke up and joined them. They went on sitting there, watching the increasing traffic of cars and people going past and overhearing loud talk and argument about trivial matters. Then it grew quiet again, except for some distant yelling and screaming. Mary saw an old man stumble past, then try to conceal himself in the oleander bushes while he stared over at Kathie's place.

Next moment Kathie flew down the veranda steps, moving with astonishing speed and agility for someone so old. A stack of small rocks assembled against the fence turned out to be her arsenal. She threw these rocks at the man with great force. "Get on your way, you dirty old fool!" The abuse kept flying back and forth between them, Kathie's sounding nasal, his more guttural. The score seemed even but eventually the old man moved on reluctantly, after yelling to Kathie that he'd be back later to give her what she was always begging him for. "I'll fight you with no clothes on, mission woman!" was his last shot.

Kathie returned to Mary. "Evil old man. Better it happened to him than poor old Delainy." She capped the old man's last delivery, yelling out "Whyn't ya go and have a stroke!" and slapping her hands with exultant glee before she sat down again. She talked about Delainy. "Poor old fella. Just went like that. He wasn't a bad man. Oh, bad enough when he was younger. His one time away, goes off to some political meeting. Musta really scared him. Comes home like a vegetable. You can see him torturing himself, wanting to say something. But no words come out." Kathie sighed. "While rotten people just live on."

Next morning Victor came by. He stopped the Council

jeep in the driveway and beeped the horn. Mary came outside to talk to him.

"Well, looks like you'll be sticking around for a while," Victor told her. "The Tribal Council met with the Community Council this morning. Surprise, surprise! They thought they should give you a try. See how it goes for a while ... if that's alright with you." Victor sounded happy and told her to jump in beside him. Then he yelled out to Jessie that Uncle was here to see her, and Jessie ran out of the house and into the jeep. She needed no coaxing when it came to this new man in her life.

They went to meet the Council of Elders. Mary explained who she was, what she could achieve, and stressed that she would act only with their permission. The elders remained silent. Then she changed to a new tack. She told them that she believed she had been taken away from St Dominic's as a baby, and hoped they would help her to find her mother. They looked at her for a while and then over to Jessie, who refused to get out of the jeep and sat there with a sulky face. One or two of the elders glanced uncomfortably at each other. Still they gave no response.

Nobody wanted to have the past suddenly foisted upon them. The memories were too sad. It was easier to avert their eyes and watch the elderly women walking home with bunches of white plastic bags loaded with shopping, or the children of card-playing mothers, running wild. The elders were used to strangers coming here and saying they were going to change the world. Then leaving. Presently, two identical-looking old men sitting next to each other told Victor in a slow, serious voice that everything would be fine. Mary and Victor were dismissed for the time being.

Office space was arranged for Mary in the Community Council building. Victor showed her around the community and she was introduced to a lot of people, and afterwards she went to stock up on provisions from the community store. The old man who had been hit by stones and insulted by Kathie was waiting in the back of the jeep when Mary and Victor, with Jessie, emerged from the store, laden with plastic bags of groceries.

"More missionary people comin' here what for?" The old man leant over and mumbled into Victor's ear with his throaty voice, giving Mary a cursory sidelong glance.

"No, no! Those days are well and truly finished, Dad. No, she's one of us. Going to be working here for a while." Victor laughed, but there was an undercurrent of strain in his voice. Then he introduced Mary to Elliot.

Mary could tell from Elliot's stone-set face that he did not take kindly to anyone laughing at him. His was a face the sun had parched and creased. A man prematurely old, with a vacant stare and signs of major illness. Obviously an alcoholic. A stench of fermenting beer exuded from every pore — a lit match and he might have gone up in flames. Elliot held out a shaky hand to Mary, and the handshake lasted several seconds longer than politeness demanded. Her own hand felt bruised from his clamp-like grip. He stared into her eyes, his face only inches from hers. His breath vaporised across her when he said "Hello". He looked down at Jessie, who was in the back seat beside him. He moved farther over to his own side and told Victor to drive him home.

As soon as Victor turned on the ignition, Elliot held onto the back of Mary's seat and stared straight ahead. He remained like this until the vehicle stopped outside his place. There was no goodbye, he just grunted that he was tired and walked slowly towards his house. Victor waited until the old man had disappeared into the small grey Besser-block construction on its concrete slab, then drove off.

This was the start of the adoption of Mary and Jessie into the community. First by Grannie Kathie and Auntie Gloria, the fragile old woman who lived at Kathie's place. Mary

found out that Gloria used to be Delainy's wife until after
many years he kicked her out in disgrace and turned all
their children against her. Gloria looked and acted like a
black version of Mae West in old age. She always stayed
inside the house and behaved like a recluse. Visitors to
Kathie's house never spoke to Gloria, and she never spoke
to them. However, when Mary went over to Kathie's place
one day, Gloria decided to turn on full theatrics, telling
wonderful stories about her disastrously crippled life, about
her maladies, her loves, her worries ... Mary kept the tea
coming because Auntie Gloria did not make herself tea.
After it was all over and Mary had gone home, Kathie
trotted across the road and told Mary not to believe a word
Gloria had said. It was all lies.

"She forgets the truth — which is best forgotten, anyhow." But Kathie clammed up about Gloria's true life. After
this Mary sent away for mail-order catalogues and helped
Gloria choose cosmetics.

Later on, while Mary was having an on-off affair with
Victor, she accidently found out that he was Gloria's son
and the strong and capable Victoria was her daughter. The
eldest of Gloria's children. She was shunned by them both
although they sometimes would recognise Elliot as their
real father. It was just a passing remark, brave with drink,
made in the canteen, but it triggered an eruption of disputes and rivalries, many of them decades old, that existed
within the community. The unspoken had been spoken
and gave rise to a free-for-all fight between opposing families that took place on the football oval. Crowbars ... hunting sticks ... boomerangs ... shanghais ... all were used as
weapons of war. The battle went on all night. Children went
to sleep to the sounds of screaming and abuse carried by
the night wind across their parentless houses, drifting further away to add to the manifold stored in the cavities of
rocks and the sulking ground. The badly wounded were

flown off to hospital next day. No one could fully explain why and what had happened during the days that followed.

Mary learned that no one referred to Gloria as anyone's mother, although Kathie was known universally as "Grannie". Along with almost everyone else in the community, Victor and Victoria often visited Grannie Kathie, but like everyone else who came to her house, they never spoke to Gloria. Like all the other visitors, they acted as if she was not there. Apart from Kathie and Mary herself, it seemed that Gloria was invisible to the whole community.

The one time Mary tried to discuss Gloria with Victor his reply was terse. "Don't ever talk to me about that woman. She's a slut." End of conversation. To make his point clear, he stayed away from Mary for over a week, driving straight past her house. Then he came back late one night as if nothing had happened. Mary kept her feelings for Victor in check after that.

After she met Elliot for the first time, he also became a frequent visitor to her place. He told her to call him "Uncle". He would often sit on her veranda steps, staring vacantly towards Kathie's place. Mary noticed a gradual decrease in his drinking, which made him sicker before he began to feel better. Sometimes he helped Mary in the garden. If Kathie caught sight of him in Mary's yard, sweeping or watering, she would come into the street yelling out nonsensical abuse. But she always stopped short of entering the yard, a respectful gesture. Mary would encourage Elliot not to be abusive himself, to go inside with her for a cup of tea or something to eat.

Elliot never talked much to Mary or Jessie at first, but as he grew to know them they became his audience. If Victor or his sister called in while he was there, he would say a few words then leave, returning later on when he was sure they had gone. In the end, Mary figured there had been great difficulties in the past relationship between Elliot and Gloria, and that was why he haunted Kathie's place and hurled abuse at her. And Kathie reciprocated, coming out onto the street to return his abuse.

19

In December, a haze of spores from the wings of tiger moths filled the night air. It was nearly Christmas: Mary's three months at St Dominic's was drawing to a close. Like a wasted spore, inconsequential, she floated about, unconnected.

There was nothing she could discover that connected her with the community. She spoke of her search to anyone, at every opportunity, sometimes forgetting that she had told her story to the same person before. Soon everyone knew what she was after, and that she would ask their help before she started talking. No one knew of her mother — "I wouldn't know anything about that, dear": all the old women said the same.

History was history. The memories were too sad, too bad. Records were incomplete. There were no clues, official or otherwise, to prove if she had actually been taken away from St Dominic's. Somehow, no one felt she had been born there. It was rare for anyone who had been taken away to return — if they did, people muttered they should have stayed away. And no one had ever returned looking as successful as Mary. She was like a white woman, and everyone came straight out and said so.

The Council of Elders viewed her with a quiet petulance whenever she gave her reports to them. One of the elderly twins would merely say, "That will be fine". Their interest lay in their personal scrutiny of her rather than her work.

Although Mary realised her work was considered insignificant to the scheme of things at St Dominic's, she was still determined to make some sort of breakthrough. It would take time to penetrate those barriers, continually reinforced to lock out strangers. Beneath their polite exteriors, she felt that most people treated her as though she might be carrying some deadly infectious disease. Too many of them were mixed up by years of displacement themselves. The authorities had brought too many people to the Mission in wire cages decades ago, and forced them to become assimilated into the local language group. Not that it really worked. People just became more engrossed with their inner spirit and closed all doors behind them.

Mary was unable to create within herself a sense of belonging, or to feel that she was related to any of the families. Not that she knew what sort of feeling made someone know that they belonged. It did not worry her unduly. Life was good enough, tenuously "normal". She felt at home in her little fibro house. She had found a family that had adopted her right from the start. Yes, she was an adopted child: it was the story of her life. Things were alright for the moment.

In the hot weather she had made her bed in a corner of the front yard. In the long shadows cast by the oleanders she listened to new cassettes of classical music which she had obtained from a mail-order catalogue. Starry nights, the heavens so close to her face, like no other place on earth. At the first signs of rain, the ants would be on the move, building nest after nest and finally crawling out of their holes in a disorderly procession to take flight with small, silvery wings. With the build-up of storms she slept inside again while the heavy rain poured down, deafening on the tin roof. A damp atmosphere spread through the house, the smell of wet earth coming through half-closed louvres.

Elliot's dawn arrival would be heralded by flocks of

galahs taking flight from the branches of high trees along the track he took to reach her place. When Mary woke up she would find Elliot there, so early, raking up dead moths or leaves that had fallen in the storms, or yesterday's footprints. She made breakfast and he ate with her and Jessie. Then he would sit around outside with his pannikin of tea while she and Jessie went off for the day. Instead of going off to the canteen most days, the way he used to, he would return later to sit on the veranda in the late afternoon. In the evening he would sometimes tell stories or give detailed accounts of hunting trips and other significant events that had brought change to the community.

Mary and Jessie would often leave him and go over to Grannie Kathie's place to listen to the talk. Gloria did most of the talking, when she was up to it. Her voice was childlike, punctuated with a nervous laugh. Mary collected new catalogues from far and wide for the three of them to pore over — sometimes there would be small parcels for Gloria. Mary had no idea why she kept on producing new wonders for Gloria: perhaps it was simply to share the sheer joy they gave her old drama queen friend. And Jessie loved her. The women were like three children poring over those catalogues, even if it was only a Coles' brochure advertising price cuts for prime stead at the nearest town, 600 kilometres away, which they would never visit. Mission-trained in the Queen's language, Gloria mimicked the white people she imagined in that small country town.

"I want two pounds of that cut-price steak," she'd say, real slow. "Two pounds of that good sirloin and spare the fat, dearie." She would get Kathie and Mary to repeat it after her, asking them with puffed cheeks: "Whatta ya want?" She told them she had been to that town years ago, and in the butcher's shop they had talked to her real loud and slow, thinking she was just a black nig-nog: "Whatta it be today, ma'am?" Young Jessie laughed and laughed, trying to sound like Gloria.

*   *   *

"You know I can't go over there myself," Elliot told Mary one evening as he sat on her steps sipping hot tea held to his lips with shaky hands. This alternative to the canteen had its own drawbacks. The packet of gingernuts on the veranda floor was fast disappearing inside his diabetic body. "My favourites," he'd tell Mary, dropping a biscuit down his gob. *Snap!* Like fish into a pelican's gut.

Mary would sit on the veranda hoping Victor would show up. She knew that Elliot was too proud ever to ask her about the house across the road. She made sure he received one or two snippets of information, whatever seemed appropriate in her judgment. Nothing that would insult his seniority. He always feigned disinterest, making polite responses. — "Gloria sang that song 'Silver Threads' beautifully today, didn't she, Jessie?" Mary might say. Then he would hum a line or two. If he was in a good mood, he would sing old country and western songs to Jessie in his best gravelly mock-up of Al Martino in full flight. — "Gloria had a migraine yesterday," Mary would tell him. He would nod sympathetically, and he'd be "feeling off-colour" for days afterwards to muster up sympathy for himself. Sometimes Mary felt he knew everything she did without going near the house across the street.

One night, Elliot was prepared to trade secrets. Not about the past — that had nothing to do with anyone, he told her once. "An eye for an eye," he quoted. She knew he carried his own hurt. She could imagine the hidden passion that had sustained his adultery with Gloria. Both of them would have been treated harshly in the former Mission, where an abnormal life was enforced by white laws. But in any case traditional values would have opposed their behaviour. Neither the religious zealots nor the administrators of traditional values would have turned a blind eye to adulterers.

"I have little friends who help me," Elliot told Mary,

chomping gingernuts two at a time. He pointed to a few little moths sitting on his shirt. "These are my messengers. I can tell them to do things for me."

Mary never knew when to believe him. "But they are just like any moths," she said. She noticed she had a few sitting on her own clothes. One she had to pluck out of her teacup.

"It's what you see," he replied. He flicked his fingers and the moths flew off into the night.

Watching the moths leave, Mary reasoned it had something to do with a change in the light. A shadow cast by his arm.

"You don't see, do you? Jessie will."

Mary said nothing, and went on hoping that Victor would turn up soon.

"You won't be seeing Victor tonight," Elliot told her.

"Why not?"

"He's out in the bush."

"Out in the bush?" She had seen him only a few hours ago and he had told her he was going to help a friend fix his car.

"He's out in the bush now. Drinking with other men."

Mary tried to argue that Victor hardly drank, then thought how stupid she was. She hardly knew Victor or anyone else who lived here.

"I sent my little friends. He's near my outstation. Get him to tell you, if you like. Anyway, I made him sick for lying to you about his drinking." Elliot was serious. he did not appreciate anyone doubting his words.

Victor arrived at Mary's place drunk, in the early hours of the morning. He had gone stumbling into her house to look for her, not realising she was sleeping in the front yard with Jessie. She watched him as he came out of the house, tripping over things. He vomited over the veranda railing then fell on the floorboards. Mary went back to sleep, only to be awakened several times during the night by moans, more vomiting and snoring. Both Mary and Jessie were deeply asleep when Elliot arrived as usual, early in the morning. He prodded Victor, who lay asleep on the ground, with the end of the rake. When Victor stirred, Elliot told him he should be ashamed of himself, and told him to go home. He then cleaned up Victor's mess, and went home himself.

It was an overcast Christmas Day, strangely cool. In the early afternoon Victor arrived at Mary's house wearing his usual navy blue shorts, with bare chest and bare feet. He was an agile man in his thirties. More capable and practical than Buddy. With less ego. He knew how to read things for what they truly were. Two fathers sat in the jeep. Elliot in the front seat in his usual clean pale-blue shirt and long, worn, brown trousers. Delainy was sitting up straight in the back, tied in place by a length of rope. He had a bright yellow Fourex cap neatly placed on his head.

"Get Jessie. We're going for a ride," Victor told Mary.

"Where to?"

"Dad's place. His country camp. We got a bit of an outstation there."

Mary glanced at Delainy as she got into the jeep. His face was contorted like a devil's, seeing all but looking straight ahead. Mary looked away. She sat in the back, in the middle, and each time they hit a bump and she accidentally touched his side she felt him cringe.

It wasn't an easy drive in the old jeep. The road trailed into non-existence and it became a matter of slowly negotiating a path through sharp rocks that jutted out of the ground. The jeep swayed, thumped and groaned its way over hills and down steep gullies. Mary felt queasy. She held the thought of Victor's vomit in her mind, although she hadn't actually seen it. Jessie, who had inherited her mother's propensity for motion sickness, hung over the side the entire journey, vomiting until she had nothing left of Christmas fare, and dry-retched a trail of saliva in the dust.

All the way Elliot talked in a prophetic voice about the stories that belonged to this country. He pointed out his spiritual ancestral sites, constantly asking Mary to look this way and that. He was in his element. She swallowed, gulped, breathed deeply: anything to avoid the embarrassment of vomiting. After an hour or so they finally reached a better road, winding through long grasses towards trees, with a creek or river in the distance.

They drove past a clearing where a lonely stream of smoke still rose from the dying fire of someone's camp the previous night. Empty beer cans lay everywhere on the dry, prickly earth. Elliot turned around, tapped Mary on the knee and pointed towards the rubbish with pursed lips. "I wonder what that was?" he remarked.

Victor said nothing.

"They should clean up after themselves. Going about messing up the country like that. No respect." The old man rattled on in tune with the motor.

Finally, after a minute or two, Victor slammed his foot on the brake. Everyone lurched forward except for Delainy, securely roped in his seat. Mary watched Victor's lean arm slam the gears into reverse. Then, looking angry, he roared the jeep back to the abandoned camp. He jumped out, picked up a bag from the back, and began walking around picking up the cans. Jessie went to help him while the others sat and watched. The full bag was thrown into the back of the vehicle and they continued their journey.

The outstation, a lonely place with a look of abandonment, stood beside a dry creek bed. On the flat there were a couple of corrugated iron sheds which the family had constructed from government kits designed to provide housing for Aboriginal people, it was believed they would feel comfortable living in them. They bore a curious resemblance to the dog houses provided by the missionaries at the turn of the century.

A family of crows were larking in the rivergums to the

beat of loose sheets of corrugated iron clashing in the wind. A few iron-frame beds sat out in the open, beside a mound of dead ashes stirred by the wind. Nestlé milk tins, used as billies and burnt black, rolled noisily around.

Elliot was first out of the car; he went up ahead surveying the area and picking up billies, with Jessie running behind him. Mary did not feel comfortable here; there was an eerie feeling to this place. To her it seemed as though something drastic might have happened and the people had simply got up and walked away, leaving everything behind.

Victor untied the rope from around Delainy, who looked quite shaken up by the trip. Mary started to follow Elliot and Jessie. She noticed a piebald dog coming out of the undergrowth of saltbush. A young dog, a decent sort of animal. Maybe she'd pat it once it got closer. In the moments that followed, she was aware of a number of things happening. The swift movement of Elliot bending to the ground then rising upwards. Like a video on fast-forward. Suddenly his feet lifted from the ground. The pitchfork travelled in a straight line. Impaled through the head, the dog fell not far from her feet. Dark red blood sprang out like a fountain before a picturesque scene in colours of olive, white, lemon and black against a purple sky.

"Augustine's dog, Dad," Victor said, looking down at the dead animal. He placed one foot on its body and removed the pitchfork.

"*Was*," Mary thought.

"Fuckin' told that Augustine not to let his dogs around here," Elliot muttered, taking the pitchfork and throwing it towards the dead fireplace.

"They know I hate camp dogs," Elliot said. "So they only got themselves to blame."

Mary asked if the owner would be upset. Victor asked her if it mattered, then answered his own question. "It doesn't matter."

Mary looked at the dead dog and tried to get Jessie to

leave it alone. She was busy poking a hole in its head with a stick. Disgusted, Mary tried to drag her away, but Victor said to let her be. Kids are like that, he said, they like to see how things work. "She'll tire of it. Don't worry."

It was easy to see who was taking over here, Mary thought to herself with annoyance. Jessie seemed halfway to becoming a local already. Maybe that applied to herself as well.

Victor walked away after telling Jessie she could help him bury the dog later on. But Elliot said they should take the carcass back to Augustine's place. It was his dog, let him do his own burying. Mary knew that Augustine was a poor old fella, not much left in his two legs to get around with. She would help him herself if she had to.

Victor carried Delainy to the shady side of one of the huts to lie down on a mattress. He fell asleep almost at once. Elliot boiled the billy and they had tea and fruit cake made by Grannie Kathie. The cake had a thick layer of marzipan that the store ordered specially for Christmas cake bakers. Each year there was a competition, started years ago by Beverly Jipp. Kathie had won the Beverly Jipp competition this year, in fact she'd won it for a good number of years. Kathie could tell you in detail the exact decoration of Mrs Jipp's cakes from year to year, as far back as she could remember anything. How many little reindeers or snowmen; a sweet little robin in '53, and so on. Jessie had left the dog, now she whizzed about holding all the pieces of icing sugar she had managed to pick from her piece of cake. She ended up in tears after stubbing her toe on a sharp rock. Her cries triggered off a racketing chorus from the crows assembled on a nearby tree. Jessie screamed louder to be heard over the din of the crows.

"We're here for the night now," Victor told Mary curtly. She wished she could put their relationship into a proper perspective — she wished she could figure out why she had started a relationship with him in the first place.

The day was drawing quickly to a close with the onset of

black storm clouds. Wild lightning forked across the sky. Mary calculated how far away the thunder was, counting down from the lightning flashes. Possibly two kilometres away, she thought. A lone butcher bird hopped around looking for scraps and emitting a song like bells from the steeple, competing with the squawking crows as they flew away from the storm.

The back of the jeep was unloaded. There were enough essential supplies to last for weeks. Victor carried the cardboard boxes into one of the huts and Mary followed him. Elliot found some flour and went off to make damper with Jessie in tow. Mary unpacked the supplies. Besides flour, the boxes contained packets of Redhead matches, sugar, tea, tins of soup and camp pie, rice, biscuits, Sunlight soap, lollies and tins of tobacco — and a twenty-kilo bag of potatoes. As well as a drum of kerosene. She stacked the goods on the shelves, next to a few tins and cartons that were either unopened or half-used. There were other items such as crockery and cutlery, cooking pots and a couple of lamps. Dried up bird and bat droppings were scattered over the shelves, table and earth floor. The recent rains had brought a humid smell to the interior of the hut.

Suddenly Victor grabbed her from behind and began to fondle her breasts. Mary resisted, trying to release herself as his arms tightened around her. She told him to stop. "Why?" he whispered, breathing into her ear. She reminded him that his dad or Jessie might come in, but he replied they were all busy. She said the place was dirty and stank, though she was already giving in. He told her to be quiet and held his hand over her mouth to make his point. Standing up, their love-making was fast, overdue. It had been on his mind since the previous night.

Shortly afterwards they all ate hot damper with jam and butter by the light of the fire. Steak and potatoes were cooked in the coals and washed down with beer. Jessie fell asleep next to Delainy, who had been fed and had fallen back to sleep. Thinking of all the groceries she had un-packed, Mary asked Elliot whether he intended to stay out here for the Christmas break. Otherwise, what would be-come of all that food? She noticed how Victor stared at Elliot, while Elliot himself did not appear to have heard what she said.

"Mary wants to know if you are going to stay here for a while, Dad." Victor raised his voice as he flipped the tab off another can of beer.

"No, I won't be staying here," Elliot answered quickly. Strangely, his body had started to shake and his lips quiv-ered.

"She's not making you stay, Dad. She's just asking, that's all." He looked at Elliot. "It was you who decided we should stay here tonight."

"Well, we can still go home. You can drive at night."

"Ah, come on! What if we get caught in a storm and lose the track. It's best if we stay."

Bats began to circle above them.

"We got to think of Uncle. He's had enough for the day. His Christmas treat. Isn't that right, Dad?" Victor patted Delainy on the leg; in return he got a hostile grunt between snores. Victor laughed, tickled that his Uncle was unable to speak but could grunt when he was snoring.

"Dad's turning into a big scared pussycat at night," Victor chuckled to Mary. He was full of bravado. On top of the situation. Taking the stuffing out of the old man.

Elliot mumbled that it was alright for young people, but he was an old man and he did not feel right in this place. He came nearer the fire, although it was a warm night, and lay down close to Delainy. He told Mary to camp near the fire as well.

Victor pointed to another spot for Mary and himself to sleep farther away, but she refused. She wanted to be near the light of the fire, for all of them to stay together. She knew now that she was right about the feeling she'd had when she first saw this place. Something must have happened here. She lay down near Jessie and Victor gave up and lay down beside her.

Long after everyone else was asleep, Mary lay awake watching the bats circling above. They had built up in numbers, flying around on many levels. She wondered why they did not land, watching them move round and round in slow motion until she became dizzy, and then drifted into sleep. The air was quiet except for the thunder of distant storms rumbling on in the still, dark night.

She woke in fright. Something had touched her face, her arms. What was it? She felt a repulsion. She reached out for Jessie, but could not find her. The wind was blowing sparks from the fire onto their beds. Lightning flashed across the sky, and in the sudden light Mary could see Jessie tucked in between herself and Victor, at the end of their bed. She must have scrambled over them while they were sleeping. The others were waking up too. She saw Delainy's mad eyes staring at her. Balls of dry spinifex rolled along the ground and hurtled through the air, passing through the coals to be ignited by loose sparks, then floating over their bodies like fireballs.

Guided by flashes of lighting seconds apart, Mary grabbed Jessie in her arms and ran to the closest hut for shelter, while Victor carried Delainy into the other hut, with Elliot close behind. Victor hurried to collect all the bedding before the storm broke, then went to help his father.

At first Mary thought it was an animal. A wild animal cowering in one corner. A 'roo or emu, with long, matted fur or feathers. She screamed for Victor. By now heavy rain had started to pelt down, with pebbles of hail. It flew through the door as Victor came and he pushed it shut.

"Stay still! I'll light the lamp." His short breaths filled the closed hut over the sound of the rain hammering the roof.

Mary and Jessie froze in the moments while they waited

for a match to strike. Mary felt her heart beating against Jessie's head.

"Auntie — is it you?" Victor spoke softly to the bundle in rags, a creature with matted white hair. She looked at them briefly and Jessie screamed at the awesome face revealed by the light of the lamp. The old woman jammed herself farther into the corner, her face locked beneath her folded arms.

"Don't be scared, Auntie. We have to stay in here until the rain stops. Just for a while. Then we'll go outside again and leave you alone." Victor spoke in a slow, calm voice. The old woman growled like a wild animal. Mary had never heard anything like it. She felt cold shivers running through her body. Jessie started screaming again. Mary tried to calm Jessie, but her shivers grew wilder and she began to tremble all over. Then Jessie started trembling too, choking on her uncontrollable screams. It occurred to Mary that both Jessie and the old woman were about to explode from their violent convulsions.

Suddenly the door burst open. Elliot's large frame stood in the doorway. Victor, still trying to calm down the old woman, was unaware of the state Mary and Jessie were in. Elliot took one glance at them, moved past Victor, and in almost the same instant grabbed the old woman by one of her bony arms and pulled her to her feet. She was like a small child beside him. Curled up like a diseased leaf, not much bigger than Jessie. She was so frightened of Elliot that her growls stopped instantly. Her yellowish eyes protruding from their sockets claimed all the fear on earth. She fell silent long before Elliot told her in a rough voice that she had better stop it. At last, when everything had calmed down, he released her and she fell back into a heap on the ground. Mary started to go to her aid, but Victor held her back.

"Ivy, you listening to me?" Elliot barked at the woman.

"I want you to meet Mary and little Jessie here. They are our family."

The old woman did not look up.

"Just say hello to her, Mary," Victor said, yawning, wanting to get back to bed.

"Hello, Ivy." Mary did as she was told. And was surprised to find herself rewarded by a gentler look from the old woman, peeping over her folded arms position.

"This is Jessie," Mary went on, but the child had gone back to sleep in her arms. The woman peeped out again then turned away. Mary felt a sudden surge of disappointment and depression which she could not explain to herself.

Elliot said he had to go and look after Delainy. He told Ivy not to cause any more trouble, otherwise he would be back quick smart. Victor and Mary, sitting up on their mattress with their backs against the wall, fell half-asleep. Jessie lay across them. As soon as the rain stopped, Victor gave Mary a nudge and whispered that they should move outside. She knew he meant they should leave the old woman by herself. Very quietly they moved out with their piece of foam mattress and the sleeping child. Mary was sure the old woman was watching them.

Next morning Mary and Jessie were still fast asleep as the men, who had long been up, were boiling the billy and making damper for breakfast. It was a beautifully cool day, though overcast with the hint of a light drizzle in the air. Victor woke Mary with a pannikin of steaming tea. She sat up and immediately stared towards the hut where they'd taken shelter in the night.

"Forget it," Victor told her. "She's gone."

"Did you see her go?"

"No. But Dad said he told her to go first thing, when he got up."

"Why?"

"Didn't want her around frightening everyone, I suppose."

"Does she live here? Is this her place or something?" Mary asked, thinking about all the supplies she had unpacked.

"If you must know, she was Dad's first wife. And she's as crazy as a loop. They sent her away from St Dominic's because she was mad, but then she was brought back. By the looks of her, she's worse than ever now."

"Then why is she out here alone? Doesn't she need medical treatment? Shouldn't she be in a hospital or institution?"

"We are not set up for welfare. We don't have special hospitals or institutions. She was in a loony bin but they didn't want her. Besides, she's happy here. Dad looks after her because he wants to. He buys all her food with her pension cheque and I drive him out here. There's plenty of water from the bore. She's safe here and no one has to worry about her causing trouble around the community."

"What sort of trouble?"

"Oh, nothing much … Let's get started. We'd better get old Uncle back before it gets too hot. Dad thinks this cloud will clear up soon. Better for Jessie, too, if it's cool on the road."

Mary gave Jessie some tea and damper for breakfast. Who could tell if the old woman was happy? What was "happy" in Victor's terms? She resigned herself to thinking it probably wasn't such a bad spot. It looked pleasant enough at this time of day.

The car was loaded up with the eskies and, on Elliot's insistence, the dead piebald dog. Once again Elliot sang softly as they drove, songs of the country. Jessie was fine all the way back, whispering story after story about the old woman in Mary's ear. She asked questions about her too, but Mary wouldn't respond, telling her to wait until later.

Back at the community, Mary and Jessie were dropped

off first. Delainy looked fine, roped up in his seat. He didn't even look half-mad, and Mary thought she caught a smile on his face. Victor had to attend to giving Augustine his dog back.

At home again, Jessie told her mother about how she had heard the other kids talking about a mad witch with long white hair who used to walk around the streets trying to catch them. A dirty old woman who could kill people. Now they played pretend games, making Jessie take the part of the witch. Jessie didn't understand why she had to be the witch all the time. Now Jessie was afraid that the old woman would come to their house and kill them. "But she doesn't know where we live," Mary told her. But Jessie said she'd seen an old woman just like the one in the hut near their house one day. It happened when they first came to the community, when Mary was across the road. The old woman came into their house and gave her a lolly, Jessie said. Mary said she couldn't have, but Jessie protested it was true. The lolly was green, with a red stripe. A hard lolly. And when the old woman smiled at her she had no teeth. When Mary heard this a shiver ran down her spine and she snapped at Jessie. How many times she had told her not to take things from strangers? This set Jessie off sobbing.

Later on, Mary went over the road and told Kathie and Gloria where she had been, and about the storm that made them stay the night there, and meeting Elliot's first wife. Kathie was furious when she heard this. "He did the wrong thing!" she said. Mary realised she simply did not understand the dynamics of relationships which appeared to have finished up bitterly decades ago. In one hard lesson in local history, she learned that you needed to have been through it all in order to understand. You were never going to be told.

"Never mention that wicked woman's name in this house!" Kathie snapped, whirling around her kitchen. But immediately she apologised to Mary, saying that she

couldn't possibly know about the troubles of Gloria. Gloria
was there, looking like a crumpled paper doll. Her little hat
of green imitation flowers sat lopsided on her head and
then fell off. At this point she began sobbing in a quiet,
composed way, and Kathie led her off to her bedroom, then
hurried back to get a glass of water and some Aspros. "You'd
better go home now," she told Mary, adding that she would
come over to see her later.

No one came later on and Mary went on playing classical
music to herself. There was no one she could think of worth
the walk up to the office to telephone long distance. She
had read all her books. So she and Jessie made a cake, iced
it and waited until the icing had set before eating it by
themselves.

When Mary arrived at work next day, a heated argument
was going on in the local language on the lawn beside the
community offices. The full Council of Elders was present,
including the old twins Gabriel and Mervin. Mary secretly
thought of them as the twelve apostles. Each night members of the community were lashing out at one another
under the effects of prolonged alcohol abuse. By day, St
Dominic's was a holy place where the bell tolled and righteous messages about paradise were blasted over loud speakers. God could arrive at any moment and feel that he had
never left heaven. The community administration relied on
memories of Mission practice and beliefs when it considered white man issues.

Elliot and Victor were with the elders. So was Augustine.
The elders were arguing with Elliot and he was arguing with
Augustine. The killing of the dog was being taken very
seriously indeed. Mary went straight into the office, trying
not to notice what was going on. The other staff pretended
they were busy, and said they didn't know what it was all
about when she asked them. She got the message. By

mid-morning the plane had arrived and the newspapers were delivered.

Her heart dropped when she reached page three of the national paper. The organisation had dumped on her. Johnno's desperation for votes, which he knew were more obtainable in the city-based areas, was behind it. He had done a deal with the federal government to move Aboriginal people in the southern states towards establishing the grounds for a treaty. On another page there was a profile on Johnno where he had given information Mary had collected on northern communities in her first months with the Coalition. He had deliberately, or naively, singled out St Dominic's as a place so conditioned to the white man's mentality that it would be light years away before they were ready to join the rest of the country in reclaiming their rights.

Mary, shaking, dialled STD. The argument, conducted in the language she was the only one unable to understand, was still firing outside. She thought of yesterday. Elliot should not have taken her out there. The woman was evil. She had only to use those yellow eyes once to transfer evil. Mary was sizing the situation up pretty quickly. Had Elliot and everyone else here heard Johnno whistle-blowing on the radio this morning? What she did not know was that the elders were accusing Elliot of making trouble by bringing Mary and the child together with Ivy. He had made a promise to them to not re-unite Mary and her mother. Now the promise was broken. They had told him *only one*, now the power would be too strong. They had told him to quickly choose which one he wanted to stay if he had wanted redemption from God. *Not three. Just one.*

The office workers gave excuses to leave, asking Mary's permission even though she was not their boss. Their eyes had a vacant look, practised so that no one could tell what they were thinking. Mary, oblivious to what was happening outside, went on dialling. The number was continuously engaged. She could imagine reporters busting at the seams. Angry Aboriginal leaders ready to kill. Northern politicians in opposition jockeying to offer support. Turncoats with their backs against the wall. All trying to get through. The secret dealers silent, stealthily clawing around the halls of power. She wanted to murder Johnno and everyone else in the organisation.

She stopped trying to get through. Then the phone rang.

"Before you start, save it and listen good. More of this shit in the papers is going to hit the fan. You're out. I've checked there's a plane today and if you want to avoid troubles from the locals, make sure you and Jessie are on it. It leaves at two. The tickets are paid for. We're dealing with Johnno from this end."

"Thanks a lot." She was almost in tears. "What about my stuff?"

"We'll get that out later, when everything calms down," Buddy told her. She found it difficult to hear him because of the racket outside. She couldn't believe her life was being turned upside-down again.

"Sorry, kid, I know you feel at a complete loss. This has meant a lot to you. But Johnno has let us all down." Buddy said he had to go. There was a lot of repair work to be done. *Click.*

About to leave, she was met at the door by Victor and the elderly twins. A crowd of people stood around the elders in the full sun. All of them were staring at her. Elliot was nowhere to be seen.

"I will be leaving on the plane at two. I am very, very sorry about this. I didn't know. I should have, I suppose, but I didn't." She spoke to all of them, but to Victor in particular.

Victor nodded. "Yeah, well, I'm sorry too. But the elders have decided it is best for everyone if you leave straight away."

"I am truly sorry. I thought the organisation wanted the best for you. I want to help you fight them. To make them support you." Mary forced out the words, trying not to cry in front of everyone, to show the old men her weakness.

"We don't want anyone's conscience by prescription, Mary. We will do it ourselves," Victor told her.

"You got to go now before you make more trouble," one of the twins said to her. She had never been able to tell one from the other.

Victor helped her to pack and get Jessie organised. He didn't say much, just did what had to be done. He understood the decision, but found it difficult to tie it in with the reality of this woman and the child he had come to know. "Everything will be taken care of," he told Mary finally, giving her a hug as the three of them left together for the airstrip.

As the car pulled out of the driveway, Mary saw Kathie sitting on a kerosene drum in her yard. She had rubbed white paint all over herself and was singing a traditional farewell in her own language. Mary and Jessie waved to her as they passed by. The old woman gave a limp response with her hand, continuing her song uninterrupted. No one saw the tears in her eyes.

"Say goodbye to your dad for us. I'm going to miss him."

"He was too sad to come," Victor told her. He smiled at her. "I'll come and see you one day for sure."

"I know you will." She knows they will bump into one another again, perhaps at a meeting somewhere, but they will be different people who must live in different worlds.

The twin-engined plane flies over Elliot's outstation. Mary looks down and sees the old woman sitting under the shade of a tree. She is busy with something on the ground, perhaps playing with a stick. It is impossible to see. But Mary can feel her contentment. *"Besides, she's happy here ..."* She hears Victor's kind voice.

The plane lands at the town with the butcher shop

specials. A small, award-winning tidy town. "Coon Town" is
written on the reservoir, a message condoned by the population for a good many years. Mary cannot wait to leave, to
resume the journey. But she and Jessie go to look at the
butcher shop. They stand by the window laughing, thinking
of Gloria all done up with her green roses hat, cutting the
best deal.

"It's a beautiful sight. A beautiful sight." The pilot's voice
interrupts the multi-channel inflight music and entertain-
ment. The big plane jives to one side. "Everyone look down
the right side, if you please," he says. No one could fail to
do this when the plane is flying side-on. "This is pure magic,
ladies and gentlemen. What you are witnessing is the water
once again coming to the surface of what we call the
'Disappearing Lake'. It has been dry for at least thirty years.
A rare sight, and it is my privilege to show it to you."

Mary wishes the pilot would shut up and concentrate on
his flying. She is not convinced that he is doing such a good
job. Jessie echoes her thought, bursting out with "Shut up,
why don't you!" She starts crying. Then she looks down at
the lake. "I want to go there," she says.

Mary and Jessie both look down in wonder at the brown-
and blue-streaked shimmering water of a large lake in the
midst of flat plains and foothills. They see dark clouds
moving towards the lake. Once they reach the water they
fall apart. Then Mary sees that each solid mass is made up
of thousands of waterbirds returning to the lake, as if they
had known the waters were returning.

"I'll take you there one day," she suddenly finds herself
promising Jessie.

As Mary watches, she can hear Elliot's voice of farewell.
She recalls him sitting in the dark with the bright starry
night almost on top of them as they drank their tea, while
he told her a story which he swore was true ...

If a beautiful bird was to miss the moment when the rest of its kind lifted from the Great Lake as the water was about to disappear, it would be lost. It may have been ready for days, even months, alongside the others. But when each day the birds lifted to the skies, perhaps the wind was not behind them, so they landed on the water again, waiting for the next day and the day after that, and so on ...

If a young bird was left behind it might have died. That is what happens when these kind of birds don't make the great flight. They die very quickly. But if it does not die, then this is what could have happened.

The tribes of crows wait in the spindly bush to take over the empty lake. Near the centre a little mud hole is all that is left of the great waters. There stands the lonely bird that was left behind. The crows fight over who shall have the bird for their own. It is such a beautiful little thing. After a battle that lasts for days and nights, no one has won, no one has lost. They will battle again to claim the powers of the waterbird: it is given the gift of life.

The waterbirds returned when the great lake reappeared. The young bird left behind had been able to devise a secret way to make the water flow. The crows were unable to unlock this secret themselves, even though the knowledge was theirs. They were too lazy. In any case, they had not much use for water except for a mud hole good enough for drinking.

Then the young waterbird had a child. So that the disappearing lake could be made to reveal its waters each year when the birds returned. The secret was passed on to the child. This meant that they should always live near the lake.

But the crows, greedy and evil, needed to live in new places. Their magic was so strong that they could take on whatever form they wished, and they made the little waterbird and its child, and the child's child and so forth go with them; to do

304 Plains of Promise

as the evil ones pleased. And the secret of the lake went away with them. But the waterbird's children sent the secret back to the lake each year by unsuspecting carriers.

Over time, however, the waterbird's children's children's child went mad, because she lost her daughter in a terrible place. And the secret of the lake was lost because the crows were too interested in evil things and could not control the waterbird's madness.

So the great lake dried up and is no more.

UQP BLACK AUSTRALIAN WRITERS SERIES

UQP's Black Australian Writers Series continues strong its commitment to Aboriginal and Torres Strait Islander writing. The Series opens up exciting opportunities in Black writing and makes this emerging literature more widely available.

This significant series testifies to the diversity of Black writing. Launched in 1990, it evolved out of the annual David Unaipon Award which attracts texts by unpublished Black authors from across the nation and is judged by a panel of well-known Indigenous authors. Jack Davis, Mudrooroo and the late Oodgeroo of the tribe Noonuccal are founding judges and series consultants. The Black Australian Writers Series is made up of the award winners and other Aboriginal and Torres Strait Islander authors.

This unique paperback range celebrates and proclaims the literary achievements of Black Australia.

WARRIGAL'S WAY

Warrigal Anderson

Warrigal has every reason to believe that the Suits from the Department are coming to take him away, with five pounds from his mother and hasty instructions he hops on what he thinks is a train to Swan Hill. Instead he finds himself on a life-long journey.

Winner of the 1995 David Unaipon Award

Memoir   ISBN 0 7022 2909 1

DREAMING IN URBAN AREAS

Lisa Bellear

Lyn McCredden in her introduction to *Dreaming in Urban Areas* captures the essence of Bellear's poetry.

"These poems are anything but motionless. Their emotions cut, determined to map out another possibility, a place of personal and social reconciliation. The tools of this poetry range from wild analogy, to smart-arse juxtaposition, from calculated advice, to articulate imagery. Let it unravel you."

Poetry   ISBN 0 7022 2856 7

MY KIND OF PEOPLE

Achievement, Identity and Aboriginality
Wayne Coolwell

Profiled in this exciting book by ABC journalist Wayne Coolwell are actor Ernie Dingo, TV journalists Rhoda Roberts and Stan Grant, artist Gordon Bennett, opera singer Maroochy Barambah, rugby union coach Mark Ella, singer-songwriter Archie Roach, and land rights advocate Noel Pearson, teachers, a medical doctor, and a classical dancer. Includes photographs.

Profiles   ISBN 0 7022 2543 6

BLACK LIFE

Jack Davis

"I write of life as I see it. Whether it is the beauty of the bush or the difficulties which my people find in living in the cities and the towns. I want my audience to feel the hurt and the pain of being born black as well as to feel the beauty of the countryside."

— Jack Davis

"This latest collection of poems is, in my opinion, Jack Davis's greatest."

— Oodgeroo

Poetry   ISBN 0 7022 2247 X

PAPERBARK

A Collection of Black Australian Writings
edited by Jack Davis, Stephen Muecke, Mudrooroo and Adam Shoemaker

Thirty-six Aboriginal and Islander authors are represented including David Unaipon, Oodgeroo Noonuccal, Gerry Bostock, Ruby Langford, Robert Bropho, Jack Davis, Hyllus Maris, William Ferguson, Sally Morgan, Mudrooroo and Archie Weller. Many more are represented through community writings. — Prose, poetry, song, drama and polemic —
"A watershed in Australian literature."

—Irruluma Guruliwini Enemburu

Anthology   ISBN 0 7022 2180 5

HOLOCAUST ISLAND
Graeme Dixon

Graeme Dixon's ballads speak out on contemporary and controversial issues, from Black deaths in custody to the struggles of
single mothers. Contrasted with these are poems of spirited
humour and sharp satire.

Winner of the 1989 David Unaipon Award

Poetry   ISBN 0 7022 2320 4

BROKEN DREAMS
Bill Dodd

When eighteen-year-old Bill Dodd dived into the Maranoa River
his life changed in an instant. This young larrikin had enjoyed
many adventures as a stockman on a remote cattle station; now
he was a quadriplegic. His boxing, running and football days
were over, and he would never ride his beloved horses again.

Winner of the 1991 David Unaipon Award

Autobiography   ISBN 0 7022 2428 6

NO REGRETS
Mabel Edmund

"Mabel Edmund is a gifted writer as well as an artist. She tells
her story with determination, courage and humour. Overwhelm-
ingly, the reader is left humbled by Mabel's deep compassion for
her fellow human beings."

—Sally Morgan

Autobiography   ISBN 0 7022 2426 X

CONNED!
A Koorie Perspective
Eve Mumewa D. Fesl

Language is power — it can describe and direct events fictional
and true. This is a look at the history of its use and the way in
which it has conned a nation. Linguist Dr Eve Fesl reveals the
invisible text used in perpetuating a false and oppressive image
of indigenous Australians.

History   ISBN 0 7022 2497 9

SON OF ALYANDABU
My Fight for Aboriginal Rights
Joe McGinness

From his involvement with the trade union movement of the 1930s through to the black rights movement of the 1960s and 70s, Joe McGinness has often been labelled a troublemaker. *Highly commended in the inaugural David Unaipon Award, this personal journey is also a landmark history of political struggle and achievement in the area of human rights.*

Autobiography   ISBN 0 7022 2335 2

THE SAUSAGE TREE
Rosalie Medcraft and Valda Gee

The title celebrates the favourite childhood game of authors Rosalie and Valda. This memoir tells of the sisters' childhood during the Depression in smalltown Tasmania. For the family of nine, thrift was a virtue and home-grown food and hand-made clothing a necessity. In later years, they learned of their heritage as descendants of Manalargenna, leader of the Trawlwooway people of Cape Portland in north-east Tasmania.

Winner of the 1994 David Unaipon Award

Memoir   ISBN 0 7022 2783 8

SWEET WATER — STOLEN LAND
Philip McLaren

Winner of the 1992 Unaipon Award for unpublished Black writers, this is a thriller, a historical novel, a story of conflict and triumph. Black and white lives are swept up in an epic tale of romance, greed and murder in 19th century New South Wales.

Fiction   ISBN 0 7022 2551 7

PACIFIC HIGHWAY BOO-BLOOZ
Mudrooroo

This powerful collection of poetry exhibits the interconnectedness of the cultural and the personal.

Poetry   ISBN 0 7022 2834 6

BRIDGE OF TRIANGLES
John Muk Muk Burke

A story of family struggle and cultural allegiance told by Chris who is a tender witness to poverty and despair. The torment of a young boy living black in a white world is truthfully told in writing both lyrical and wise.

Winner of the 1993 David Unaipon Award

Fiction   ISBN 0 7022 2639 4

CAPRICE
A Stockman's Daughter
Doris Pilkington/Nugi Garimara

One woman's journey to recover her family and heritage.
"In the life of an Aboriginal woman, no one is more important than her mother when she is young, her daughters when she is old …"

Winner of the 1990 David Unaipon Award

Fiction   ISBN 0 7022 2400 6

FOLLOW THE RABBIT-PROOF FENCE
Doris Pilkington/Nugi Garimara

Doris Pilkington's second novel tells of extraordinary courage and faith. It is based on the actual experiences of three Aboriginal girls who fled from the repressive life of Moore River Native Settlement, following along the rabbit-proof fence back to their homelands.

Fiction   ISBN 0 7022 2709 9

UP RODE THE TROOPERS
The Black Police in Queensland
Bill Rosser

A chilling story of the infamous Queensland Native Police Force, a murderous band of black troopers led by white officers. Their activities contributed to the extermination of whole tribes of Aborigines.

Winner of the 1991 Ruth Adeney Koori Award

History   ISBN 0 7022 2224 0

UNBRANDED

Herb Wharton

From the riotous picnic races in the famous Mt Isa rodeo, from childhood in the yumba to gutsy outback pubs, *Unbranded* presents a strikingly original vision of Australia.

"One of the most important Black texts ... A creative work of significance."

— Mudrooroo

Fiction   ISBN 0 7022 2444 8

CATTLE CAMP

Murrie Drovers and Their Stories
Herb Wharton

These droving stories by ten Murrie stockmen and women record the vital yet seldom sung contribution of Australia's Aboriginal stock workers. Entertaining and informative. Includes photographs.

History   ISBN 0 7022 2638 6

WHERE YA' BEEN MATE

Herb Wharton

Unforgettable characters emerge from this vintage Herb Wharton collection which ranges from city to bush.

Short Stories   ISBN 0 7022 2803 6